Abo

Cat Schield lives in N
opiniated Burmese cats, and a silly Doberman puppy.
Winner of the Romance Writers of America 2010 Golden
Heart® for series contemporary romance, when she's not
writing sexy, romantic stories for Mills & Boon Desire,
she can be found sailing with friends on the St. Croix
River or in more exotic locales like the Caribbean and
Europe. You can find out more about her books at:
catschield.net

Sheri WhiteFeather is an award-winning, national
bestselling author. Her novels are generously spiced with
love and passion. She has also written under the name
Cherie Feather. She enjoys travelling and going to art
galleries, libraries, and museums. Visit her website,
sheriwhitefeather.com, where you can learn more about
her books and find links to her Facebook and Twitter
pages. She loves connecting with readers.

Avril Tremayne became a writer via careers in
shoe-selling, nursing, teaching, and public relations.
Along the way, she studied acting, singing, pottery, oil
painting, millinery, German, and Arabic (among other
things). A committed urbanite, her favourite stories are
fast-paced contemporary city stories told with sass and
humour. Married with one daughter, Avril lives in Sydney,
Australia. When not writing or reading, she's thinking
about food, wine, and shoes.

Sinfully Yours

Sinfully Yours:
The Best Friend

CAT SCHIELD

SHERI WHITEFEATHER

AVRIL TREMAYNE

MILLS & BOON

First Published in Great Britain 2023
by Mills & Boon, an imprint of HarperCollins*Publishers* Ltd,
1 London Bridge Street, London, SE1 9GF

www.harpercollins.co.uk

HarperCollins*Publishers*
Macken House, 39/40 Mayor Street Upper,
Dublin 1, D01 C9W8, Ireland

Sinfully Yours: The Best Friend © 2023 Harlequin Enterprises ULC.

A Tricky Proposition © 2013 Catherine Schield
Paper Wedding, Best-Friend Bride © 2017 Sheree Henry-WhiteFeather
Getting Lucky © 2018 Belinda de Rome

ISBN: 978-0-263-31932-3

MIX
Paper | Supporting responsible forestry
FSC™ C007454

This book is produced from independently certified FSC™ paper to ensure responsible forest management.

For more information visit: www.harpercollins.co.uk/green

Printed and Bound in the UK using 100% Renewable Electricity at CPI Group (UK) Ltd, Croydon, CR0 4YY

A TRICKY PROPOSITION

CAT SCHIELD

To my best friend, Annie Slawik.
I can't thank you enough for all the laughter and support.
Without you I wouldn't be who I am.

One

Ming Campbell's anxiety was not soothed by the restful trickle of water from the nearby fountain or by the calming greenery hanging from baskets around the restaurant's outdoor seating area. With each sip of her iced pomegranate tea she grew more convinced she was on the verge of making the biggest mistake of her life.

Beneath the table, her four-pound Yorkshire terrier lifted her chin off Ming's toes and began her welcome wiggle. Muffin might not be much of a guard dog, but she made one hell of an early warning system.

Stomach tightening, Ming glanced up. A tall man in loose-fitting chinos, polo shirt and casual shoes approached. Sexy stubble softened his chiseled cheeks and sharp jaw.

"Sorry I'm late."

Jason Sterling's fingertips skimmed her shoulder, sending a rush of goose bumps speeding down her arm. Ming cursed her body's impulsive reaction as he sprawled in the chair across from hers.

Ever since breaking off her engagement to his brother, Evan, six months ago, she'd grown acutely conscious of any and all contact with him. The friendly pat he gave her arm. His shoulder bumping hers as he sat beside her on the couch. The affable hugs he doled so casually that scrambled her nerve endings. It wasn't as if she could tell him to stop. He'd want to know what was eating at her, and there was no way she was going to tell him. So, she silently endured and hoped the feelings would go away or at least simmer down.

Muffin set her front paws on his knee, her brown eyes fixed on his face, and made a noise that was part bark, part sneeze. Jason slid his hand beneath the terrier's belly and lifted her so she could give his chin a quick lick. That done, the dog settled on his lap and heaved a contented sigh.

Jason signaled the waitress and they ordered lunch. "How come you didn't start without me?"

Because she was too keyed up to be hungry. "You said you were only going to be fifteen minutes late."

Jason was the consummate bachelor. Self-involved, preoccupied with amateur car racing and always looking for the next bit of adventure, whether it was a hot girl or a fast track. They'd been best friends since first grade and she loved him, but that didn't mean he didn't occasionally drive her crazy.

"Sorry about that. We hit some traffic just as we got back into town."

"I thought you were coming home yesterday."

"That was the plan, but then the guys and I went out for a couple beers after the race and our celebration went a little long. None of us were in any shape to drive five hours back to Houston." With a crooked smile he extended his long legs in front of him and set his canvas-clad foot on the leg of her chair.

"How is Max taking how far you are ahead of him in points?" The two friends had raced domestic muscle cars in events sanctioned by the National Auto Sports Association since they were sixteen. Each year they competed to see who could amass the most points.

"Ever since he got engaged, I don't think he cares."

She hadn't seen Jason this disgruntled since his dad fell for a woman twenty years his junior. "You poor baby. Your best buddy has grown up and gotten on with his life, leaving you behind." Ming set her elbow on the table and dropped her chin into her palm. She'd been listening to Jason complain about the changes in his best friend ever since Max Case had proposed to the love of his life.

Jason leaned forward, an intense look in his eyes. "Maybe I need to find out what all the fuss is about."

"I thought you were never going to get married." Sudden anxiety crushed the air from her lungs. If he fell madly in love with someone, the dynamic of their friendship would change. She'd no longer be his best "girl" friend.

"No worries about that." His lopsided grin eased some of her panic.

Ming turned her attention to the Greek salad the waitress set in front of her. In high school she'd developed a crush on Jason. It had been hopeless. Unrequited. Except for one brief interlude after prom—and he'd taken pains to assure her that had been a mistake—he'd never given her any indication that he thought of her as anything but a friend.

When he headed off to college, time and distance hadn't blunted her feelings for him, but it had provided her with perspective. Even if by some miracle Jason did fall madly in love with her, he wasn't going to act on it. Over and over, he'd told her how important her friendship was to him and how he didn't want to do anything to mess that up.

"So, what's up?" Jason said, eyeing her over the top of his hamburger. "You said you had something serious to discuss with me."

And in the thirty minutes she'd sat waiting for him, she'd

talked herself into a state of near panic. Usually she told him everything going on in her life. Well, almost everything.

When she'd starting dating Evan there were a few topics they didn't discuss. Her feelings for his brother being the biggest. Holding her own council about such an enormous part of her life left her feeling as if a chunk of her was missing, but she'd learned to adjust and now found it harder than she expected to open up to him.

"I'm going to have a baby." She held her breath and waited for his reaction.

A French fry paused midway between his plate and his mouth. "You're pregnant?"

She shook her head, some of her nervousness easing now that the conversation had begun. "Not yet."

"When?"

"Hopefully soon."

"How? You're not dating anyone."

"I'm using a clinic."

"Who's going to be the father?"

She dodged his gaze and stabbed her fork into a kalamata olive. "I've narrowed the choices down to three. A lawyer who specializes in corporate law, an athlete who competes in the Ironman Hawaii challenge every year and a wildlife photographer. Brains. Body. Soul. I haven't decided which way to go yet."

"You've obviously been thinking about this for a while. Why am I only hearing about it now?" He pushed his plate away, abandoning his half-eaten burger.

In the past she'd been able to talk to Jason about anything. Getting involved with his brother had changed that. Not that it should have. She and Jason were friends with no hope of it ever being anything more.

"You know why Evan and I broke up." She'd been troubled that Evan hadn't shared her passion for family, but she thought he'd come around. "Kids are important to me. I wouldn't do what I do if they weren't."

She'd chosen to become an orthodontist because she loved kids. Their sunny view of the world made her smile, so she gave them perfect teeth to smile back.

"Have you told your parents?"

"Not yet." She shifted on her chair.

"Because you know your mother won't react well to you getting pregnant without being married."

"She won't like it, but she knows how much I want a family of my own, and she's come to accept that I'm not going to get married."

"You don't know that. Give yourself a chance to get over your breakup with Evan. There's someone out there for you."

Not likely when the only man she could see herself with was determined never to marry. Frustration bubbled up. "How long do I wait? Another six months? A year? In two months I turn thirty-two. I don't want to waste any more time weighing the pros and cons or worrying about my mom's reaction when in my heart I know what I want." She thrust out her chin. "I'm going to do this, Jason."

"I can see that."

Mesmerizing eyes studied her. Galaxy blue, the exact shade of her '66 Shelby Cobra convertible. He'd helped her convince her parents to buy the car for her seventeenth birthday and then they'd spent the summer restoring it. She had fond memories of working with him on the convertible, and every time she drove it, she couldn't help but feel connected to Jason. That's why she'd parked the car in her garage the day she started dating his brother and hadn't taken it out since.

"I'd really like you to be on board with my decision."

"You're my best friend," he reminded her, eyes somber. "How can I be anything but supportive?"

Even though she suspected he was still processing her news and had yet to decide whether she was making a mistake, he'd chosen to back her. Ming relaxed. Until that second she hadn't realized how anxious she was about Jason's reaction.

"Are you done eating?" she asked a few minutes later, catching the waitress's eye. Jason hadn't finished his lunch and showed no signs of doing so. "I should probably get back to the clinic. I have a patient to see in fifteen minutes."

He snagged the bill from the waitress before she set it on the table and pulled out his wallet.

"I asked you to lunch." Ming held her hand out imperiously. "You are not buying."

"It's the least I can do after being so late. Besides, the way you eat, you're always a cheap date."

"Thanks."

While Jason slipped cash beneath the saltshaker, she stood and called Muffin to her. The Yorkie refused to budge from Jason's lap. Vexed, Ming glared at the terrier. She was not about to scoop the dog off Jason's thighs. Her pulse hitched at the thought of venturing anywhere near his muscled legs.

Air puffing out in a sigh, she headed for the wood gate that led directly to the parking lot. Jason was at her side, dog tucked beneath his arm, before she reached the pavement.

"Where's your car?" he asked.

"I walked. It's only two blocks."

Given that humidity wasn't a factor on this late-September afternoon, she should have enjoyed her stroll to the restaurant. But what she wanted to discuss with Jason had tied her up in knots.

"Come on. I'll drive you back." He took her hand, setting off a shower of sparks that heightened her senses.

The spicy scent of his cologne infiltrated her lungs and caused the most disturbing urges. His warm, lean body bumped against her hip. It was moments like these when she was tempted to call her receptionist and cancel her afternoon appointments so she could take Jason home and put an end to all the untidy lust rampaging through her body.

Of course, she'd never do that. She'd figure out some other way to tame the she-wolf that had taken up residence beneath her skin. All their lives she'd been the conservative one. The one who studied hard, planned for the future, organized her life down to the minute. Jason was the one who acted on impulse. Who partied his way through college and still managed to graduate with honors. And who liked his personal life unfettered by anyone's expectations.

They neared his car, a 1969 Camaro, and Jason stepped forward to open the passenger door for her. Being nothing more than friends didn't stop him from treating her with the same chivalry he afforded the women he dated. Before she could sit down he had to pluck an eighteen-inch trophy off her seat. Despite the cavalier way he tossed the award into the backseat, Ming knew the win was a source of pride to him and that the trophy would end up beside many others in his "racing" room.

"So what else is on your mind?" Jason asked, settling behind the wheel and starting the powerful engine. Sometimes he knew what she was thinking before she did.

"It's too much to get into now." She cradled Muffin in her arms and brushed her cheek against the terrier's silky coat. The dog gave her hand a happy lick.

"Give me the CliffsNotes version."

Jason accelerated out of the parking lot, the roar of the 427 V-8 causing a happy spike in Ming's heart rate. Riding shotgun in whatever Jason drove had been a thrill since the year he'd turned sixteen and gotten his first muscle car. Where other boys in school had driven relatively new cars, Jason and Max preferred anything fast from the fifties, sixties and seventies.

"It doesn't matter because I changed my mind."

"Changed your mind about what?"

"About what I was going to ask you." She wished he'd just drop it, but she knew better. Now that his curiosity had been aroused, he would bug her until he got answers. "It doesn't matter."

"Sure it does. You've been acting odd for weeks now. What's up?"

Ming sighed in defeat. "You asked me who was going to be the father." She paused to weigh the consequences of telling him. She'd developed a logical explanation that had nothing to do with her longing to have a deeper connection with him. He never had to know how she really felt. Her heart a battering ram against her ribs, she said, "I wanted it to be you."

Silence dominated until Jason stopped the car in front of the medical building's entrance. Ming's announcement smacked into him like the heel of her hand applied to his temple. That she wanted to have a baby didn't surprise him. It's what had broken up her and Evan. But that she wanted Jason to be the father caught him completely off guard.

Had her platonic feelings shifted toward romance? Desire? Unlikely.

She'd been his best friend since first grade. The one person he'd let see his fear when his father had tried to commit suicide. The only girl who'd listened when he went on and on about his goals and who'd talked sense into him when doubts took hold.

In high school, girlfriends came and went, but Ming was always there. Smart and funny, her almond-shaped eyes glowing with laughter. She provided emotional support without complicating their relationship with exasperating expectations. If he canceled plans with her she never pouted or ranted. She never protested when he got caught up working on car engines or shooting hoops with his buddies and forgot to call her. And more often than not, her sagacity kept Jason grounded.

She would have made the perfect girlfriend if he'd been willing to ruin their twenty-five-year friendship for a few months of romance. Because eventually his eye would wander and she'd be left as another casualty of his carefully guarded heart.

He studied her beautiful oval face. "Why me?"

Below inscrutable black eyes, her full lips kicked up at the corners. "You're the perfect choice."

The uneasy buzz resumed in the back of his mind. Was she looking to change their relationship in some way? Link herself to him with a child? He never intended to marry. Ming knew that. Accepted it. Hadn't she?

"How so?"

"Because you're my best friend. I know everything about you. Something about having a stranger's child makes me uncomfortable." She sighed. "Besides, I'm perfectly comfortable being a single parent. You are a dedicated bachelor. You won't have a crisis of conscience and demand your parental rights. It's perfect."

"Perfect," he echoed, reasoning no matter what she claimed, a child they created together would connect them in a way that went way beyond friendship.

"You're right. I don't want marriage or kids. But fathering your child…" Something rumbled in his subconscious, warning him to stop asking questions. She'd decided against asking him to help her get pregnant. He should leave it at that.

"Don't say it that way. You're making it too complicated. We've been friends forever. I don't want anything to change our relationship."

Too late for that. "Things between us changed the minute you started dating Evan."

Jason hadn't welcomed the news. In fact, he'd been quite displeased, which was something he'd had no right to feel. If she was nothing more than his friend, he should have been happy that she and Evan had found each other.

"I know. In the beginning it was awkward, but I never would have gone out with him if you hadn't given me your blessing."

What other choice did he have? It wasn't as if he intended to claim her as anything other than a friend. But such rational thinking hadn't stood him in good stead the first time he'd seen his brother kiss her.

"You didn't need my blessing. If you wanted to date Evan, that was your business." And he'd backed off. Unfortunately, distance had lent him perspective. He'd begun to see her not only as his longtime friend, but also as a desirable woman. "But let's get back to why you changed your mind about wanting me."

"I didn't want *you,*" she corrected, one side of her mouth twitching. "Just a few of your strongest swimmers."

She wanted to make light of it, but Jason wasn't ready to oblige her. "Okay, how come you changed your mind about wanting my swimmers?"

She stared straight ahead and played with the Yorkie's ears, sending the dog into a state of bliss. "Because we'd have to keep it a secret. If anyone found out what we'd done, it would cause all sorts of hard feelings."

Not anyone. Evan. She'd been hurt by his brother, yet she'd taken Evan's feelings into consideration when making such an important decision. She'd deserved better than his brother.

"What if we didn't keep it a secret? My dad would be thrilled that one of his sons made him a grandfather," Jason prompted.

"But he'd also expect you to be a father." Her eyes soft with understanding, she said, "I wouldn't ask that of you."

He resented her assumption that he wouldn't want to be involved. Granted, until ten minutes earlier he'd never considered being a parent, but suddenly Jason didn't like the idea that his child would never know him as his father. "I don't suppose I can talk you out of this."

"My mind is set. I'm going to have babies."

"Babies?" He ejected the word and followed it up with a muttered curse. "I thought it was a baby. Now you're fielding a baseball team?"

A goofy snort of laughter escaped her. Unattractive on ninety-nine percent of women, the sound was adorable erupting from her long, thin nose. It probably helped that her jet-black eyes glittered with mischief, inviting him to join in her amusement.

"What's so funny?" he demanded.

She shook her head, the action causing the ebony curtains of hair framing her exotic Asian features to sway like a group of Latin dancers doing a rumba. "You should see the look on your face."

He suppressed a growl. There was not one damn thing about this that was funny. "I thought this was a one-time deal."

"It is, but you never know what you're going to get when you go in vitro. I might have triplets."

Jason's thoughts whirled. "Triplets?" Damn. He hadn't adjusted to the idea of one child. Suddenly there were three?

"It's possible." Her gaze turned inward. A tranquil half smile curved her lips.

For a couple, triplets would be hard. How was she going to handle three babies as a single mom?

Images paraded through his head. Ming's mysterious smile as she placed his hand on her round belly. Her eyes sparkling as she settled the baby in his arms for the first time. The way the pictures appealed to him triggered alarm bells. After his father's suicide attempt, he'd closed himself off to being a husband and a father. Not once in the years since had he questioned his decision.

Ming glanced at the silver watch on her delicate wrist. "I've got seven minutes to get upstairs or I'll be late for my next appointment."

"We need to talk about this more."

"It'll have to be later." She gathered Muffin and exited the car.

"When later?"

But she'd shut the door and was heading away, sleek and sexy in form-fitting black pants and a sleeveless knit top that showed off her toned arms.

Appreciation slammed into his gut.

Uninvited.

Unnerving.

Cursing beneath his breath, Jason shut off the engine, got out of the car and headed for the front door, but he wasn't fast enough to catch her before she crossed the building's threshold.

Four-inch heels clicking on the tile lobby floor, she headed toward the elevator. With his longer legs, Jason had little trouble keeping pace. He reached the elevator ahead of her and put his hand over the up button to keep her from hitting it.

"The Camaro will get towed if you leave it there."

He barely registered her words. "Let's have dinner."

A ding sounded and the doors before them opened. She barely waited for the elevator to empty before stepping forward.

"I already have plans."

"With whom?"

She shook her head. "Since when are you so curious about my social life?"

Since her engagement had broken off.

On the third floor, they passed a door marked Dr. Terrance Kincaid, DDS, and Dr. Ming Campbell, DDS. Another ten feet and they came to an unmarked door that she unlocked and breezed through.

One of the dental assistants hovered outside Ming's office. "Oh, good, you're here. I'll get your next patient."

Ming set down Muffin, and the Yorkie bounded through the hallway toward the waiting room. She headed into her office and returned wearing a white lab coat. When she started past him, Jason caught her arm.

"You can't do this alone." Whether he meant get pregnant or raise a child, he wasn't sure.

Her gentle smile was meant to relieve him of all obligations. "I'll be fine."

"I don't doubt that." But he couldn't shake the sense that she needed him.

A thirteen-year-old boy appeared in the hallway and waved to her.

"Hello, Billy," she called. "How did your baseball tournament go last month?"

"Great. Our team won every game."

"I'd expect nothing else with a fabulous pitcher like you on the mound. I'll see you in a couple minutes."

As often as Jason had seen her at work, he never stopped being amazed that she could summon a detail for any of her two hundred clients that made the child feel less like a patient and more like a friend.

"I'll call you tomorrow." Without waiting for him to respond, she followed Billy to the treatment area.

Reluctant to leave, Jason stared after her until she disappeared. Impatience and concern urged him to hound her until he was satisfied he knew all her plans, but he knew how he'd feel if she'd cornered him at work.

Instead, he returned to the parking lot. The Camaro remained at the curb where he'd left it. Donning his shades, he slid behind the wheel and started the powerful engine.

Two

When Ming returned to her office after her last appointment, she found her sister sitting cross-legged on the floor, a laptop balanced on her thighs.

"There are three chairs in the room. You should use one."

"I like sitting on the ground." With her short, spiky hair and fondness for natural fibers and loose-fitting clothes, Lily looked more than an environmental activist than a top software engineer. "It lets me feel connected to the earth."

"We're three stories up in a concrete building."

Lily gave her a "whatever" shoulder shrug and closed the laptop. "I stopped by to tell you I'm heading out really early tomorrow morning."

"Where to this time?"

For the past five years, her sister had been leading a team of consultants involved with transitioning their company's various divisions to a single software system. Since the branches were all over the country, she traveled forty weeks out of the year. The rest of the time, she stayed rent-free in Ming's spare bedroom.

"Portland."

"How long?"

"They offered me a permanent position."

Her sister's announcement came as an unwelcome surprise. "Did you say yes?"

"Not yet. I want to see if I like Portland first. But I gotta tell you, I'm sick of all the traveling. It would be nice to buy a place and get some appliances. I want a juicer."

Lily had this whole "a healthy body equals a healthy mind" mentality. She made all sorts of disgusting green concoctions that smelled awful and tasted like a decomposing marsh. Ming's eyes watered just thinking about them. She preferred to jump-start her day with massive doses of caffeine.

"You won't get bored being stuck in one city?"

"I'm ready to settle down."

"And you can't settle down in Houston?"

"I want to meet a guy I can get serious about."

"And you have to go all the way to Portland to find one?" Ming wondered what was really going on with her sister.

Lily slipped her laptop into its protective sleeve. "I need a change."

"You're not going to stick around and be an auntie?" She'd hoped once Lily held the baby and saw how happy Ming was as a mom, her sister could finally get why Ming was willing to risk their mother's wrath about her decision.

"I think it's better if I don't."

As close as the sisters were, they'd done nothing but argue since Ming had divulged her intention of becoming a single mom. Her sister's negative reaction had come as a complete surprise. And on the heels of her broken engagement, Ming was feeling alone and blue.

"I wish I could make you understand how much this means to me."

"Look, I get it. You've always wanted children. I just think that a kid needs both a mother and a father."

Ming's confidence waned beneath her sister's criticism. Despite her free-spirited style and reluctance to be tied down, Lily was a lot more traditional than Ming when it came to family. Last night, when Ming had told her sister she was going to talk to Jason today, Lily had accused Ming of being selfish.

But was she? Raising a child without a father didn't necessarily mean that the child would have problems. Children needed love and boundaries. She could provide both.

It wasn't fair for Lily to push her opinions on Ming. She hadn't made her decision overnight. She'd spent months and months talking to single moms, weighing the pros and cons, and using her head, not her emotions, to make up her mind about raising a child on her own. Of course, when it came right down to it, her longing to be a mother was a strong, biological urge that was hard to ignore.

Ming slipped out of her lab coat and hung it on the back of her office door. "Have you told Mom about the job offer?"

"No." Lily countered. "Have you told her what you're going to do?"

"I was planning to on Friday. We're having dinner, just the two of us." Ming arched an eyebrow. "Unless you'd like to head over there now so we can both share our news. Maybe with two of us to yell at, we'll each get half a tongue lashing."

"As much as I would love to be there to see the look on Mom's face when she finds out you're going to have a baby without a husband, I'm not ready to talk about my plans. Not until I'm completely sure."

It sounded as if Lily wasn't one hundred percent sold on moving away. Ming kept relief off her face and clung to the hope that her sister would find that Portland wasn't to her liking.

"Will I see you at home later?"

Lily shook her head. "Got plans."

"A date?"

"Not exactly."

"Same guy?" For the past few months, whenever she was in town, her sister had been spending a lot of time with a mystery man. "Have you told him your plans to move?"

"It's not like that."

"It's not like what?"

"We're not dating."

"Then it's just sex?"

Her sister made an impatient noise. "Geez, Ming. You of all people should know that men and women can be just friends."

"Most men and women can't. Besides, Jason and I are more like brother and sister than friends."

For about the hundredth time, Ming toyed with telling Lily about her mixed feelings for Jason. How she loved him as a friend but couldn't stop wondering if they could have made it as a couple. Of course, she'd blown any chance to find out when she'd agreed to have dinner with Evan three years ago.

But long before that she knew Jason wouldn't let anything get in the way of their friendship.

"Have you told him about your plans to have a baby yet?"

"I mentioned it to him this afternoon."

She was equally disappointed and relieved that she'd decided against asking Jason to help her get pregnant. Raising his child would muddle her already complicated emotions where he was concerned. It would be easier to get over her romantic yearnings if she had no expectations.

"How did he take it?"

"Once he gets used to the idea, I think he'll be happy for me." Her throat locked up. She'd really been counting on his support.

"Maybe this is the universe's way of telling you that you're on the wrong path."

"I don't need the universe to tell me anything. I have you." Although Ming kept her voice light, her heart was heavy. She was torn between living her dream and disrupting her relationships with those she loved. What if this became a wedge between her and Lily? Or her and Jason? Ming hated the idea of being pulled in opposite directions by her longing to be a mom and her fear of losing the closeness she shared with either of them.

To comfort herself, she stared at her photo wall, the proof of what she'd achieved these past seven years. Hundreds of smiles lightened her mood and gave her courage.

"I guess you and I will just have to accept that neither one of us is making a decision the other is happy with," Ming said.

Jason paced from one end of his large office to the other. Beyond his closed door, the offices of Sterling Bridge Company emptied. It was a little past six, but Jason had given up working hours ago. As the chief financial officer of the family's bridge construction business, he was supposed to be looking over some last-minute changes in the numbers for a multimillion-dollar project they were bidding on next week, but he couldn't focus. Not surprising after Ming's big announcement today.

She'd be a great mom. Patient. Loving. Stern when she had to be. If he'd voiced doubts it wasn't because of her ability to parent, but how hard it would be for her to do it on her own. Naturally Ming wouldn't view any difficulty as too much trouble. She'd embrace the challenges and surpass everyone's expectations.

But knowing this didn't stop his uneasiness. His sense that he should be there for her. Help her.

Help her what?

Get pregnant.

Raise his child?

His gut told him it was the right thing to do even if his brain warned him that he was embarking on a fool's journey. They were best friends. This was when best friends stepped up and helped each other out. If the situation was reversed and he wanted a child, she'd be the woman he'd choose to make that happen.

But if they did this, things could get complicated. If his brother found out that Jason had helped Ming become a mother, the hurt they caused might lead to permanent estrangement between him and Evan.

On the other hand, Ming deserved to get the family she wanted.

Another thirty minutes disappeared with Jason lost in thought. Since he couldn't be productive at the office, he decided to head home. A recently purchased '73 Dodge Charger sat in his garage awaiting some TLC. In addition to his passion for racing, he loved buying, fixing up and selling classic muscle cars. It's why he'd chosen his house in the western suburbs. The three-acre estate had afforded him the opportunity to build a six-car garage to house his rare collection.

On the way out, Jason passed his brother's office. Helping Ming get pregnant would also involve keeping another big secret from his brother. Jason resented that she still worried about Evan's feelings after the way he'd broken off their engagement. Would it be as awkward for Evan to be an uncle to his ex-fiancée's child as it had been for Jason to watch his best friend fall in love with his brother?

From the moment Ming and Evan had begun dating, tension had developed between Jason and his brother. An unspoken rift that was territorial in nature. Ming and Jason were best friends. They were bonded by difficult experiences. Inside jokes. Shared memories. In the beginning, it was Evan who was the third wheel whenever the three of them got together. But this wasn't like other times when Ming had dated. Thanks to her long friendship with Jason, she was practically family. Within months, it was obvious she and Evan were perfectly matched in temperament and outlook, and the closer Ming and Evan became, the more Jason became the outsider. Which was something he resented. Ming was his best friend and he didn't like sharing her.

Entering his brother's office, Jason found Evan occupying the couch in the seating area. Evan was three years older and carried more weight on his six-foot frame than Jason, but otherwise, the brothers had the same blue eyes, dark blond hair and features. Both resembled their mother, who'd died in a car accident with their nine-year-old sister when the boys were in high school.

The death of his wife and daughter had devastated their father. Tony Sterling had fallen into a deep depression that lasted six months and almost resulted in the loss of his business. And if Jason hadn't snuck into the garage one night to "borrow" the car for a joyride and found his father sitting behind the wheel with the garage filling with exhaust fumes, Tony might have lost his life.

This pivotal event had happened when Jason was only fifteen years old and had marked him. He swore he would never succumb to a love so strong that he would be driven to take his own life when the love was snatched away. It had been an easy promise to keep.

Jason scrutinized his brother as he crossed the room, his footfalls soundless on the plush carpet. Evan was so focused on the object in his hand he didn't notice Jason's arrival until he spoke.

"Want to catch dinner?"

Evan's gaze shot toward his brother, and in a furtive move, he pocketed the earrings he'd been brooding over. Jason recognized them as the pearl-and-diamond ones his brother had given to Ming as an engagement present. What was his brother doing with them?

"Can't. I've already got plans."

"A date?"

Evan got to his feet and paced toward his desk. With his back to Jason, he spoke. "I guess."

"You don't know?"

That was very unlike his brother. When it came to living a meticulously planned existence, the only one more exacting than Evan was Ming.

Evan's hand plunged into the pocket he'd dropped the earrings into. "It's complicated."

"Is she married?"

"No."

"Engaged?"

"No."

"Kids?"

"Let it go." Evan's exasperation only increased Jason's tension.

"Does it have something to do with Ming's earrings in your pocket?" When Evan didn't answer, Jason's gut clenched, his suspicions confirmed. "Haven't you done enough damage there? She's moving on with her life. She doesn't need you stirring things up again."

"I didn't plan what happened. It just did."

Impulsive behavior from his plan-everything-to-death brother? Jason didn't like the sound of that. It could only lead to Ming getting hurt again.

"What exactly happened?"

"Lily and I met for a drink a couple months ago."

"You and Lily?" He almost laughed at the odd pairing. While Evan and Ming had been perfectly compatible, Evan and Lily were total opposites. Then he sobered. "Just the once?"

"A few times." Evan rubbed his face, bringing Jason's attention to the dark shadows beneath his eyes. His brother looked exhausted. And low. "A lot."

"Have you thought about what you're doing?" When it came to picking sides, Jason would choose Ming every time. In some ways, she was more like family to him than Evan. Jason had certainly shared more of himself with her. "Don't you think

Ming will be upset if she finds out you and her sister are dating?"

Before Evan could answer, Jason's cell began to ring. With Ming's heart in danger and his brother in his crosshairs, Jason wouldn't have allowed himself to be distracted if anyone else on the planet was calling. But this was Ming's ringtone.

"We'll talk more about this later," he told his brother, and answered the call as he exited. "What's going on?"

"It's Lily." There was no mistaking the cry for help in Ming's voice.

Jason's annoyance with his brother flared anew. Had Ming found out what was going on? "What about her?"

"She's moving to Portland. What am I going to do without her?"

What a relief. Ming didn't yet know that her sister was dating Evan, and if Lily moved to Portland then her relationship with her sister's ex-fiancé would have to end.

"You still have me." He'd intended to make his tone light, but on the heels of his conversation with his brother moments before, his declaration came out like a pledge. "Do you want to catch a drink and talk about it? We could continue our earlier conversation."

"I can't. Terry and I are having dinner."

"Afterward?"

"It's been a long day. I'm heading home for a glass of wine and a long, hot bath."

"Do you want some company?"

Unbidden, his thoughts took him to an intoxicating, sensual place where Ming floated naked in warm, fragrant water. Candles burned, setting her delicate, pale shoulders aglow above the framing bubbles of her favorite bath gel. The office faded away as he imagined trailing his lips along her neck, discovering all the places on her silky skin that made her shiver.

"Jason?" Ming's voice roused him to the fact that he was standing in the elevator. He didn't remember getting there.

Damn it. He banished the images, but the sensations lingered.

"What?" he asked, disturbed at how compelling his fantasy had been.

"I asked if I could call you later."

"Sure." His voice had gone hoarse. "Have a good dinner."

"Thanks."

The phone went dead in his hand. Jason dropped the cell back into his pocket, still reeling from the direction his thoughts had gone. He had to stop thinking of her like that. Unfortunately, once awakened, the notion of making love to Ming proved difficult to coax back to sleep.

He headed to his favorite bar, which promised a beer and a dozen sports channels as a distraction from his problems. It failed to deliver.

Instead, he replayed his conversations with both Ming and Evan in his mind. She wanted to have a baby, wanted Jason's help to make that happen, but she'd decided against it before he'd had a chance to consider the idea. All because it wouldn't be fair to Evan if he ever found out.

Would she feel the same if she knew Evan was dating Lily and that he didn't care if Ming got hurt in the process? That wouldn't change her mind. Even if it killed her, Ming would want Evan and Lily to be happy.

But shouldn't she get to be selfish, too? She should be able to choose whatever man she wanted to help her get pregnant. Even the brother of her ex-fiancé. Only Jason knew she'd never go there without a lot of convincing.

And wasn't that what best friends were for?

Fifteen minutes after she'd hung up on Jason, Ming's heart was still thumping impossibly fast. She'd told herself that when he'd asked if she wanted company for a glass of wine and a hot bath, he hadn't meant anything sexual. She'd called him for a shoulder to cry on. That's all he was offering.

But the image of him sliding into her oversize tub while candlelight flickered off the glass tile wall and a thousand soap bubbles drifted on the water's surface…

"Ready for dinner?"

Jerked out of her musing, Ming spun her chair away from her computer and spied Terry Kincaid grinning at her from the doorway, his even, white teeth dazzling against his tan skin. As well as being her partner in the dental practice and her best girl friend's father, he was the reason she'd chosen to become an orthodontist in the first place.

"Absolutely."

She closed her internet browser and images of strollers disappeared from her screen. As crazy as it was to shop for baby stuff before she was even pregnant, Ming couldn't stop herself from buying things. Her last purchase had been one of those mobiles that hangs above the crib and plays music as it spins.

"You already know how proud I am of you," Terry began after they'd finished ordering dinner at his favorite seafood place. "When I brought you into the practice, it wasn't because you were at the top of your class or a hard worker, but because you're like family."

"You know that's how I feel about you, too." In fact, Terry was so much better than her own family because he offered her absolute support without any judgment.

"And as a member of my family, it was important to me that I come to you with any big life-changing decisions I was about to make."

Ming gulped. How had he found out what she was going to do? Wendy couldn't have told him. Her friend knew how to keep a secret.

"Sure," she said. "That's only fair."

"That's why I'm here to tell you that I'm going to retire and I want you to take over the practice."

This was the last thing she expected him to say. "But you're only fifty-seven. You can't quit now."

"It's the perfect time. Janice and I want to travel while we're still young enough to have adventures."

In addition to being a competitive sailor, Terry was an expert rock climber and pilot. Where Ming liked relaxing spa vacations in northern California, he and his wife went hang gliding in Australia and zip lining through the jungles of Costa Rica.

"And you want me to have the practice?" Her mind raced at the thought of all the things she would have to learn, and fast. Managing personnel and finances. Marketing. The practice thrived with Terry at the helm. Could she do half as well? "It's a lot."

"If you're worried about the money, work the numbers with Jason."

"It's not the money." It was an overwhelming responsibility to take on at the same time she was preparing for the challenge of being a single mom. "I'm not sure I'm ready."

Terry was unfazed by her doubts. "I've never met anyone who rises to the challenge the way you do. And I'm not going to retire next week. I'm looking at the middle of next year. Plenty of time for you to learn what you need to know."

The middle of next year? Ming did some rapid calculation. If everything went according to schedule, she'd be giving birth about the time when Terry would be leaving. Who'd take over while she was out on maternity leave? She'd hoped for twelve glorious weeks with her newborn.

Yet, now that the initial panic was fading, excitement stirred. Her own practice. She'd be crazy to let this opportunity pass her by.

"Ming, are you all right?" Concern had replaced delight. "I thought you'd jump at the chance to run the practice."

"I'm really thrilled by the opportunity."

"But?"

She was going to have a baby. Taking over the practice would require a huge commitment of time and energy. But Terry believed in her and she hated to disappoint him. He'd taken her under his wing during high school when she and Wendy had visited the office and shown her that orthodontia was a perfect career for someone who had an obsession with making things straight and orderly.

"No *buts*." She loaded her voice with confidence.

"That's my girl." He patted her hand. "You have no idea how happy I was when you decided to join me in this practice. There's no one but you that I'd trust to turn it over to."

His words warmed and worried her at the same. The amount of responsibility overwhelmed her, but whatever it took, she'd make sure Terry never regretted choosing her.

"I won't let you down."

Crickets serenaded Jason as he headed up the walk to Ming's front door. At nine o'clock at night, only a far-off bark disturbed the peaceful tree-lined street in the older Houston suburb. Amongst the midcentury craftsman homes, Ming's contemporary-styled house stood out. The clean lines and geometric landscaping suited the woman who lived there. Ming kept her surroundings and her life uncluttered.

He couldn't imagine how she was going to handle the sort of disorder a child would bring into her world, but after his conversation with Evan this afternoon, Jason was no longer deciding whether or not he should help his oldest friend. It was more a matter of how he was going to go about it.

Jason rang her doorbell and Muffin began to bark in warning. The entry light above him snapped on and the door flew open. Jason blinked as Ming appeared in the sudden brightness. The scent of her filled his nostrils, a sumptuous floral that made him think of making love on an exotic tropical island.

"Jason? What are you doing here?" Ming bent to catch the terrier as she charged past, but missed. "Muffin, get back here."

"I'll get her." Chasing the frisky dog gave him something to concentrate on besides Ming's slender form clad in a plum silk nightgown and robe, her long black hair cascading over one shoulder. "Did I wake you?" he asked, handing her the squirming Yorkie.

His body tightened as he imagined her warm, pliant form snuggled beside him in bed. His brother had been a complete idiot not to give her the sun, moon and whatever stars she wanted.

"No." She tilted her head. "Do you want to come in?"

Swept by the new and unsettling yearning to take her in his arms and claim her lush mouth, Jason shook his head. "I've been thinking about what we talked about earlier today."

"If you've come here to talk me out of having a baby, you can save your breath." She was his best friend. Back in high school they'd agreed that what had happened after prom had been a huge mistake. They'd both been upset with their dates and turned to each other in a moment of weakness. Neither one wanted to risk their friendship by exploring the chemistry between them.

But in the back of Jason's mind, lying in wait all these years, was curiosity. What would it be like between them? It's why he'd decided to help her make a baby. Today she'd offered him the solution to satisfy his need for her and not complicate their friendship with romantic misunderstandings. He'd be a fool not to take advantage of the opportunity.

"I want to help."

"You do?" Doubt dominated her question, but relief hovered nearby. She studied him a long moment before asking, "Are you sure?"

"I've been thinking about it all afternoon and decided I'd be a pretty lousy friend if I wasn't there when you needed me."

A broad smile transformed her expression. "You don't know how much this means to me. I'll call the clinic tomorrow and make an appointment for you."

Jason shook his head. "No fertility clinic. No doctor." He hooked his fingers around the sash that held her robe closed and tugged her a half step closer. Heat pooled below his belt at the way her lips parted in surprise. "Just you and me."

Something like excitement flickered in her eyes, only to be dampened by her frown. "Are you suggesting what I think you're suggesting?"

"Let's make a baby the old-fashioned way."

Three

"Old-fashioned way?" Ming's brain sputtered like a poorly maintained engine. What the hell was he…? "Sex?"

"I prefer to think of it as making love."

"Same difference."

Jason's grin grew wolfish. "Not the way I do it."

Her mind raced. She couldn't have sex—make love—with Jason. He was her best friend. Their relationship worked because they didn't complicate it by pretending a friends-with-benefits scenario was realistic. "Absolutely not."

"Why not?"

"Because…" What was she supposed to give him for an excuse? "I don't feel that way about you."

"Give me an hour and I'm sure you'll feel exactly that way about me."

The sensual light in his eyes was so intense she could almost feel his hands sliding over her. Her nipples tightened. She crossed her arms over her chest to conceal her body's involuntary reaction.

"Arrogant jackass."

His cocky grin was her only reply. Ming scowled at him to conceal her rising alarm. He was enjoying this. Damn him. Worse, her toes were curling at the prospect of making love with him.

"Be reasonable." *Please be reasonable.* "It'll be much easier if you just go to the clinic. All you have to do is show up, grab a magazine and make a donation."

"Not happening."

The air around them crackled with electricity, raising the hair at the back of her neck.

"Why not?" She gathered the hair hanging over her shoulder and tugged. Her scalp burned at the harsh punishment. "It's not as if you have any use for them." She pointed downward.

"If you want them, you're going to have to get them the old-fashioned way."

"Stop saying that." Her voice had taken on a disturbing squeak.

Jason naked. Her hands roaming over all his hard muscles. The slide of him between her thighs. She pressed her knees together as an ache built.

"Come on," he coaxed. "Aren't you the least bit curious?"

Of course she was curious. During the months following senior prom, it's all she'd thought about. "Absolutely not."

"All the women I've dated. Haven't you wondered why they kept coming back for more?"

Instead of being turned off by his arrogance, she found his confidence arousing. "It never crossed my mind."

"I don't believe that. Not after the way you came on to me after prom."

"I came on to you? You kissed me."

"Because you batted those long black eyelashes of yours and went on and on about how no one would ever love you and how what's-his-name wasn't a real man and that you needed a real man."

Ming's mouth fell open. "I did no such thing. You were the one who put your arm around me and said the best way to get over Kevin was to get busy with someone else."

"No." He shook his head. "That's not how it happened at all."

Damn him. He'd given his word they'd never speak of it again. What other promises would he break?

"Neither one of us is going to admit we started it, so let's just agree that a kiss happened and we were prevented from making a huge mistake by my sister's phone call."

"In the interests of keeping you happy," he said, his tone sly and patronizing, "I'll agree a kiss happened and we were interrupted by your sister."

"And that afterward we both agreed it was a huge mistake."

"It was a mistake because you'd been dumped and I was fighting with my girlfriend. Neither one of us was thinking clearly."

Had she said that, or had he? The events of the night were blurry. In fact, the only thing she remembered with crystal clarity was the feel of his lips on hers. The way her head spun as he plunged his tongue into her mouth and set her afire.

"It was a mistake because we were best friends and hooking up would have messed up our relationship."

"But we're not hormone-driven teenagers anymore," he reminded her. "We can approach the sex as a naked hug between friends."

"A naked hug?" She wasn't sure whether to laugh or hit him.

What he wanted from her threatened to turn her emotions into a Gordian knot, and yet she found herself wondering if she could do as he asked. If she went into it without expectations, maybe it was possible for her to enjoy a few glorious nights in Jason's bed and get away with her head clear and her heart unharmed.

"Having…" She cleared her throat and tried again. "Making…" Her throat closed up. Completing the sentence made the prospect so much more real. She wasn't ready to go there yet.

Jason took pity on her inability to finish her thought. "Love?"

"It's intimate and…" Her skin tingled at the thought of just how intimate.

"You don't think I know that?"

Jason's velvet voice slid against her senses. Her entire body flushed as desire pulsed hot and insistent. How many times since her engagement ended had she awakened from a salacious dream about him, feeling like this? Heavy with need and too frustrated to go back to sleep? Too many nights to count.

"Let me finish," she said. "We know each other too well. We're too comfortable. There's no romance between us. It would be like brushing each other's teeth."

"Brushing each other's teeth?" he echoed, laughter dancing in his voice. "You underestimate my powers of seduction."

The wicked light in his eye promised that he was not going to be deterred from his request. A tremor threatened to upend the small amount of her confidence still standing.

"You overestimate my ability to take you seriously."

All at once he stopped trying to push her buttons and his humor faded. "If you are going to become a mother, you don't want that to happen in the sterile environment of a doctor's office. Your conception should be memorable."

She wasn't looking for memorable. Memorable lasted. It clogged up her emotions and made her long for impossible things. She wanted clinical. Practical. Uncomplicated.

Which is why her decision to ask him to be her child's father made so little sense. What if her son or daughter inherited his habit of mixing his food together on the plate before eating because he liked the way it all tasted together? That drove her crazy. She hated it when the different types of food touched each other.

Would her baby be cursed by his carefree nature and impulsiveness? His love of danger and enthusiasm for risk taking?

Or blessed with his flirtatious grin, overpowering charisma, leadership skills and athletic ability.

For someone who thought everything through, it now occurred to her that she'd settled too fast on Jason for her baby's father. As much as she'd insisted that he wouldn't be tied either legally or financially to the child, she hadn't considered how her child would be part of him.

"I would prefer my conception to be fast and efficient," she countered.

"Why not start off slow and explore where it takes us?"

Slow?

Explore?

Ming's tongue went numb. Her emotions simmered in a pot of anticipation and anxiety.

"I'm going to need to think about it."

"Take your time." If he was disappointed by her indecisiveness, he gave no indication. "I'm not going anywhere."

Three days passed without any contact from Ming. Was she considering his proposal or had she rejected the idea and was too angry at his presumption to speak to him? He shouldn't care what she chose. Either she said yes and he could have the opportunity to satisfy his craving for her, or she would refuse and he'd get over the fantasy of her moaning beneath him.

"Jason? Jason?" Max's shoulder punch brought Jason back to the racetrack. "Geez, man, where the hell's your head today?"

Cars streaked by, their powerful engines drowning out his unsettling thoughts. It was Saturday afternoon. He and Max were due to race in an hour. Driving distracted at over a hundred miles an hour was a recipe for trouble.

"Got something I didn't resolve this week."

"It's not like you to worry about work with the smell of gasoline and hot rubber on the wind."

Max's good-natured ribbing annoyed Jason as much as his

slow time in the qualifying round. Or maybe more so because it wasn't work that preoccupied Jason, but a woman.

"Yeah, well, it's a pretty big something."

Never in his life had he let a female take his mind off the business at hand. Especially when he was so determined to win this year's overall points trophy and show Max what he was missing by falling in love and getting engaged.

"Let me guess, you think someone's embezzling from Sterling Bridge."

"Hardly." As CFO of the company his grandfather began in the mid-fifties, Jason had an eagle eye for any discrepancies in the financials. "Let's just say I've put in an offer and I'm waiting to hear if it's been accepted."

"Let me guess, that '68 Shelby you were lusting after last month?"

"I'm not talking about it," Jason retorted. Let Max think he was preoccupied with a car. He'd promised Ming that he'd keep quiet about fathering her child. Granted, she hadn't agreed to let him father the child the way he wanted to, but he sensed she'd come around. It was only a matter of when.

"If it's the Shelby then it's already too late. I bought it two days ago." Max grinned at Jason's disgruntled frown. "I had a space in my garage that needed to be filled."

"And whose fault is that?" Jason spoke with more hostility than he meant to.

A couple of months ago Jason had shared with Max his theory that the Lansing Employment Agency was not in the business of placing personal assistants with executives, but in matchmaking. Max thought that was crazy. So he wagered his rare '69 'Cuda that he wouldn't marry the temporary assistant the employment agency sent him. But when the owner of the placement company turned out to be the long-lost love of Max's life, Jason gained a car but lost his best buddy.

"Why are you still so angry about winning the bet?" Despite his complaint, Max wore a good-natured grin. Everything about Max was good-natured these days. "You got the car I spent five years convincing a guy to sell me. I love that car."

He loved his beautiful fiancée more.

"I'm not angry," Jason grumbled. He missed his cynical-about-love friend. The guy who understood and agreed that love and marriage were to be avoided because falling head over heels for a woman was dangerous and risky.

"Rachel thinks you feel abandoned. Like because she and I are together, you've lost your best friend."

Jason shot Max a skeptical look. "Ming's my best friend. You're just some guy I used to hang out with before you got all stupid about a girl."

Max acted as if he hadn't heard Jason's dig. "I think she's right."

"Of course you do," Jason grumbled, pulling his ball cap off and swiping at the sweat on his forehead. "You've become one of those guys who keeps his woman happy by agreeing with everything she says."

Max smirked. "That's not how I keep Rachel happy."

For a second Jason felt a stab of envy so acute he almost winced. Silent curses filled his head as he shoved the sensation away. He had no reason to resent his friend's happiness. Max was going to spend the rest of his life devoted to a woman who might someday leave him and take his happiness with her.

"What happened to you?"

Max looked surprised by the question. "I fell in love."

"I know that." But how had he let that happen? They'd both sworn they were never going to let any woman in. After the way Max's dad cheated on his wife, Max swore he'd never trust anyone enough to fall in love. "I don't get why."

"I'd rather be with Rachel than without her."

How similar was that to what had gone through his father's mind after he'd lost his wife? His parents were best friends. Soul mates. Every cliché in the book. She was everything to him. Jason paused for breath. It had almost killed his dad to lose her.

"What if she leaves you?"

"She won't."

"What if something bad happens to her?"

"This is about what happened to your mom, isn't it?" Max gave his friend a sympathetic smile. "Being in love doesn't guarantee you'll get hurt."

"Maybe not." Jason found no glimmers of light in the shadows around his heart. "But staying single guarantees that I won't."

A week went by before Ming responded to Jason's offer to get her pregnant. She'd spent the seven days wondering what had prompted him to suggest they have sex—she just couldn't think of it as making love—and analyzing her emotional response.

Jason wasn't interested in complicating their friendship with romance any more than she was. He was the one person in her life who never expected anything from her, and she returned the favor. And yet, they were always there to help and support each other. Why risk that on the chance that the chemistry between them was out-of-this-world explosive?

Of course, it had dawned on her a couple of days ago that he'd probably decided helping her get pregnant offered him a free pass. He could get her into bed no strings attached. No worries that expectations about where things might go in the future would churn up emotions.

It would be an interlude. A couple of passionate encounters that would satisfy both their curiosities. In the end, she would be pregnant. He would go off in search of new hearts to break, and their friendship would continue on as always.

The absolute simplicity of the plan warned Ming that she was missing something.

Jason was in his garage when Ming parked her car in his

driveway and killed the engine. She hadn't completely decided to accept his terms, but she was leaning that way. It made her more sensitive to how attractive Jason looked in faded jeans and a snug black T-shirt with a Ford Mustang logo. Wholly masculine, supremely confident. Her stomach flipped in full-out feminine appreciation as he came to meet her.

"Hey, what's up?"

Light-headed from the impact of his sexy grin, she indicated the beer in his hand. "Got one of those for me?"

"Sure."

He headed for the small, well-stocked fridge at the back of the garage, and she followed. When he bent down to pull out a bottle, her gaze locked on his perfect butt. Hammered by the urge to slide her hands over those taut curves, she knew she was going to do this. Correction. She *wanted* to do this.

"Thanks," she murmured, applying the cold bottle to one overheated cheek.

Jason watched her through narrowed eyes. "I thought you didn't drink beer anymore."

"Do you have any wine?" she countered, sipping the beer and trying not to grimace.

"No."

"Then I'm drinking beer." She prowled past racing trophies and photos of Jason and Max in one-piece driving suits. "How'd your weekend go?"

"Come upstairs and see."

Jason led the way into the house and together they ascended the staircase to Jason's second floor. He'd bought the home for investment purposes and had had it professionally decorated. The traditional furnishings weren't her taste, but they suited the home's colonial styling.

He'd taken one of the four bedrooms as his man cave. A wall-to-wall tribute to his great passion for amateur car racing. On one wall, a worn leather couch, left over from his college days, sat facing a sixty-inch flat-screen TV. If Jason wasn't racing his Mustang or in the garage restoring a car, he was here, watching NASCAR events or recaps of his previous races.

He hit the play button on the remote and showed Ming the clip of the race's conclusion.

The results surprised her. "You didn't win?" He'd been having his best season ever. "What happened?"

His large frame slammed into the old couch as he sat down in a disgruntled huff. A man as competitive as Jason had a hard time coming in second. "Had a lot on my mind."

The way his gaze bore into her, Ming realized he blamed her for his loss. She joined him on the couch and jabbed her finger into his ribs. "I'm not going to apologize for taking a week to give your terms some thought."

"I would've been able to concentrate if I'd known your answer."

"I find that hard to believe," she said, keeping her tone light. Mouth Sahara dry, she drank more beer.

He dropped his arm over the back of the couch. His fingertips grazed her bare shoulder. "You don't think the thought of us making love has preoccupied me this last week?"

"Then you agree that we run the risk of changing things between us."

"It doesn't have to." Jason's fingers continued to dwell on her skin, but now he was trailing lines of fire along her collarbone. "Besides, that's not what preoccupied me."

This told Ming all she needed to know about why he'd suggested they skip the fertility clinic. For Jason this was all about the sex. Fine. It could be all about the sex for her, too.

"Okay. Let's do it." She spoke the words before she could second-guess herself. She stared at the television screen. It would be easier to say this next part without meeting his penetrating gaze. "But I have a few conditions of my own."

He leaned close enough for her to feel his breath on her neck. "You want me to romance you?"

As goose bumps appeared on her arms, she made herself

laugh. "Hardly. There is a window of three days during which we can try. If I don't get pregnant your way, then you agree to do it my way." Stipulating her terms put her back on solid ground with him. "I'm not planning on dragging this out indefinitely."

"I agree to those three days, but I want uninterrupted time with you."

She dug her fingernails beneath the beer label. In typical Jason fashion, he was messing up her well-laid plans.

She'd been thinking in terms of three short evenings of fantastic sex here at his house and then heading back home to relive the moments in the privacy of her bedroom. Not days and nights of all Jason all the time. What if she talked in her sleep and told him all her secret fantasies about him? What if he didn't let her sleep and she grew so delirious from all the hours of making love that she said something in the heat of passion?

"You're crazy if you think our families are going to leave us alone for three days."

"They will if we're not in Houston."

This was her baby. She should be the one who decided where and when it was conceived. The lack of control was making her edgy. Vulnerable.

"I propose we go somewhere far away," he continued. "A secluded spot where we can concentrate on the business at hand."

The business at hand? He caressed those four words with such a high degree of sensuality, her body vibrated with excitement.

"I'll figure out where and let you know." At least if she took charge of where they went she wouldn't have to worry about her baby being conceived in whatever town NASCAR was racing that weekend.

She started to shift her weight forward, preparing to stand, when Jason's hand slid across her abdomen and circled around to her spine.

"Before you go."

He tugged her upper half toward him. The hand that had been skimming her shoulder now cupped the back of her head. She was trapped between the heat of his body and his strong arm, her breasts skimming his chest, nipples turning into buds as desire plunged her into a whirlpool of longing. The intent in his eyes set her heart to thumping in an irregular rhythm.

"What do you think you're doing?" she demanded, retreating from the lips dipping toward hers.

"Sealing our deal with a kiss."

"A handshake will work fine."

Her brusque dismissal didn't dim the smug smile curving his lips. She put her hand on his chest. Rock-hard pecs flexed beneath her fingers. The even thump of his heart mocked her wildly fluctuating pulse.

"Not for me." He captured and held her gaze before letting his mouth graze hers. With a brief survey of her expression, he nodded. "See, that wasn't so bad."

"Right." Her chest rose and fell, betraying her agitation. "Not bad."

"If you relax it will get even better." He shifted his attention to her chin, the line of her jaw, dusting his lips over her skin and making her senses whirl.

"I'm not ready to relax." She'd geared up to tell him that she'd try getting pregnant his way. Getting physical with him would require a different sort of preparation.

"You don't have to get ready." His chest vibrated with a low chuckle. "Just relax."

"Jason, how long have we known each other?"

"Long time." He found a spot that interested him just below her ear and lingered until she shivered. "Why?"

Her voice lacked serenity as she said, "Then you know I don't do anything without planning."

His exhalation tickled her sensitive skin and made holding still almost impossible. "You don't need to plan. Just let go."

Right. And risk him discovering her secret? Ever since she'd decided to ask his help in getting pregnant, she'd realized that what she felt for him was deeper than friendship. Not love. Or not the romantic sort. At least she didn't think so. Not yet. But it could become that sort of love if they made love over and over and over.

And if he found out how her feelings had changed toward him, he'd bolt the way he'd run from every other woman who'd tried to claim his heart.

Ming tensed to keep from responding to the persuasive magic of his touch. Just the sweep of his lips over her skin, the strength of his arms around her, raised her temperature and made her long for him to take her hard and fast.

"I'll let go when we're out of town," she promised. Well, lied really. At least she hoped she was lying. "What are you doing?"

In a quick, powerful move, he'd shifted her onto her back and slid one muscular leg between her thighs. Her body reacted before her mind caught up. She bent her knees, planted her feet on the couch cushions and rocked her hips in the carnal hope of easing the ache in her loins.

"While you make arrangements for us to go away, I thought you'd feel better if you weren't worried about the chemistry between us."

His heat seeped into her, softening her muscles, reducing her resistance to ash. "No worries here. I'm sure you're a fabulous lover." She trembled in anticipation of just how fabulous. With her body betraying her at his every touch, she had to keep her wits sharp. "Otherwise, why else would you have left a trail of broken hearts in your wake?"

Jason frowned. "I didn't realize that bothered you so much."

"It doesn't."

He hummed his doubt and leaned down to nibble on her earlobe. "Not sure I believe you."

With her erogenous zones on full red alert, she labored to keep her legs from wrapping around his hips. She wanted to feel him hard and thick against the thudding ache between her thighs. Her fingernails dug into the couch cushions.

"You're biting your lip." His tongue flicked over the tender spot. "I don't know why you're fighting this so hard."

And she didn't want him to find out. "Okay. I'm not worried about your sexual prowess. I'm worried that once we go down this path, there'll be no turning back."

"Oh, I see. You're worried you're going to fall in love with me."

"No." She made a whole series of disgruntled, dismissive noises until she realized he was teasing her. Two could play at this game. "I'm more concerned you'll fall in love with me."

"I don't think that's going to happen."

"I don't know," she said, happy to be on the giving end of the ribbing. "I'm pretty adorable."

"That you are." He scanned her face, utterly serious. "Close your eyes," he commanded. "We're going to do this."

She complied, hoping the intimacy they shared as friends would allow her to revel in the passion Jason aroused in her and keep her from worrying about the potential complications. Being unable to see Jason's face helped calm the flutters of anxiety. If she ignored the scent of sandalwood mingled with car polish, she might be able to pretend the man lying on top of her was anyone else.

The sound of his soft exhalation drifted past her ears a second before his lips found hers. Ming expected him to claim her mouth the way he had fifteen years ago and kiss her as if she was the only woman in the world he'd ever wanted. But this kiss was different. It wasn't the wild, exciting variety that had caused her to tear at Jason's shirt and allow him to slip his hand down the bodice of her dress to bare her breasts.

Jason's lips explored hers with firm but gentle pressure. If she'd worried that she'd be overcome with desire and make a complete fool of herself over him, she'd wasted her energy.

This kiss was so controlled and deliberate she wondered if Jason was regretting his offer to make love to her.

An empty feeling settled in her chest.

"See," Jason said, drifting his lips over her eyelids. "That wasn't so bad."

"I never expected it would be."

"Then what are you so afraid of?"

What if her lust for him was stronger than his for her? What if three days with him only whet her appetite for more?

"The thought of you seeing me naked is one," she said, keeping her tone light to hide her dismay.

His grin bloomed, mischievous and naughty. "I've already seen you naked."

"What?" Lust shot through Ming, leaving her dazzled and disturbed. "When?"

"Remember that family vacation when we brought you with us to Saint John? The outdoor shower attached to my bedroom?"

"Everyone was snorkeling. That's why I came back to the villa early." She'd wanted the room Jason ended up with because of the outdoor shower. Thinking she was alone, she'd used it. "You spied on me?"

"More like stumbled upon you."

She shoved at his beefy shoulder but couldn't budge him. "Why did you have to tell me that?"

"To explain why you have no need to be embarrassed. I've seen it all before." And from his expression, he'd liked what he saw.

Ming flushed hot. Swooning was impossible if she was lying down, right?

"How long did you watch me?"

"Five, maybe ten minutes."

Her mouth opened, but no words came out. Goose bumps erupted at the way his gaze trailed over her. Was she wrong about the kiss? Or was she the only one who caught fire every time they touched?

He stood and offered her his hand. She let him pull her to her feet and then set about straightening her clothes and finger-combing her hair.

Already she could feel their friendship morphing into something else. By the time their three days together were up, she would no longer be just his friend. She would be his ex-lover. That would alter her perspective of their relationship. Is that really what she wanted?

"I've been charting my cycle for the last six months," she said, uncaring if he'd be disinterested in her feminine activities. "The next time I ovulate is in ten days. Can you get away then?"

"Are you sure you want to go through with this?"

Had he hoped his kiss would change her mind? "I really want this baby. If sleeping with you is the only way that's going to happen, I'm ready to make the sacrifice."

He grinned. "Make the arrangements."

Four

Ming had chosen Mendocino, California, for her long weekend with Jason because the only person who knew it was her favorite getaway spot was Terry's daughter, Wendy, her closest girlfriend from high school. Wendy had moved to California with her husband seven years earlier and had introduced Ming to the town, knowing she would fall in love with the little slice of New England plopped onto a rugged California coast. The area featured some of the most spectacular scenery Ming had ever seen, and every year thereafter she returned for a relaxing long weekend.

That all had ended two years ago. She'd arrived early in September for a few days of spa treatments and soul-searching. Surrounded by the steady pulse of shore life, she lingered over coffee, browsed art galleries and wine shops, and took a long look at her relationship with Evan. They'd been going out for a little over a year and he'd asked her to decide between becoming a fully committed couple or parting ways.

That long weekend in Mendocino she'd decided to stop feeling torn between the Sterling brothers. She loved Evan one way. She loved Jason another. He'd been nothing but supportive of her dating Evan and more preoccupied than ever with his career and racing hobby. Ming doubted Jason had even noticed that Evan took up most of her time and attention. Or maybe she just wished it had bothered him. That he'd tell his brother to back off and claim Ming as his own.

But he hadn't, and it had nagged at her how easily Jason had let her go. She'd not viewed a single one of his girlfriends as casually. Each new love interest had meant Jason had taken his friendship with Ming even more for granted.

In hindsight, she understood how she'd fallen for Evan. He'd showered her with all the attention she could ever want.

Despite how things worked out between them, she'd never regretted dating Evan or agreeing to be his wife. So what if their relationship lacked the all-consuming passion of a romance novel. They'd respected each other, communicated logically and without drama. They'd enjoyed the same activities and possessed similar temperaments. All in all, Evan made complete sense for her as a life partner. But had everything been as perfect as it seemed?

A hundred times in the past six months she'd questioned whether she'd have gone through with the wedding if Evan hadn't changed his mind about having kids and ended their engagement.

They'd dated for two years, been engaged for one.

Plenty of time to shake off doubts about the future.

Plenty of time to decide if what she felt for Evan was enduring love or if she'd talked herself into settling for good enough because he fit seamlessly into her picture of the perfect life.

They were ideally suited in temperament and ideology. He never challenged her opinions or bullied her into defending her beliefs. She always knew where she stood with him. He'd made her feel safe.

A stark contrast to the wildly shifting emotions Jason aroused in her.

The long drive up from San Francisco gave Ming too much time to think. To grow even more anxious about the weekend with Jason. Already plagued by concern that letting him help her conceive a baby would complicate their relationship, now she had to worry that making love with him might just whip up a frenzy of emotions that would lead her to disappointment.

Knowing full well she was stalling, Ming stopped in Mendocino and did some window-shopping before she headed to the inn where she and Jason would be staying. To avoid anyone getting suspicious about the two of them doing something as unusual as heading to California for the weekend, they'd travelled separately. Ming had flown to San Francisco a few days ago to spend some time with Wendy. Jason had headed out on Friday morning. As much as Ming enjoyed visiting with her friend, she'd been preoccupied with doubts and worries that she couldn't share.

Although Wendy was excited about Ming's decision to have a baby, she wouldn't have approved of Ming's choice of Jason as the father. So Ming kept that part of her plans to herself. Wendy had been there for all Ming's angst in the aftermath of the senior prom kiss and believed she had wasted too much energy on a man who was never going to let himself fall in love and get married.

Add to this her sister's disapproval, and the fact that the one person she'd always been able to talk to when something was eating at her was the source of her troubles, and Ming was drowning in uncertainty.

The sun was inching its way toward the horizon when Ming decided she'd dawdled long enough. She paid the gallery owner for the painting of the coast she'd fallen in love with and made arrangements to have it shipped back to her house. Her feet felt encased in lead as she headed down the steps toward her rental car.

She drove below the speed limit on the way to the inn. Gulls wheeled and dove in the steady winds off the Pacific as the car rolled down the driveway, gravel crunching beneath the tires. Silver Mist Inn was composed of a large central lodge and a collection of small cottages that clung to the edge of the cliffs. The spectacular views were well matched by the incredible cuisine and the fabulous hospitality of the husband-and-wife team who owned the inn and spa.

Rosemary was behind the check-in desk when Ming entered the lodge. "Hello, Ming," the fifty-something woman exclaimed. "How wonderful to see you."

Ming smiled. Already the relaxing, familiar feel of the place was sinking into her bones. "It's great to see you, too, Rosemary. How have you been?"

Her gaze drifted to the right of reception. The lodge's main room held a handful of people sipping coffee, reading or talking while they enjoyed the expansive views of the ocean. Off to the left, a door led to a broad deck that housed lounge chairs where waitresses were busy bringing drinks from the bar.

"Busy as always." Rosemary pushed a key toward Ming. "Your friend checked in three hours ago. You're staying in Blackberry Cottage."

The change of plans revived Ming's earlier uneasiness. "I booked my regular room in the lodge."

Rosemary nodded. "After your friend saw all we had to offer, he wanted to upgrade your accommodations. It's a little bigger, way more private and the views are the best we have."

"Thank you." Ming forced her lips into a smile she wasn't feeling.

Why had Jason disrupted her arrangements? Whenever she vacationed here, she always stayed in the same room, a comfortable suite with a large balcony that overlooked the ocean. This weekend in particular she'd wanted to be in familiar surroundings.

Ming parked her car beside the one Jason had rented and

retrieved her overnight bag from the trunk. Packing had taken her three hours. She'd debated every item that had gone into the carry-on luggage.

What sort of clothes would set the correct tone for the weekend? She'd started with too much outerwear. But the purpose of the trip wasn't to wander the trails by the cliffs but to explore Jason's glorious, naked body.

So, she'd packed the sexy lingerie she'd received as a bridal shower gift but never gotten the chance to wear. As she'd folded the silky bits of lace and satin, she realized the provocative underwear sent a message that Ming hoped to drive Jason wild with passion, and that struck her as very nonfriendlike.

In the end, she'd filled the suitcase with leggings and sweaters to combat the cool ocean breezes and everyday lingerie because she was making too big a deal out of what was to come.

Ming entered the cottage and set her suitcase by the front door. Her senses purred as she gazed around the large living room decorated in soothing blues and golds. Beyond the cozy furnishings was a wall of windows that revealed a deck gilded by the setting sun and beyond, the indigo ocean.

To her right something mouthwatering was cooking in the small, well-appointed kitchen. An open door beside the refrigerator led outside. Nearing the kitchen, she spied Jason enjoying the ocean breezes from one of the comfortable chairs that flanked a love seat on the deck.

For an undisturbed moment she observed him. He was as relaxed as she'd seen him in months, expression calm, shoulders loose, hands at ease on the chair's arms. A sharp stab of anticipation made her stomach clench. Shocked by the excitement that flooded her, Ming closed her eyes and tried to even out her breathing. In a few short hours, maybe less, they would make love for the first time. Her skin prickled, flushed. Heat throbbed through her, forging a path that ended between her thighs.

Panic followed. She wasn't ready for this. For him.

Telling her frantic pulse to calm down, Ming stepped onto the deck. "Hi."

Jason's gaze swung her way. A smile bloomed. "Hi yourself." He stood and stepped toward her. "You're later than I expected."

His deep voice and the intense light in his eyes made her long to press herself into his arms and pretend they were a real couple and that this was a magical getaway. She dug her nails into her palms.

"It's been over a year since I've seen Wendy. We had a lot to catch up on."

"What was her take on your decision to have a baby?"

"Total support." Ming slipped past him and leaned her elbows on the railing. As the sapphire-blue ocean churned against rugged cliffs, sending plumes of water ten feet into the air, she put her face into the breeze and let it cool her hot cheeks. "After the week I had, it was a relief to tell someone who didn't go all negative on me."

"I wasn't negative."

Ming tore her gaze from the panorama and discovered Jason two feet away. Attacked by delicious tingles, she shook her head. "No, but you created trouble for me, nonetheless."

"Did you tell her about us?"

Ming shook her head. "We're supposed to keep this a secret, remember? Besides, she never liked you in high school."

"Everybody liked me in high school."

Although he'd been a jock and one of the most popular guys in school, Jason hadn't been mean to those less blessed the way his football buddies had been.

"Don't you mean all the girls?" Blaming nerves for her disgruntled tone, Ming pressed her lips together and redirected her attention to the view. The sun was still too bright to stare at, but the color was changing rapidly to orange.

"Them, too." Jason reached out and wrapped the ends of her scarf around his fists.

He tugged, startling her off balance, and stepped into her space. Her hormones shrieked in delight as the scent of cologne and predatory male surrounded her. She gulped air into her lungs and felt her breasts graze his chest. A glint appeared in his eyes, sending a spike of excitement through her.

"Something smells great in the kitchen. What's for dinner?" she asked, her voice cracking on the last word. Her appetite had vanished in the first rush of desire, but eating would delay what came later.

"Coq au vin." Although his lips wore a playful smile, his preoccupation with her mouth gave the horseplay a sexual vibe. He looked prepared to devour her in slow, succulent bites. "Your favorite. Are you hungry?"

He looked half-starved.

"I haven't eaten since breakfast." Her stomach had been too knotted to accept food.

"Then I'd better feed you." He softened his fists and let her scarf slip through his fingers, releasing her. "You'll need your strength for what I have planned for you tonight."

Freed, Ming couldn't move. The hunger prowling through her prevented her from backing to a safe distance. His knowing smirk kept her tongue-tied. She silently cursed as she trailed after him into the kitchen.

"I found a really nice chardonnay in town." He poured two glasses of wine and handed one to Ming. "I figured we'd save the champagne for later."

Great. He was planning to get her liquored up. She could blame the alcohol for whatever foolish thing she cried out in the heat of passion. She swallowed half the pale white wine in a single gulp and made approving noises while he pulled a wedge of brie out of the fridge. Grapes. Crackers. Some sort of pâté. All the sort of thing she'd served him at some point. Had he paid attention to what she liked? Asking herself the question had an adverse effect on her knees and led to more dangerous ruminating. What else might he have planned for her?

"Dinner should be ready in half an hour." He had everything assembled on a plate and used his chin to gesture toward the deck. "It's a gorgeous night. Let's not waste the good weather."

Early September in northern California was a lot cooler than what they'd left behind in Houston, and Ming welcomed the break from the heat. "It really is beautiful." She carried their glasses outside. "We should take a long walk after dinner."

Jason set down the plate and shot her a look. "If you have any strength in your legs after I'm done with you, we'll do that."

Despite the hot glance that accompanied his suggestive words, she shivered. Is this how the weekend was going to go? One long flirtation? It took them away from their normal interaction. Made her feel as if they'd grown apart these past few years and lost the comfortable intimacy they'd once shared.

"You're cold. Come sit with me and I'll warm you up."

Her scattered wits needed time to recover before she was ready to have his arms around her. "I'll grab my wrap."

"Let me get it."

"It's on my suitcase by the door."

How was she supposed to resist falling under his spell if he continued being so solicitous? This was the Jason she'd glimpsed with other women. The one she'd longed to have for her own. Only this Jason never stayed to charm any one woman for more than a few months, while Ming had enjoyed her fun-loving, often self-involved friend in her life for over twenty years. She sighed. Was it possible for him to be the thoughtful, romantic lover and a great friend all in one?

Was she about to find out? Or would making love with him complicate her life? Was he close to discovering she'd harbored a secret, unrequited crush on him for years? At best he'd not take it seriously and tease her about it. At worst, he'd put up walls and disappear the way he always did when a girlfriend grew too serious. Either way, she wasn't ready for his pity or his alarm.

Jason returned with her dark blue pashmina. "I put your suitcase in the bedroom."

Foolishly her heart jerked at the last word. Every instinct told her to run. Altering their relationship by becoming sexually intimate was only going to create problems.

Then he was wrapping the shawl around her and grazing her lips with his. All thoughts of fleeing vanished, lost in the heat generated by her frantic heart.

She put a hand on his arm. "Jason—"

He put a finger against her lips and silenced her. "Save it for later."

The twinkle in his eye calmed some of the frenzy afflicting her hormones. She reminded herself that he was way more experienced in the art of seduction, having had vast numbers of willing women to practice on. He liked the chase. It was routine that turned him off. And right now, he was having a ball pursuing her. Maybe if she stopped resisting, he'd turn down the charisma.

So, she took half a dozen slow, deep breaths and forced herself to relax. Nibbling cheese, she stared at their view and kept her gaze off the handsome man with the dazzling blue eyes. But his deep voice worked its way inside her, its rumble shaking loose her defenses. She let him feed her grapes and crackers covered with pâté. His fingers skimmed her lips, dusted sensation over her cheeks and chin. By the time they were bumping hips in the small kitchen while transferring coq au vin and potatoes to plates, pouring more wine and assembling cutlery, Ming had gotten past her early nerves.

This was the Jason she adored. Funny, completely present, a tad bit naughty. The atmosphere between them was as easy as it had ever been. They'd discussed Terry's offer to take over the practice. Her sister's decision to buy a house in Portland. And stayed away from the worrisome topic of what was going to happen after dessert.

"This is delicious," Ming murmured, closing her eyes in

rapture as the first bite of coq au vin exploded on her taste buds. "My favorite."

"I thought you'd appreciate it. Rosemary told me the restaurant was known for their French cuisine." Jason had yet to sample the dinner.

She indicated his untouched plate. "Aren't you hungry?" He sure looked half-starved.

"I'm having too much fun watching you eat."

And just like that the sizzle was back in the room. Ming's mouth went dry. She bypassed her wine and sipped water instead. After her first glass of the chardonnay, she'd barely touched her second. Making love to Jason for the first time demanded a clear head. She wanted to be completely in the moment, not lost in an alcoholic fog.

"How can watching me eat be fun?" She tried to make her tone light and amused, but it came out husky and broken.

"It's the pleasure you take in each bite. The way you savor the flavors. You're usually so matter-of-fact about things, I like knowing what turns you on."

He wasn't talking about food. Ming felt her skin heat. Her blood moved sluggishly through her veins. Even her heart seemed to slow. She could feel a sexy retort forming on her tongue. She bit down until she had it restrained. They were old friends who were about to have sex, not a man and a woman engaged in a romantic ritual that ended in passionate lovemaking. Ming had to be certain her emotions stayed out of the mix. She could count on Jason to do the same.

"The backs of my knees are very ticklish." She focused on cutting another bite of chicken. "I've always loved having my neck kissed. And there's a spot on my pelvis." She paused, cocked her head and tried to think about the exact spot. "I guess I'll have to show you when we get to that point." She lifted her fork and speared him with a matter-of-fact gaze. "And you?"

His expression told her he was on to her game. "I'm a guy.

Pretty much anywhere a beautiful woman touches me, I'm turned on."

"But there has to be something you really like."

His eyes narrowed. "My nipples are very sensitive."

She pressed her lips together to keep from laughing. "I'll pay special attention to them," she said when she trusted her voice.

If they could talk like this in the bedroom, Ming was confident she could emerge from the weekend without doing something remarkably stupid like mentioning how her feelings for him had been evolving over the last few months. She'd keep things casual. Focus on the physical act, not the intimacy. Use her hands, mouth and tongue to appreciate the perfection of Jason's toned, muscular body and avoid thinking about all those tiresome longings she'd bottled up over the years.

Savor the moment and ignore the future.

While Jason cleared the dishes from the table, Ming went to unpack and get ready for what was to come. Her confidence had returned over dinner. She had her priorities all in a row. Her gaze set on the prize. The path to creating a baby involved being intimate with Jason. She would let her body enjoy making love with him. Emotion had no place in what she was about to do.

Buoyed by her determination, Ming stopped dead in the doorway between the living room and bedroom. The scene before her laid waste to all her good intentions. Here was the stuff of seduction.

The centerpiece of the room was a king-size bed with the white down comforter pulled back and about a hundred red rose petals strewn across the white sheets. Candles covered every available surface, unlit but prepared to set a romantic mood when called upon. Piano music, played by her favorite artist, poured from the dresser, where portable speakers had been attached to an iPod. Everything was perfect.

Her chest locked up. She could not have designed a better setting. Jason had gone to a lot of trouble to do this. He'd planned, taken into account all her favorite things and executed all of this to give her the ideal romantic weekend.

It was so unlike him to think ahead and be so prepared. To take care of her instead of the other way around. It was as if she was here with a completely different person. A thoughtful, romantic guy who wanted something more than three days of great sex and then going back to being buddies. The sort of man women fell for and fell for hard.

"What do you think?"

She hadn't heard Jason's approach over the thump of her heart. "What I think is that I can't do this."

Jason surveyed the room, searching for imperfections. The candles were vanilla scented, her favorite. The rose petals on the bed proclaimed that this weekend was about romance rather than just sex. The coq au vin had been delicious. Everything he'd done was intended to set the perfect stage for romance.

He'd given her no indication that he intended to rush her. He'd promised her a memorable weekend. She had to know he'd take his time with her, drive her wild with desire. This wasn't some spontaneous hookup for him. He took what they were about to do seriously.

What the hell could possibly be wrong?

"I'm sorry," she said into the silence. Sagging against the door frame, she closed her eyes and the weight of the world appeared to descend on her.

"I don't understand."

"I don't, either." She looked beautiful and tragic as she opened her eyes and met his gaze. "I want to do this."

He was very glad to hear that because anticipation had been eating him alive these past few days. He wanted her with an intensity he'd never felt before. Maybe that was because ever since he'd kissed her, he'd been fantasizing about this moment. Or maybe he'd never worked this hard to get a woman into bed before.

"Being a mom is all I think about these days. I know if I want your help to get pregnant, we have to do it this weekend." Ming lapsed into silence, her hunched shoulders broadcasting discomfort.

"I didn't realize making love with me required so much sacrifice on your part." He forced amusement into his tone to keep disappointment at bay.

Her words had cut deep. When he'd insisted they make her baby this way instead of going to a clinic, he thought this would be the perfect opportunity to satisfy his longing for her. The kiss between them a few days earlier confirmed the attraction between them was mutual. Why was she resisting when the vibe between them was electric? What was she afraid of?

"I didn't mean it that way." But from her unhappy expression his accusation hadn't been far off.

"No?" Jason leaned against the wall and fought the urge to snatch her into his arms and kiss her senseless. He could seduce her, but he didn't want just her body, he wanted... "How exactly did you mean it?"

"Look, we're best friends. Don't you think sleeping together will make things awkward between us?"

"Not possible. It's because we're just friends that it will work so great." He sounded as if he was overselling used cars of dubious origin. "No expectations—"

"No strings?"

He didn't like the way she said that. As if he'd just confirmed her worst fears. "Are you worried that I'm in this just for the sex?" She wasn't acting as if she hoped it would lead to something more.

"Yes." She frowned, clearly battling conflicting opinions. "No."

"But you have some sort of expectation." Jason was surprised that his flight response wasn't stimulated by her question. Usually when a woman started thinking too much, it was time to get out.

"Not the sort you mean." She gave her head a vigorous shake. "I know perfectly well that once we have sex—"

"Make love."

"Whatever." She waved her hand as if she was batting away a pesky fly. "That once we…become intimate, you will have your curiosity satisfied—"

"Curiosity?" The word exploded from him. That's not how he'd describe the hunger pulsing through him. "You think all I feel is curiosity?"

She gave him a little shoulder shrug. Frustration clawed at him. The bed was feet away. He was damned tempted to scoop her up in his arms and drop her onto the softly scented sheets. Give her a taste of exactly what he was feeling.

He pushed off the wall and let his acute disappointment and eight-inch height advantage intimidate her into taking a step back. "And what about you? Aren't you the least bit curious how hot this thing between us will burn?"

"Oh, please. I'm not one of the women you date."

The second she rolled her eyes at him, Jason knew he'd hit a soft spot. Ming overthought everything. She liked her life neat and orderly. That was great for her career, but in her personal life she could use a man who overwhelmed her senses and short-circuited her thoughts. His brother hadn't been able to do it. Evan had once complained that his fiancée had a hard time being spontaneous and letting go. He'd never come right out and said that she'd been reserved in bed. Evan had too much respect for Ming to be so crass, but Jason had been able to read between the lines.

"What is that supposed to mean?"

"Has it ever occurred to you to look at the sort of women you prefer to date?"

"Beautiful. Smart. Sexy."

"Needy. Clinging. Terrified of abandonment." She crossed her arms over her chest and stared him down as no one else did. "You choose needy women to get your ego stroked and then, when you start to pull away because they're too clingy, they fear your abandonment and chase you."

"That's ridiculous." Jason wasn't loving the picture she was painting of him. Nor was this conversation creating the romantic mood he'd hoped for, but he refused to drop the subject until he'd answered her charges.

"Jennifer was a doctor," he said, listing the last three women he'd dated. "Amanda owned a very successful boutique and Sherri was a vice president of marketing. Independent, successful women all."

"Jennifer had daddy issues." She ticked the women off on her fingers. "Her father was a famous cardiologist and never let her feel as if she was good enough even though she finished second in her class at med school. Amanda was a middle child. She had four brothers and sisters and never felt as if her parents had time for her. As for Sherri, her mom left when she was seven. She had abandonment issues."

"How did you know all that?"

Ming's long-suffering look made his gut tighten. "Who do you think they come to when the relationship starts to cool?"

"What do you tell them?"

"That as wonderful as you are, any relationship with you has little chance of becoming permanent. You are a confirmed bachelor and an adrenaline junky with an all-consuming hobby who will eventually break their heart."

"Do they listen to you?"

"The healthy ones do."

"You know, if we weren't such old and dear friends, I might be tempted to take offense."

"You won't," she said confidently. "Because deep down you know you choose damaged women so eventually their issues will cause trouble between you and you have the perfect excuse to break things off."

Deep down he knew this? "And here I thought I dated them because they were hot." About then, Jason realized Ming had picked a fight with him. "I don't want to talk about all the women I've dated." But it was too late.

Ming wore the mulish expression he'd first encountered on the playground when one of his buddies had shoved her off the swings.

"This weekend was a mistake." She slipped sideways into the bedroom and headed straight for her suitcase.

To Jason's bafflement, she used it as a battering ram, clearing him from her path to the front door.

"You're leaving?"

"You thought conceiving a baby should be memorable, but the only thing I'm going to remember about being here with you is this fight."

"We're not fighting." She was making no sense, and Jason wasn't sure how trying to provide her with a romantic setting for their first time together had sparked her wrath. "Where do you think you're going?"

"Back to San Francisco. There's a midnight flight that will put me back in Houston by morning."

How could she know that unless…? "You'd already decided you weren't going to stay."

"Don't be ridiculous." Her voice rang with sincerity, but she was already out the door and her face was turned away from him. "I just happened to notice it when I was booking my flight."

Ming was approaching the trunk of her rental car as Jason barreled through the front door and halted. His instincts told him to stop her. He was reasonably certain he could coax her mood back to romance with her favorite dessert and a stroll through the gardens, but her words had him wondering about his past choices when it came to relationships.

In the deepening twilight, a full harvest moon, robust and orange from the sunset, crested the trees. A lovers' moon. Pity it would go to waste on them.

Jason dug his fingers into the door as Ming turned her car

around. Was giving her time to think a good idea? He was gambling that eventually she'd remember that she needed him to get pregnant.

Five

Ming hadn't been able to sleep on the red-eye from San Francisco to Houston. The minute her car had reached the Mendocino city limits, she'd begun to feel the full weight of her mistake. She had three choices: convince Jason to use a clinic for her conception, give up on him being her child's father or stop behaving like a ninny and have sex with him. Because it was her nature to do so, she spent the flight home making pro and con lists for each choice. Then she weighted each item and analyzed her results.

Logic told her to head for the nearest sperm bank. Instead, as soon as the wheels of the plane hit the runway, she texted him an apology and asked him to call as soon as he was able.

The cab from the airport dropped her off at nine in the morning. She entered her house and felt buffeted by its emptiness. With Lily in Portland and Muffin spending the weekend with Ming's parents, she had the place to herself. The prospect depressed her, but she was too exhausted to fetch the active Yorkshire terrier.

Closing the curtains in her room, she slid between the sheets but didn't fall asleep as soon as her head touched the pillow. She tortured herself with thoughts of making love with Jason. Imagined his strong body moving against her, igniting her passion. Her body pulsed with need. If she hadn't panicked, she wouldn't feel like a runaway freight train. She'd be sated and sleepy instead of wide awake and horny.

Ming buried her face in the pillow and screamed her frustration until her throat burned. That drained enough of her energy to allow her to sleep. She awakened some hours later, disoriented by the dark room, and checked the clock. It was almost five. She pushed to a sitting position and raked her long hair away from her face. Despite sleeping for six hours, she was far from rested. Turbulent dreams of Jason returned her to that unfulfilled state that had plagued her earlier.

If not for the evocative scents of cooking, she might have spent what remained of the day in bed, but her stomach growled, reminding her she hadn't had anything to eat except the power bar she'd bought at the airport. She got dressed and went to the kitchen to investigate.

"Something smells great." Ming stepped off the back stairs and into her kitchen, surprising her sister.

The oven door closed with a bang as she spun to face Ming. "You're home." Lily's cheeks bore a rosy flush, probably put there by whatever simmered on the stove.

Even though both girls had learned to cook from their mother, only Lily had inherited their mother's passion for food. Ming knew enough to keep from starving, but for her cooking was more of a necessity than an infatuation.

"You're cooking."

"I was craving lamb."

"Craving it?" The dish was a signature item Lily prepared when she was trying to impress a guy. It had been over a year since she'd made it. "I thought you were going to be house hunting in Portland this weekend."

"I changed my mind about spending the weekend."

"Does this mean you're changing your mind about moving?" Ming quizzed, unable to contain the hope in her voice.

"No." Lily pulled a bottle of wine from the fridge and dug in a drawer for the corkscrew. "How come you're home so early? I thought you were gone all weekend."

Ming thought of the chardonnay she and Jason had shared. How he'd fed her grapes and how she'd enjoyed his hands on her skin. "I wasn't having any fun so I thought I'd come home." Not the whole truth, but far from a lie. "I didn't get a chance to tell you before you left town last week, but Terry wants to sell me his half of the practice. He's retiring."

"How are you going to manage a baby and the practice all by yourself?"

"I can handle it just fine."

"I think you're being selfish." Lily's words, muffled by the refrigerator door, drove a spear into Ming's heart. She pulled a bowl of string beans out and plunked them on the counter. "How can you possibly have enough time for a child when you're running the practice?"

"There are a lot of professional women who manage to do both." Ming forced back the doubts creeping up on her, but on the heels of her failure with Jason this weekend, she couldn't help but wonder if her subconscious agreed with Lily.

What if she couldn't do both well? Was she risking complete failure? No. She could do this. Even without a partner in her life to help her when things went wrong, or to celebrate the triumphs?

She was going to be awfully lonely. Sure, her parents would help when they could, but Lily was moving and Jason had his racing and his career to occupy him. What was she thinking? She would have her child and the practice to occupy her full attention. What about love? Marriage?

She brushed aside the questions. What good did it do to

focus on something she couldn't control? Planning and organization led to success, and she was a master of both.

With her confidence renewed, she poured wine from the bottle Lily had opened. As it hit her taste buds, she made a face. She checked the label and frowned at her sister.

"Since when do you drink Riesling?"

"I'm trying new things."

"This is Evan's favorite wine."

"He recommended it so I bought a bottle."

"Recently?"

"No." Her sister frowned. "A while ago. Geez, what's with all the questions? I tried a type of wine your ex liked. Big deal."

Lily's sharpness rocked Ming. Was her sister so upset with her that it threatened to drive a wedge between them?

Ming set down her wineglass. "I'm going to run over to Mom and Dad's and pick up Muffin. Is there anything you need me to get while I'm out?"

"How about a bottle of wine you prefer?"

Flinching at her sister's unhappy tone, Ming grabbed her keys and headed for the door. "You know, I'm not exactly thrilled with your decision to move to Portland, but I know it's something you feel you have to do, so I'm trying to put aside my selfish wish for you to stay and at least act like I'm supportive."

Then, without waiting for her sister's reply, Ming stepped into her garage and shut the door firmly behind her. With her hands shaking, she had a hard time getting the key into the ignition of the '66 Shelby Cobra. She'd chosen to drive the convertible tonight, hoping the fresh air might clear away all the confusion in her mind.

The drive to her parents' house was accomplished in record time thanks to the smoothly purring 425 V8 engine. She really should sell the car. It was an impractical vehicle for a mother-to-be, but she had such great memories of the summer she and Jason had spent fixing it up.

After her spat with Lily, she'd planned to join her parents for dinner, but they were meeting friends at the country club, so Ming collected her dog and retraced her path back to her house. A car sat in her driveway. In the fading daylight, it took her a second to recognize it as Evan's.

Because she and Jason were best friends and she knew there'd be occasions when she'd hang out with his family, Ming had made a decision to keep her interactions with Evan amicable. In fact, it wasn't that hard. Their relationship lacked the turbulent passion that would make her hate him for dumping her. But that didn't mean she was okay about him showing up without warning.

Ming parked the convertible in the garage. Disappointment filled her as she tucked Muffin under her arm and exited the car. She'd been hoping Jason had stopped by. He hadn't called her or responded to her text.

When she entered the house, the tension in the kitchen stopped her like an invisible wall. What the heck? Evan and her sister had chosen opposite sides of the center island. An almost empty wine bottle sat between them. Lily's mouth was set in unhappy lines. Her gaze dropped from Evan to the bowl of lettuce on the counter before her.

"Evan, this is a surprise." Ming eyed the vase of flowers beside the sink. Daisies. The same big bunch he always gave her after they'd had a difference of opinion. He thought the simple white flower represented a sweet apology. He was nothing if not predictable. Or maybe not so predictable. Why had he shown up on her doorstep without calling?

Lily didn't look Ming's way. Had her sister shared with Evan her dismay about Ming's decision to have a baby? Stomach churning, she set Muffin down. The terrier headed straight for her food bowl.

"What brings you here?" Ming asked.

"I came by to… Because…" He appeared at a loss to explain his reason for visiting.

"Are you staying for dinner? Lily's making rack of lamb. I'm sure there's enough for three, or I should say four, since usually she makes it for whomever she's dating at the time."

Evan's gaze sliced toward Lily. "You're dating someone?"

"Not dating exactly, just using him for sex." Ming lowered her voice. "Although I think she's ready to find someone she can get serious about. That's why she's moving to Portland."

"And the guy she's seeing." Since Lily refused to look up from the lettuce she was shredding, Evan directed the question at Ming. "She can't get serious about him?"

"She says they're just friends." The Yorkie barked and Ming filled Muffin's bowl. "Isn't that right, Lily?"

"I guess." Lily's gaze darted between Ming and Evan.

"So, when are you expecting him to show?"

"Who?"

"The guy you're preparing the lamb for."

"There's no guy," Lily retorted, her tone impatient. "I told you I was craving lamb. No big deal."

Ming felt the touch of Evan's gaze. She'd been using Lily's love life to distract him from whatever purpose he had for visiting her tonight. Something about Evan had changed in the past year. The closer they got to their wedding, the more he'd let things irritate him. A part of her had been almost relieved when he called things off.

What was he doing here tonight? She glanced at the daisies. If he was interested in getting back together, his timing was terrible.

"I'm going to head upstairs and unpack," she told them, eager to escape. "Evan, make sure you let me know if Lily's mystery man shows up. I'm dying to meet him."

"There's no mystery man," her sister yelled up the stairs at her.

Ming set her suitcase on the bed and began pulling clothes out of it. She put everything where it belonged, hamper and dry cleaning pile for the things she'd worn, drawers and hang-ers for what she hadn't. When she was done, only one item remained. A white silk nightie. Something a bride might wear on her wedding night. She'd bought it in San Francisco two days ago specifically for her weekend with Jason.

Now what was she supposed to do with it?

"Ming?"

She spun around at the sound of Evan's voice. "Is Lily's date here?"

His gaze slid past her to the lingerie draped over the foot of her bed. He stared at it for a long moment before shifting his attention back to her.

"I've wanted to talk to you about something."

Her pulse jerked. He was so solemn. This couldn't be good. "You have? Let's go have dinner and chat."

He put up his hands as she started for the door. "This is something we need to discuss, just us."

Nothing that serious could ever be good. "You know, I'm in a really good place right now." She pulled her hair over one shoulder and finger-combed it into three sections. "The practice is booming. Terry wants me to buy him out." Her fingers made quick work of a braid and she snagged a scrunchy off her nightstand. "I'm happy."

"And I don't want that to change. But there's something you need to know—"

"Dinner's ready."

Ming cast her sister a grateful smile. "Wonderful. Come on, Evan. You're in for a treat." She practically raced down the stairs. Her glass of wine was on the counter where she'd left it and Ming downed the contents in one long swallow. Wincing at the taste, she reached into her wine cooler and pulled out a Shiraz.

Over dinner, Evan's sober expression and Lily's preoccupation with her own thoughts compelled Ming to fill the awkward silence with a series of stories about her trip to San Francisco and amusing anecdotes about Wendy's six-year-old daughter.

By the time the kitchen was cleaned up and the dishwasher happily humming, she was light-headed from too much wine and drained from carrying the entire conversation.

Making no attempt to hide her yawns, Ming headed upstairs and shut her bedroom door behind her. In the privacy of her large master suite, she stripped off her clothes and stepped into the shower. The warm water pummeled her, releasing some of the tension from her shoulders. Wrapped in a thick terry-cloth robe, she sat cross-legged on her window seat and stared out over her backyard. She had no idea how long her thoughts drifted before a soft knock sounded on her door.

Lily stuck her head in. "You okay?"

"Is Evan gone?"

Lily nodded. "I'm sorry about what I said to you earlier."

"You're not wrong. I am being selfish." Ming patted the seat beside her. "But at the same time you know that once I decide to do something, I give it my all."

Lily hugged Ming before sitting beside her on the window seat. "If anyone is going to be supermom it's you."

"Thanks." Ming swallowed past the tightness in her throat. She hated fighting with Lily. "So, what's up with Evan?"

"What do you mean?"

"When I came in tonight, he looked as grim as I've ever seen him. I figured he was explaining why he showed up out of the blue." Ming knew her sister had always been partial to Jason's older brother. Often in the past six months, Ming thought Lily had been the sister most upset about the broken engagement. "You two became such good friends these last few years. I thought maybe he'd share with you his reason for coming here tonight."

"Do you think Jason told him that you want to have a baby?"

"He wouldn't do that." Ming's skin grew warm as she imagined where she'd be right at this moment if she hadn't run out on Jason. Naked. Wrapped in his arms. Thighs tangled. Too happy to move. "I know this sounds crazy, but what if Evan wants to get back together?"

"Why would you think he'd want to do that?" Lily's voice rose.

"I don't. Not really." Ming shook her head. "It's just that after I told Jason I wanted to get pregnant, he was so insistent that I'm not over Evan."

"Are you?" Her sister leaned forward, eyebrows drawn together. "I mean Evan broke up with you, not the other way around."

Ming toyed with the belt of her robe. The pain of being dumped eased a little more each day, but it wasn't completely gone. "It really doesn't matter how I feel. The reasons we broke up haven't changed."

"What if they did? What if the problems that came between you were gone? Out of the picture?" Lily was oddly intent. "Would you give him another chance?"

Ming tried to picture herself with Evan now that she'd tasted Jason's kisses. She'd settled for one brother instead of fighting for the other. That was a mistake she wouldn't make again. She'd rather be happy as a single mom than be miserable married to a man she didn't love.

"I've spent the last six months reimagining my life without Evan," she told her sister. "I'd rather move forward than look back."

At a little after 8:00 p.m., Jason sat in his car and stared at Ming's house. When she'd left him in Mendocino, his pride had kept him from chasing after her for a little over two hours. He'd come to California to spend the weekend with Ming, not to pace a hotel room in a frenzy of unsatisfied desire. Confident she wouldn't miraculously change her mind and return to him, Jason had gotten behind the wheel and returned to the San Francisco airport, where he'd caught a 6:00 a.m. flight back to Houston.

He hadn't liked the way things had been left between them, and her text message gave him hope she hadn't, either. After catching a few hours of sleep, he'd come here tonight to talk her into giving his strategy one last shot.

But the sight of his brother's car parked in Ming's driveway distracted him. What the hell was Evan doing here? Had he come to tell Ming that he was dating her sister? If so, Jason should get in there because Ming was sure to be upset.

He had his hand on the door release when her front door opened. Despite the porch light pouring over the couple's head, he couldn't see Lily's expression, but her body language would be visible from the moon.

Ming's sister was hung up on his brother. And from the way Evan slid his hands around her waist and pulled her against him for a deep, passionate kiss, the feeling was mutual.

It took no more than a couple of seconds for an acid to eat at Jason's gut. He glanced away from the embracing couple, but anger continued to build.

What the hell did Evan think he was doing? Didn't he care about Ming's feelings at all? Didn't he consider how hurt she'd be if she saw him kissing Lily? Obviously not. Good thing Jason was around to straighten out his brother before the situation spun out of control.

A motor started, drowning out Jason's heated thoughts. Evan backed out of the driveway. Jason had missed the chance to catch his brother in the act. Cursing, he dialed Evan's number.

"Jason, hey, what's up?"

"We need to talk."

"So talk." Considering the fact that Evan had just engaged in a long, passionate kiss, he wasn't sounding particularly chipper.

"In person." So he could throttle his brother if the urge arose. "O'Malley's. Ten minutes."

The tension in Jason's tone must have clued in his brother to Jason's determination because Evan agreed without protest. "Sure. Okay."

Jason ended the call and followed his brother's car to the neighborhood bar. He chose the parking spot next to Evan's and was standing at his brother's door before Evan had even turned off the engine.

"You and Lily are still seeing each other?" Jason demanded, not allowing his brother to slide from behind the wheel.

"I never said I was going to stop."

"Does Ming know?"

"Not yet."

"She'll find out pretty quickly if you keep kissing Lily in full view of Ming's neighbors."

"I didn't think about that." Evan didn't ask how Jason knew. "I was sure Ming wouldn't see us. She'd gone up to her room."

"So that made it okay?" Fingers curling into fists, Jason stabbed his brother with a fierce glare. "If you intend to flaunt your relationship, you need to tell her what you and Lily are doing."

"I started to tonight, but Lily interrupted me. She doesn't want Ming to know." And Evan didn't look happy about it. "Can we go inside and discuss this over a beer?"

Considering his mood, Jason wasn't sure consuming alcohol around his brother was a wise idea, but he stepped back so Evan could get out of the car. With an effort Jason unclenched his fists and concentrated on soothing his bad temper. By the time they were seated near the back, Jason's fury had become a slow burn.

"Why doesn't Lily want Ming to know?" Jason sat with his spine pressed against the booth's polished wood back while Evan leaned his forearms on the table, all earnest and contrite.

"Because I don't think she intends for it to go anywhere."

If Evan wasn't running the risk of hurting Ming all over again, Jason could have sympathized with his brother's pain. "Then you need to quit seeing her."

"I can't." Despite the throb in his brother's voice, the corners of his mouth relaxed. "The sex is incredible. I tell myself a hundred times a day that it's going nowhere and that I should get out before anyone is hurt, but then I hear her voice or see her and I have to…" He grimaced. "I don't know why I'm telling you this."

"So you two are combustible together." Resentment made Jason cross. He and Ming had great chemistry, too, but instead of exploring some potentially explosive lovemaking, they were at odds over what effect this might have on their friendship.

"It's amazing."

"But…?" Jason prompted.

"I don't know if we can make it work. We have completely different ideas about what we want." Evan shook his head. "And now she's moving to Portland."

Which should put an end to things, but Jason sensed the upcoming separation was causing things to heat up rather than cool down.

"Long-range relationships don't work," Jason said.

"Sometimes they do. And I love her." Something Evan looked damned miserable about.

"Is she in love with you?"

"She claims it's nothing but casual sex between us. But it sure as hell doesn't feel casual when we're at it."

Love was demonstrating once again that it had no one's best interests at heart. Evan was in love with Lily, but she obviously didn't feel the same way, and that made him unhappy. And finding out that her ex-fiancé was in love with her sister was going to cause Ming pain. Nothing good came of falling in love.

"All the more reason you should quit seeing Lily before Ming finds out."

"That's not what I want."

"What *you* want?"

Jason contemplated the passion that tormented his brother. The entire time Evan and Ming were dating, not once had Evan displayed the despair that afflicted him now.

"How about what's good for Ming?" Jason continued.

"Don't you think you did enough damage to her when you broke off your engagement two weeks before the wedding?"

"Yeah, well, that was bad timing on my part." Evan paused for a beat. "We weren't meant to be together."

"You and Lily aren't meant to be together, either."

"I don't agree." Evan sounded grim. "And I want a chance to prove it. Can I count on you to keep quiet?"

"No." Seeing his brother's expression, Jason relented. "I'm not going to run over there tonight and tell her. Talk to Lily. Figure this out. You can have until noon tomorrow."

As his anger over Evan's choice of romantic partner faded, Jason noticed the hollow feeling in his chest was back. He sipped the beer the waitress had set before him and wondered why Ming had chosen to pick a fight with him in California instead of surrendering to the heat between them.

Was she really afraid their relationship would be changed by sex? How could it when they'd been best friends for over twenty years? Sure, there'd been sparks the night of senior prom, but they'd discussed the situation and decided their friendship was more important than trying to date only to have it end badly.

And what they were about to do wasn't dating. It was sex, pure and simple. A way for Ming to get pregnant. For Jason to purge her from his system.

For him to satisfy his curiosity?

Maybe her accusation hadn't been completely off the mark. He wouldn't be a guy if he hadn't looked at Ming in a bathing suit and recognized she was breathtaking. From prom night his fingers knew the shape of her breasts, his tongue the texture of her nipples. The soft heat of her mouth against his. That wasn't something he could experience and then never think about again.

But he wasn't in love with her. He'd never let that happen. Their friendship was too important to mess up with romance. Love had almost killed his father. And Evan wasn't doing too well, either.

Nope. Better to keep things casual. Uncomplicated.

Which didn't explain why he'd offered to help Ming get pregnant and why he'd suggested they do it the natural way. And Jason had no easy answer.

Six

By Sunday afternoon Ming still hadn't heard from Jason, and his lack of response to her phone calls and texts struck her as odd. She'd apologized a dozen times. Why was he avoiding her? After brunch with Lily, she drove to Jason's house in the hope of cornering him and getting answers. Relief swept her as she spied him by the 'Cuda he'd won off Max a few months ago. She parked her car at the bottom of the driveway and stared at him for a long moment.

Bare except for a pair of cargo shorts that rode low on his hips, he was preoccupied with eliminating every bit of dust from the car's yellow paint. His bronzed skin glistened with a fine mist of water from the hole in the nearby garden hose. The muscles across his back rippled as he plunged the sponge into the bucket of soapy water near his bare feet.

Ming imagined gliding her hands over those male contours, digging her nails into his flesh as he devoured her. The fantasy inspired a series of hot flashes. She slid from behind the wheel and headed toward him.

"I think you missed a spot," she called, stopping a couple feet away from the back bumper. Hearing the odd note in her own voice brought about by her earlier musing, she winced. When he frowned at her, she pointed to a nonexistent smudge on the car's trunk.

Since waking at six that morning, she'd been debating what tack to take with Jason. Did she scold him for not calling her back? Did she pretend that she wasn't hurt and worried that he'd ignored her apologies? Or did she just leave her emotional baggage at the door and talk to him straight like a friend?

Jason dropped the sponge on the car's roof and set his hands on his hips. "I'm pretty sure I didn't."

She eyed the car. "I'm pretty sure you did." When he didn't respond, she stepped closer to the car and pointed. "Right here."

"If you think you can do better..." He lobbed the dripping sponge onto the trunk. It landed with a splat, showering her with soapy water. "Go ahead."

Unsure why he got to act unfriendly when she'd been the one to apologize only to be ignored, she picked up the sponge and debated what to do with it. She could toss it back and hope it hit him full in the face, or she could take the high road and see if they could talk through what had happened in California.

Gathering a calming breath, she swept the sponge over the trunk and down toward the taillights. "I've left you a few messages," she said, focusing on the task at hand.

"I know. Sorry I haven't called you back."

"Is there a reason why you didn't?"

"I've been busy."

Cleaning an already pristine car was a pointless endeavor. So was using indirect methods to get Jason to talk about something uncomfortable. "When you didn't call me back, I started wondering if you were mad at me."

"Why would I be mad?"

Ming circled the car and dunked the sponge into the bucket. Jason had retreated to the opposite side of the 'Cuda and was spraying the car with water. Fine mist filled the air, landing on Ming's skin, lightly coating her white blouse and short black skirt. She hadn't come dressed to wash a car. And if she didn't retreat, she risked ruining her new black sandals.

"Because of what happened in Mendocino."

"You mean because you freaked out?" At last he met her gaze. Irritation glittered in his bright blue eyes.

"I didn't freak…exactly."

"You agreed we'd spend three days together and when you got there, you lasted barely an hour before picking a fight with me and running out. How is that not freaking?"

Ming scrubbed at the side mirror, paying careful attention to the task. "Well, I wouldn't have done that if you hadn't gone all Don Juan on me."

"Don Juan?" He sounded incredulous.

"Master of seduction."

"I have no idea what you're talking about."

"The roses on the bed. The vanilla candles. I'm surprised you didn't draw me a bubble bath." In the silence that followed her accusation, she glanced up. The expression on his face told her that had also been on his agenda. "Good grief."

"Forgive me for trying to create a romantic mood."

"I didn't ask for romance," she protested. "I just wanted to get pregnant."

In a clinic. Simple. Uncomplicated.

"Since when do you have something against romance? I seem to remember you liked it when Evan sent you flowers and took you out for candlelit dinners."

"Evan and I were dating." They'd been falling in love.

She picked up the bucket and moved to the front of the car. This time Jason stayed put.

"I thought you'd appreciate the flowers and the candlelight."

Ming snorted. "Men do stuff like that to get women into bed. But you already knew we were going to have sex. So what was with the whole seduction scene?"

"Why are you making such an issue out of this?"

She stopped scrubbing the hood and stared at him, hoping she could make him understand without divulging too much. "You created the perfect setting to make me fall in love with you."

"That's not what I was doing."

"I know you don't plan to make women fall for you, but it's what happens to everyone you date." She applied the sponge to the hood in a fury. "You overwhelm them with romantic gestures until they start picturing a future with you and then you drop them because they want more than you can give them."

The only movement in his face was the tic in his jaw. "You make it sound like I deliberately try to hurt them."

"That's not it at all. I don't think you have any idea what it's like when you turn on the Sterling charm."

"Are you saying that's what I did to you?"

It was the deliberate nature of what he'd done that made her feel like a prize to be won, not a friend to be helped. Another conquest. Another woman who would fall in love with him and then be dumped when she got too serious. When she wanted too much from him.

"Yes. And I don't get why." She dropped the sponge into the bucket and raked her fingers through her damp hair, lifting the soggy weight off her neck and back so the breeze could cool her. "All I wanted was to have a baby. I didn't want to complicate our friendship with sex. Or make things weird between us." Dense emotions weighed on her. Her shoulders sagged beneath the burden. She let her arms fall to her sides. "That's why I've decided to let you off the hook."

"What do you mean?"

"I'm going forward as originally planned. I'll use an anonymous donor and we can pretend the last two weeks never happened."

"I'm tired of pretending."

Before she'd fully processed his statement, chilly water rained down on her. Ming shrieked and stepped back.

"Hey." She wiped water from her eyes and glared at Jason. "Watch it."

"Sorry." But he obviously wasn't.

"You did that on purpose."

"I didn't."

"Did, too."

And abruptly they were eight again, chasing each other around her parents' backyard with squirt guns. She grabbed the sponge out of the bucket and tossed it at his head. He dodged it without even moving his feet, and a smattering of droplets showered down on her.

The bucket of water was at her feet. Seconds later it was in her hands. She didn't stop to consider the consequences of what she was about to do. How long since she'd acted without thought?

"If you throw that, I'll make sure you'll regret it," Jason warned, his serious tone a stark contrast to the dare in his eyes.

The emotional tug-of-war of the past two weeks had taken a toll on her. Her friendship with Jason was the foundation that she'd built her life on. But the longing for his kisses, the anticipation of his hands sliding over her naked flesh... She was on fire for him. Head and heart at war.

"Damn you, Jason," she whispered.

Soapy water arced across the six feet separating them and landed precisely where she meant it to. Drenched from head to groin, Jason stood perfectly still for as long as it took for Ming to drop the bucket. Then he gave his head a vigorous shake, showering soapy droplets all around him.

Ming watched as if in slow motion as he raised the hose in his hand, aimed it at her and squeezed the trigger. Icy water sprayed her. Sputtering with laughter, she put up her hands and backed away. Hampered by her heels from moving fast enough to escape, she shrieked for Jason to stop. When the deluge continued, she kicked off her shoes and raced for the house.

Until she stood dripping on Jason's kitchen floor, it hadn't occurred to her why she hadn't made a break for her car. The door leading to the garage slammed shut.

Shivering in the air-conditioning, Ming whirled to confront Jason.

He stalked toward her. Eyes on fire. Mouth set in a grim line. She held her ground as he drew near. Her trembling became less about being chilled and more about Jason's intensity as he stepped into her space and cupped her face in his hands.

"I'm sorry about California…"

The rest of her words were lost, stopped by the demanding press of his lips to hers. Electrified by the passion in his kiss, she rose up on tiptoe and wrapped her arms around his neck and let him devour her with lips, tongue and teeth.

Yes. This is what she'd been waiting for. The crazy wildness that had gripped them on prom night. The urgent craving to rip each other's clothes off and couple like long-lost lovers. Fire exploded in her loins as pulse after pulse drove heat to her core.

She drank from the passion in his kiss, found her joy in the feint and retreat of his tongue with hers. His hands left her face and traveled down her throat to her shoulders. And lower. She quaked as his palms moved over her breasts and caressed her stomach. Before she knew what he was after, he'd gathered handfuls of her blouse. She felt a tremor ripple through his torso a second before he tore her shirt open.

Flinging off her ruined shirt, Ming arched her back and pressed into his palms as he cupped her breasts through her sodden bra and made her nipples peak. Between her thighs an ache built toward a climax that would drive her mad if she couldn't get him to hurry. Impatience clawed at her. She needed his skin against hers. Reaching behind her, Ming released her bra clasp.

Jason peeled it away and drew his fingertips around her

breasts and across her aching nipples. "Perfect." Husky with awe, his voice rasped against her nerves, inflaming her already raging desire.

He bent his head and took one pebbled bud into his mouth, rolling his tongue over the hard point before sucking hard. The wet pulling sensation shot a bolt of sensation straight to where she hungered, wrenching a gasp from Ming.

"Do that again," she demanded, her fingers biting into his biceps. "That was incredible."

He obliged until her knees threatened to give out. "I've imagined you like this for so long," he muttered against her throat, teeth grazing the cord in her neck.

"Like what, half-naked?"

"Trembling. On fire." He slipped his hand beneath her skirt and skimmed up her thigh. "For me."

Shuddering as he closed in on the area where she wanted him most, Ming let her own fingers do some exploring. Behind the zipper of his cargo shorts he was huge and hard. As her nails grazed along his length, Jason closed his eyes. Breath escaped in a hiss from between his clenched teeth.

Happy with his reaction, but wanting him as needy as he'd made her, she unfastened his shorts and dived beneath the fabric to locate skin. A curse escaped him when she sent his clothes to pool at his feet. She grasped him firmly.

Abandoning his own exploration, he pulled her hands away and carried them around to his back. His mouth settled on hers again, this time stealing her breath and her sense of equilibrium. She was spinning. Twirling. Lost in the universe. Only Jason's mouth on hers, his arms banding her body to his, gave her any sense of reality.

This is what she'd been missing on the couch in his den and on the deck in California. The line between friend and lover wasn't just blurred, it was eradicated by hunger and wanton impulses. Hesitations were put aside. There was only heat and urgency. Demand and surrender.

Her back bumped against something. She opened her eyes as Jason's lips left hers.

"I need you now," she murmured as he nibbled down her neck.

"Let's go upstairs."

Her knees wouldn't survive the climb. "I can't make it that far."

"What do you have in mind?"

His kitchen table caught her eye. "How about this?"

Her knees had enough strength to back him up five feet. He looked surprised when she shoved him onto one of the four straight-back chairs.

"I'm game if you are."

She hadn't finished shimmying out of her skirt when she felt his fingers hook in the waistband of her hot pink thong and begin drawing it down her thighs. Naked, she stared down at him, her heart pinging around in her chest.

There was no turning back from this moment.

Jason's fingers bit into her hips as she straddled the chair. Meeting his gaze, she positioned herself so the tip of him grazed her entrance. Looking into his eyes, she could see straight to his soul. No veils hid his emotions from her.

She lowered herself, joining them in body as in spirit, let her head fall back and gloried at the perfection of their fit.

He'd died and gone to heaven. With Ming arched over his arm, almost limp in his grasp, he'd reached a nirvana of sorts. The sensation of being buried inside her almost blew the top of his head off. He shuddered, lost in a bewildering maze of emotions.

"This is the first time," he muttered, lowering his lips to her throat, "I've never done this before."

She tightened her inner muscles around him and he groaned. Her chest vibrated in what sounded like a laugh. With her fingers digging into his shoulders, she straightened and stared deep into his eyes.

"I have it on good authority," she began, leaning forward to draw her tongue along his lower lip, "that this is not your first time." She spoke without rancor, unbothered by the women he'd been with before.

He stroked his hands up her spine, fingers gliding over her silken skin, feeling the ridges made by her ribs. "It's the first I've ever had sex without protection."

"Really?" She peered at him from beneath her lashes. "I'm your first?"

"My only."

The instant the words were out, Jason knew he'd said too much. Delight flickered in her gaze. Her glee lasted only for the briefest of instances, but he'd spotted it, knew what he'd given away.

"I like the sound of that."

"Only because I am never going to get anyone but you pregnant."

Her smile transformed her from serene and mysterious to animated and exotic. "I like the sound of that, too." This time when she kissed him, there was no teasing in her actions. She took his mouth, plunged her tongue deep and claimed him.

Fisting a hand in her hair, Jason answered her primal call. Their tongues danced in familiar rhythm, as if they hadn't had their first kiss over a decade before. He knew exactly how to drive her wild, what made her groan and tremble.

"I'll let you in on a little secret," she whispered, her breath hot in his ear. "You're my first, too."

Incapable of speech as she explored his chest, her clever fingers circling his nipples, nails raking across their sensitive surface, he arched his brow at her in question.

"I've never had sex on a kitchen chair before." She rotated her hips in a sexy figure eight that wrenched a groan from his throat. "I rather like it."

Pressure built in his groin as she continued to experiment with her movements. Straddling his lap, she had all the control she could ever want to drive him mad. Breath rasping, eyes half-closed, Jason focused on her face to distract himself from the pleasure cascading through his body. In all the dreams he'd had of her, nothing had been this perfect.

Arching her back, she shifted the angle of her hips and moved over him again. "Oh, Jason, this is incredible."

"Amazing." He garbled the word, provoking a short laugh from her. "Perfect."

"Yes." She sat up straight and looked him square in the eyes. "It's never been like this."

"For me, either."

Deciding they'd done enough talking, Jason kissed her, long and deep. Her movements became more urgent as their passion burned hotter. His fingers bit into her hips, guiding her. A soft cry slipped from her parted lips. Jason felt her body tense and knew she was close. That's all it took to start his own climax. Gaze locked on her face, he held back, waiting for her to pitch over the cliff. The sheer glory of it caught him off guard. She gave herself completely to the moment. And called his name.

With his ears filled with her rapture, he lost control and spilled himself inside her. They were making more than a baby. They were making a moment that would last forever. The richness of the experience shocked him. Never in a million years would he have guessed that letting himself go so completely would hit him with this sort of power.

Shaking, Jason gathered Ming's body tight against his chest and breathed heavily. As the last pulses of her orgasm eased, he smoothed her hair away from her face and bestowed a gentle kiss on her lips.

"I'm glad I was your first," she murmured, her slender arms wrapped around his neck.

He smiled. "I'm glad you're my only."

* * *

Taking full advantage of Jason's king-size bed, Ming lay on her stomach lengthwise across the mattress. With her chin on his chest, her feet kicking the air, she watched him. Naked and relaxed, he'd stretched out on his back, his hands behind his head, eyes closed, legs crossed at the ankle. An easy smile tipped the corners of his lips upward. Ming regarded his satisfied expression, delighted that she'd been the one to bring him to this state. Twice.

While her body was utterly drained of energy, the same couldn't be said for her mind. "Now that we have that out of the way, perhaps you can explain why you've been avoiding me for two days."

Jason's expression tightened. "Have you talked to your sister?"

"Lily?" Ming pushed herself into a sitting position. "We had brunch before I came here. Why?"

His lashes lifted. "She didn't tell you."

She had no idea what he was talking about. "Tell me what?"

"About her and Evan." Jason looked unhappy. "They've been seeing each other."

"My sister and your brother?" Ming repeated the words but couldn't quite get her mind around the concept. "Seeing each other...you mean dating?"

Her gaze slid over Jason. Two weeks ago she'd have laughed at anyone who told her she and Jason were going to end up in bed together. The news of Evan and Lily was no less unexpected.

"Yes." He touched her arm, fingers gentle as they stroked her skin. "Are you okay?"

His question startled her. But it was the concern on his face that made her take stock of her reaction. To her dismay she felt a twinge of discomfort. But she'd be damned if she'd admit it.

"If they get married we'll end up being brother and sister." She was trying for levity but fell short of the mark.

Jason huffed out an impatient breath. "Don't make light of this with me. I'm worried that you'll end up getting hurt."

Ming's bravado faded. "But it can't be that serious. Lily is moving to Portland. She wouldn't be doing that if they had a future together." Her voice trailed away. "That's why she's leaving, isn't it? They're in love and my sister can't break it off and stick around. She needs to move thousands of miles away to get over him."

"I don't know if your sister is in love with Evan."

"But Evan's in love with her."

Jason clamped his mouth shut, but the truth was written all over his face.

Needing a second to recover her equilibrium, Ming left the bed and snagged Jason's robe off the bathroom door. She put it on and fastened the belt around her waist. By the time she finished rolling up the sleeves, she felt calmer and more capable of facing Jason.

"How long have you known?" Ming heard the bitterness in her voice and tried to reel in her emotions. Evan hadn't exactly broken her heart when he'd ended their engagement, but that didn't mean she hadn't been hurt. She'd been weeks away from committing to him for the rest of her life.

"I've known they were going out but didn't realize how serious things had gotten until I spoke with Evan last night." Jason left the bed and came toward her. "Are you okay?"

"Sure." Something tickled her cheek. Ming reached up to touch the spot and her fingers came away wet. "I'm fine."

"Then why are you crying?"

Her heart pumped sluggishly. "I'm feeling sorry for myself because I'm wondering if Evan ever loved me." She stared at the ceiling, blinking hard to hold back the tears. "Am I so unlovable?"

Jason's arms came around her. His lips brushed her cheek. "You're the furthest thing from unlovable."

Safe in his embrace, she badly wanted to believe him, but

the facts spoke loud and clear. She was thirty-one, had never been married and was contemplating single motherhood.

"One of these days you'll find the right guy for you. I'm sure of it."

Hearing Jason's words was like stepping on broken glass. Pain shot through her, but she had nowhere to run. The man her heart had chosen had no thought of ever falling in love with her.

Ming pushed out of Jason's arms. "Did you really just say that minutes after we finished making love?"

His expression darkened. "I'm trying to be a good friend."

"I get that we're never going to be a couple, but did it ever occur to you that I might not be thinking about another man while being naked with you?" Her breath rushed past the lump in her throat.

"That's funny." His voice cracked like a whip. "Because just a second ago you were crying over the fact that my brother is in love with your sister."

Ming's mouth popped open, but no words emerged. Too many statements clogged the pathway between her brain and her lips. Everything Jason had said to her was perfectly reasonable. Her reactions were not. She was treating him like a lover, not like a friend.

"You're right. I'm a little thrown by what's happening between Lily and Evan. But it's not because I'm in love with him. And I can't even think about meeting someone and starting a relationship right now."

"Don't shut yourself off to the possibility."

"Like you have?" Ming couldn't believe he of all people was giving her advice on her love life. Before she blurted out her true feelings, she gathered up all her wayward emotions and packed them away. "I'd better get home and check on Muffin."

"I'm sure Muffin is fine." Jason peered at her, his impatience banked. "Are you?"

"I'm fine."

"Why don't I believe you?"

She wanted to bask in his concern, but they were in different places in their relationship right now. His feelings for her hadn't changed while she was dangerously close to being in love with him.

"No need to worry about me." Ming collected her strength and gave him her best smile. Crossing to his dresser, she pulled out a T-shirt. "Is it okay if I borrow this since you ruined my blouse?"

Jason eyed her, obviously not convinced by her performance. "Go ahead. I don't want to be responsible for any multicar pile-ups if you drive home topless." His tone was good-natured, but his eyes followed her somberly as she exchanged shirt for robe and headed toward the door.

"I'll call you later," she tossed over her shoulder, hoping to escape before unhappiness overwhelmed her.

"You could stay for dinner." He'd accompanied her downstairs and scooped up her black skirt and her hot pink thong before she could reach them, holding them hostage while he awaited her answer.

"I have some case files to look over before tomorrow," she said, conscious of his gaze on her as she tugged her underwear and skirt from his hands.

"You can work on them after dinner. I have some reports to go over. We can have a study date just like old times."

As tempting as that sounded, she recognized that it was time to be blunt. "I need some time to think."

"About what?"

"Things," she murmured, knowing Jason would never let her get away with such a vague excuse. Like how she needed to adjust to being friends *and* lovers with Jason. Then there was the tricky situation with her sister. She needed to get past being angry with Lily, not because she was dating Ming's ex-fiancé, but because her sister might get what Ming couldn't: a happily-ever-after with a man who loved her.

"What is there to think about?" Jason demanded. "We made love. Hopefully, we made a baby."

Her knees knocked together. Could she be pregnant already? The idea thrilled her. She wanted to be carrying Jason's child. Wanted it now more than ever. Which made her question her longing to become a mother. Would she be as determined if it was any other man who was helping her get pregnant? Or was she motivated by the desire to have something of Jason otherwise denied to her?

"I hope that, too." She forced a bright smile.

His bare feet moved soundlessly on the tile floor as he picked up her ruined blouse and carried it to the trash. Slipping back into her clothes, she regarded him in helpless fascination.

In jeans and a black T-shirt, he was everything she'd ever wanted in a man, flaws and all. Strong all the time, sensitive when he needed to be. He demonstrated a capacity for tenderness when she least expected it. They were incredible together in bed and the best of friends out of it.

"Or are you heading home to fret about your sister and Evan seeing each other?"

"No." But she couldn't make her voice as convincing as she wanted it to sound. "Evan and I are over. It was inevitable that he would start dating someone."

She just wished it hadn't happened with her sister.

Ming lifted on her tiptoes and kissed Jason. "Thanks for a lovely afternoon." The spontaneous encounter had knocked her off plan. She needed to regroup and reassess. Aiming for casual, she teased, "Let me know if you feel like doing it again soon."

He grabbed her hand and pushed it against his zipper. "I feel like doing it again now." His husky voice and the intense light in his eyes made her pulse rocket. "Stay for dinner. I promise you won't leave hungry."

The heat of him melted some of the chill from her heart. She leaned into his chest, her fingers curving around the bulge in his pants. He fisted his hand in her hair while his mouth slanted over hers, spiriting her into a passionate whirlwind. This afternoon she'd awakened to his hunger. The power of it set her senses ablaze. She was helpless against the appeal of his hard body as he eased her back against the counter. On the verge of surrendering to the mind-blasting pleasure of Jason's fingers sliding up her naked thigh, his earlier words came back to her.

One of these days you'll find the right guy for you.

She broke off the kiss. Gasping air into her lungs, she put her hands on Jason's chest and ducked her head before he could claim her lips again.

"I've really got to go," she told him, applying enough pressure to assure him she wasn't going to be swayed by his sensual persuasion.

His hands fell away. As hot as he'd been a moment ago, when he stepped back and plunged his hands into his pockets, his blue eyes were as cool and reflective as a mountain lake.

"How about we have dinner tomorrow?" she cajoled, swamped by anxiety. As perfect as it was to feel his arms tighten around her, she needed to sort out her chaotic emotions before she saw him again.

"Sure." Short and terse.

"Here?"

"If you want." He gave her a stiff nod.

She put her hand on his cheek, offered him a glimpse of her longing. "I want very much."

His eyes softened. "Five o'clock." He pressed a kiss into her palm. "Don't be late."

Seven

Ming parked her car near the bleachers that overlooked the curvy two-mile track. Like most of the raceways where Jason spent his weekends, this one was in the middle of nowhere. At least it was only a couple of hours out of Houston. Some of the tracks he raced at were hundreds of miles away.

Jason was going to be surprised to see her. It had been six or seven years since she'd last seen him race. The sport didn't appeal to her. Noisy. Dusty. Monotonous. She suspected the thrills came from driving, not watching.

So, what was she doing here?

If she was acting like Jason's "friend," she would have remained in Houston and spent her Saturday shopping or boating with college classmates. Driving over a hundred miles to sit on a metal seat in the blazing-hot sun fell put her smack dab in the middle of "girlfriend" territory. Would Jason see it as such? Ming took a seat in the stands despite the suspicion that coming here had been a colossal mistake.

The portion of track in front of her was a half-mile drag

strip that allowed the cars to reach over a hundred miles an hour before they had to power down to make the almost ninety-degree turn at the end. The roar was impressive as twenty-five high-performance engines raced past Ming.

Despite the speed at which they traveled, Jason's Mustang was easy to spot. Galaxy-blue. When he'd been working on the car, he'd asked for her opinion and she'd chosen the color, amused that she'd matched his car to his eyes without him catching on.

In seconds, the cars roared off, leaving Ming baking in the hot sun. With her backside sore from the hard bench and her emotions a jumble, it was official. She was definitely exhibiting "girlfriend" behavior.

And why? Because the past week with Jason had been amazing. It wasn't just the sex. It was the intimacy. They'd talked for hours. Laughed. She'd discovered a whole new Jason. Tender and romantic. Naughty and creative. She'd trusted him to take her places she'd never been, and it was addictive.

Which is why she'd packed a bag and decided to surprise him. A single day without Jason had made her restless and unable to concentrate.

Ming stood. This had been a mistake. She wasn't Jason's girlfriend. She had no business inserting herself into his guy time because she was feeling lonely and out of sorts. She would just drive back to Houston and he'd never know how close she'd come to making a complete fool of herself over him.

The cars roared up the straightaway toward her once again. From past experience at these sorts of events, she knew the mornings were devoted to warm-up laps. The real races would begin in the afternoon.

She glanced at the cars as they approached. Jason's number twenty-two was in the middle of the pack of twenty-five cars. He usually saved his best driving for the race. As the Mustang reached the end of the straightaway and began to slow down for the sharp turn, something happened. Instead of curving to the left, the Mustang veered to the right, hit the wall and spun.

Her lungs were ready to burst as she willed the cars racing behind him to steer around the wreckage so Jason didn't suffer any additional impact. Once the track cleared, his pit crew and a dozen others hurried to the car. Dread encased Ming's feet in concrete as she plunged down the stairs to the eight-foot-high chain-link fence that barred her from the track.

With no way of getting to Jason, she was forced to stand by and wait for some sign that he was okay. She gripped the metal, barely registering the ache in her fingers. The front of the Mustang was a crumpled mess. Ming tried to remind herself that the car had been constructed to keep the driver safe during these sorts of crashes, but her emotions, already in a state of chaos before the crash, convinced her he would never hear how she really felt about him.

"Wow, that was some crash," said a male voice beside her. "Worst I've seen in a year."

Ming turned all her fear and angst on the skinny kid with the baseball cap who'd come up next to her. "Do you work here?"

"Ah, yeah." His eyes widened as the full brunt of her emotions hit him.

"I need to get down there, right now."

"You're really not supposed—"

"Right now!"

"Sure. Sure." He backed up a step. "Follow me." He led her to a gate that opened onto the track. "Be careful."

But she was already on the track, pelting toward Jason's ruined car without any thought to her own safety. Because of the dozen or so men gathered around the car, she couldn't see Jason. Wielding her elbows and voice like blunt instruments, she worked her way to the front of the crowd in time to see Jason pulled through the car's window.

He was cursing as he emerged, but he was alive. Relief slammed into her. She stopped five feet from the car and watched him shake off the hands that reached for him when he swayed. He limped toward the crumpled hood, favoring his left knee.

Jason pulled off his helmet. "Damn it, there's the end of my season."

It could have been the end of him. Ming sucked in a breath as a sharp pain lanced through her chest. It was just typical of him to worry about his race car instead of himself. Didn't he realize what losing him would do to the people who loved him?

She stepped up and grabbed his helmet from his hands, but she lost the ability to speak as his eyes swung her way. She loved him. And not like a friend. As a man she wanted to claim for her own.

"Ming?" Dazed, he stared at her as if she'd appeared in a puff of smoke. "What are you doing here?"

"I came to watch you race." She gripped his helmet hard enough to crack it. "I saw you crash. Are you okay?"

"My shoulder's sore and I think I did something to my knee, but other than that, I'm great." His lips twisted as he grimaced. "My car's another thing entirely."

Who cares about your stupid car? Shock made her want to shout at him, but her chest was so tight she had only enough air for a whisper. "You really scared me."

"Jason, we need to get the car off the track." Gus Stover and his brother had been part of Jason's racing team for the past ten years. They'd modified and repaired all his race cars. Ming had lost track of how many hours she and Jason had spent at the man's shop.

"That's a good idea," she said.

"A little help?" Jason suggested after his first attempt at putting weight on his injured knee didn't go so well.

Ming slipped her arm around his waist and began moving in the direction of the pit area. As his body heat began to warm her, Ming realized she was shaking from reaction. As soon as they reached a safe distance from the track, Jason stopped walking and turned her to face him.

"You're trembling. Are you okay?"

Not even close. She loved him. And had for a long time. Only she'd been too scared to admit it to herself.

"I should be asking you that question," she said, placing her palm against his unshaven cheek, savoring the rasp of his beard against her skin. She wanted to wrap her arms around him and never let go. "You should get checked out."

"I'm just a little banged up, that's all."

"Jason, that was a bad crash." A man in his late-thirties with prematurely graying hair approached as they neared the area where the trailers were parked. He wore a maroon racing suit and carried his helmet under one arm. "You okay?"

"Any crash you can walk away from is a good one." Leave it to Jason to make light of something as disastrous as what she'd just witnessed. "Ming, this is Jim Pearce. He's the current points leader in the Texas region."

"And likely to remain on top now that Jason's done for the season."

Is that all these men thought about? Ming's temper began to simmer again until she saw the worry the other driver was masking with his big, confident grin and his posturing. It could have been any of these guys. Accidents didn't happen a lot, but they were part of racing. This was only Jason's second in the entire sixteen years he'd been racing. If something had gone wrong on another area of the track, he might have ended up driving safely onto the shoulder or he could have taken out a half dozen other cars.

"Nice to meet you." As she shook Jim's hand, some of the tension in her muscles eased. "Were you on the track when it happened?"

"No. I'm driving in the second warm-up lap." His broad smile dimmed. "Any idea what happened, Jason? From where I stood it looked like something gave on the right side."

"Felt like the right front strut rod. We recently installed Agent 47 suspension and might have adjusted a little too aggressively on the front-end alignment settings."

Jim nodded, his expression solemn. "Tough break."

"I'll have the rest of the year to get her rebuilt and be back better than ever in January."

Ming contemplated the hours Jason and the Stover brothers would have to put in to make that happen and let her breath out in a long, slow sigh. If she'd seen little of him in the past few months since he'd made it his goal to take the overall points trophy, she'd see even less of him with a car to completely rebuild.

"The Stovers will get her all fixed up for you." Jim thumped Jason on the back. "They're tops."

As Jim spoke, Jason's car was towed up to the trailer. The men in question jumped off the truck and began unfastening the car.

"What happened?" Jason called.

"The strut rod pulled away from the helm end," Gus Stover replied. "I told you the setting was wrong."

His brother, Kris, shook his head. "It's so messed up from the crash, we won't know for sure until we get her on the lift."

"Do you guys need help?" Jason called.

Jim waved and headed off. Ming understood his exit. When Jason and the Stovers started talking cars, no one else on the planet existed. She stared at the ruined car and the group of men who'd gathered to check out the damage. It would be the talk of the track for the rest of the weekend.

"Looks like you've got your hands full," she told Jason, nodding toward a trio of racers approaching them. "I'm going to get out of here so you can focus on the Mustang."

"Wait." He caught her hand, laced his fingers through hers. "Stick around."

She melted beneath the heat of his smile. "I'll just be in the way."

"I need you—"

"Jason, that was some crash," the man in the middle said.

Ming figured she'd take advantage of the interruption to escape, but Jason refused to relinquish her hand. A warm feeling set up shop in her midsection as Jason introduced her. She'd expected once his buddies surrounded him, he wouldn't care if she took off.

But after an hour she lost all willpower to do so. Despite the attention Jason received from his fellow competitors, he never once forgot that she was there. Accustomed to how focused Jason became at the track, Ming was caught off guard by the way he looped his arm around her waist and included her in the conversations.

By the time the car had been packed up later that afternoon, she was congratulating herself on her decision to come. They sat side by side on the tailgate of his truck. Jason balanced an icepack on his injured knee. Despite the heat, she was leaning against his side, enjoying the lean strength of his body.

"What prompted you to come to the track today?" he questioned, gaze fixed on the Stover brothers as they argued over how long it would take them to get the car ready to race once more.

The anxiety that had gripped her before his crash reappeared and she shrugged to ease her sudden tension. "It's been a long time since I've seen you race." She eyed the busted-up Mustang. "And now it's going to be even longer."

"So it seems."

"Sorry your season ended like this. Are you heading back tonight?"

"Gus and Kris are. I've got a hotel room in town. I think I'll ice my knee and drive back tomorrow."

She waited a beat, hoping he'd ask her to stay, but no invitation was forthcoming. "Want company?"

"In the shape I'm in, I'd be no use to you." He shot her a wry smile.

As his friend, she shouldn't feel rejected, but after accepting that she was in love with him and being treated like his girlfriend all day, she'd expected he'd want her to stick around. She recognized that he was in obvious pain and needed a restful night's sleep. A friend would put his welfare above her own desires.

"Then I guess I'll head back to Houston." She kissed him on the cheek and hopped off the tailgate.

He caught her wrist as her feet hit the ground. "I'm really glad you came today."

It wasn't fair the way he turned the sex appeal on and off whenever it suited him. Ming braced herself against the lure of his sincere eyes and enticing smile. Had she fallen in love with his charm? If so, could she go back to being just his friend once they stopped sleeping together?

She hoped so. Otherwise she'd spend the rest of her life in love with a man who would never let himself love her back.

"Supporting each other is what friends are for," she said, stepping between his thighs and taking his face in her hands.

Slowly she brought her lips to his, releasing all her pent-up emotions into the kiss. Her longing for what she could never have. Her fear over his brush with serious injury. And pure, sizzling desire.

After the briefest of hesitations, he matched her passion, fingers digging into her back as he fed off her mouth. The kiss exhilarated her. Everything about being with Jason made her happy. Smiling, she sucked his lower lip into her mouth and rubbed her breasts against his chest. As soon as she heard his soft groan, she released him.

Stepping back, Ming surveyed her handiwork. From the dazed look in his eyes, the flush darkening his cheekbones and the unsteady rush of breath in and out of his lungs, the kiss had packed a wallop. A quick glance below his belt assured her he would spend a significant portion of the evening thinking about her. Good.

"Careful on the drive home tomorrow," she murmured, wiping her fingertip across her damp lips in deliberate seduction. "Call me when you get back."

And with a saucy wave, she headed for her car.

The sixty-eight-foot cruiser Jason had borrowed for Max's bachelor party barely rocked as it encountered the wake of the large powerboat that had sped across their bow seconds earlier. Cigar in one hand, thirty-year-old Scotch in the other, Jason tracked the boat skimming the dark waters of Galveston Bay from upstairs in the open-air lounge. On the opposite rail, Max's brothers were discussing their wives and upcoming fatherhood.

"She's due tomorrow," Nathan Case muttered, tapping his cell phone on his knee. "I told her it was crazy for me come to this bachelor party, but she was determined to go out dancing with Missy, Rachel and her friends."

Nathan's aggrieved tone found a sympathetic audience in Jason. Why were women so calm about the whole pregnancy-and-giving-birth thing? Ming wasn't even pregnant, and Jason was already experiencing a little coil of tension deep in his gut. He hadn't considered how connected he'd feel to her when he'd agreed to father her baby. Nor could he stop wondering if he'd feel as invested if they'd done it her way and he'd never made love to her.

"I'm sure Emma knows what she's doing," Sebastian Case said. Older than Max and Nathan by a few years, Sebastian was every inch the confident CEO of a multimillion-dollar corporation.

"I think she's hoping the dancing will get her contractions started." Nathan stared at the cell phone as if he could make it ring by sheer willpower. "What if her water breaks on the dance floor?"

"Then she'll call and you can meet her at the hospital." Sebastian's soothing tones were having little effect on his agitated half brother.

"You're barely into your second trimester," Nathan scoffed. "Let's see how rational you are when Missy hasn't been able to see her feet for a month, doesn't sleep more than a few hours a night and can't go ten minutes without finding a bathroom."

Sebastian's eyes grew distant for a few seconds as if he was imagining his wife in the final weeks before she was due.

"Do you know what you're having?" Even as Jason asked Nathan the question, he realized that a month ago he never would have thought to inquire.

"A boy."

Jason lifted his Scotch in a salute. "Congratulations."

"You're single, aren't you?" Sebastian regarded him like a curiosity. "How come you're not downstairs with Max and his buddies slipping fives into the ladies' G-strings instead of hanging out with a couple old family men?"

Because he wasn't feeling particularly single at the moment.

Jason raised the cigar. "Charlie said no smoking in the salon."

"But you're missing the entertainment." Nathan gestured toward the stairs that led below.

Some entertainment. Max might be downstairs with a half dozen of their single friends and a couple of exotic dancers someone had hired, but Jason doubted his best friend was having any fun. Max wasn't interested in any woman except Rachel.

Up until two weeks ago Jason hadn't understood what had come over his friend. Now, after making love with Ming, his craving for her had taken on a life of its own. His body stirred at the memory of her dripping wet in his kitchen. The way her white blouse had clung to her breasts, the fabric rendered sheer by the water. He wasn't sure what he would have done if she'd denied him then. Gotten down on his knees and begged?

Probably.

Jason shoved aside the unsettling thought and smirked at Nathan. "When you're free to hit a strip club any night of the week, the novelty wears off. You two are the ones who should be downstairs."

"Why's that?" Nathan asked.

"I just assumed with your wives being pregnant..."

Sebastian and Nathan exchanged amused looks.

"That our sex lives are nonexistent?" Sebastian proposed. He looked as relaxed and contented as a lion after consuming an antelope.

The last emotion pestering Jason should be envy. He was the free one. Unfettered by emotional ties that had the potential to do damage. Unhampered by monotony, he was free to sleep with a different woman every night of the week if he wanted. He had no demanding female complicating his days.

"Did it surprise either of you that Max is getting married?" Jason asked.

Sebastian swirled the Scotch in his glass. "If I had to wager which one of you two would be getting married first, I would have bet on you."

"Me?" Jason shook his head in bafflement.

"I thought for sure you and Ming would end up together."

"We're close friends, nothing more."

Sebastian's thumb traced the rim of his glass. "Yeah, it took me a long time to see what was waiting right under my nose, too."

Rather than sputter out halfhearted denials, Jason downed the last of his drink and stubbed out the cigar. The Scotch scorched a trail from his throat to his chest.

"I think I'll go see if Max needs rescuing."

They'd been cruising around Galveston for a little over an hour and Jason was as itchy to get off the boat as Nathan. He wanted to blame his restlessness on the fact that the bachelor party meant a week from now his relationship with his best buddy would officially go on the back burner as Max took on his new responsibilities as a husband. But Max had been splitting his loyalty for three months now, and Jason was accustomed to being an afterthought.

No, Jason's edginess was due to the fact that like Nathan, Sebastian and Max, he'd rather be with the woman he was intimate with than whooping it up with a bunch of single guys and a couple of strippers.

What had happened to him?

Only two weeks ago he'd been moaning that Max had abandoned him for a woman. And here he was caught in the same gossamer net, pining for a particular female's companionship.

He met Max on the narrow stairs that connected the salon level to the upper deck, where Nathan and Sebastian remained.

"Feel like getting off this boat and hooking up with our ladies?" Max proposed. "I just heard from Rachel. They've had their fill of the club."

Jason glanced at his watch. "It's only ten-thirty. This is your bachelor party. You're supposed to get wild one last time before you're forever leg-shackled to one woman."

"I'd rather get wild with the woman I'm going to be leg-shackled to." Max punched Jason in the shoulder. "Besides, I don't see you downstairs getting a lap dance from either Candy or Angel."

"Charlie said no smoking in the salon. I went upstairs to enjoy one of the excellent cigars Nathan brought."

"And this has nothing to do with the warning you gave Ming tonight?"

Jason cursed. "You heard that?"

"I thought it was cute."

"Jackass." Swearing at Max was a lot easier than asking himself why he'd felt compelled to tell Ming to behave herself and not break any hearts at the club. He'd only been half joking. The thought of her contemplating romance with another man aroused some uncomfortably volatile emotions.

"And it doesn't look like she listened to you."

"What makes you say that?"

Max showed him his cell phone screen. "I think this guy's pretty close to having his heart broken."

Jason swallowed a growl but could do nothing about the frown that pulled his brows together when he glimpsed the photo of Ming dancing with some guy. Irritation fired in his gut. It wasn't the fact that Ming had her head thrown back and her arms above her head that set Jason off. It was the way the guy had his hands inches from her hips and looked prepared to go where no one but Jason belonged.

Max laughed. "I know Nathan and Sebastian are ready to leave. Are you up for taking the launch in and leaving the boys to play by themselves?"

Damn right he was. "This is your party. Where you go, I go."

Eight

Rachel Lansing, bride-to-be, laughed at the photo her fiancé sent her from his bachelor party. Sitting across the limo from her, Ming wasn't the least bit amused. Her stomach had been churning for the last half an hour, ever since she'd found out that there were exotic dancers on the boat. And her anxiety hadn't been relieved when she hadn't spotted Jason amongst the half dozen men egging on the strippers. He could be standing behind Max, out of the camera's range.

She had no business feeling insecure and suspicious. It wasn't as if she had a claim to Jason beyond their oh-so-satisfying baby-making activities. Problem was, she couldn't disconnect her emotions. And heaven knew she'd been trying to. Telling herself over and over that it was just sex. Incredibly hot, passionate, mind-blowing sex, but not the act of two people in love. Just a couple of friends trying to make a baby together.

Whom was she kidding?

For the past two weeks, she'd been deliriously happy and anxiety-ridden by turn. Every time he slid inside her it was a struggle not to confide that she was falling in love with him, and her strength was fading fast. Already she was rationalizing why she and Jason should continue to be intimate long after she was pregnant.

It was only a matter of time before she confessed what she truly wanted for her future and he'd sit her down and remind her why they'd made love in the first place. Then things would get awkward and they'd start to avoid each other. No. Better to stay silent and keep Jason as her best friend rather than lose him forever.

"If you're worried about Jason, Max texted me and said he's on the upper deck with Nathan and Sebastian." Rachel gave Ming a reassuring smile.

"I'm not worried about Jason," Ming hastily assured her as she sagged in relief. She mustered a smile. "No need for me to be. We're just friends. Have been for years."

A fact Rachel knew perfectly well since the four of them had gone out numerous times since she and Max had gotten engaged. Ming had no idea why she had to keep reminding people that she and Jason were not an item.

"Jason's a great guy."

"He sure is." Ming saw where this was going and knew she had to cut Rachel off. "But he's the sort of guy who isn't ever going to fall in love and get married."

Rachel cocked her head. "Funny, that's what I thought about Max and yet he lost his favorite car to Jason over a wager that he wouldn't get married." Her blue eyes sparkled with mischief. "What's to say Jason won't change his mind, too?"

Ming smiled back, but she knew there was a big difference between the two men. Max hadn't found his father trying to kill himself because he was so despondent over the loss of his wife and daughter. And after getting the scoop about how Max and Rachel had met five years earlier, Ming suspected the reason Max had been so down on love and marriage was that he'd already lost his heart to the woman of his dreams.

"I don't know," Ming said. "He's pretty set in his ways. Besides, you weren't around when my engagement to Jason's brother ended. It made me realize that I'm happier on my own."

"Yeah, before Max, I was where you are. All I have to say is that things change." Rachel nudged her chin toward her soon-to-be-sisters-in-law. "Ask either of those two if they believed love was ever going to happen for them. I'll bet both of them felt the way you do right now."

Ming glanced toward the back of the limo, where Emma, nine months pregnant and due any second, and Missy, four months pregnant and radiant, sat side by side, laughing. They had it all. Gorgeous, devoted men. Babies on the way. Envy twisted in Ming's heart.

She sighed. "I'm really happy for all of you, but love doesn't find everyone."

"If you keep an open mind it does."

The big diamond on Rachel's hand sparkled in the low light. Ming stared at it while her fingers combed her hair into three sections. As she braided, she mused that being in love was easy when you were a week away from pairing your engagement ring with a wedding band. Not that she begrudged any of the Case women their happiness. Each one had gone through a lot before finding bliss, none more so than Rachel. But Ming just wasn't in a place where she could feel optimistic about her own chances.

She was in love with a man who refused to let his guard down and allow anyone in, much less her. Because she couldn't get over her feelings for Jason, she'd already lost one man and almost made the biggest mistake of her life. And as of late, she was concerned that having Jason father her child was going to lead to more heartache in the future.

Ming mulled Rachel's words during the second half of the forty-five-minute drive from downtown Houston to the Galveston marina where the men would be waiting. Maybe she should have gone home from the club like Rachel's sister, Hailey, instead of heading out to meet up with Jason. They'd made no plans to rendezvous tonight. She was starting to feel foolish for chasing him all the way out here.

If Jason decided to stay on the yacht with the bachelor party instead of motoring back to the dock on the launch with Max and his brothers, would she be the odd girl out when the couples reunited? Her chest tightened. Ming closed her eyes as they entered the marina parking lot.

The limo came to a stop. Ming heard the door open and the low rumble of male voices. She couldn't make her eyes open. Couldn't face the sight of the three couples embracing while she sat alone and unwanted.

"What's the matter? Did all the dancing wear you out?"

Her eyes flew open at Jason's question. His head and shoulders filled the limo's open door. Heart pounding in delight, she clasped her hands in her lap to keep from throwing herself into his arms. That was not how friends greeted each other.

"I'm not used to having that much fun." She scooted along the seat to the door, accepting Jason's hand as her foot touched the pavement. His familiar cologne mingled with the faint scent of cigars. She wanted to nuzzle her nose into his neck and breathe him in. "How about you? Did you enjoy your strippers?"

"They preferred to be called exotic dancers." He showed her his phone. "They weren't nearly as interesting as this performance."

She gasped at the picture of herself dancing. How had Jason gotten ahold of it? So much for what happens at a bachelorette party stays at a bachelorette party. She eyed the women behind Jason. Who'd ratted her out?

"It was just some guy who asked me to dance," she protested.

"Just some guy?" He kept his voice low, but there was no denying the edge in his tone. "He has his hands all over you."

She enlarged the image, telling herself she was imagining the possessive glint in Jason's eye. "No he doesn't. And if this had been taken five seconds later you would have seen me shove him away and walk off the dance floor."

"Whoa, sounds like a lover's spat to me," Rachel crowed.

Confused by the sparks snapping in Jason's blue eyes, Ming realized a semicircle of couples had formed five feet away. Six faces wore various shades of amusement as they looked on.

Jason composed his expression and turned to face the group. "Not a lover's spat."

"Just a concerned friend," Max intoned, his voice dripping with dry humor.

"Come on, we're all family here." Sebastian's gesture encompassed the whole group. "You can admit to us that you're involved."

"We're not involved." Ming found her voice.

"We're friends," Jason said. "We look out for each other."

"I disagree," Max declared, slapping Jason on the back. "I think you've finally realized that your best friend is the best thing that ever happened to you." He glanced around to see if the others agreed with him. "About time, too."

"You don't know what you're talking about." Jason was making no attempt to laugh off his friend's ribbing.

Ming flinched at Jason's resolute expression. If he'd considered moving beyond friendship, Max would be the one he'd confide in. With Jason's adamant denial, Ming had to face the fact that she was an idiot to hope that Jason might one day realize they belonged together.

"Oh!"

All eyes turned to Emma, who'd bent over, her hand pressed to her round belly.

"Are you okay?" Nathan put his arm around her waist. "Was it a contraction?"

"I don't know. I don't think so." Emma clutched his arm. "Maybe you'd better take me home."

To Ming's delight everyone's focus had shifted to Emma. What might or might not be going on between Ming and Jason was immediately forgotten. As Nathan opened the passenger door for Emma, she looked straight at Ming and winked. Restraining a grin, Ming wondered how many times Emma had used the baby in such a fashion.

"Alone at last," Jason said, drawing her attention back to him. "And the night is still young."

Ming shivered beneath his intense scrutiny. "What did you have in mind?"

"I was thinking maybe you could show me your dancing skills in private."

"Funny. I was thinking maybe you could give me a demonstration of the techniques you picked up from your strippers tonight."

"Exotic dancers," he corrected, opening the passenger door on his car so she could get in. "And I didn't pick up anything because I wasn't anywhere near their dancing."

The last of her tension melted away. "I don't believe you," she teased, keeping her relief hidden. She leaned against his chest and peered up at him from beneath her lashes. "Not so long ago you wouldn't have missed that kind of action."

"Not so long ago I didn't have all the woman I could handle waiting for me at home."

"Except I wasn't waiting for you." Lifting up on tiptoe, she pressed her lips to his and then dropped into the passenger seat.

"No, you were out on the town breaking hearts."

The door shut before her retort reached Jason's ears. Was he really annoyed with her for dancing with someone? Joy flared and died. She was reading too much into it.

"So, where are we heading?" Jason turned out of the marina parking lot and got them headed toward the bridge off the island.

"You may take me home. After all that heartbreaking, my feet are sore." She tried to smile, but her heart hurt too much. "Besides, Muffin is home alone."

"Where's Lily?"

"Supposedly she's out of town this weekend."

"Why supposedly?"

"Because I drove past Evan's house and her car was in the driveway."

"You drove past Evan's house?" Jason shifted his gaze off the road long enough for her to glimpse his alarm. "Are you sure that was a good idea?"

She bristled at his disapproving tone. "I was curious if my sister had lied to me."

"You were curious." He echoed her words doubtfully. "Not bothered that they're together?"

"No."

"Because you two were engaged not that long ago and now he's dating your sister."

"Why do you keep bringing that up?" Her escalating annoyance came through loud and clear. She'd known Jason too long not to recognize when he was picking a fight.

"I want you to be honest with yourself so this doesn't blow up between you and your sister in the future."

"You don't think I'm being honest with myself?"

"Your sister is dating the man who broke off your engagement two weeks before the wedding. I think you're trying too hard to be okay with it."

He took her hand and she was both soothed and frustrated by his touch. No matter what else was happening between them, Jason was her best friend. He knew her better than anyone. Sometimes better than she knew herself. But the warm press of his fingers reminded her that while he could act like a bossy boyfriend, she came up against his defenses every time she started to play girlfriend.

"Right now I've got my hands full with you." Ming wasn't exaggerating on that score. "Can we talk about something else? Please?"

The last thing she wanted was to argue with him when her hopes for the evening required them to be in perfect accord.

"Sure." Even though he agreed, she could tell he wasn't happy about dropping the subject. "What's on your mind?"

"I have the house to myself until late Sunday if you want to hang out."

"That sounds like an invitation to sleep over."

She made a sandwich of his hand and hers and ignored the anxious flutter in her stomach.

"Maybe it is." Flirting with Jason was fun and dangerous. It was easy to lose track of reality and venture into that tricky romantic place best avoided if she wanted their friendship to remain uncomplicated.

Or maybe she was too far gone for things to ever be the same between them again.

The part of her that wanted them to be more than just friends was growing stronger every day. It was a crazy hope, but she couldn't stop the longing any more than Jason could get past his reluctance to fall in love.

"Ming..."

She heard the wariness in his voice and held up her hand. They hadn't spent a single night together this whole week. That had been a mutual decision based on practicality. Neither of them wanted Evan to pop over late one night and find her at Jason's house. Plus, Lily had been in Houston all week and would have noticed if Ming had stayed out all night.

But she was dying to spend the night snuggled in his arms. And the craving had nothing to do with making a baby.

"Forget I said anything." Her breath leaked out in a long, slow sigh. "This past week has been fun. But you and I both know I'm past my prime fertility cycle. It makes no sense for us to keep getting together when I'm either pregnant or I'm too late in my cycle to try."

"Wait. Is that what this week has been about?" He sounded put out. "You're just using me to make a baby?"

Startled, she opened her mouth to deny his claim and realized he was trying to restore their conversation to a lighter note by teasing her. "And a few weeks from now we'll see if you've succeeded." She faked a yawn. "I guess I'm more tired than I thought."

Jason nodded and turned the topic to the bachelorette party. Ming jumped on board, glad to leave behind the tricky path they'd been treading.

By the time he turned the car into her driveway, she'd man-handled her fledgling daydreams about turning their casual sex into something more. She was prepared to say good-night and head alone to her door.

"Call me tomorrow," he told her. "I've got to go shopping for Max and Rachel's wedding present."

"You haven't done that yet?"

"I've been waiting for you to offer to do it for me."

Robbed of a dreamy night in Jason's arms and the pleasure of waking up with him in the morning, Ming let her irritation shine. "You said no about going in on a gift together, so you're on your own."

"Please come shopping with me." He put on his most appealing smile. "You know I'm hopeless when it comes to department stores."

How could she say no when she'd already agreed to help him before they'd started sleeping together. It wasn't fair to treat him differently just because she felt differently toward him.

"What time tomorrow?"

"Eleven? I want to be home to watch the Oilers at three."

"Fine," she grumbled.

With disappointment of her own weighing her down, she plodded up the stairs and let herself into her house. Muffin met her in the foyer. She danced around on her back legs, wringing a small smile from Ming's stiff lips.

"I'll take you out back in a second." She waited by the front door long enough to see Jason's headlights retreating down her driveway, then headed toward the French doors that led from her great room to the pool deck.

While the Yorkie investigated the bushes at the back of her property, Ming sat down on a lounge chair and sought the tranquility often gained by sitting beside her turquoise kidney-shaped pool. She revisited her earlier statement to Jason. It made no sense for them to rendezvous each afternoon and have the best sex ever if all they were trying to do was make a baby. Only, if she was completely honest with herself, she'd admit that a baby isn't all she wanted from Jason.

Her body ached with unfulfilled desire. Her soul longed to find the rhythm of Jason's heart beating in time with hers. From the beginning she'd been right to worry that getting intimate with her best friend was going to lead her into trouble. But temptation could be avoided for only so long when all you've ever wanted gets presented to you on a silver platter. She would just have to learn to live with the consequences.

Finding nothing of interest in the shrubbery, Muffin came back to the pool, her nails clicking on the concrete. Sympathetic to her mistress's somber mood, the terrier jumped onto Ming's lap and nuzzled her nose beneath Ming's hand.

"I am such an idiot," she told the dog, rubbing Muffin's head.

"That makes two of us."

Jason hadn't even gotten out of Ming's neighborhood before he'd realized what a huge error he'd made. In fact, he hadn't made it to the end of her block. But just because he'd figured it out didn't mean returning to Ming wasn't an even bigger mistake. So, he'd sat at a stop sign for five minutes, listening to Rascal Flatts and wondering when his life had gotten so damned complicated. Then, he'd turned the car around, used his key to get into Ming's house and found her by the pool.

"Let's go upstairs," he said. "We need to talk."

Ming pulled her hair over one shoulder and began to braid it. "We can't talk here?"

Was she being deliberately stubborn or pretending to be dense?

Without answering, he pivoted on his heel and walked toward the house. Muffin caught up as he crossed the threshold. Behind him, Ming's heels clicked on the concrete as she rushed after him.

"Jason." She sounded breathless and uncertain. She'd stopped in the middle of her kitchen and called after him as he got to the stairs. "Why did you come back?"

Since talking had only created problems between them earlier, he was determined to leave conversation for later. Taking the stairs two at a time, he reached her bedroom in record time. Unfastening his cuffs, he gazed around the room. He hadn't been up here since he'd helped her paint the walls a rich beige. The dark wood furniture, rich chestnut bedspread and touches of sage green gave the room the sophisticated, expensive look of a five-star hotel suite.

"Jason?"

He'd had enough time to unfasten his shirt buttons. Now, as she entered the room, he let the shirt drop off his shoulders and draped it over a chair. "Get undressed."

While she stared at him in confounded silence, he took Muffin from her numb fingers and deposited the dog in the hallway.

"She always sleeps with me," Ming protested as he shut the door.

"Not tonight."

"Well, I suppose she can sleep on Lily's bed. Jason, what's gotten into you?"

His pants joined his shirt on the chair. With only his boxer briefs keeping his erection contained, he set his hands on his hips.

"You and I have been best friends for a long time." Since she wasn't making any effort to slip out of that provocative halter-top and insanely short skirt, he prowled toward her. "And

I've shared with you some of the hardest things I've ever had to go through."

She made no attempt to stop him as he tugged at the thin ribbon holding up her top, but she did grab at the fabric as it began to fall away from her breasts. "If you're saying I know you better than anyone except Max, I'd agree."

Jason hooked his fingers in the top and pulled it from her fingers, exposing her small, perfect breasts. His lungs had to work hard to draw in the air he required. Damn it. They had been together all week, but he still couldn't get over how gorgeous she was, or how much he wanted to mark her as his own.

"Then it seems as if I'm doing our friendship an injustice by not telling you what's going on in my head at the moment."

Reaching around her, he slid down the zipper on her skirt and lowered it past her hips. When it hit the floor, she stepped out of it.

"And what's that?"

Jason crossed his arms over his chest and stared into her eyes. It was nearly impossible to keep his attention from wandering over her mostly naked body. Standing before him in only a black lace thong and four-inch black sandals, she was an exotic feast for the eyes.

"I didn't like seeing you dancing with another man."

The challenge in her almond-shaped eyes faded at his admission. Raw hope rushed in to replace it. "You didn't?"

Jason ground his teeth. He should have been able to contain the truth from her. That he'd admitted to such possessive feelings meant a crack had developed in the well-constructed wall around his heart. But a couple weaknesses in the structure didn't mean he had to demolish the whole thing. He needed to get over his annoyance at her harmless interaction with some random guy. Besides, wasn't he the one who'd initially encouraged her that there was someone out there for her?

To hell with that.

Taking her hand, he drew her toward the bed.

"Not one bit." It reminded him too much of how he'd lost her to his brother. "It looked like you were having fun without me."

"Did it, now?" His confession had restored her confidence. With a sexy smile, she coasted her nails from his chest to the waistband of his underwear. "I guess I was imagining that you were otherwise occupied with your exotic dancers. Did they get you all revved up? Is that why we're here right now?"

He snorted. "The only woman I have any interest in seeing out of her clothes is you."

Heaven help him—it was true. He hadn't even looked at another woman since this business of her wanting to become a mother came up. No. It had been longer than that. Since his brother had broken off their engagement.

The level of desire he felt for her had been eating at him since last weekend when she'd kissed him good-bye at the track. That had been one hell of a parting and if his knee hadn't been so banged up he never would've let her walk away.

This isn't what he'd expected when he'd proposed making love rather than using a clinic to help her conceive. He'd figured his craving for her was strictly physical. That it would wane after his curiosity was satisfied.

What he was feeling right now threatened to alter the temper of their friendship. He should slow things down or stop altogether. Yeah. That had worked great for him earlier. He'd dropped her off and then raced back before he'd gotten more than a couple blocks away.

Frustrated with himself, he didn't give her smug smile a chance to do more than bud before picking her up and dumping her unceremoniously on the bed. Without giving her a chance to recover, he removed first one then the other of her shoes. As each one hit the floor, her expression evolved from surprised to anticipatory.

It drove him crazy how much he wanted her. Every cell in his body ached with need. Nothing in his life had ever compared. Was it knowing her inside and out that made the sexual chemistry between them stronger than normal?

While he snagged her panties and slid them down her pale thighs, she lifted her arms above her head, surrendering herself to his hot gaze. The vision of her splayed across the bed, awaiting his possession, stirred a tremor in his muscles. His hands shook as he dropped his underwear to the floor.

Any thought of taking things slow vanished as she reached for him. A curse made its way past his lips as her confident strokes brought him dangerously close to release.

"Stop." His harsh command sounded desperate.

He took her wrist in a firm grip and pinned it above her head. Lowering himself into the cradle between her thighs, he paused before sliding into her. Two things were eating at him tonight: that picture of her dancing and her preoccupation with Evan and Lily's romance.

"You're mine." The words rumbled out of him like a vow. Claiming her physically hadn't rattled his safe bachelor existence, but this was a whole different story.

"Jason." She waggled her hips and arched her back, trying to entice him to join with her, but although it was close to killing him, he stayed still.

"Say it." With his hands keeping her wrists trapped over her head and his body pinning hers to the mattress, she was at his mercy.

"I can't…" Her eyes went wide with dismay. "…say that."

"Why not?" He rocked against her, giving her a taste of what she wanted.

A groan erupted past her parted lips. She watched him through half-closed eyes. "Because…"

"Say it," he insisted. "And I'll give you what you want."

Her chest rose and fell in shallow, agitated breaths. "What I want…"

He lowered his head and drew circles around her breast with his tongue. His willpower had never felt so strong before. When she'd started dating his brother, he'd been in the worst sort of hell. Deep in his soul, Jason had always believed if she'd choose anyone, she'd pick him. They were best friends. Confidants. Soul mates. And buried where neither had ventured before prom night was a flammable sexual chemistry.

Both of them had been afraid at the power of what existed between them, but he'd been the most vocal about not ruining their friendship. So vocal, in fact, she'd turned to his brother before Jason had had time to come to his senses.

"Mine." He growled the word against her breast as his mouth closed around her nipple.

She gasped at the strong pull of his mouth. "Yours." She wrapped her thighs around his hips. "All yours."

"All mine."

Satisfied, he plunged into her. Locked together, he released her wrists and kissed her hard and deep, sealing her pledge before whisking them both into unheard of pleasure.

Nine

Moving slowly, her legs wobbly from the previous night's exertions, Ming crossed her bedroom to the door, where Muffin scratched and whined. She let the Yorkie in, dipping to catch the small dog before Muffin could charge across the room and disturb the large, naked man sprawled facedown in the middle of the tangled sheets.

"Let's take you outside," she murmured into the terrier's silky coat, tearing her gaze away from Jason.

Still shaken from their passionate lovemaking the night before, she carefully navigated the stairs and headed for the back door. After cuddling against Jason's warm skin all night, the seventy-degree temperature at 7:00 a.m. made her shiver. She should have wrapped more than a silky lavender robe around her naked body.

While Muffin ran off to do her business and investigate the yard for intruders, Ming plopped down on the same lounge she'd occupied the night before and opened her mind to the thoughts she'd held at bay all night long.

What the hell had possessed Jason to demand that she admit to belonging to him? Battling goose bumps, she rubbed at her arms. The morning air brushed her overheated skin but couldn't cool the fire raging inside her. *His.* Even now the word made her muscles tremble and her insides whirl like a leaf caught in a vortex. She dropped her face into her hands and fought the urge to laugh or weep. He made her crazy. First his vow to never fall in love and never get married. Now this.

Muffin barked at something, and Ming looked up to find her dog digging beneath one of the bushes. Normally she'd stop the terrier. Today, she simply watched the destruction happen.

What was she supposed to make of Jason's territorial posturing last night? Why had he reacted so strongly to the inflammatory photo? She'd understand it if they were dating. Then he'd have the right to be angry, to be driven to put his mark on her.

Jason hadn't changed his mind about falling in love. Initially last night he hadn't even wanted to spend the night. So, what had brought him back? It was just about the great sex, right? It wasn't really fair to say he only wanted her body, but he'd shown no interest in accepting her heart.

Ming called Muffin back to the house and started a pot of coffee. She wasn't sure if Jason intended to head home right away or if he would linger. She hoped he'd stick around. She had visions of eating her famous cinnamon raisin bread French toast and drinking coffee while they devoured the Sunday paper. As the day warmed they could go for a swim in her pool. She'd always wanted to make love in the water. Or they could laze in bed. It would be incredible to devote an entire day to hanging out.

Afternoon and evening sex had been more fun and recreational than serious and committed. Ming could pretend they were just enjoying the whole friends-with-benefits experience. Sleeping wrapped in each other's arms had transported them into "relationship" territory. Not to mention the damage done to her emotional equilibrium when Jason admitted to feeling jealous.

She brought logic to bear on last night's events, and squashed the giddy delight bubbling in her heart. She'd strayed a long way from the reason she was in this mess in the first place. Becoming a mom. Time to put things with Jason in perspective. They were friends. Physical intimacy might be messing with their heads at this point, but once she was pregnant all sex would cease and their relationship would go back to being casual and supportive.

"I started coffee," she announced as she stepped into her bedroom and stopped dead at the sight of the person standing by her dresser.

Lily dropped something into Ming's jewelry box and smiled at her sister. "I borrowed your earrings. I hope that's okay."

"It's fine." From her sister, Ming's gaze went straight to the bed and found it empty. Relief shot through her, making her knees wobble. "I thought you were in Portland."

"I came back early."

Since Lily wasn't asking the questions Ming was expecting, she could only assume her sister hadn't run into Jason. "Ah, great."

Where the hell was he?

"How come Jason's car is in the driveway?" Lily asked.

Ming hovered near the doorway to the hall, hoping her sister would take the hint and come with her. "Max's bachelor party was last night. He had a little too much to drink so I drove him home and brought the car back here."

Too late she realized she could have just said he was staying in the guest room. That would at least have given him a reason to be in the house at this hour. Now he was trapped until she could get away from Lily.

Her sister wandered toward the window seat. "I put an offer in on a house."

"Really?" What was going to happen between her and Evan if she was moving away?

Lily plopped down on the cushioned seat and set a pillow in her lap, looking as if she was settling in for a long talk. "You sound surprised."

Ming shot a glance toward the short hallway, flanked by walk-in closets, that led to her bathroom. He had to be in there.

"I guess I was hoping you'd change your mind." She pulled underwear and clothes from her dresser and headed toward the bathroom. "Let me get dressed and then you can tell me all about it."

Her heart thumped vigorously as she shut the bathroom door behind her.

Jason leaned, fully clothed and completely at ease, against her vanity. "I thought you said she was spending the weekend with Evan."

"She was." Ming frowned when she realized he clearly thought she'd lied to him. "Something must have happened. She seems upset." Ming dropped her robe and stepped into her clothes, ignoring his appreciative leer. "Did she see you?"

"I was already dressed and in here when I heard you start talking." Readying himself to make a break for it.

"You were leaving?" Ming shouldn't have been surprised. Last night was over. Time to return their relationship to an easygoing, friendly place. Hadn't she been thinking the same thing? So why did her stomach feel like she'd been eating lead? "Did you intend to say goodbye or just sneak out while I was downstairs with Muffin?"

"Don't be like that."

"Why don't you tell me exactly how I'm supposed to be."

Not wanting her sister to get suspicious, Ming returned to the bedroom without waiting for Jason's answer. Her heart ached, but she refused to give in to the pain pressing on the edge of her consciousness.

Since Lily seemed entrenched in Ming's room, she sat beside her sister on the window seat. To catch Lily's attention, Ming put her hand on her knee. "Tell me about the house."

"House?"

"The one you put an offer in on."

"It's just a house."

"How many bedrooms does it have?"

"Two."

Curious about whatever was plaguing her sister, Ming was distracted by Muffin investigating her way toward the bathroom. "Nice neighborhood?"

"I think I made a huge mistake."

"Then withdraw the offer." She held her breath and waited for the terrier to discover Jason and erupt in a fit of barking.

"Not the house. The guy I've been seeing."

With an effort, Ming returned her full attention to her sister. "I thought you were just friends."

"It's gone a little further than that."

"You're sleeping together?" She asked the question even though she suspected the answer was yes.

Although the fact that her ex-fiancé was dating her sister continued to cause Ming minor discomfort, she was relieved that her strongest emotion was concern for her sister. When jealousy had been her first reaction to the realization that Lily and Evan were involved, Ming had worried that she was turning into a horrible person.

And lately, on top of all her other worries, Ming had started to wonder how Evan would feel if he found out about her and Jason. Something that might just happen if they weren't more careful.

"Yes. But it's not going anywhere."

Ming's gaze strayed to the bathroom door she hadn't completely closed. Muffin had yet to return to the bedroom. What was going on in there?

"Because you don't want it to?"

"I guess."

That tight spot near Ming's heart eased a little. "You guess? Or you know?" When her sister didn't answer, Ming asked, "Do you love him?"

"Yes." Lily stared at her hands.

Ming's throat locked up, but she couldn't blame her sister for falling for Evan. The heart rarely followed a logical path. And it must be tearing Lily apart to love the man who'd almost married her sister.

"I think you should forget about moving to Portland."

"It's not that simple."

Time to rattle her sister's cage a little. "Funny, Jason told me Evan's dating someone, but his situation is complicated, too." Ming gave a little laugh. "Maybe you two should get together and compare notes."

"I suppose we should." Lily gave her a listless smile.

Was there a way for Ming to give her sister permission to have a future with Evan? "You know, I was glad to hear that Evan had found someone and was moving on with his life."

"Really?" Despite Lily's skeptical tone, her eyes were bright with hope.

"He and I weren't mean to be. It happens."

"That's not how you felt six months ago."

"I'm not going to say that having him break off our engagement two weeks before the wedding was any fun, but I'd much rather find out then that we weren't meant to be than to get married and try to make it work only to invest years and then have it fail."

Ming's cell phone rang. She plucked it off the nightstand and answered it before Lily could respond.

"If I'm going to be stuck in your bathroom all morning, I'd love a cup of coffee and some breakfast."

"Good morning to you, too," she said, mouthing Jason's name to Lily. "How are you feeling?"

"Tired and a little aroused after checking out the lingerie drying in your shower."

"Sure, I can return your car." She rolled her eyes in Lily's direction. "Are you sober enough to drive me back here?"

"I guess I don't need to ask what excuse you gave your sister for why my car is at your house." Jason's voice was dry.

"I can follow you over there and bring you back," Lily offered.

"Hey, Lily just offered to follow me to your house so I can drop the car off."

"You're a diabolical woman, do you know that?"

"I'm sure it's no bother," Ming continued. "We're going to make breakfast first though."

"French toast with cinnamon raisin bread?"

"That's right. Your favorite." And one of the few things Ming enjoyed cooking. "Pity you aren't here this morning to have some."

"Just remember that paybacks can be painful."

"Oh, I didn't realize you needed your car to go shopping for Max and Rachel's wedding gift this morning. I'll see you in fifteen minutes." She disconnected the call. "I'm going to run Jason's car over to him and then I'll come back and we can make breakfast."

"Are you sure you don't want me to drive you over there?"

"No. I think the fresh air will do him some good."

She escorted Lily to the kitchen and settled her with a cup of green tea before she headed for the front door. Jason was already in the car when she arrived.

"Lily sounded upset this morning," Jason said. "Did I hear her say she put an offer on a house?"

"In Portland. But she seems really unsure what her next move is." She drove the car into the parking lot of a coffee shop in her neighborhood and cut the engine. "She's conflicted about going." She paused a beat. "Did you know they're sleeping together?"

Silence filled the space between her and Jason. Ming listened to the engine tick as it cooled, her thoughts whirling.

"Yes." He was keeping things from her. That wasn't like him.

"And you didn't tell me?"

"I didn't want you to get upset."

"I'm not upset." Not about Lily and Evan.

Last weekend she'd discovered what she really wanted from Jason. It wasn't a baby she would raise on her own. It was a husband who'd adore her and a bunch of kids to smother with love. She was never going to have that with him, and accepting that was tearing her apart.

"Well, you don't look happy."

"I want my sister to stay in Houston." The air inside the car became stuffy and uncomfortable. Ming shoved open the door and got out.

By the time she reached the Camaro's front bumper, Jason was there, waiting for her. "What happens if Lily and Evan decide to get married?"

Then she would be happy for them. "Evan and I were over six months ago."

"You and Evan broke up six months ago."

"Are you insinuating I'm not over him?"

"Are you?" He set his hand on his hips, preventing her from going past.

"Don't be ridiculous." She tried to sidestep him, but he shifted to keep her blocked. "Would I be sleeping with you if I was hung up on your brother?"

"If I recall, the only reason you're sleeping with me is so you can get pregnant."

She should be relieved that he believed that. It alleviated the need for complicated explanations. But what had happened between them meant so much more to her than that she couldn't stay silent.

"Perhaps you need to think a little harder about that first afternoon in your kitchen." She leaned into his body, surrendering her pride. "Did it seem as if all I was interested in was getting pregnant?"

"Ming." The guilt in his voice wrenched at her. He cupped her shoulders, the pressure comforting, reassuring.

She stared at his chest and hoped he wouldn't see the tears burning her eyes. "I knew it was going to get weird between us."

"It's not weird."

"It's weird." She circled around him and headed to the passenger side. "I should probably get back."

For a moment Jason stood where she'd left him. Ming watched him through the windshield, appreciating the solitude to collect her thoughts. It was her fault that their relationship was strained. If she'd just stuck with her plan and used a clinic to get pregnant, she wouldn't have developed a craving for a man who could never be hers. And she wouldn't feel miserable for opening herself to love.

As Jason slid behind the wheel, she composed her expression and gathered breath to tell him that they needed to go back to being friends without benefits, but he spoke first.

"Last night." He gripped the steering wheel hard and stared straight ahead. "I crossed the line."

To fill the silence that followed his confession, Jason started the Camaro, but for once the car's powerful engine didn't make him smile.

"Because of what you wanted me to say." Ming sounded irritated and unsure.

"Yes." Moments earlier, he'd considered skirting the truth, but she'd been honest about her feelings toward him.

"Then why did you?"

Making love to her had flipped a switch, lighting him up like a damned merry-go-round. He kept circling, his thoughts stuck on the same track, going nowhere. He liked that they were lovers. At the same time he relied on the stability of their friendship. So far he'd been operating under the belief that he could have it both ways. Now, his emotions were getting away from him. Logic told him lust and love were equally powerful and easily confused. But he'd begun to question his determination to never fall in love.

"Because it's how I feel."

"And that's a bad thing?"

He saw the hope in her eyes and winced. "It isn't bad. We've been close a long time. My feelings for you are strong." How did he explain himself without hurting her? "I just don't want to lead you on and I think that's what I did."

"Lead me on?" She frowned. "By making me think that you wanted to move beyond friendship into something…more?" Her fingers curled into fists. "I'm not sure who I'm more angry with right now. You or me."

If he'd known for sure that sleeping with her would complicate their friendship, would he have suggested it? Yes. Even now he wasn't ready to go back to the way things were. He had so much he longed to explore with Ming.

If he was honest with himself, he'd admit that helping her get pregnant was no longer his primary motivation for continuing their intimate relationship. He'd have to weigh a deeper connection with Ming against the risk that someday one of them would wake up and realize they were better off as friends. If emotions were uneven, their friendship might not survive.

"Do you want to stop?" He threw the car into gear and backed out of the parking spot.

"You're making me responsible for what does or doesn't happen between us? How is that fair?"

Below her even tone was a cry for help. Jason wanted to pull her close and kiss away her frown. If today they agreed to go back to the way things were, how long would he struggle against the impulse to touch her the way a lover would?

"I want you to be happy," he told her. "Whatever that takes."

"Do you?" She looked skeptical. "Last night I wanted you to stay, but you got all tense and uncomfortable." A deep breath helped get her voice back under control. When she continued, she seemed calmer. "I know it's because you have a rule against spending the night with the women you see."

"But I spent last night with you."

"And this morning you couldn't put your clothes on fast enough." She stared at him hard enough to leave marks on his face.

"So what do you want from me?"

"I'd like to know what you want. Are we just friends? Are we lovers?"

Last night he'd denied their relationship to his friends and felt resistance to her suggestion that he stay the night with her. As happy as Max and his brothers were to be in love with three terrific women, Jason could only wonder about future heartbreak when he looked at the couples. He didn't want to live with the threat of loss hanging over his head, but he couldn't deny that the thought of Ming with another man bugged him. So did her dismay that Evan had fallen in love with Lily.

"I won't deny that I think we're good together," he said. "But you know how I feel about falling in love."

"You don't want to do it."

"Can't we just keep enjoying what we have? You know I'll always be there for you. The chemistry between us is terrific. Soon you'll be busy being a mom and won't have time for me." He turned the car into her driveway and braked but didn't put the Camaro in Park. He needed to get away, to mull over what they'd talked about today. "Let's have dinner tomorrow."

"I can't. It's the Moon Festival. Lily and I are having dinner with our parents tomorrow. I'm going to tell them my decision to have a baby, and she's going to tell them she's moving." Ming sighed. "We promised to be there to support each other."

Jason didn't envy either sister. Helen Campbell was a stubborn, opinionated woman who believed she knew what was best for her daughters. At times, Ming had almost collapsed beneath the weight of her mother's hopes and dreams for her.

She hadn't talked about it, but Jason knew the breakup of her engagement had been a major blow to Ming's mother.

"What about Tuesday?" he suggested.

She put her hand on the door release, poised to flee. "It's going to be a hectic week with Max and Rachel's wedding next weekend."

Jason felt a sense of loss, but he didn't understand why. He and Ming were still friends. Nothing about that had changed.

"What's wrong?"

"It's too much to go into now."

Jason caught her arm as she pushed the door open and prevented her from leaving. "Wait."

Ming made him act in ways that weren't part of his normal behavior. Today, for example. He'd hid in her bathroom for fifteen minutes while she and her sister had occupied the bedroom. There wasn't another woman on earth he would have done that for.

Now he was poised to do something he'd avoided with every other woman he'd been involved with. "You're obviously upset. Tell me what's going on."

"I feel like an idiot." Her voice was thick with misery. "These last couple weeks with you have been fantastic and I've started thinking of us as a couple."

Her admission didn't come as a complete shock. Occasionally over the years he too had considered what they'd be like together. She knew him better than anyone. He'd shared with her things no one else knew. His father's suicide attempt. How he'd initially been reluctant to join the family business. The fact that the last words he'd spoken to his little sister before she'd died had been angry ones.

"Even knowing how you feel about love—" She stopped speaking and blinked rapidly. "Turns out I'm just like all those other women you've dated. No, I'm worse, because I knew better and let myself believe…" Her chin dropped toward her chest. "Forget it, okay?"

Was she saying she was in love with him? Her declaration hit him like a speeding truck. He froze, unable to think, unsure what to feel. Had she lost her mind? Knowing he wasn't built for lasting relationships, she'd opened herself up to heartbreak?

And where did they go from here? He couldn't ask her to continue as they'd been these past two weeks. But he'd never had such mind-blowing chemistry with anyone before, and he was a selfish bastard who wasn't going to give that up without a fight.

"Saturday night, after the wedding, we're going to head to my house and talk. We'll figure out together what to do." But he suspected the future was already written. "Okay?"

"There's nothing to figure out." She slid out of the car. "We're friends. Nothing is going to change that."

But as he watched her head toward her front door, Jason knew in the space of a few minutes, everything had changed.

Ten

Ming caught her sister wiping sweaty palms on her denim-clad thighs as she stopped the car in front of her parents' house and killed the engine. She put her hand over Lily's and squeezed in sympathy.

"We'll be okay if we stick together."

Arm in arm they headed up the front walk. No matter what their opinions were about each other's decisions, Ming knew they'd always form a unified front when it came to their mother.

Before they reached the front door, it opened and a harlequin Great Dane loped past the handsome sixty-year-old man who'd appeared in the threshold.

"Dizzy, you leave that poor puppy alone," Patrick Campbell yelled, but his words went unheeded as Dane and Ming's Yorkie raced around the large front yard.

"Dad, Muffin's fine." In fact, the terrier could run circles around the large dog and dash in for a quick nip then be gone again before Dizzy knew what hit her. "Let them run off a little energy."

After surviving rib-bruising hugs from their father, Ming and Lily captured the two dogs and brought them inside. The house smelled like heaven, and Ming suspected her mother had spent the entire weekend preparing her favorite dishes as well as the special moon cakes.

Ming sat down at her parents' dining table and wondered how the thing didn't collapse under the weight of all the food. She'd thought herself too nervous to eat, but once her plate was heaped with a sample of everything, she began eating with relish. Lily's appetite didn't match hers. She spent most of the meal staring at her plate and stabbing her fork into the food.

After dinner, they took their moon cakes outside to eat beneath the full moon while their mother told them the story of how the festival came to be.

"The Mongolians ruled China during the Yuan Dynasty," Helen Campbell would begin, her voice slipping naturally into storytelling rhythm. She was a professor at the University of Houston, teaching Chinese studies, language and literature. "The former leaders from the Sung dynasty wanted the foreigners gone, but all plans to rebel were discovered and stopped. Knowing that the Moon Festival was drawing near, the rebel leaders ordered moon cakes to be baked with messages inside, outlining the attack. On the night of the Moon Festival, the rebels successfully overthrew the government. What followed was the establishment of the Ming dynasty. Today, we eat the moon cakes to remember."

No matter how often she heard the tale, Ming never grew tired of it. As a first-generation American on her mother's side, Ming appreciated the culture that had raised her mother. Although as children both Ming and Lily had fought their mother's attempts to keep them attached to their Chinese roots, by the time Ming graduated from college, she'd become fascinated with China's history.

She'd visited China over a dozen times when Helen had returned to Shanghai, where her family still lived. Despite growing up with both English and Chinese spoken in the house, Ming had never been fluent in Mandarin. Thankfully her Chinese relatives were bilingual. She couldn't wait to introduce her own son or daughter to her Chinese family.

Stuffed to the point where it was difficult to breathe, Ming sipped jasmine tea and watched her sister lick sweet bean paste off her fingers. The sight blended with a hundred other memories of family and made her smile.

"I've decided to have a baby," she blurted out.

After her parents exchanged a look, Helen set aside her plate as if preparing to do battle.

"By yourself?"

Ming glanced toward Lily, who'd begun collecting plates. Ever since they'd been old enough to reach the sink, it was understood that their mother would cook and the girls would clean up.

"It's not the way I dreamed of it happening, but yes. By myself."

"I know how much you want children, but have you thought everything through?" Her mother's lips had thinned out of existence.

"Helen, you know she can handle anything she sets her mind to," her father said, ever supportive.

Ming leaned forward in her chair and looked from one parent to the other. "I'm not saying it's going to be a picnic, but I'm ready to be a mom."

"A single mom?" Helen persisted.

"Yes."

"You know my thoughts on this matter." Her mother's gaze grew keen. "How does Jason feel about what you're doing?"

Ming stared at the flowers that surrounded her parents' patio. "He's happy for me."

"He's a good man," her mother said, her expression as tranquil as Ming had ever seen it. "Are you hoping he'll help you?"

"I don't expect him to." Ming wondered if her mother truly

understood that she was doing this on her own. "He's busy with his own life."

Patrick smiled. "I remember how he was with your cousins. He's good with kids. I always thought he'd make a great father."

"You did?" The conversation had taken on a surreal quality for Ming. Since he never intended to get married, she'd never pictured Jason as a father. But now that her dad had mentioned it, she could see Jason relishing the role.

"What I meant about Jason…is he going to help you make the baby?" her mother interjected.

"Why would you think that?"

"You two are close. It seems logical."

Ming kept her panic off her face, but it wasn't easy. "It would mess up our friendship."

"Why? I'm assuming you're going to use a clinic."

This was all hitting a little too close to home. "That's what I figured I'd do." Until Jason came up with the crazy notion of them sleeping together. "I'd better give Lily a hand in the kitchen."

Leaving her parents to process what she'd told them, Ming sidled up to her sister.

"I shared my news." She started rinsing off dishes and stacking them in the dishwasher. "Are you going to tell them you've bought a house in Portland?"

"I changed my mind."

"About the house or Portland?"

"Both."

"Evan must be thrilled." The words slipped out before Ming realized what she was saying. In her defense, she was rattled by her father's speculation about Jason being a great dad and her mother's guess that he was going to help her get pregnant.

"Evan?" Lily tried to sound confused rather than anxious, but her voice buckled beneath the weight of her dismay. "Why would Evan care?"

The cat was out of the bag. Might as well clear the air. "Because you two are dating?"

Ming was aware that keeping a secret about her and Jason while unveiling her sister's love life was the most hypocritical thing she'd done in months.

"Don't be ridiculous."

"Evan admitted it to Jason and he told me."

"I'm sorry I didn't tell you."

"Don't you think you should have?" She didn't want to resent Lily for finding happiness.

"I honestly didn't think anything was going to happen between us."

"Happen between you when, exactly?" Ming's frustration with her own love life was bubbling to the surface. "The first time you went out? The first time he kissed you?"

"I don't want this to come between us."

"Me, either." But at the moment it was, and Ming couldn't dismiss the resentment rumbling through her.

"But I don't want to break up with him." Beneath Lily's determined expression was worry. "I can't."

Shock zipped across Ming's nerve endings. "Is it that serious?"

"He told me he loves me."

"Wow." Ming exhaled in surprise.

It had taken almost a year of dating for Evan to admit such deep feelings for her. As reality smacked her in the face, she was overcome by the urge to curl into a ball and cry her eyes out. What was wrong with her? She wasn't in love with Evan. She'd made her peace with their breakup. Why couldn't she be happy for her sister?

"Do you feel the same?"

Lily wouldn't meet her gaze. "I do."

"How long have you been going out?"

"A couple months. I know it seems fast, but I've been interested in Evan since high school. Until recently, I had no idea he saw me as anything more than your baby sister. Emphasis on the *baby*." Lily's lips curved down at the corners.

There was a five-year difference in their ages. That gap would have seemed less daunting as Lily moved into her twenties and became a successful career woman.

"I guess he's seen the real you at last."

"I want you to know, I never meant for this to happen."

"Of course you didn't."

"It's just that no one has control over who they fall in love with."

What Lily had just told Ming should have relieved her own guilt over what she and Jason were doing. Evan had moved on. He was in love. If he ever discovered what was happening between her and Jason, Evan should be completely accepting. After all, he'd fallen for her sister. All Ming was doing was getting pregnant with Jason's child. It wasn't as if they were heading down the path to blissfully-ever-after.

Struck by the disparity between the perfect happiness of every couple she knew and the failure of her own love life, Ming's heart ached. Her throat closed as misery battered her. Her longing for a man she could never have and her inability to let him go trapped her. It wasn't enough to have Jason as her best friend. She wanted to claim him as her lover and the man she'd spend the rest of her life committed to. On her current path, Ming wasn't sure how she was ever going to find her way out of her discontent, but since she wasn't the sort who moldered in self-pity, she'd better figure it out.

Unwinding in her office after a hectic day of appointments, Ming rechecked the calendar where she'd been keeping track of her fertility cycle for the past few months. According to her history, her period should have started today.

Excitement raced through her. She could be pregnant. For a second she lost the ability to breathe. Was she ready for this? Months of dreaming and hoping for this moment hadn't prepared her for the reality of the change in her life between one heartbeat and the next.

Ming stared at her stomach. Did Jason's child grow inside her? She caught herself mid-thought. This was her child. Not hers and Jason's. She had to stop fooling herself that they were going to be a family. She and Jason were best friends who wanted very different things out of life. They were not a couple. Never would be.

"Are you still here?" Terry leaned into the room and flashed his big white smile. "I thought you had a wedding rehearsal to get to."

Ming nodded. "I'm leaving in ten minutes. The church is only a couple miles away."

"Did those numbers I gave you make you feel better or worse?"

Earlier in the week Terry had opened up the practice's books so she could see all that went into the running of the business. Although part of her curriculum at dental school had involved business courses that would help her if she ever decided to open her own practice, her college days were years behind her.

"I looked them over, but until I get Jason to walk me through everything, I'm still feeling overwhelmed."

"Understandable. Let me know if you have any questions."

After Terry left, Ming grabbed her purse and headed for the door. Until five minutes ago, she'd been looking forward to this weekend. Max and Rachel were a solid couple.

Thanks to Susan Case, Max's mother, the wedding promised to be a magical event. After both Nathan and Sebastian had skipped formal ceremonies—Nathan marrying Emma on a Saint Martin beach and Sebastian opting for an impromptu Las Vegas elopement—Susan had threatened Max with bodily harm if she was denied this last chance at a traditional wedding.

Most brides would have balked at so much input from their future mother-in-law, but Rachel's only family was her sister, and Ming thought the busy employment agency owner appreciated some of the day-to-day details being handled by Max's mother.

When Ming arrived at the church, most of the wedding party was already there. She set her purse in the last pew and let her gaze travel up the aisle to where the minister was speaking to Max. As the best man, Jason stood beside him, listening intently. Ming's breath caught at the sight of him clad in a well-cut dove-gray suit, white shirt and pale green tie.

Was she pregnant? It took effort to keep her fingers from wandering to her abdomen. When she'd embarked on this journey three weeks ago, she'd expected that achieving her goal would bring her great joy and confidence. Joy was there, but it was shadowed by anxiety and doubt.

She wasn't second-guessing her decision to become a mom, but she no longer wanted to do it alone. Jason would freak out if he discovered how much she wanted them to be a real family. Husband, wife, baby. But that's not how he'd visualized his future, and she had no right to be disappointed that they wanted different things.

As if her troubled thoughts had reached out to him, Jason glanced in her direction. When their eyes met, some of her angst eased. Raising his eyebrows, he shot her a crooked grin. Years of experience gave her insight into exactly what he was thinking.

Max couldn't be talked out of this crazy event.

She pursed her lips and shook her head.

You shouldn't even try. He's found his perfect mate.

"Are you two doing that communicating-without-words thing again?"

Ming hadn't noticed Missy stop beside her. With her red hair and hazel eyes, Sebastian's wife wore chocolate brown better than anyone Ming had ever met.

"I guess we are." Ming's gaze returned to Jason.

"Have you ever thought about getting together? I know you

were engaged to his brother and all, but it seems as if you'd be perfect for each other."

"Not likely." Ming had a hard time summoning energy to repeat the tired old excuses. She was stuck in a rut where Jason was concerned, with no clue how to get out. "We're complete opposites."

"No one is more different than Sebastian and I." Missy grinned. "It can be a lot of fun."

Based on the redhead's saucy smile, Ming had little trouble imagining just how much fun the newlyweds were having. She sighed. Prior conversations with Emma, Missy and Rachel had shown her that not everyone's road to romance was straight and trouble-free, but Ming knew she wasn't even on a road with Jason. More like a faint deer trail through the woods.

"He doesn't want to fall in love."

Missy surveyed the three Case men as the minister guided them into position near the front of the church. "So make him."

Rather than lecture Missy about how hopeless it was to try changing Jason's mind about love and marriage, Ming clamped her lips together and forced a smile. What good would it do to argue with a newly married woman who was a poster child for happily ever after?

As she practiced her walk up the aisle on Nathan's arm, she had a hard time focusing on the minister's instructions. Casting surreptitious glances at Jason, standing handsome and confident beside Max, she fought against despair as she realized there would never be a day when the man she loved waited for her at the front of the church. She would never wear an elegant gown of white satin and shimmering pearls and speak the words that would bind them together forever.

"And then you separate, each going to your place." The minister signaled to the organist. "Here the music changes to signal that the bride is on her way."

While everyone watched Rachel float up the aisle, her happiness making it appear as if her feet didn't touch the ground,

Ming stared down at the floor and fought against the tightness in her throat. She was going to drive herself mad pining for an ending that could never be.

Twenty minutes later, the wedding party was dismissed. They trooped back down the aisle, two-by-two, with Nathan and Ming bringing up the rear.

"How's Emma doing?" she asked. Nathan's wife was five days past her due date.

"She's miserable." Nathan obviously shared his wife's discomfort. "Can't wait for the baby to come."

"I didn't see her. Is she here tonight?"

"No." A muscle jumped in his jaw. "I told her to stay home and rest up. Tomorrow is going to be a long day." Nathan scowled. "But if I know her, she's working on the last of her orders to get them done before the baby arrives."

Nathan's wife made some of the most unique and beautiful jewelry Ming had ever seen. Missy's wedding set was one of her designs. From what Jason had told her, Max and Rachel's wedding rings had been created by Emma as well.

"I'm worried she's not going to slow down even after the baby arrives," Nathan continued, looking both exasperated and concerned. "She needs to take better care of herself."

"Why, when she has you to take care of her?"

Nathan gave her a wry grin. "I suppose you're right. See you tomorrow."

Smiling thoughtfully at Nathan's eagerness to get home to his wife, Ming went to fetch her purse. When she straightened, she discovered Jason standing beside her. He slipped his fingers through hers and squeezed gently.

"I missed you this week."

Shivers danced along her spine at his earnest tone. "I missed you, too."

More than she cared to admit. Although they'd talked every day on the phone, their conversations had revolved around the dental practice financials and other safe topics. They hadn't discussed that Evan was in love with Lily, and Ming wasn't sure Jason even knew.

"I don't suppose I could talk you into coming home with me tonight," he murmured, drawing her after the departing couples.

Although tempted by his offer, she shook her head. "I promised Lily we'd hang out, and I have an early appointment to get my hair and makeup done tomorrow." She didn't like making up excuses, but after what she'd started to suspect earlier, the only thing she wanted to do was take the pregnancy test she'd bought on the way to the church and see if it was positive. "Tomorrow after the reception."

Jason walked her to her car and held her door while she got behind the wheel. He lingered with his hand on the door. The silence between them grew heavy with expectation. Ming's heart slowed. The crease between his brows told her that something troubled him.

She was the first to break the silence. "Evan's in love with Lily and she's decided to stay in Houston."

"How do you feel about that?"

"I'm thrilled."

"I mean about how Evan feels about her."

With a determined smile she shook her head. "I'm happy for him and Lily."

"You're really okay with it?"

"I'm going to be a mom. That's what I'm truly excited about. That's where I need to put all my energy."

"Because you know I'm here if you want to talk."

"Really, I'm fine," she said, keeping her voice bright and untroubled. She knew he was just being a good friend, but she couldn't stop herself from wishing his concern originated in the same sort of love she felt for him. "See you at the restaurant."

He stared at her for a long moment more before stepping back. "Save me a seat."

And with that, he closed her car door.

Eleven

Jason had never been so glad to be done with an evening. Sitting beside Ming while toast after toast had been made to the bride and groom, he'd never felt more alone. But it's what he wanted. A lifetime with no attachments. No worries that he'd ever become so despondent over losing a woman that he'd want to kill himself.

Logic and years of distance told him that his father had been in an extremely dark place after the death of his wife and daughter. But there was no reason to believe that Jason would ever suffer such a devastating loss. And if he did, wasn't he strong enough to keep from sinking into a hole and never coming out?

And yet, his reaction to that photo of her dancing hadn't exactly been rational. Neither had the way he'd demanded that she declare herself to be his. Oh, he'd claimed that he didn't want to lead her on. The truth was he was deathly afraid of losing her.

"I'm heading home." Ming leaned her shoulder against his.

Her breath brushed his neck with intoxicating results. "Can you walk me to my car?"

"I think I'll leave, too." The evening was winding down. Sebastian and Missy had already departed.

As soon as they cleared the front door, he took her hand. Funny how such a simple act brought him so much contentment. "Did I mention you look beautiful tonight?"

"Thank you." Only her eyes smiled at him. The rest of her features were frozen into somber lines.

They reached her car and before he could open her door, she put a hand on his arm. "This is probably not the best place for this…" She glanced around, gathered a breath and met his gaze. Despite her tension, joy glittered in her dark eyes. "I'm pregnant."

Her declaration crushed the air from his lungs. He'd been expecting it, but somehow now, knowing his child grew inside her, he was beyond thrilled.

"You're sure?"

"As sure as an early pregnancy test can be." Her fingers bit into his arm. "I took one at the restaurant." She laughed unsteadily. "How crazy is that? I couldn't even wait until I got home."

Jason wrapped his arms around her and held her against him. A baby. Their baby. He wanted to rush back into the restaurant and tell everyone. They were going to be parents. Reality penetrated his giddy mood. Except she didn't want to share the truth with anyone. She intended to raise the child on her own.

"I'm glad you couldn't wait," he told her, his words muffled against her hair. "It's wonderful news."

From chest to thigh, her long, lean body was aligned with his. How many months until holding her like this he'd feel only her rounded stomach? Or would he even get to snuggle with her, her head resting on his shoulder, her arms locked around his waist?

"Of course, this means…"

Knowing what was coming next, Jason growled. "You aren't seriously going to break up with me on the eve of Max's wedding."

"Break up with you?" She tipped her head back so he could see her smile, but she wouldn't meet his eyes. "That would require us to be dating."

But they'd sworn never to explore that path. Would they miss a chance to discover that the real reason they were such good friends was because they were meant to be together?

Are you listening to yourself? What happened to swearing you'd never fall in love?

Frustrated by conflicting desires, Jason's hold on her tightened. Her breath hitched as he lowered his head and claimed her mouth. Heat flared between them. Their tongues tangled while delicious sensations licked at his nerves. She was an endless feast for his senses. A balm for his soul. She challenged him and made him a better person. And now she was pregnant with his child. They could be happy together.

All he needed to do was let her in.

He broke off the kiss and dragged his lips across her cheek. What existed in his heart was hers alone. He could tell her and change everything.

The silence between them lengthened. Finally, Ming slid her palm down his heaving chest and stepped back.

"We're just good friends who happen to be sleeping together until one of us got pregnant," she said, her wry tone at odds with her somber eyes.

"And we promised nothing would get in the way of our friendship."

She sagged against him. "And it won't."

"Not ever."

Our baby.

Jason's words the previous night had given her goose bumps.

Almost ten hours later, Ming rubbed her arms as the sensation lingered.

My baby.

She tried to infuse the declaration with conviction, but couldn't summon the strength. Not surprising, when his claim filled her with unbridled joy. It was impossible to be practical when her heart was singing and she felt lighter than air.

Pulling into the parking lot of the salon Susan Case had selected based on their excellent reputation, Ming spent a few minutes channeling her jubilation over her baby news into happiness for Rachel and Max. It was easy to do.

The bride was glowing as she chatted with her sister, Hailey, Missy and Susan. As Ming joined the group, two stylists took charge of Rachel, escorting her to a chair near the back. Rachel had let her hair grow out from the boyish cut she'd had when Ming had first met her. For her wedding look, the stylists pinned big loops of curls all over her head and attached tiny white flowers throughout.

Unaccustomed to being the center of attention, Rachel endured being fussed over with good grace. Watching the stylists in action, Ming was certain the bride would be delighted with the results.

Because all the bridesmaids had long hair, they were styled with the front pulled away from their face and soft waves cascading down their back. When the four girls lined up so Susan could take a photo, the resulting picture was feminine and romantic.

Although the wedding wasn't until four, the photographer was expecting them to be at the church, dressed in their wedding finery by one. With a hundred or more photos to smile for and because she'd skipped breakfast after oversleeping, Ming decided she'd better grab lunch before heading to the church. She ended up being the last to arrive.

Naturally her gaze went straight to Jason. Standing halfway up the aisle, model-gorgeous in his tuxedo, he looked far more stressed than the groom. Ming flashed back to their senior prom, the evening that marked the beginning of the end for her in terms of experiencing true love.

"Don't you look handsome," she exclaimed as he drew near. Over the years, she'd had a lot of practice pretending she wasn't infatuated with him. That stood her in good stead as Jason pulled her into his arms for a friendly hug.

"You smell as edible as you look," he murmured. "Whose insane idea was it to dress you in a color that made me want to devour you?"

For her fall wedding, Rachel had chosen strapless empire waist bridesmaid dresses in muted apple green. They would all be carrying bouquets of orange, yellow and fuchsia.

Ming quivered as his sexy voice rumbled through her. If he kept staring at her with hungry eyes, she might not be able to wait until after the wedding to get him alone. A deep breath helped Ming master her wayward desires. Today was about Max and Rachel.

"Susan proposed apple green, I believe." She'd never know how she kept her tone even given the chaos of her emotions.

"Remind me to thank her later."

Ming restrained a foolish giggle and pushed him to arm's length so she could check him out in turn. "I like you in a tux. You should wear one more often."

"If I'd known how much fun it would be to have you undress me with your eyes, I would have done so sooner."

"I'm not undressing—" She stopped the flow of words as Emma waddled within earshot.

"I don't know what you're planning on taking off," the very pregnant woman said as she stepped into the pew beside them, "but I'd start with what he's wearing."

Jason smirked at Ming, but there was no time for her to respond because the photographer's assistant called for the wedding party to come to the front of the church.

With everyone in a festive mood, it was easy for Ming to

laugh and joke with the rest of Rachel's attendants as they posed for one photo after another. The photographer's strict schedule allowed little time for her to dwell on how close she'd been to her own wedding six months earlier, or whether she might be in this same position months from now if things continued to progress with Lily and Evan.

But in the half-hour lull between photos and ceremony, she had more than enough quiet to contemplate what might have been for her and to ponder the future.

She kept apart from the rest of the group, not wanting her bout of melancholy to mar the bride and groom's perfect day. Shortly before the ceremony was supposed to start, Jason approached her and squeezed her hand.

"You look pensive."

"I was just thinking about the baby."

"Me, too." His expression was grave. "I want to tell everyone I'm the father."

Ming's heart convulsed. Last night, after discovering she was pregnant, she'd longed to stand at Jason's side and tell everyone they were having a baby. Of course, doing it would bring up questions about whether or not they were together.

"Are you sure this is a good idea?"

"The only reason you wanted to keep quiet was because you didn't want to hurt Evan. But he's moved on with your sister."

"So you decided this because Evan and Lily are involved?"

"It isn't about them. It's about us. I'm going to be in the child's life on a daily basis." His expression was more determined than she'd ever seen it. "I think I should be there as his dad rather than as Uncle Jason."

He'd said *us*.

Only it wasn't about her and Jason. Not in the way she wanted. Ming's heart shuddered like a damaged window battered by strong winds. At any second it could shatter into a thousand pieces. She loved the idea that he wanted to be a father, but she couldn't ignore her yearning to have him be there for her as well.

"Come on, you two," Missy called as the wedding party began moving into position near the church's inner door. "We're on."

Jason strode to his position in line and Ming relaxed her grip on her bouquet before the delicate stems of the Gerber daisies snapped beneath the intensity of her conflicting emotions.

As maid of honor, Rachel's sister, Hailey, was already in place behind Max and his parents. The music began signaling the trio to start down the aisle. The groom looked relaxed and ready as he accompanied his parents to their places at the front of the church.

The bright flowers in Ming's hands quivered as she stood beside Nathan. He appeared on edge. His distress let Ming forget about her own troubles.

"Are you okay?" she asked.

Lines bracketed his mouth. "I tried to convince Emma to stay home. Although she wouldn't admit it, she's really having a difficult time today. I'm worried about her."

"I'm sure it's natural to be uncomfortable when you're past your due date," Ming said and saw immediately that her words had little effect on the overprotective father-to-be. "She'll let you know if anything is wrong."

"I'm concerned that she won't." He glanced behind him at the bride. "She didn't want anything to disturb your day."

Rachel put her hand on Nathan's arm, her expression sympathetic. "I appreciate both of you being here today, but if you think she needs to be at home, take her there right after the ceremony."

Nathan leaned down and grazed Rachel's cheek with his lips. "I will. Thank you."

He seemed marginally less like an overwound spring as they took their turn walking down the aisle. It might have helped that his wife beamed at him from the second row. Ming's stomach twisted in reaction to their happiness. Even for someone who wasn't newly pregnant and madly in love with a man who refused to feel the same way, it was easy to get overwhelmed by emotions at a wedding. Holding herself together became easier as she watched Rachel start down the aisle.

The bride wore a long strapless dress unadorned by beading or lace. Diamond and pearl earrings were her only jewelry. Her styling was romantic and understated, allowing the bride's beauty and her utter happiness to shine.

With her father dead and her mother out of her life since she was four, Rachel had no one to give her away. Ming's sadness lasted only until she realized this was the last time Rachel would walk alone. At the end of the ceremony, she would be Max's wife and part of his family.

Ming swallowed past the lump in her throat as the minister began talking. The rest of the ceremony passed in a blur. She was roused out of her thoughts by the sound of clapping. Max had swept Rachel into a passionate kiss. The music began once more and the happy couple headed back down the aisle, joined for life.

Because they'd been the last up the aisle, Nathan and Ming were the last to return down it. They didn't get far, however. As they drew near Emma, Ming realized something was wrong. Nathan's wife was bending forward at the waist and in obvious pain. When Nathan hastened to her side, she clutched his forearm and leaned into his strength.

"I think it might be time to get to the hospital," she said, her brown eyes appearing darker than ever in her pale face.

"How long has this been going on?" he demanded.

"Since this morning."

Nathan growled.

"I'm fine. I wanted both of us to be here for Rachel and Max. And now I'd like to go to the hospital and give birth to our son."

"Stubborn woman," Nathan muttered as he put a supporting arm around his wife and escorted her down the aisle.

"Do you want us to come with you?" Max's mother asked, following on their heels. She reached her hand back to her husband.

"No." Emma shook her head. "Stay and enjoy the party. The baby probably won't come anytime soon." But as she said it, another contraction stopped her in her tracks.

"I'm going to get the car." Handing his wife off to Ming, Nathan raced out of the church.

Ming and Emma continued their slow progress.

"Has he always been like this?" Ming asked, amused and ever so envious.

"It all started when my father decided to make marrying me part of a business deal Nathan was doing with Montgomery Oil. Since then he's got this crazy idea in his head that I need to be taken care of."

"I think it's sweet."

Emma's lips moved into a fond smile. "It's absolutely wonderful."

By the time Ming got Emma settled into Nathan's car and returned to the church, half the guests had made it through the reception line and had spilled onto the street. Since she wasn't the immediate family of the bride and groom, she stood off to one side and waited until the wedding party was free so she could tell them what had happened to Nathan and Emma.

"The contractions seemed fairly close together," Ming said in answer to Susan Case's question regarding Emma's labor. "She said she'd started having them this morning, so I don't know how far along she is."

"Hopefully Nathan will call us from the hospital and let us know," Max's father said.

Sebastian nodded. "I'm sure he will."

"In the meantime," Max said, smiling down at his glowing wife, "we have a reception to get to."

A limo awaited them at the curb to take the group to The Corinthian, a posh venue in downtown Houston's historical district. Ming had never attended an event there, but she'd heard nothing but raves from Missy and Emma. And they were right. The space took its name from the fluted Corinthian columns that flanked the long colonnade where round tables of ten had been placed for the reception. Once the lobby for the First National Bank, the hall's thirty-five-foot ceilings and tall windows now made it an elegant place to hold galas, wedding receptions and lavish birthday parties.

Atop burgundy damask table cloths, gold silverware flanked gilded chargers and white china rimmed with gold. Flickering votive candles in glass holders nestled amongst flowers in Rachel's chosen palette of gold, yellow and deep orange.

Ming had never seen anything so elegant and inviting.

"Susan really outdid herself," Missy commented as she and her husband stopped beside Ming to admire the view. "It almost makes me wish Sebastian and I hadn't run off to Las Vegas to get married." She grinned up at her handsome husband. "Of course, having to wait months to become his wife wouldn't have been worth all this."

Sebastian lifted her hand and brushed a kiss across her knuckles. The heat that passed between them in that moment made Ming blink.

She cleared her throat. "So, you don't regret eloping?"

Missy shook her head, her gaze still locked on her husband's face. "Having a man as deliberate and cautious as Sebastian jump impulsively into a life-changing event as big as marriage was the most amazing, romantic, sexy thing ever."

"He obviously knew what he wanted," Ming murmured, her gaze straying to where Jason laughed with Max's father.

Sebastian's deep voice resonated with conviction as he said, "Indeed I did."

Twelve

Keeping Ming's green-clad form in view as she chatted with their friends, Jason dialed his brother's cell. Evan hadn't mentioned skipping the wedding, and it was out of character for him to just not show. When voice mail picked up, Jason left a message. Then he called his dad, but Tony hadn't heard from Evan, either. Buzzing with concern, Jason slid the phone back into his pocket and headed for Ming.

She was standing alone, her attention on the departing Sebastian and Missy, a wistful expression on her face. Their happiness was tangible. Like a shot to his head, Jason comprehended Ming's fascination. Despite her insistence that she wasn't cut out for marriage, it's what she longed for. Evan had ended their engagement and broken her heart in the process. Her decision to become a single mom was Ming's way of coping with loneliness.

How had he not understood this before? Probably because he didn't want it to be true. He hated to think that she'd find someone new to love and he'd lose her all over again.

Over dinner, while Rachel and Max indulged the guests by kissing at every clinking of glassware, Jason pondered his dinner companion and where the future would take them after tonight. He'd been happier in the past couple of weeks than he'd been in years. It occurred to him just how much he'd missed the closeness that had marked their relationship through high school.

He wasn't ready to give up anything that he'd won. He wanted Ming as the best friend whom he shared his hopes and fears with. He wanted endless steamy nights with the sexy temptress who haunted his dreams. Most of all, he wanted the family that the birth of their baby would create.

All without losing the independence he was accustomed to. Impossible.

He wasn't foolish enough to think Ming would happily go along with what he wanted, so it was up to Jason to figure out how much he was comfortable giving up and for her to decide what she was willing to live with.

By the time the dancing started, Jason had his proposition formed. Tonight was for romance. Tomorrow morning over breakfast he would tell her his plan and they would start hashing out a strategy.

"Hmm," she murmured as they swayed together on the dance floor. "It's been over a decade since we danced together. I'd forgotten how good you are at this."

"There are things I'm even better at." He executed a spin that left her gasping with laughter. "How soon can we get out of here?"

"It's barely nine." She tried to look shocked, but her eyes glowed at his impatience.

"It's the bride and groom's party." In the crush on the dance floor, he doubted if anyone would notice his hand venturing over her backside. "They have to stick around. We can leave anytime."

Her body quivered, but she grabbed his hand and repositioned it on her waist. "I don't think Max and Rachel would appreciate us ducking out early."

Jason glanced toward the happy newlyweds. "I don't think they'll even notice."

But in the end, they stayed until midnight and saw Max and Rachel off. The newlyweds were spending the night at a downtown hotel and flying on Monday to Gulf Shores, Alabama, where Max owned a house. The location had seemed an odd choice to Jason until he heard the story of how Max and Rachel met in the beach town five years earlier.

As the guests enjoyed one last dance, Jason slid his palm into the small of Ming's back. "Did your sister say anything about Evan's plan to miss the wedding today?"

A line appeared between Ming's finely drawn eyebrows. "No. Did you try calling him?"

"Yes. And I spoke with my dad, too. He hadn't heard from him. This just isn't like Evan."

"Let me call Lily and see if she knows what's going on." Ming dialed her sister's cell and waited for her to pick up. "Evan didn't make the wedding. Did he tell you he was planning on skipping it?" Ming met Jason's eyes and shook her head.

"Find out when she last spoke to him."

"Jason wants to know when you last heard from him. I'm going to put you on speaker, okay?"

"Last night."

It was odd for his brother to go a whole day without talking to one of them. "Is something going on with him?"

"Last night he proposed." Lily sounded miserable.

"Wow," Ming exclaimed, her excitement sounding genuine.

"I told him I couldn't marry him."

Anxiety kicked Jason in the gut. "I guess I don't need to ask how he took that."

Twice he'd seen Evan slip into the same self-destructiveness their father had once exhibited. The first time as a senior in high school when his girlfriend of three years decided to end things a week after graduation. Evan had spent the entire summer in a black funk. The second time was about a year before he and Ming had started dating. His girlfriend of two years had dumped him and married her ex-boyfriend. But Jason suspected neither of those events had upset Evan to the extent that losing Lily would.

"I don't understand," Ming said. "I thought you loved him."

"I do." Lily's voice shook. "I just can't do that to you."

Ming looked to Jason for help. "I don't blame either of you for finding each other."

While the sisters talked, Jason dialed his brother again. When he heard Evan's voice mail message, he hung up. He'd already left three messages tonight. No need to leave another.

"Do you mind if I stop by Evan's before I head home?" Jason quizzed Ming as he escorted her to where she'd left her car. "I'll feel better if I see that he's all right."

"Sure."

"Just let yourself in. I shouldn't be more than fifteen minutes behind you."

But when he got to his brother's house, he discovered why Evan hadn't made it to the wedding and hadn't called him back. His brother was lying unconscious on his living room floor while an infomercial played on the television.

An open bottle of pain pills was tipped over on the coffee table. Empty. In a flash Jason became a fifteen-year-old again, finding his father passed out in the running car, the garage filled with exhaust. With a low cry, Jason dropped to his knees beside his brother. The steady rise and fall of Evan's chest reassured Jason that his brother wasn't dead. Sweat broke out as he grabbed his brother's shoulder and shook.

"Evan. Damn it. Wake up." His throat locked up as he searched for some sign that his brother was near consciousness. Darkness closed over his vision. He was back in the shadow-filled garage, where poisonous fumes had raked his throat and filled his lungs. His chest tightened with the need to cough. His brother couldn't die. He had to wake him. With both hands on Evan's shoulders, Jason shook him hard. "Evan."

A hand shoved him in the chest, breaking through the walls of panic that had closed in on Jason.

"Geez, Jason." His brother blinked in groggy confusion. "What the hell?"

Chest tight, Jason sat on the floor and raked his fingers through his hair. Relief hadn't hit him yet. He couldn't draw a full breath. Oxygen deprivation made his head spin. He dug the heels of his palms against his eyes and felt moisture.

Grabbing the pill bottle, he shook it in his brother's face. "How many of these did you take?"

"Two. That's all I had."

And if there had been more? Would he have taken them? "Are you sure?"

Evan batted away his brother's hand. "What the hell is wrong with you?"

"You didn't make the wedding. So I came over to check on you. Then I saw you on the floor and I thought..." He couldn't finish the thought.

"I didn't make the wedding because I wasn't in the mood."

"And these?"

"I went for a bicycle ride this morning to clear my head and took a spill that messed up my back. That's why I'm lying on the floor. I seized up."

"I left three messages." Jason's hands trembled in the aftermath of the adrenaline rush. "Why didn't you call me back?"

"I turned my phone off. I didn't want to talk to anyone." Evan rolled to his side and pushed into a sitting position. "What are you doing here?"

"Lily said she turned down your proposal. I thought maybe you'd done something stupid."

But Evan wasn't listening. He sucked in a ragged breath. "She's afraid it'll hurt her sister if we get married." He blinked three times in rapid succession. "And she wouldn't listen to me when I said Ming wouldn't be as upset as Lily thinks."

Jason couldn't believe what he was hearing. Was this Evan's way of convincing himself he wasn't the bad guy in this scenario? "How do you figure? It's only been six months since your engagement ended."

Evan got to his feet, and Jason glimpsed frustration in his brother's painful movements. "I know you think I messed up, but I did us both a favor."

"How do you figure?" Jason stood as well, his earlier worry lost in a blast of righteous irritation.

"She wasn't as much in love with me as you think she was."

Jason couldn't believe his brother was trying to shift some of the blame for their breakup onto Ming. "You forget who you're talking to. I know Ming. I saw how happy she was with you."

"Yeah, well. Not as happy as she could have been."

"And whose fault was that?" He spun away from Evan and caught his reflection in the large living room windows. He looked hollow. As if the emotion of a moment before had emptied him of all energy.

"I worked hard at the relationship," he said, his voice dull.

"And Ming didn't?"

A long silence followed his question. When Jason turned around, his brother was sitting on the couch, his head in his hands.

"Ming and I were a mistake. I know that now. It's Lily I love." He lifted his head. His eyes were bleak. "I don't know how I'm supposed to live without her."

Jason winced at his brother's phrasing. His cell rang. Ming was calling.

"Is everything okay with Evan?" The concern in her soft voice was a balm to Jason's battered emotions. "It's been almost a half an hour."

He couldn't tell her what he thought was going on while

Evan could overhear. "He threw his back out in a bicycle-riding accident this morning."

"Oh, no. There should be some ice packs in his freezer."

"I'll get him all squared away and be there in a half an hour."

"Take your time. It's been a long couple of days and I'm exhausted. Wake me when you get here."

He ended the call and found himself smiling at the image of Ming asleep in his bed. This past week without her had been hell. Not seeing her. Touching her. He hadn't been able to get her out of his mind.

"Ming told me to put you on ice." Talking to her had lightened his mood. He needed to get his brother settled so he could get home. "Do you want me to bring the ice packs to you here or upstairs?'

"What the hell do I care?"

Evan's sharp retort wasn't like him. Lily's refusal had hit him hard. Fighting anxiety over his brother's dark mood, Jason bullied Evan upstairs and settled him in his bed. Observing his brother's listless state, Jason was afraid to leave him alone.

"Are you going to be okay?"

Evan glared at him. "Why aren't you gone?"

"I thought maybe I should stick around a bit longer."

"Sounds like Ming is waiting for you." Evan deliberately looked away from Jason, making him wonder if Evan suspected what Jason and Ming had been up to.

"She is."

"Then get out of here."

Jason headed for the door. "I'll be back to check on you in the morning."

"Don't bother. I'd rather be alone."

The fifteen-minute drive home offered Jason little time to process what had happened with Evan. What stood out for him was his brother's despair at losing the woman he loved.

He stepped from his garage into the kitchen, and stood in the dark, listening. The silence soothed him, guided him toward the safe place he'd created inside himself. The walled fortress that kept unsettling emotions at bay.

He glanced around the kitchen and smiled as his gaze landed on the chair where he and Ming had made love for the first time. Just one of the great moments that had happened in this room. In almost every room in the house.

He had dozens of incredible memories featuring Ming, and not one of them would be possible if he hadn't opened the doors to his heart and let himself experience raw, no-holds-barred passion.

But desire he could handle. It was the other strong feelings Ming invoked that plagued him. Being with her these past few weeks had made him as happy as he ever remembered. He couldn't stop imagining a life with her.

And this morning he'd been ready to make his dreams reality.

But all that had changed tonight when he'd mistaken what was going on with Evan and relived the terror of the night he'd found his father in the garage. The fear had been real. His pledge to never fall in love—the decision that had stopped making sense these last few weeks—became rational once more.

He couldn't bear to lose Ming. If they tried being a couple and it didn't work out, the damage done to their friendship might never heal. Could he take that risk?

No.

Jason marched up the stairs, confident that he was making the right decision for both of them. He'd expected to find her in his bed, but the soft light spilling from the room next door drew him to the doorway. In what had been his former den, Ming occupied the rocking chair by the window, a stuffed panda clutched against her chest, her gaze on the crib. Encased in serenity, she'd never looked more beautiful.

"Where's all your stuff?" she asked, her voice barely above a whisper.

"It's in the garage."

Gone was the memorabilia of his racing days. In its place stood a crib, changing table and rocker. The walls had been painted a soft yellow. The bedding draped across the crib had pastel jungle animals parading between palm trees and swinging from vines.

She left the chair and walked toward him past the pictures that had graced her childhood bedroom. He'd gotten them from her parents. Her father was sentimental about things like that.

"Who helped you do this?"

"No one." His arms went around her slim form, pulling her against his thudding heart. He rested his chin on her head. "Except for the paint and new carpet. I hired those out."

"You picked all this out by yourself?"

Jason had never shopped for a Christmas or birthday present without her help, and Ming was obviously having a hard time wrapping her head around what he'd accomplished in such a short time.

"Do you like it?" he prompted, surprised by how much he wanted her approval.

"It's perfect."

Nestled in Jason's arms, Ming wouldn't have believed it was possible to fall any deeper in love with him, but at that moment she did. The room had been crafted with loving care by a guy who was as comfortable in a department store as a cat in a kennel of yapping dogs.

He was an amazing man and he would be a terrific father. She was lucky to have such a good friend.

Jason's arms tightened. "I'm glad you like the room. It turned out better than I expected."

"I love you." The courage to say those words had been building in her ever since Jason told her he wanted to go public about his part in her pregnancy. She'd always been truthful with Jason. She'd be a fool and a coward to hide something so important from him.

He tensed.

She gestured at the room. "Seeing this, I thought…" Well, that wasn't true. She'd been reacting emotionally to Jason's decision to be an active father and to his decorating this room to surprise her. "I want to be more than your best friend. I want to be a family with you and our baby."

Fear that he'd react badly didn't halt her confession. As her love for him strengthened with each day that passed, she knew she was going to bare her soul at some point. It might as well be sooner so they could talk it through. "I know that's not what you want to hear," she continued. "But I can't keep pretending I'm okay with just being your best friend."

When his mouth flattened into a grim line, Ming pulled free of his embrace. Without his warmth, she was immediately chilled. She rubbed her arms, but the cold she felt came from deep inside.

"Evan knew how you felt, didn't he?" Jason made it sound like an accusation. "Tonight. He told me you weren't as in love with him as I thought."

"Why did he tell you that?"

"I assumed because he was justifying falling for Lily."

"I swear I never gave him any reason to suspect how I felt about you. I couldn't even admit it to myself until I saw you crash. You've always been so determined not to fall in love or get married." Ming's eyes burned as she spoke. "I knew you'd never let yourself feel anything more for me than friendship, so I bottled everything up and almost married your brother because I was completely convinced you and I could never be."

He was silent a long time. "I haven't told you what happened with Evan tonight."

"Is he okay?"

"When I got to his house I found him on the floor with an empty bottle of painkillers beside him. I thought he was so upset over Lily refusing to marry him that he tried to kill himself."

Ming's heart squeezed in sympathy. The wound he'd suffered when he'd found his father in the garage with the car running had cut deeper than anyone knew. The damage had been permanent. Something Jason would never be free from.

"Did he?" She'd been with Evan for three years and had never seen any sign of depression, but Jason's concern was so keen, she was ready to believe her ex-fiancé had done something to harm himself.

"No. He'd only taken a couple." A muscle jumped in Jason's jaw. He stared at the wall behind her, his gaze on a distant place. "I've never seen him like this. He's devastated that Lily turned him down."

"They're not us."

"What does that mean?" Annoyance edged his voice, warning her that he wasn't in the mood to listen.

She refused to be deterred. "Just because they might not be able to make it work doesn't mean we can't."

"Maybe. But I don't want to take the risk." He gripped her hands and held on tight.

"Have you considered what will happen if we go down that road and it doesn't work out between us? You could come to hate me. I don't want to lose my best friend."

Ming had thought about it, but she had no easy answer. "I don't want to lose you, either, but I'm struggling to think of you as just my best friend. What I feel for you is so much deeper and stronger than that."

And here's where things got tricky. She could love Jason to the best of her ability, but he was convinced that loving someone meant opening up to overwhelming loss, and she couldn't force him to accept something different. But she could make him face what he feared most.

"I love you," she said, her voice brimming with conviction. "I need you to love me in return. I know you do. I feel it every time you touch me." She paused to let her words sink in. "And because we love each other, whether you want to admit it or not, our friendship is altered. We're no longer just best friends. We're a whole lot more."

Through her whole speech he regarded her with an unflinching stare. Now he spoke. "So, what are you saying?"

"I'm saying what you're trying to preserve by not moving our relationship forward no longer exists."

A muscle jumped in his jaw as he stared at her. Silence surrounded them.

"Is this an ultimatum?"

Was it? When she started, she hadn't meant it to be.

"No. It's a statement of intent. Our friendship as it once was is over. I love you and I want us to be a family."

"And if I don't accept that things have to change?"

She made no attempt to hide her sadness. "Then we both lose."

Half an hour after her conversation with Jason, Ming plopped onto her window seat and stared at the dark backyard. She didn't bother changing into a nightgown and sliding between the sheets. What was the point when there was no way she was going to be able to sleep? Her conversation with Jason played over and over in her mind.

Could she have handled it better? Probably not. Jason was never going to relish hearing the truth. He liked their relationship exactly the way it was. Casual. Comfortable. Constant. No doubt he'd resent her for shaking things up.

Dawn found her perched on a stool at the breakfast bar, her gaze on the pool in her backyard. She cradled a cup of coffee in her hands.

"You're up early." Lily entered the kitchen and made a beeline for the cupboard where she kept the ingredients for her healthy breakfast shake. "Couldn't sleep?"

"You're an idiot." Ming knew it wasn't fair to take her frustration out on her sister, but Lily was throwing away love.

Her sister leaned back against the countertop. "Good morning to you, too."

"I'm sorry." Ming shook her head. Her heart hurt. "I'm sitting here thinking how lucky you are that Evan wants to marry you. And it just makes me so mad that you turned him down."

"Are you sure that's what you're mad about?"

Ming blinked and focused her gaze on Lily. "Of course."

"The whole time you were with Evan I was miserable."

Seeing where her sister was going, Ming laughed. "And you think I'm unhappy because Evan loves you?"

"Are you?"

"Not even a little."

"Then why are you so upset?"

With shaky hands, Ming set her cup down and rubbed her face. "I'm pregnant."

After all the arguments she'd had with her sister, the last thing Ming expected was for Lily to rush over and hug her. Ming's throat closed.

"Aren't you going to scold me for doing the wrong thing?" Ming asked.

"I'm sorry I've been so unsupportive. It wasn't fair of me to impose my opinions on you. I'm really happy for you." Lily sounded sincere. "Why didn't you didn't tell me you'd gone to the clinic?"

"Because I didn't go."

"Then how...?" Lily's eyes widened. "Jason?"

"Yes." Ming couldn't believe how much it relieved her to share the truth.

"Have you thought about what this is going to do to Evan?" It was natural that this would be Lily's reaction. She loved Evan and wanted to protect him.

"I was more worried about it before I knew he'd moved on with you." Ming crossed her arms. "But now you've turned down his proposal, and neither Jason nor I want to keep his involvement a secret."

"Why did you have to pick Jason?" Lily shook her head.

Ming refrained from asking Lily why Evan had picked her. "When I decided to have a baby, I wasn't keen on having a stranger's child. Jason understood, and because he's my best friend, he agreed to help."

"So you slept with him."

Ming's cheeks grew warm. "Yes."

"Does that mean you two are a couple?"

"No. As much as I want more, I understood that us being together was a temporary thing. Once I got pregnant, we'd stop."

"But now you're in love with him." Not a question, a statement. "Does he know?"

"I told him last night."

Lily squeezed Ming's hands. "How did he react?"

"Exactly how I'd expected him to." Ming put on her bravest smile. "He has his reasons for never falling in love."

"What are you talking about? He loves you."

"I know, but he won't admit to anything stronger than friendship."

"A friend he wants to sleep with." Lily's smile was wry.

"We have some pretty fabulous chemistry." The chuckle that vibrated in Ming's chest was bittersweet. "But he won't let it become anything more."

"Oh, Ming."

"It's not as if I didn't know how he feels." Ming slid off her stool and looped her arm through Lily's. She tugged her sister toward the stairs. "It just makes it that much more important for you to accept Evan's proposal." Closing her ears to her sister's protests, Ming packed Lily an overnight bag and herded her into the garage. "One of us deserves to be madly in love."

Fifteen minutes later, they pulled up in front of Evan's house. The longing on Lily's face told Ming she'd been right to meddle. She scooped up her sister's overnight bag and breezed up the front walk, Lily trailing slowly behind.

"Are you sure about this?" Lily questioned as they waited for Evan to answer the door.

"Positive. What a horrible sister I would be to stand in the way of your happiness."

Evan opened his door and leaned on it. He looked gray beneath his tan. "Ming? What are you doing here?"

"My sister tells me she turned down your marriage proposal."

His gaze shot beyond Ming to where Lily lingered at the bottom of his steps, but he said nothing.

Not being able to fix what was wrong in her own love life didn't mean she couldn't make sure Lily got her happily-ever-after. "She claims she turned you down because she thinks I would be hurt, but I'm moving on with my life and I don't want to be her excuse for not marrying you." Ming fixed her ex-fiancé with a steely gaze. "Do you promise you'll love her forever?"

"Of course." Evan was indignant.

Fighting to keep her composure intact, Ming headed down the steps to hug her sister. Confident they were out of Evan's hearing, she whispered, "Don't you dare come home until you've got an engagement ring on your finger."

Lily glanced at Evan. "Are you going to take your own advice and go talk to Jason?"

Ming shook her head. "Too much has happened over the last few days. We both need some time to adjust."

"He'll come around. You'll see."

But Ming didn't see. She merely nodded to pacify her sister. "I hope you're right."

Finding Evan passed out last night had reaffirmed to Jason how much better off he was alone. After such a powerful incident, Ming was convinced he'd never change his mind.

"Hey, Dad." It was late Sunday morning when Jason opened his front door and found his father standing there. "What's up?"

"Felt like having lunch with you."

From his father's serious expression, Jason wondered what he was in for, but he grabbed his keys and locked the house. "Where to?"

"Where else?"

They drove to his dad's favorite restaurant, where the pretty brunette hostess greeted Tony by name and flirted with him the whole way to the table.

"She's young enough to be your daughter," Jason commented, eyeing his father over the menu.

Tony chuckled. "She's young enough to be my granddaughter. And there's nothing going on. I love my wife."

When Tony had first announced that he was marrying Claire, Jason had a hard time believing his father had let himself fall in love again. But he'd reasoned that fifteen years of grieving was more than enough for anyone, and there was no question that Claire made his father happy. But his father's optimistic attitude toward love didn't stop Jason from wondering what would happen if Claire left.

Would his father collapse beneath the weight of sadness again? There was no way to know, and Jason hoped he never had to find out. "So, what's on your mind, Dad?"

"I spoke with Evan earlier today. Sounds like he and Lily are engaged."

"Since when?"

"Since this morning. Apparently Ming dropped her sister off and told her not to come home until she was engaged." Tony grinned. "I always loved that girl."

"Good for Evan. He was pretty beat up about Lily last night."

"He said you weren't doing too great, either."

Jason grimaced. "I found Evan on his living room floor, an empty bottle of pain pills next to him and I assumed..."

"That he'd tried to kill himself the way I had when you were fifteen." Tony looked older than his sixty-two years. The vibrancy had gone out of his eyes and the muscles in his face were slack. "That was the single darkest moment of my life, and I'm sorry you had to be the one to experience it with me."

"If I hadn't you'd be dead." They'd never really talked about what had happened. As a teenager Jason had been too shocked by almost losing a second parent to demand answers. And since Evan had been away at college, the secret had remained between Jason and his father while questions ate away Jason's sense of security.

"Looking back, I can't believe I allowed myself to sink so low, but I wasn't aware that I needed help. All I could see was a black pit with steep sides that I couldn't climb out of. Every day the hole seemed deeper. The company was months away from layoffs. I was taking my professional worries out on your mother, and that was eating me up. Then the car accident snatched her and Marie away from us. I was supposed to have driven them to the dress rehearsal for Marie's recital that night, but I was delayed at the office." Tony closed his eyes for a few seconds before resuming. "Those files could have waited until morning. If I had put my family first, they might still be alive. And in the end, all my work came to nothing. The job we'd bid went elsewhere and the company was on the verge of going under. I was to the point where I couldn't live with my failure as a husband, father or businessman."

So, this was the burden his father had carried all these years. Guilt had driven him to try to take his life because he'd perceived himself a failure?

And just like that, Jason's doctrine citing the dangers of falling in love lost all support.

"I thought you were so desperately in love with Mom that you couldn't bear to live without her anymore."

"Her death was devastating, but it wasn't why I started drinking or why I reached the point where I didn't want to go on. It was the guilt." His father regarded Jason in dismay. "Is that why you and Ming never dated? Were you afraid you'd lose her one day?"

"We didn't date because we're friends."

"But you love her."

"Of course I love her." And he did. "She's my—"

His father interrupted to finish. "Best friend." He shook his head in disgust. "Evan had another bit of news for me." Tony leaned his forearms on the table and pinned Jason with hard eyes. "Something Lily told him about Ming."

Now Jason knew why his father had shown up at his house. "She's pregnant."

"And?"

"The baby's mine."

So was Ming. His. Just as he'd told her the night of Max's bachelor party. He'd claimed her and then pushed her away because of a stupid pledge he'd made at fifteen. Had he really expected her to remain his best friend just because that's how it had always been for them?

And now that he knew the truth behind his father's depression, Jason could admit that he wanted the same things she did. Marriage. Children. The love of a lifetime.

But after he pushed her away last night, would she still want those things with him?

Jason's chair scraped the floor as he got to his feet. He threw enough money on the table to cover their tab and gestured for his father to get up. "We have to go."

"Go where?" Tony followed his son out the door without receiving an answer. "Go where?" he repeated, sliding behind the wheel of his BMW.

"I have an errand to run. Then I'm going to go see Ming. It's way past time I tell her how I really feel."

Ming swam beneath the pool's surface, stroking hard to reach the side before her breath gave out. After leaving Evan's house hours earlier, she'd been keyed up. After cleaning her refrigerator and vacuuming the whole upstairs, she'd decided to burn off her excess energy, hoping the cool water would calm both her body and her mind.

The exercise did its job. By the time she'd completed her twentieth lap, her thoughts had stopped racing. Muffin awaited her at the edge of the pool. As soon as Ming surfaced, the Yorkie raced forward and touched her nose to Ming's. The show of affection made her smile.

"What would I do without you?" she asked the small dog and received a lick in response.

"I've been asking myself the same question since you left last night."

A shadow fell across her. Ming looked up, her stomach flipping at the determined glint in Jason's blue eyes. Relief raced through her. The way their conversation had ended the previous night, she'd worried their friendship was irrevocably damaged.

"Luckily you aren't ever going to find that out." She accepted Jason's hand and let him pull her out of the water.

He wrapped her in a towel and pulled her against him. Dropping his lips to hers, he kissed her slow and deep. Ming tossed aside all the heartache of the past twelve hours and surrendered to the powerful emotions Jason aroused.

"I was wrong to dump all that stuff about Evan on you last night," he told her.

"I'm your friend. You know I'm always there for you."

"I know I take that for granted."

He took her by the hand and led her inside. To Ming's delight he pulled her toward the stairs. This wasn't what she'd expected from him after she confessed her feelings. She figured he'd distance himself from her as he'd done with women in the past.

But when they arrived in her bedroom, he didn't take her in his arms or rip the covers off the mattress and sweep her onto the soft sheets.

Instead, he kissed her on the forehead. "Grab a shower. I have an errand to run and could use your help."

An errand? Disappointment sat like a bowling ball in her stomach. "What sort of an errand?"

"I never got Max and Rachel a wedding present."

"Oh, Jason." She rolled her eyes at him.

"I'm hopeless without you," he reminded her, nudging her in the direction of the bathroom. "You know that."

"Does it have to be today?"

"They're leaving for Alabama tomorrow morning. I want them to have it before then." He scooped up the Yorkshire terrier and the dog's stuffed squirrel toy. "Muffin and I will be waiting for you downstairs."

"Fine."

Half an hour later Ming descended her stairs and found Jason entertaining Muffin with a game of fetch. She'd put on a red sundress with thin straps and loved the way Jason's eyes lit up in appreciation.

She collected the Yorkie's leash and her purse and headed out the front door. When she spotted the car in front of her house, she hesitated. "Why are you driving the 'Cuda?"

"I told you, I never got Max and Rachel a wedding present."

Understanding dawned. "You're giving him back the car?"

"The bet we made seems pretty stupid in light of recent events."

"What recent events?"

He offered her his most enigmatic smile. "Follow me and you'll find out."

When they arrived at Max and Rachel's house, Jason didn't even have a chance to get out of the car before the front door opened. To his amusement, Max looked annoyed.

"Why are you driving the 'Cuda?" he demanded as Jason slowly got to his feet. "Do you have any idea what the car's worth?"

"I don't, since you never told me what you paid for it." Jason took Ming's hand as she reached his side and pulled her close.

"Look, I'm sorry that I didn't get you anything for your wedding. Ming was supposed to help me pick something, but she backed out at the last minute."

"Jason." She bumped her hip against him in warning. "You are perfectly capable of shopping on your own."

"No, he's not," Max put in.

"No, I'm not. So, here." Jason held out the keys.

"You're giving me back the 'Cuda?" Max's thunderstruck expression was priceless.

"I realize now that I had an unfair advantage when we made the bet. You were already in love with Rachel, just too stubborn to realize it."

Max took the keys and nodded. "Being stubborn when it comes to love means you lose out on all sorts of things."

Jason felt the barb hit home. He had missed a lot with Ming. If he hadn't been so determined never to be hurt, she might have married his brother, and Jason could have ended up with a lifetime of pain.

Rachel had come out to join them. She snuggled against her husband's side and looked fondly at the bright yellow car. "What's going on?"

"Jason's giving me back the 'Cuda," Max explained with a wry grin. "Can I interest you in a ride?"

To Jason's surprise, the blonde's cheeks turned pink. Unwilling to delve too deeply into whatever subtext had just passed between husband and wife, he reached for the passenger seat and pulled out a box wrapped in white-and-silver paper and adorned with a silver bow.

"And because the car is a really lousy wedding present," he continued, handing the gift to Rachel, "I got this for you."

Rachel grinned. "I think the car is a lovely present, but thank you for this."

Jason shut the 'Cuda's door and gave the car one last pat. "Take good care of her," he told Max.

"I intend to." Max leaned down and planted a firm kiss on his wife's lips.

"I meant the car," Jason retorted, amused.

"Her, too."

After spending another ten minutes with the newlyweds, Ming and Jason returned to her car.

"What was that about?" she asked, standing beside the driver's door. "You didn't need me to help deliver the car. You could have had Max come pick it up."

"It was symbolic." He could feel her tension growing and decided he'd better tell her what was on his mind before she worked herself into a lather. "I won the car because I bet against love. It sits in my garage, a testament to my stubbornness and stupidity. So I decided to give it back to Max. Apparently in addition to its financial value it has some sentimental value to him, as well."

Her lips curved. "I'm happy to hear you admit that you were idiotic and pigheaded, but what caused your enlightenment?"

He leaned against the car and drew her into his arms.

"My dad swung by my house earlier and we had a long talk about what happened after my mother and sister died."

She sighed and relaxed against him. "You've talked with him about it before, haven't you?"

"We talked about his depression, but I never understood what was at the root of him trying to take his life."

"I thought it was because he was so much in love with your mom that he couldn't live without her."

"That's what I believed. Turns out I didn't know the whole story."

"There's more?"

"Today I found out why he was so depressed after my mother and sister died. Apparently he stayed at work when he was supposed to drive them the night they died. He thinks if he'd chosen his family over the business they might still be alive. It was eating him up."

"You mean he felt guilty?"

Jason nodded. "Guilty because he'd failed her. Not devastated by loss. All these years I was wrong to think love only led to pain." He watched Ming's expression to gauge her reaction to his tale. "When my dad fell in love with Claire, I thought he was nothing more than an optimistic fool." Jason winced. He'd spoken up against his father marrying her and a rift had formed between them. "Then Max fell in love with Rachel. Until he met her, he'd had a block of ice where his heart should be."

"But Rachel's great."

Jason nodded. "And she's perfect for Max, but when he fell head over heels for her, I was even more convinced that love made everyone else crazy and that I was the only sane one."

It scared her how firmly he clung to his convictions. "And now your brother has gone mad for Lily."

"That he has." He gave her a sheepish smile. "Max and his brothers. My dad. Evan. They're all so damned happy."

"You're happy."

"When I'm with you." He set his forehead against hers. "I've been a stubborn idiot. All this time I've been lying to myself about what I wanted. I thought if you and I made love, I could keep things the way they were between us and manage to have the best of both worlds."

"Only I had to go and fall in love with you."

"No. You had to go and tell me you wanted us to be together as a family." At last he was free to share with her what lay in his heart. "Did you know when you chose me to help you get pregnant that a baby would bind us together forever?"

"It crossed my mind, but that isn't why I decided on you." She frowned defensively. "And I'd like to point out that you agreed to help me. You also had to realize that any child I gave birth to would be part of us."

"From the instant you said you wanted me to be your baby's father, all I could think about was how much I wanted you." He took her hand and kissed her palm, felt her tension ease.

"After prom night I ran from the way I felt about you. It went against everything I believed. I've been running for the last fifteen years."

"And what is it you want?"

"You. More than anything. Marry me. I want to spend the rest of my life showing you how much I love you." He produced a diamond ring and held it before her eyes.

Heart pounding, she stared at the fiery gem as he took her left hand and slid the ring onto her finger. It fit perfectly.

"Yes. Yes. Of course, yes."

Before she finished her fervent acceptance, he kissed her. As his lips moved with passionate demand against hers, she melted beneath the rush of desire. He took his time demonstrating how much he loved her until his breath was rough and ragged. At last he lifted his head and stared into her eyes. Her stark joy stopped his heart.

Grinning, he hugged her hard. "And just in case you're worried about everyone's reaction, I cleared this with your sister and parents and my brother. The consensus seems to be that it's about time we take things from friends..."

"To forever." She laughed, a glorious sound of joy. "How lucky can a girl be?" she murmured. "I get to marry my best friend and the man I adore."

Jason cupped her face and kissed her gently. "What could be better than that?"

Ming lifted onto her tiptoes and wrapped her arms around his neck. "Not one single thing."

Epilogue

One year later

Bright afternoon sunshine glinted off the brand new paint on the galaxy blue Mustang parked in the driveway. Ming adjusted the big red bow attached to the roof and waved goodbye to the Stover brothers, who'd dropped the repaired race car off moments before. With her anniversary present for Jason looking absolutely perfect, she glanced toward the colonial's front door. The delivery had not been particularly quiet and she was surprised her husband of one year hadn't come out to see what the commotion was about.

She headed inside and paused in the foyer. From the family room came the sounds of revving engines so she followed the sound. Jason sat on the couch in front of the sixty-inch TV, absorbed in a NASCAR race. Muffin slept on the back of the couch near his shoulder.

"Jason?"

Muffin's head came up and her tail wagged, but Jason didn't

react at all. She circled the couch and discovered why he hadn't heard the delivery. He was fast asleep. So were their twin three-month-old sons, Jake and Connor, one on either side of him, snuggled into the crooks of his arms.

Ming grinned at the picture of her snoozing men and hoped this nap meant Jason would have lots of energy later tonight because she had plans for him that required his full strength. But right now she was impatient to show him his gift.

"Jason." She knelt between his knees and set her hands on his thighs. Muffin stretched and jumped down to lick Connor's cheek. "Wake up and see what I got you for our anniversary." When her words didn't rouse him, she slid her palms up his thigh. She was more than halfway toward her goal when his lips twitched upward at the corners.

"Keep going."

"Later."

He sighed, but didn't open his eyes. "That's what you always say." But despite his complaint, his smile had blossomed into a full-blown grin.

"And I always come through." She stood and slapped his knee. "Now come see your present."

She scooped up Jake and waited until Jason draped Connor over his shoulder and got to his feet before she headed back through the house. Muffin raced ahead of them to the foyer. Tingling with anticipation, Ming pulled open the front door and stepped aside so Jason could look out. The shock on his face when he spotted the car was priceless.

"You had the Mustang repaired?" He wrapped his free arm around her waist and pulled her tight against him.

"I did." She smiled up at him and his lips dropped onto hers for a passion-drenched kiss that curled her toes. When he let her breath again, she caught his hand and dragged him down the steps. "I think you should start racing again."

He hadn't been anywhere near the track since he'd crashed the Mustang over a year ago. Between getting married, her taking over the dental practice and the birth of their twins, they'd been plenty busy.

"Are you sure that's what you want?" Jason ran his hand along the front fender with the same appreciation he'd lavished on her thigh the previous night. "It'll take me away some weekends."

"I never wanted you to stop doing what you love."

"What I love is being your husband and a father to Jake and Connor."

"And I love that, too." She nudged her body against his. "But racing is your passion, and Max is bored to death without you to compete against."

He coasted his palm over her hip and cupped her butt, drawing her up on her toes for a slow, thorough kiss. The babies began to fuss long before Ming was done savoring her husband's fabulous technique and they broke apart with matching regretful sighs.

"More of that to come later," she assured him, soothing Jake.

While they were distracted, a car had pulled up behind the Mustang. Max and Rachel got out. "Get a room you two," Max called good-naturedly, picking up the excited terrier.

"That's the plan," Ming retorted, handing off her son to Rachel.

"Great to see you guys." Jason switched Connor to his other arm so he could give Max a man hug. "Are you staying for dinner?"

"They're staying," Ming said. "We're leaving. They're going to babysit while we celebrate our anniversary." Since the twins were born, uninterrupted time together was pretty much nonexistent, and Ming was determined that she and Jason should make a memorable start to their second year of marriage.

Jason eyed Max. "Are you sure you're up for this?"

"I think I could use a little parenting practice."

"I'm pregnant," Rachel announced, beaming.

While Jason congratulated Max, and Rachel cooed over

Jake, Ming marveled at her good fortune. She'd married her best friend and they had two healthy baby boys. Her practice was thriving. Lily and Evan were getting married in the spring. Everything that had been going wrong a little over a year ago was now sorted out. It wasn't perfect, but it was wonderful.

Jason looked over and caught her watching him. The blaze that kindled in his eyes lit an answering inferno deep inside her. For twenty-five years he'd been her best friend and that had been wonderful, but for the rest of her life he was going to be her husband and that was perfect.

* * * * *

PAPER WEDDING, BEST-FRIEND BRIDE

SHERI WHITEFEATHER

One

Lizzie McQueen emerged from a graceful dip in Max Marquez's black-bottom pool, water glistening on her bikini-clad body.

Reminiscent of a slow-motion scene depicted in a movie, she stepped onto the pavement and reached for a towel, and he watched every long-legged move she made. While she dried herself off, he swigged his root beer and pretended that he wasn't checking out her perfectly formed cleavage or gold pierced navel or—

"Come on, Max, quit giving me *the look*."

Caught in the act, he dribbled the stupid drink down his chin. She shook her head and tossed him her towel. He cursed beneath his breath and wiped his face.

The look was code for when either of them ogled the other in an inappropriate manner. They'd agreed quite a while ago that sex, or anything that could possibly lead to it, was off the table. They cared too much about each other to ruin their friendship with a few deliciously hot romps in the sack. Even now, at thirty years old, they held a platonic promise between them.

She smoothed back her fiery red hair, placed a big, floppy hat on her head and stretched out on the chaise next to him. Max lived in a 1930s Beachwood Canyon mansion, and Lizzie resided in an ultra-modern condo. She spent more time at his place than he did at hers because he preferred it that way. His Los Angeles lair was bigger, badder and much more private.

He returned the towel, only now it had his soda stain on it. She rolled her eyes, and they shared a companionable grin.

He handed her a bottle of sunscreen. "You better reapply this."

She sighed. "Me and my sensitive skin."

He liked her ivory complexion. But he'd seen her get some nasty sunburns, too. He didn't envy her that. She slathered on the lotion, and he considered how they'd met during their senior year in high school. They were being paired up on a chemistry project, and, even then, she'd struck him as a debutant-type girl.

Later he'd learned that she was originally from Savannah, Georgia, with ties to old money. In that regard, his assessment of her had been correct, and just being near her had sent his boyhood longings into a tailspin. Not only was she gorgeous; she was everything he'd wanted to be: rich, prestigious, popular.

But Max had bottomed out on the other end of the spectrum: a skinny, dorky Native American foster kid with a genius IQ and gawky social skills, leaving him open to scorn and ridicule.

Of course, Lizzie's life hadn't been as charmed as he'd assumed it was. Once he'd gotten to know her, she'd revealed her deepest, darkest secrets to him, just as he'd told her his.

Supposedly during that time, when they were pouring their angst-riddled hearts out to each other, she'd actually formed a bit of a crush on him. But even till this day, he found that hard to fathom. In what alternate universe did prom queens get infatuated with dorks?

She peered at him from beneath the fashionable brim of her pale beige hat. Her bathing suit was a shimmering shade of copper with a leopard-print trim, and her meticulously manicured nails were painted a soft warm pink. Every lovely thing about her purred, "trust fund heiress," which was exactly what she was.

"What are you thinking about?" she asked.

He casually answered, "What a nerd I used to be."

She teased him with a smile. "As opposed to the sexy billionaire you are today?"

"Right." He laughed a little. "Because nothing says beefcake like a software designer and internet entrepreneur."

She moved her gaze along the muscle-whipped length of his body. "You've done all right for yourself."

He raised his eyebrows. "Now who's giving who *the look*?"

She shrugged off her offense. "You shouldn't have become such a hottie if you didn't want to get noticed."

That wasn't the reason he'd bulked up, and she darned well knew it. Sure, he'd wanted to shed his nerdy image, but he'd started hitting the gym after high school for more than aesthetic purposes. His favorite sport was boxing. Sometimes he shadowboxed and sometimes he pounded the crap out of a heavy bag. But mostly he did it to try to pummel the demons that plagued him. He was a runner, too. So was Lizzie. They ran like a tornado was chasing them. Or their pasts, which was pretty much the same thing.

"Beauty and the brainiac," he said. "We were such a teenage cliché."

"Why, because you offered to tutor me when I needed it? That doesn't make us a cliché. Without your help, I would never have gotten my grades up to par or attended my mother's alma mater."

Silent, Max nodded. She'd also been accepted into her mom's old sorority, which had been another of her goals. But none of that had brought her the comfort she'd sought.

"The twentieth anniversary is coming up," she said.

Of her mom's suicide, he thought. Lizzie was ten when her high-society mother had swallowed an entire bottle of sleeping pills. "I'm sorry you keep reliving it." She mentioned it every year around this time, and even now he could see her childhood pain.

She put the sunscreen aside, placing it on a side table, where her untouched iced tea sat. "I wish I could forget about her."

"I know." He couldn't get his mom out of his head, either, especially the day she'd abandoned him, leaving him alone in their run-down apartment. He was eight years old, and she'd parked him in front of the TV, warning him to stay there until she got back. She was only supposed to be gone for a few hours, just long enough to score the crack she routinely smoked. Max waited for her return, but she never showed up. Scared out of his young mind, he'd fended for himself for three whole days, until he'd gone to a neighbor for help. "My memories will probably never stop haunting me, either."

"We do have our issues."

"Yeah, we do." Max was rescued and placed in foster

care, and a warrant was issued for his mom's arrest. But she'd already hit the road with her latest loser boyfriend, where she'd partied too hard and overdosed before the police caught up with her.

"What would you say to your mother if she was still alive?" Lizzie asked.

"Nothing."

"You wouldn't tell her off?"

"No." He wouldn't say a single word to her.

"You wouldn't even ask her why she used to hurt you?"

Max shook his head. There wasn't an answer in the world that would make sense, so what would be the point? When Mom hadn't been kicking him with her cheap high heels or smacking him around, she'd taken to burning him with cigarette butts and daring him not to cry. But her most common form of punishment was locking him in his closet, where she'd told him that the Lakota two-faced monsters dwelled.

The legends about these humanoid creatures varied. In some tales, it was a woman who'd been turned into this type of being after trying to seduce the sun god. One of her faces was beautiful, while the other was hideous. In other stories, it was a man with a second face on the back of his head. Making eye contact with him would get you tortured and killed. Cannibalism and kidnapping were among his misdeeds, too, with a malevolent glee for preying on misbehaving children.

The hours Max had spent in his darkened closet, cowering from the monsters and praying for his drugged-out mother to remove the chair that barred the door, would never go away.

He cleared his throat and said, "Mom's worst crime was her insistence that she loved me. But you already know all this." He polished off the last of his root beer and crushed the can between his palms, squeezing the aluminum down to nearly nothing. He repeated another thing she already knew. "I swear, I never want to hear another woman say that to me again."

"I could do without someone saying that to me, too. Sure, love is supposed to be the cure-all, but not for..."

"People like us?"

She nodded, and he thought about how they tumbled in and out of affairs. Max went through his lovers like wine. Lizzie wasn't any better. She didn't get attached to her bedmates, either.

"At least I have my charity work," she said.

He was heavily involved in nonprofits, too, with it being a significant part of his life. "Do you think it's enough?"

"What?" She raised her delicately arched brows. "Helping other people? Of course it is."

"Then why am I still so dissatisfied?" He paused to study the sparkling blue of her eyes and the way her hair was curling in damp waves around her shoulders. "And why are you still stressing over your mom's anniversary?"

She picked up her tea, sipped, put it back down. "We're only human."

"I know. But I should be ashamed of myself for feeling this way. I got everything I ever wanted. I mean, seriously, look at this place." He scowled at his opulent surroundings. How rich and privileged and spoiled could he be?

"I thought your sabbatical helped." She seemed to be evaluating how long he'd been gone, separating himself from her and everyone else.

He'd taken nearly a year off to travel the world, to search for inner peace. He'd also visited hospitals and orphanages and places where he'd hoped to make a difference. "The most significant part of that experience was the months I spent in Nulah. It's a small island country in the South Pacific. I'd never been there before, so I didn't really know what to expect. Anyway, what affected me was this kid I came across in an orphanage there. A five-year-old boy named Tokoni."

She cocked her head. "Why haven't you mentioned him before now?"

"I don't know." He conjured up an image of the child's big brown eyes and dazzling smile. "Maybe I was trying to keep him to myself a little longer and imagine him with the family his mother wanted him to have. When he was two, she left him at the orphanage, hoping that someone would adopt him and give him a better life. She wasn't abusive to him, like my mother was to me. She just knew that she couldn't take proper care of him. Nulah is traditional in some areas, with old-world views, and rough and dangerous in others. It didn't used to be so divided, but it started suffering from outside influences."

"Like drugs and prostitution and those sorts of things?"

"Yes, and Tokoni's mother lived in a seedy part of town and was struggling to find work. She'd already lost her family in a boating accident, so there was no one left to help her."

"What about the boy's father?" she asked. "How does he fit into this?"

"He was an American tourist who made all sorts of promises, saying he was going to bring her to the States and marry her. But in the end, he didn't do anything, except ditch her and the kid."

"Oh, how awful." Lizzie's voice broke a little. "That

makes me sad for her, living on a shattered dream, waiting for a man to whisk her away."

It disturbed Max, too. "She kept in touch with the orphanage for a while, waiting to see if Tokoni ever got a permanent home, but then she caught pneumonia and died. The old lady who operates the place told me the story. It's a private facility that survives on charity. I already donated a sizable amount to help keep them on track."

She made a thoughtful expression. "I can write an article about them to drum up more support, if you want."

"That would be great." Max appreciated the offer. Lizzie hosted a successful philanthropy blog with tons of noble-hearted followers. "I just wish someone would adopt Tokoni. He's the coolest kid, so happy all the time." So different from how Max was as a child. "He's at the age where he talks about getting adopted and thinks it's going to happen. He's been working on this little picture book, with drawings of the mommy and daddy he's convinced he's going to have. They're just stick figures with smiley faces, but to him, they're real."

"Oh, my goodness." She tapped a hand against her heart. "That's so sweet."

"He's a sweet kid. I've been wanting to return to the island to see him again. Just to let him know that I haven't forgotten about him."

"Then you should plan another trip soon."

"Yeah, I should." Max could easily rearrange his schedule to make it happen. "Hey, here's an idea. Do you want to come to Nulah with me to meet him?" He suspected that Lizzie could manage her time to accommodate a trip, as well. She'd always been a bit of a jet-setter, a spontaneous society girl ready to leave town on a whim. But mostly she traveled for humanitarian causes, so this was right up her alley. "While we're there, you can interview the woman who operates the orphanage for the feature you're going to do on your blog."

"Sure. I can go with you. I'd like to see the orphanage and conduct an in-person interview. But I should probably spend most of my time with her and let you visit with Tokoni on your own. You know how kids never really take to me."

"You just need to relax around them." Although Lizzie championed hundreds of children's charities, she'd never gotten the gist of communicating with kids, especially the younger ones. A side effect from her own youth, he thought, from losing her mom and forcing herself to grow up too fast. "For the record, I think you and Tokoni will hit it off just fine. In fact, I think he's going to be impressed with you."

"You do?" She adjusted her lounge chair, moving it to a more upright position. "What makes you say that?"

"In his culture redheads are said to descend from nobility, from a goddess ruler who dances with fire, and your hair is as bright as it gets." Max sat forward, too, and leaned toward her. "He'll probably think you're a princess or something. But you were homecoming queen. So it's not as if you didn't have your reign."

Her response fell flat. "That doesn't count."

He remembered going to the football game that night, sitting alone in the bleachers, watching her receive her crown. He'd skipped the homecoming dance. He wouldn't have been able to blend in there. Getting a date would have been difficult, too. As for Lizzie, she'd attended the dance with the tall, tanned star of the boys' swim team. "It counted back then."

"Not to me, not like it should have. It wasn't fair that my other friends didn't accept you."

"Well, I got the last laugh, didn't I?"

She nodded, even if neither of them was laughing.

Before things got too morose, he reached out and tugged on a strand of her hair. "Don't fret about being royalty to me. The only redhead that influenced my culture was a woodpecker."

She sputtered into a laugh and slapped his hand away. "Gee, thanks, for that compelling tidbit."

He smiled, pleased by her reaction. "It's one of those old American Indian tales. I told it to Tokoni when he was putting a puzzle together with pictures of birds." Max stopped smiling. "The original story involves love. But I left off that part when I told Tokoni. I figured he was too young to understand it. Plus, it would have been hypocritical of me to tell it that way."

She took a ladylike sip of her tea. "Now I'm curious about the original version and just how lovey-dovey it is."

"It's pretty typical, I guess." He went ahead and recited it, even if he preferred it without the romance. "It's about a hunter who loves a girl from his village, but she's never even noticed him. He thinks about her all the time. He even has trouble sleeping because he can't get her off his mind. So he goes to the forest to be alone, where he hears a beautiful song that lulls him to sleep. That night, he dreams about a woodpecker who says, 'Follow me and I'll show you how to make this song.' In the morning, he sees a real woodpecker and follows him. The bird is tapping on a branch and the familiar song is coming from it. Later, the hunter returns home with the branch and tries to make the music by waving it in the air, but it doesn't work."

Lizzie removed her hat. By now the sun was shifting in the sky, moving behind the trees and dappling her in scattered light. But mostly what Max noticed was how intense she looked, listening to the silly myth. Or was her intensity coming from the energy that always seemed to dance between them? The sexiness that seeped through their pores?

Ignoring the feeling, he continued by saying, "The hunter has another dream where the woodpecker shows him how to blow on the wood and tap the holes to make the song he'd first heard. Obviously, it's a flute the bird made. But neither the hunter nor his people had ever seen this type of instrument before."

She squinted at him. "What happens with the girl?"

"Once she hears the hunter's beautiful song, she looks into his eyes and falls in love with him, just as he'd always loved her. But like I said, I told it to Tokoni without the romance."

She was still squinting, intensity still etched on her face. "Where did you first come across this story? Was it in one of the books you used to read?"

"Yes." When he was in foster care, he'd researched his culture, hoping to find something good in it. "I hated that the only thing my mom ever talked about was the scary stuff. But I'm glad that Tokoni's mother tried to do right by him."

"Me, too." She spoke softly. "Parents are supposed to want what's best for their children."

He met her gaze, and she stared back at him, almost like the girl in the hunter's tale—except that love didn't appeal to either of them.

But desire did. If Lizzie wasn't his best friend, if she was someone he could kiss without consequence, he would lock lips with her right now, pulling her as close to him as he possibly could. And with the way she was looking at him, she would probably let him kiss the hell out of her. But that wouldn't do either of them any good.

"I appreciate you coming to Nulah with me," he said, trying to shake off the heat of wanting her. "It means a lot to me, having you there."

"I know it does," she replied, reaching for his hand.

But it was only the slightest touch. She pulled away quickly. Determined, it seemed, to control her hunger for him, too.

A myriad of thoughts skittered through Lizzie's mind. Today she and Max were leaving on their trip, and she should be done packing, as he would be arriving soon to pick her up. Yet she was still sorting haphazardly through her clothes and placing them in her suitcase. Normally Lizzie was far more organized. But for now she couldn't think clearly.

She hated it when her attraction to Max dragged her under its unwelcome spell, and lately it seemed to be getting worse. But they'd both learned to deal with it, just as she was trying to get a handle on how his attachment to Tokoni was making her feel. Even with his troubled past, being around children was easy for Max. Lizzie was terribly nervous about meeting the boy. Kids didn't relate to her in the fun-and-free way they did with him. Of course her stodgy behavior in their presence didn't help. But no matter how hard she tried, she couldn't seem to change that side of herself.

After her mother had drifted into a deathly sleep, she'd compensated for the loss by taking on the characteristics of an adult, long before she should have.

But what choice did she have? Her grieving father had bailed out on parenthood, leaving her with nannies and cooks. He'd immersed himself in his high-powered work and business travels, allowing her to grow up in a big lonely house full of strangers. Lizzie didn't have any extended family to speak of.

Even after all these years, she and her dad barely communicated. Was it any wonder that she'd gone off to Columbia University searching for a connection to her mom? She'd even taken the same journalism major. She'd walked in her mother's path, but it hadn't done a bit of good. She'd returned with the same disjointed feelings.

Her memories of her mom were painfully odd: scattered images of a beautifully fragile blonde who used to stare unblinkingly at herself in the mirror, who used to give lavish parties and tell Lizzie how essential it was for a young lady of her standing to be a good hostess, who used to laugh at the drop of a hat and then cry just as easily. Mama's biggest ambition was to be awarded the Pulitzer Prize. But mostly she just threw away her writings. Sometimes she even burned them, tossing them into the fireplace and murmuring to herself in French, the language of her ancestors.

Mama was rife with strange emotions, with crazy behaviors, but she was warm and loving, too, cuddling Lizzie at night. Without her sweet, dreamy mother by her side, Elizabeth "Lizzie" McQueen had been crushed, like a bug on a long white limousine's windshield.

After Mama killed herself, Dad sold their Savannah home, got a new job in Los Angeles and told Lizzie that she was going to be a California kid from then on.

But by that time she'd already gotten used to imitating her mother's lady-of-the-manor ways, presenting a rich-girl image that made her popular. Nonetheless, she'd lied to her new friends, saying that her socialite mother had suffered a brain aneurysm. Dad told his new workmates the same phony story. Lizzie had been coaxed by him to protect their privacy, and she'd embraced the lie.

Until she met Max.

She'd felt compelled to reveal the truth to him. But he was different from her other peers—a shy, lonely boy, who was as damaged as she was.

The doorbell rang, and Lizzie caught her breath.

She dashed to answer the summons, and there he was: Max Marquez, with his longish black hair shining like a raven's wing. He wore it parted down the middle and falling past his neck, but not quite to his shoulders. His deeply set eyes were brown, but sometimes they looked as black as his hair. His face was strong and angular, with a bone structure to die for. The gangly teenager he'd once been was gone. He'd grown into a fiercely handsome man.

"Are you ready?" he asked.

She shook her head. "Sorry. No. I'm still packing."

He entered her condo. "That's okay. I'll text my pilot and tell him we're running late."

Lizzie nodded. Max's success provided him the luxury of a private jet. She'd inherited her mother's old Savannah money, but she was nowhere as wealthy as he was. He wasn't the only Native American foster kid in LA who'd made good. He remained close to two of his foster brothers, who'd also become billionaires. Max had been instrumental in helping them attain their fortunes, loaning them money to get their businesses off the ground.

He followed her into her room, where her suitcase was on the bed, surrounded by the clothes she'd been sorting.

He lifted a floral-printed dress from the pile. "This is pretty." He glanced at a lace bra and panty set. "And those." Clearly, he was teasing her, as if making a joke was easier than anything else he could think of doing or saying.

"Knock it off." She grabbed the lingerie and shoved them into a pouch on the side of her Louis Vuitton luggage, glad that he hadn't actually touched her underwear. As for the dress, she tugged it away from him.

"Did you really have a thing for me in high school?" he asked.

Oh, goodness. He was bringing that up now? "Yes, I really did." She'd developed a quirky little crush on him, formed within the ache of the secrets they'd shared. But he'd totally blown her away when she returned from university and saw his physical transformation. He'd changed in all sorts of ways by then. While she'd been hitting the books, he'd already earned his first million, selling an app he'd designed, and he hadn't even gone to college. These days, he invested in start-ups and made a killing doing it.

"It never would have worked between us," he said.

Lizzie considered flinging her makeup bag at him and knocking him upside that computer chip brain of his. "I never proposed that it would."

"You were too classy for me." He gazed at her from across the bed. "Sometimes I think you still are."

A surge of heat shot through her blood. "That's nonsense. You date tons of socialites. They're your type."

"Because you set the standard. How could I be around you and not want that type?"

"Don't do this, Max." He'd gone beyond the realm of making jokes. "You shouldn't even be in my room, let alone be saying that sort of stuff."

"As if." He brushed it off. "I've been in your room plenty of times before. Remember last New Year's Eve? I poured you into bed when you got too drunk to stand."

She looked at him as if he'd gone mad. But maybe he had lost his grip on reality. Or maybe she had. Either way, she challenged him. "What are you talking about? I wasn't inebriated. I was coming down with the flu."

"So you kept telling me." He gave her a pointed look. "I think it was all those cosmopolitans that international playboy lover of yours kept plying you with."

Seriously? His memory couldn't be that bad. "You were tending bar at the party that night." Here at her house, with her guests.

"Was I? Are you sure? I thought it was that Grand Prix driver you met in Monte Carlo. The one all the women swooned over."

"He and I were over by then." She wagged a finger at him. "You're the one who kept adding extra vodka to my drinks."

"I must have felt sorry for you, getting dumped by that guy."

"From what I recall, it was around the same time that department store heiress walked out on you."

"She was boring, anyway."

"I thought she was nice. She was hunting for a husband, though."

"Yeah, and that ruled me out. I wouldn't get married if the survival of the world depended on it."

"Me, neither. But what's the likelihood of us ever having to do that, for saving mankind or any other reason?"

"There isn't. But I still say that you were drunk last New Year's, and I was the gentleman—thank you very much—who tucked you into this very bed." He patted her pillow for effect, putting a dent in it.

"Oh, there's an oxymoron. The guy feeding me liquor is the gentleman in the story?"

"It beats your big-fish tale about having the flu."

"Okay. Fine. I was wasted. Now stop taking it out on my pillow."

"Oops, sorry." He plumped it back up, good as new. "Are you going to finish packing or we going to sit here all day, annoying each other?"

"You started it." She filled her suitcase, stuffing it to the gills. She only wished they were going on a trip that didn't include a child she was nervous about meeting.

"Are you still worried about whether or not Tokoni will like you?" he asked, homing in on her troubled expression. "I already told you that I think you're going to impress him."

"Because he might regard me as a princess? That feels like pressure in itself."

"It'll be all right, Lizzie. And I promise, once you meet him, you'll see how special he is."

She didn't doubt that Tokoni was a nice little boy. But that didn't ease her nerves or boost her confidence about meeting him. Of course for now all she could do was remain by Max's side, supporting his cause, like the friend she was meant to be.

Two

Lizzie awakened inside a bungalow, with a tropical breeze stirring through an open window. Alone with her thoughts, she sat up and stretched.

Yesterday afternoon she and Max had arrived at their destination and checked in to the resort he'd booked for their weeklong stay. They had separate accommodations, each with its own colorful garden and oceanfront deck, equipped with everything they needed to relax, including hammocks. The interiors were also decorated to complement the environment, with beamed ceilings, wood floors, cozy couches and canopy beds.

Nulah consisted of a series of islands, and the sparsely populated island they were on was a twenty-minute boat ride to the mainland, the main island within the nation, where the capital city and all the activities in that area were: the airport, the orphanage they would be visiting, shopping and dining, dance clubs and other tourist-generated nightlife, nice hotels, cheap motels, burgeoning crime, basically what you would find in any city except on a smaller scale.

Of course at this off-the-grid resort, things were quiet. Max had stayed here before, during his sabbatical, and now Lizzie understood why it appealed to him.

With another body-rolling stretch, she climbed out of bed. She suspected that Max was already wide awake and jogging along the beach. He preferred early-morning runs. Typically, Lizzie did, too. But she'd skipped that routine today.

She showered and fixed her makeup and hair, keeping it simple. She didn't want to show up at the orphanage looking like a spoiled heiress. Or a princess. Or anything that drew too much attention to herself.

Returning to her bedroom, she donned the floral-printed dress Max had manhandled when she was packing yesterday, pairing it with T-strap sandals.

Lizzie made a cup of coffee, with extra cream, and headed outside. With a quiet sigh, she settled into a chair on her deck and gazed out at the view—the pearly white sand and aqua-blue water.

She closed her eyes, and when she opened them, Max appeared along the shore, winding down from his run. For a moment, he almost seemed like an apparition, a tall, tanned warrior in the morning light.

He glanced in her direction, and she waved him over. But before he strode toward her, he stopped to remove his T-shirt, using it like a towel to dry the sweat from his face and chest. Lizzie got a sexy little pulse-palpitating reaction from watching him. He'd already told her that his shower was outside, located in a walled section of his garden. He'd requested a bungalow with that type of amenity. So now she was going to envision him, naked in the elements, with water streaming over his sun-bronzed skin.

"Hey." He stood beside her chair. "What happened? I was expecting to see you out there. I figured you would've joined me at some point."

"I wasn't in the mood to run today." She glanced past him, making sure that she wasn't ogling his abs or giving him *the look*. Instead, she checked out a foamy wave breaking onto the shore. This island was a certified marine reserve, allowing guests to snorkel off the beach from the front of their bungalows. Lizzie hadn't been in the ocean yet, but according to Max there were heaps of fish, clams and coral reefs.

"You look pretty," he said.

His compliment gave her pulse another little jump start, prompting her to meet his gaze. "Thank you."

"I like your hair that way."

All she'd done was tie a satin ribbon around a carefully fastened ponytail, creating a girlish bow. "It's nothing, really."

"I think it gives you an interesting quality. Like a socialite trying to be incognito."

So much for her plan to be less noticeable. She changed the subject. "You must be hungry by now. I can get us something and bring it back here." Although room service was available, there was also an eat-in or takeout breakfast buffet. She didn't mind packing up their food to go. The restaurant and bar that provided their meals was a short walk along the beach.

She waited while he balled up his sweaty T-shirt and pondered her suggestion.

Finally he said, "I'll take bacon and eggs and a large tumbler of orange juice. Last time I was here, they served seafood crepes in this mouthwatering wine-cheese sauce, so fill my plate with those, too. I'm pretty sure they'll have them again. It's one of their specialties."

Apparently he'd worked up an appetite. "Anything else?"

"No. But I have to shower first."

Damn, she thought. The outdoor shower she shouldn't be thinking about. "Go ahead, and I'll see you in a few."

He left, and she watched him until he was out of sight. She finished her coffee, then headed for the buffet.

As she made the picturesque trek, she admired the purple and pink flowers she passed along the way. They flourished on abundant vines, growing wild in the sandy soil. The garden attached to her bungalow was also filled with them, along with big leafy plants and tall twisty palms.

After she got their food, she set everything up on her patio table. Inspired by the flora that surrounded her, she used a live orchid from her room as the centerpiece.

Max returned wearing a Polynesian-print shirt, board shorts and flip-flops. His thick damp hair was combed away from his face, but it was already starting to part naturally on its own. He smelled fresh and masculine, like the sandalwood soap he favored. Lizzie had used the mango-scented body wash the resort gave them.

He said, "This looks good." He sat across from her and dived into his big hearty breakfast.

For herself, she'd gotten plain yogurt and a bowl of fresh-cut fruit. But she hadn't been able to resist the crepes, so she was indulging in them, too.

He glanced up from his plate and asked, "Do you want to see a picture of Tokoni? I meant to show it to you before now. It's of the two of us."

"Yes, of course." She waited for him to pull it up on his phone, which took all of a second.

He handed it to her. The photo was of an adorable little dark-haired, tanned-skinned boy, expressing a big toothy grin. Max looked happy in the picture, too. She surmised that it was a selfie, snapped at close range. "He's beautiful."

"He's smart as a whip, too. Kindergarten starts at six here, so he isn't in school yet. But they work with the younger ones at the orphanage, preparing them for it." He took the phone back and set it aside. "I'm glad that you'll get to meet him today."

"What time are we supposed to be there?"

"We don't have an appointment. Losa said we can come any time it's convenient for us."

"That's her name? Losa? The woman who runs the orphanage?" The lady Lizzie would be interviewing today.

He nodded. "The kids call her Mrs. Losa."

"So is that her first or last name?"

"Her first. It means Rose in their native tongue."

That seemed fitting, with all the other flowers Lizzie had encountered today. "Is there a mister? Is she married?"

"She's widowed. She started the orphanage after her husband died. They were together for nearly forty years before he passed away."

She couldn't imagine being with the same person all that time. Or losing him.

"She has five kids," Max said. "They had three of their own, but they also adopted two from their village, orphaned siblings whose extended family wasn't able to care for them. But those children weren't adopted in an official way. Losa and her husband just took them in and raised them."

"Really? That's legal here?"

"Yes, but mostly it's the country folks, the traditionalists who still do that. They live in small communities where the people are tightly knit, so if there's a child or children in need, they band together to help. Losa and her husband used to be farmers. But she sold her property and moved to the capital to open the orphanage when she learned how many kids on the mainland were homeless. Her entire family supported her decision and relocated with her. All of her children and their spouses work there, along with their kids. She has two grown granddaughters and three teenage grandsons."

"They must be quite a family, taking on a project like that. Do they have any outside help?"

"At first it was just them, but now they have regular volunteers. And some who just pitch in when they can." Max drank his juice. "I volunteered when I was here before. That's how I spent the last three months of my sabbatical, helping out at the orphanage."

Lizzie hadn't realized the extent of his commitment. She'd assumed he'd merely visited the place. "No wonder you know so much about it."

He offered more of his knowledge by saying, "Nulah didn't used to allow international adoptions. But they finally decided it was in the best interest of the children. Otherwise, finding homes for these kids would be even more difficult. There aren't enough local families who have the means to take them. The older folks are dying off, and most of the younger ones are struggling to raise their own children."

He paused to watch a pair of colorful seabirds soaring along the shore. Lizzie watched them, too, thinking how majestic they were.

Then he said, "Not all of the kids at the orphanage are

up for adoption. Losa is fostering some of them, keeping them until they can return to their families. But either way, she devotes her life to the children in her care, however she can."

"She sounds like a godsend."

"She is. She spent years lobbying for the international adoption law here. Without her, it might never have happened."

Clearly, Losa had strength and fortitude, seeing things through to the end. "When we're on the mainland, I'd like to stop by a florist and get her a rose."

"You want to give her a flower that matches her name?"

"Mama always taught me that you should bring someone a gift the first time you visit." She paused to reflect. "I should bring something for the kids, too. Not just for Tokoni, but for all of them. How many are there?"

"The last time I was here, it was around thirty. It's probably still about the same."

"And what's the age range?"

"It varies, going from babies to young teens."

"That's a wide margin. I'm going to need a little time to shop for a group like that. We should leave for the mainland soon." Lizzie was anxious to get started. "We can take the next boat."

He grinned. "Then maybe we should eat a little faster."

She knew he was kidding. He'd already wolfed down most of his meal. Hers was nearly gone, too. "It's delicious." She raised her fork. "These crepes."

"This island is paradise." He stopped smiling. "If only everything on the mainland was as nice as it is here."

"Yes, if only." She'd caught glimpses of the capital city yesterday and had seen how poverty-stricken some of the areas were, the places where the kids from the orphanage had come from. And if anyone could relate to their ravaged beginnings, it was Max. He'd been born in South Dakota on one of the poorest reservations in the States, before his mother had hauled him off to an impoverished Los Angeles neighborhood.

As lonely as Lizzie's childhood had been, she'd never known the pain and fear of being poor. But that hadn't stopped her and Max from becoming friends. They'd formed a bond, regardless of how different they'd been from each other.

Trapped in emotion, she said, "Thank you."

He gave her a perplexed look. "For what?"

For everything, she thought. But she said, "For inviting me to take this trip with you."

"I'm glad you're here, too."

Their gazes met and held, but only for a moment.

Returning to their food, they fell silent, fighting the ever-present attraction neither of them wanted to feel.

Max and Lizzie got to the mainland around eleven, and he hailed a cab. Taxis weren't metered here, so they had to agree on the price of the fare before departure. Max arranged to keep the taxi at their disposal for the rest of the day. Their driver was a big, broad-shouldered twentysomething with a brilliant smile. As pleasant and accommodating as he was, he drove a bit too fast. But tons of cabbies in the States did that, too. As for the car, it was old and rickety, with seat belts that kept coming unbuckled. But it was better than no transportation at all, Max thought.

As they entered the shopping district, the car bumped and jittered along roughly paved roads. The still-smiling cabbie found a centrally located parking spot and told them he would wait there for them. To keep himself occupied, he reached for his phone. Max, of course, was consumed with technology, too. It was his world, his livelihood, his outlet. But he never buried his face in his phone when he was with Lizzie. She hated it when people ignored each other in favor of their devices, so he'd made a conscious effort not to do that to her.

Behaving like tourists, they wandered the streets, going in and out of small shops. Some of the vendors were aggressive, trying as they might to peddle their wares. But Max didn't mind. He understood that they had families to feed. He went ahead and purchased a bunch of stuff to ship back home, mostly toys and trinkets for his nieces—his foster brothers' adorable little daughters.

Lizzie wasn't faring as well. Although she'd already gotten a stack of baby goods for the infants and toddlers at the orphanage and placed them in the taxi for safekeeping, she couldn't make up her mind about the rest of the kids.

Finally she said, "Maybe I can put together a big box of art supplies that all of them can use."

"That's a great idea. Tokoni would appreciate it, too, since he loves to draw. There's an arts and crafts store around the corner. They also have a little gallery where they sell works by local artists. I always wanted to check it out."

"Then let's go." She seemed interested in the art, too. "But first I want to get what I need for the kids."

They walked to their destination. The sun was shining, glinting beautifully off her ponytailed hair. He'd teased her earlier about her looking like a socialite who was trying to go incognito. In his opinion, Lizzie wasn't the type who could downplay her breeding. She'd already spent too many years perfecting it, and by now it was ingrained into the woman she'd become.

When they came to the arts and crafts store, they went inside, and she gathered paints, brushes, crayons, markers, colored pencils, paper, blank canvases and whatever else she could find. She added crafts, too, like jewelry-making kits and model cars. The man who owned the shop was thrilled. He was a chatty old guy who introduced himself as George. Max figured it was the English translation of his birth name.

After Lizzie made her purchases, she and Max browsed the work that was for sale in the gallery section. George followed them. Hoping, no doubt, that Lizzie was an art collector.

Only it was Max who got curious about a painting. It depicted a ceremony of some sort, where a young couple was cutting pieces of each other's hair with decorative knives. In Native American and First Nations cultures, shearing one's hair was sometimes associated with death and mourning. But the people in this picture didn't appear to be grieving.

While he inspected the painting, Lizzie stood beside him. George was nearby, as well.

"What are they doing?" Max asked him.

The owner stepped forward. "Preparing for their wedding. It's an old custom, chopping a betrothed's hair. Doing this symbolizes their transitions into adulthood."

Max frowned. "I'd never do that."

"Do what? Cut your lady's hair?" By now George was gazing at Lizzie's bright red locks.

"I meant get married." Max shook his head. "And she isn't my lady. She's my friend."

"Hmm." George tapped his chin. "Is this true?" he asked Lizzie. "You're only friends with this man?"

"Yes, that's all we are," she assured him.

"It's different for me," he said. "I have a wife." He

took her hand and tugged her toward the other side of the gallery. "You come, too," he told Max. "I'll show you something else."

As soon as Max spotted the painting George wanted them to see, he stopped to stare at it. The nearly life-size image depicted a wildly primitive young woman on a moonlit beach, dancing with a male partner, only he was made completely of fire. She swayed in his burning-hot arms, with her long slim body draped in a sparkling gold dress. Her flame-red hair blew across her face, shielding her mysterious features from view.

"It's called *Lady Ari*," George said.

Max sucked in his breath. "After the royal goddess of fire." He hadn't known her name until now.

"Yes," George said. "With hair like your friend's." He glanced over at Lizzie.

Max shifted his attention to her, too, but she didn't acknowledge him. She continued looking at the painting. Was she as captivated by it as he was, or was she focusing on the picture so she didn't have to return his gaze?

He couldn't be sure. But the feverish feeling *Lady Ari* gave him was too overpowering to ignore. "I'm going to buy it." Now, he thought, today.

With a sudden jolt, Lizzie jerked her head toward his. "And do what with it?"

"I'll hang it in my house." He considered where to put it. "Above the fireplace in my den."

"You already have a nice piece of artwork there."

"So I'll replace it with this one."

She fussed with her ponytail, as if she was fighting its brazen color, and he realized how uncomfortable his attraction to *Lady Ari* was making her. But he simply couldn't let the painting go.

As they both fell silent, Max noticed that George

was watching the two of them, probably thinking what strange friends they were. But nonetheless, the older man was obviously pleased that he'd just made a significant sale.

"The artist would be enchanted by you," George told Lizzie. "You would be charmed by him, too. He's young and handsome." He then said to Max, "A lot like you."

Lizzie raised her eyebrows at that, and Max shrugged, as if the artist's virility was of no consequence. But it made him feel funny inside, with George making what seemed like romantic comparisons.

Still, it didn't change his interest in buying it. The need to have it was too strong. Max arranged to have the painting shipped home, as he'd done with the items he'd bought for his nieces.

After the transaction was complete, they said goodbye to George and returned to their taxi, piling the art supplies Lizzie had purchased into the trunk.

She scowled at Max and said, "I still have to get Losa a rose."

"Okay, but don't be mad about the painting."

"I'm not."

Yes, she was, he thought. She didn't like the idea of him owning a picture that could be mistaken for an untamed version of her. But he wasn't going to apologize for buying something he wanted.

"Do you know where the florist is?" she asked him.

"No." He didn't have a clue. He checked with their driver and was informed that it was close enough to walk, so they set out on foot again.

The florist offered a variety of exotic plants and blooms. Max waited patiently while Lizzie labored over what color of rose to buy.

She decided on a pale yellow, and they returned to the

taxi and climbed into the car. The driver started the engine and off they went, en route to the orphanage.

After a beat of silence, she said, "I wonder who modeled for it."

For it. The painting. Obviously her mind was still on *Lady Ari*. "I assumed that the artist had created her from his imagination."

She sat stiffly in her seat, clutching the rose. "I should have asked George, but I didn't think of it then. I'd prefer that she was a real person."

"Why? Because then she would seem less like you and more like the model? Just think of how I feel, knowing the artist is a handsome guy who's supposedly a lot like me."

She narrowed her eyes at him. "It serves you right. I mean, really, what were you thinking, buying something like that?"

He defended himself. "You ought to be glad that I did."

"Oh, yeah? How do you figure?"

"Because now I can lust over the painting and forget that I ever had the hots for you."

"You wish." As they rounded a corner, he leaned into her. She shoved him aside. "And stop crowding me."

Max cursed beneath his breath. He wasn't invading her space purposely. The force of the turn had done it. He wanted to tell the driver to slow down, that this wasn't the damned Autobahn. Instead he said to Lizzie, "You're nothing like Lady Ari. It's not as if you'd ever dance that way in the moonlight."

"Gee, you think?" She waved her arms around, willy-nilly. "Me and a male heap of burning fire?"

"That was the worst sensual dance I've ever seen."

"That was the idea."

"To suck?"

The taxi came to a quick halt, stopping for a group of pedestrians. Max and Lizzie both flew forward and bumped their foreheads on the seats in front of them.

He turned to look at her, and she burst out laughing. He did, too. It was impossible to keep arguing in the midst of such absurdity.

"I'm sorry for giving you a hard time," she said. "You can buy whatever artwork you want."

"I'm sorry, too." He leaned toward her and whispered in a mock sexy voice, "I didn't mean what I said about forgetting that I have the hots for you. Even if you can't dance like her, you're still a temptress."

She accepted his flirtation for what it was. But she also pushed him away from her again, keeping him from remaining too close.

Then…*vroom*! The car sped off, taking them to the grassy outskirts of town, where the orphanage was.

Three

The orphanage was in a renovated old church, large enough to accommodate its residents and perched on a pretty piece of land with a cluster of coconut trees.

A short stout lady greeted them on the porch. With plainly styled gray hair and eyes that crinkled beneath wire-rimmed glasses, she appeared to be around seventy. Max introduced her as Losa.

After they shook hands, Lizzie extended the rose. "This is for you."

"Thank you. It's lovely." The older woman accepted it with a gracious smile. Although she gazed at Lizzie's fiery red hair, she didn't comment on it.

Thankfully, that made the painting Max had bought seem less important. For now, anyway. No doubt *Lady Ari* would keep creeping back into Lizzie's mind, along with Max's sexy little joke about Lizzie tempting him.

Clearing her wayward thoughts, she said, "I also

brought gifts for the kids." She gestured to the boxes Max had placed beside the door. "I got blankets and bottles for the babies and art supplies for the rest of them."

"That's wonderful." Once again, Losa thanked her. "You seem like a nice girl."

"She is," Max said. "We've known each other since high school. We've been proper friends a long time."

Proper friends? Was that his way of making sure that Losa didn't mistake them as lovers, the way George had done? That was fine with Lizzie. She preferred to avoid that sort of confusion.

Losa invited them into her office, a simply designed space that was as understated as she was. Max brought the boxes inside and put them next to a metal file cabinet.

Losa offered them iced tea that had been chilling in a mini fridge and slices of homemade coconut bread that were already precut and waiting to be served.

They sat across from her with their food and drink, near a window that overlooked the yard.

Lizzie noticed a fenced area with picnic benches, occupied by groups of children who appeared to be between the ages of two and five. Two colorfully dressed young women watched over them.

Losa followed her line of sight and said, "The older children are in school and the babies are in the nursery. The others are having lunch, as you can see. Tokoni is among them. You can visit with him afterward."

Lizzie didn't ask which child was Tokoni or try to recognize him from the photo Max had shown her, at least not from this distance. She was still nervous about meeting him, especially with how much Max adored him.

"So," Losa went on to say, "you want to interview me for your charity blog?"

"Yes," Lizzie quickly replied, "I'd like to feature the

orphanage. To provide whatever information you're willing to give." She removed her phone from her purse. "Also, may I get your permission to do an audio recording? It's more accurate than taking written notes."

"Certainly," Losa said. "It's good of you to help. It was kind of Max to donate to us, too. He was very generous." She sent him an appreciative smile.

Although he returned her smile, he stayed quiet, drinking his tea and allowing Lizzie to do the talking.

Once the recording app was activated, she said to Losa, "Max told me that you and your family founded this orphanage after your husband passed."

"He was a dear man." Her expression went soft. "He would be pleased by what we accomplished here."

Lizzie stole another glance at the window. "Are those your granddaughters? The young women tending to the kids?"

"Yes. They're good girls, as devoted as I am to keeping this place going and matching our children in waiting with interested families. Tokoni is especially eager to be adopted. He chatters about it all the time."

Lizzie nodded. Max had said the same thing about him. "I'm hoping that my article will raise more than just money for your cause. That it will bring awareness to the kids themselves and how badly they need homes."

"We work with international adoption agencies that provide pictures and information of our children in waiting. You're welcome to post links to those websites."

"Absolutely." Lizzie intended to be as thorough as possible. "Will you email me that information, along with whatever else you think will be helpful?"

"Actually, I can give you a packet right now." Losa went to the file cabinet and removed a large gray envelope. She resumed her seat, slid it across the desk and said, "In the United States, intercountry adoption is governed by three sets of laws—the laws of the child's country of origin, your federal laws and the laws of the US state in which the child will be adopted."

"How long does the process typically take?"

"In some countries, it can take years. For us, it's between three and six months."

"Wow. That's fast." Lizzie leaned forward. "Are you the only country that's been able to expedite it that way?"

"No. There are others in this region. Small independent nations, like ours, with less red tape, as one might say."

"Will you tell me about your guidelines?"

"Certainly," Losa replied. "We don't have residency requirements, meaning that the applicants don't have to live here before they adopt. But we do require that they study our culture through the online classes we designed. Prospective parents may be married or single. They need to be at least twenty-five years of age and demonstrate a sufficient income. But what we consider sufficient is reasonable. We're not seeking out the rich. Just people who will love and care for these children. Honorable people," she added. "Their character is what's most important to us."

"Did you help develop these guidelines when you lobbied for international adoption?"

"I worked closely with the authorities, giving them my input. But in some cases, the requirements are modified to accommodate a family member's request. For example, Tokoni's mother asked that he be adopted by a married couple. She didn't want him being raised by a single parent." The older woman softly added, "So I promised her that he would be matched with the type of parents she envisioned, a young romantic couple who would devote their hearts to him, as well as to each other."

Lizzie considered Tokoni's mother and how terribly she'd struggled. Apparently she wanted her son to have a warm, cozy, traditional family, which was what she'd longed to give him when she dreamed of marrying his father.

Losa said, "Most of our applicants want girls. Studies show this to be true in other countries, as well. Unfortunately, that makes it more challenging to find homes for the boys. If Tokoni were a girl, he might have been placed by now."

Lizzie's chest went heavy, tight and twisted, in a way that was beginning to hurt. "I hope the perfect parents come along for him. But you never really know what hand life will deal you. My mom died when I was ten, and my dad raised me after she was gone. But I hardly ever saw him. He was wealthy enough to hire nannies and cooks to look after me."

"I'm sorry that your father wasn't available for you," Losa said. "It shouldn't be that way."

Lizzie noticed that Max was watching her closely now. Was he surprised that she'd offered information about herself?

After a second of silence, he said, "I told Losa about my childhood last time I was here. Not all the sordid details, but enough for her to know that I came from an abusive environment."

"So much sadness." Losa sighed. "Perhaps spending a little time with Tokoni will cheer you up. He's such a vibrant boy."

Lizzie glanced out the window. By now the children had finished eating and were playing in the grass. She watched them for a while, analyzing each one. Was Tokoni the boy in the green shirt and denim shorts? He appeared to be about the right age, with a similar haircut to that of the child in Max's picture, with his bangs skimming his eyes. He was laughing and twirling in the sun, like the happy kid he was supposed to be.

"Their recess is almost over," Losa said. "And as soon as they come inside, you can meet him."

"Yes, of course." Since the interview was coming to a close, Lizzie turned off the recorder on her phone and gathered the packet she'd been given. "I'm looking forward to it."

"Splendid." Losa stood. "You can chat with him in the library. We use it as an art room, too, so that's where the supplies you brought will be kept." She said to Max, "You know where the library is, so you two go on ahead, and I'll bring Tokoni to you."

Lizzie put on a brave face, but deep down she was still concerned that Tokoni would find her lacking. That he wouldn't take to her the way he had with Max.

But it was too late to back out. She was here to support Max—and the orphaned child they'd come to see.

The library was furnished in the typical way, with tables and chairs and shelves of books, but as Lizzie and Max stepped farther into the room, she spotted a seating area in the back that she assumed was designed for guests.

Max led her toward it, and they sat on a floral-printed sofa. She folded her hands on her lap, then unfolded them, attempting to relax.

"It feels good to be back," he said, far more comfortable than she was. "I miss volunteering here."

"What kinds of things did you do?" she asked, trying to envision him in the throes of it.

"Mostly I read to the kids or told them stories. But sometimes I helped in the kitchen. I fixed the plumbing once and mopped the floors in the bathroom when one of the toilets overflowed. Tokoni got in trouble that day because he caused the problem, flushing a toy boat down there."

She bit back a laugh. Apparently sweet little Tokoni had a mischievous side. "I guess your donation didn't make you immune to the grunt work."

"I didn't think it was fair for me to pick and choose my tasks. Besides, as much as Losa appreciated the money, she understood that I needed to be useful in other ways, too."

"The kids must have gotten used to having you around."

He smiled. "Yeah, they did. That's how Tokoni and I got so close."

Just then Losa entered the library, clutching the boy's hand. He was the kid in the green shirt and denim shorts Lizzie had noticed earlier, and up close he looked just like the picture Max had shown her, with full round cheeks and expressive eyes. As soon as Tokoni saw Max, he grinned and tried to escape Losa's hold. But she wouldn't let him go, so he stood there, bouncing in place.

Max came to his feet. Lizzie followed suit, and her nerves ratcheted up a notch.

Tokoni tried to pull Losa toward Max, but the older woman wouldn't budge. "If you want to see Max, you have to be good," she warned the child. "And then I'll come back to get you."

"Okay." He promised her that he would be "very, very good." A second later, he was free and running straight to Max.

Losa left the library, and Lizzie watched as man and child came together in a joyous reunion.

"Hey, buddy," Max said, scooping him up. "It's great to see you."

"Hi, Max!" He nuzzled the big, broad shoulder he was offered, laughing as Max tickled him.

Once the kid calmed down, he gazed curiously at Lizzie. This strange woman, she thought, who was just standing there.

She tried for a smile, but feared that it might have come off as more of a grimace. He just kept staring at her, *really* staring, to the point of barely blinking. She could tell it was her hair that caught his attention. Her dang Lady Ari hair.

With Tokoni still in his arms, Max turned to face her, too. At this point, he'd become aware of how the five-year-old was reacting to her.

"Is she a goodness?" the child asked.

"You mean a *goddess*?" Max chuckled. "No. She's just a pretty lady with red hair. But sometimes I think she looks like a goddess, too. She's my friend Lizzie."

Tokoni grinned at her and said, "Hi, Izzy."

"Hello." She didn't have the heart to correct him. But Max did.

"Her name is Lizzie," he said. "With an *L*. Like Losa. Or lizard." Max stuck out his tongue at her, making a reptile face. "I always thought her name sounded a little like that."

"Gee, thanks." She made the same goofy face at him, trying to be more kidlike. But truth of the matter, he'd nicknamed her Lizard ages ago. Just as she sometimes called him Mad Max.

Tokoni giggled, enjoying their antics.

Max said to him, "So you think we're funny, do you?"

"Yep." The child's chest heaved with excitement, with

more laughter. Then he said to Lizzie, "Know what? This is an orange-fan-age."

She smiled, amused by his pronunciation of it.

"Know what else?" he asked. "My real mommy is gone, but I'm going to get 'dopted by a new mommy. And a daddy, too."

Overwhelmed by how easily he'd rattled that off, she couldn't think of anything to say. She should have been prepared for a conversation like this, knowing what she knew about him, but she couldn't seem to find her voice.

But that didn't stop him from asking her, "Why are you at the orange-fan-age?"

"Because Max wanted me to meet you."

Tokoni reached out to touch her hair, locating a strand that had come loose from her ponytail. "How come?"

"Because of how much he likes you." She released the air in her lungs, realizing that she'd been holding her breath. "And because I'm going to write a story about the orphanage and the kids who live here."

"Can I be a superhero in it?"

Oh, dear. "It's not that kind of story."

He was still touching her hair. "It could be."

No, she thought, it couldn't. She wasn't good at writing fiction. She'd always been a reality-type gal.

"Come on, buddy," Max said, redirecting Tokoni's attention. "Let's all go over here." He carried him to the sofa and plopped him down.

Lizzie joined them, with Tokoni in the middle. She fixed her hair, tucking the loose strand behind her ear.

"I made a book of the mommy and daddy who are going to 'dopt me," he said to her. "I can show it to you."

"Sure," she replied, trying to be as upbeat about it as he was.

Tokoni climbed off the sofa and dashed over to a plastic bin that had his name on it. There appeared to be personalized bins for all the children, stacked in neat rows.

He returned and resumed his spot, between her and Max. He showed her a handmade booklet, consisting of about ten pieces of white paper with staples in the center holding it together.

He narrated each picture, explaining the activity he and his future parents were engaging in. On page one, they stood in the sun. On page two, they swam in the ocean. In the next one, they were going out to dinner, where they would eat all of Tokoni's favorite foods.

Everyone had red smiles on their faces, black dots for eyes and no noses. Dad was the tallest, Mom was wearing a triangle-shaped dress and Tokoni was the only one with hair. His folks were completely bald.

Lizzie assumed it was deliberate. That Tokoni hadn't given them hair because he didn't know what color it should be. He obviously knew that he might be adopted by people who looked different from him. Blonds, maybe? Or even redheads?

She fussed with her hair, checking the piece she'd tucked behind her ear, making sure it stayed put.

"Your book is wonderful," she said. "Your drawings are special. The best I've ever seen." She didn't know much about kids' art, but his work seemed highly developed to her, with how carefully thought out it was.

He flashed a proud smile and crawled onto her lap. She went warm and gooey inside. This child was doing things to her that she'd never felt before.

He said, "You can color inside my book if you want to."

Heavens, no, she thought. As flattered as she was by his generous offer, she couldn't handle the pressure that would cause. "That's very nice of you, but I don't think I should."

He persisted. "It's okay if you don't color very good. I'll still let you."

Her skills weren't the problem. "I just don't—"

Max bumped her shoulder, encouraging her to do it. Damn. Now how was she supposed to refuse?

"All right," she relented, her stomach erupting into butterflies. "But I'm going to sit at one of the tables." Where she could concentrate. "And I'll need some crayons." She didn't mention that she'd brought new art supplies for Tokoni and his peers, because it was up to Losa to distribute those.

After Tokoni got the crayons, he scooted next to her at the table, directly at her elbow and making it difficult for her to work. But she didn't tell him to move over. He was so darned excited to have her do this, almost as if she really was a goddess.

Max joined them, only he didn't have to draw. He got to kick back and watch. Lizzie wished she hadn't gotten roped into this. What if she ruined the boy's book? What if he didn't like what she did to it?

She opened the first page: the depiction of Tokoni and his family on a sunny day. She used an orange crayon and added more rays to the giant sun, giving it an extra pop of color. That seemed safe enough.

Tokoni grinned. What Max had told her about the boy was true. He smiled all the time.

"Do something else," he told her.

She put grass beneath the people's feet and glanced across the table at Max. He shot her a playful wink, and her pulse beat a bit faster.

Returning to the picture, Lizzie drew multicolored

flowers sprouting up from the grass. "How's this?" she asked Tokoni.

"That's nice." He turned the page for her. "Do this one."

It was the ocean scene. She embellished it with bigger waves and a school of fish. She added sand and seashells, too.

Tokoni wiggled in his seat and went to the next page, where the family was going out to dinner. He said, "Make the mommy look more like a girl."

Lizzie contemplated the request. She certainly wasn't going to give the female a bust or hips or anything like that. So she detailed the mommy's dress, making it more decorative. She also gave her jewelry, a gold necklace and dangling earrings.

"That looks pretty," Tokoni said.

"Thank you." She drew high heels onto the mommy's feet.

But the poor woman looked incomplete, all dressed up with her bald head, so Lizzie included a hat with a flower poking out of it.

"Put stuff on her mouth," Tokoni said.

"Lipstick?"

He nodded.

She reached for a pink crayon. "How about this?"

"Okay." He moved even closer, eager to see the transformation.

She reshaped the mommy's lips, making them fuller but still retaining her smile.

"I think the mom needs some hair coming out from under her hat," Max said. "The dad could use some, too. Unless he's the shaved-head type."

Seriously? Lizzie could have kicked him. With all the months he'd spent here, getting close to Tokoni, he should have known what the hairless parents were about. But sometimes men could be downright clueless, even the sensitive ones like Max.

And now poor little Tokoni was mulling over the situation, looking perplexed. "What color?" he asked Max.

Realization dawned in Max's eyes, and Lizzie squinted at him, wishing he hadn't opened this can of worms.

After a beat of outward concern, Max said, "Any color." He quickly added, "Blue, green, purple."

Tokoni laughed. "That's silly."

Max laughed, too, recovering from his blunder. "Not as silly as you think. There are people where I live who dye their hair those colors."

"You should do yours," the boy said to him.

Max ran his fingers through the blackness of his hair. "Maybe I will."

Tokoni laughed again. Then he said to Lizzie, "But not you."

She tapped the tip of his nose. As cute as he was, she couldn't seem to help herself. "You don't want me to dye my hair a funny color?"

"No. I want it to stay red."

The hair discussion ended and the mommy and daddy in Tokoni's booklet remained bald.

A short while later, Losa returned. Tokoni didn't want to go with her, but he didn't have a choice. It was naptime. All the younger kids had to nap in the middle of the day. Or at least rest their eyes and stay quiet.

"Will you and Max come back tomorrow?" he asked Lizzie.

"Yes, absolutely," she replied. "Maybe we can volunteer for the rest of the week and see you every day, if that's all right with Losa."

The older woman readily agreed, and Lizzie's heart

twirled. She wanted to spend as much time with Tokoni as she could before their trip was over. She was certain that Max did, too. He seemed pleased with her suggestion. But he'd already told her that he missed volunteering there.

"See you soon, buddy." Max got on bended knee to say goodbye to the boy, and they hugged.

Lizzie was next. Tokoni held her so warmly, so affectionately, she nearly cried. This child needed a family, and she was going to do everything within her power to help him get one.

Four

While dusk approached the sky, Lizzie and Max walked along the beach at their resort. Collecting her thoughts, she stopped to gaze at the horizon.

Reflecting on the day's events, she said what was on her mind, what she'd been consumed with since they left the orphanage. "I want to help Tokoni get adopted."

An ocean breeze stirred Max's shirt, pulling the fabric closer to his body. "You're already going to try to do that with your blog article."

"Yes, but I want to do more than just write an article that *might* help. I want to actually—" she stalled, trying to make sense of what it was she thought she was capable of "—find the perfect parents for him."

"How?" he asked. "How would you even begin to go about doing something like that?"

"I don't know." All she'd ever done was raise money for children's charities. She'd never set out to find an orphaned kid a home. "But with all my resources, with all the people I know, there has to be a way to make it happen."

He looked into her eyes, almost as if he was peering into the anxious window of her soul. "You're really serious about this."

"Yes, I am." She couldn't help how eager she was, how attached she'd already become to Tokoni. "You were right about how special he is. And I want to make a difference in his life."

His gaze continued to bore into hers. Did he think that she was getting in over her head?

Then he smiled and said, "I'll help you, Lizzie. We can do this. Both of us together. We can find him a home."

Her pulse jumped, her mind raced. Suddenly the beach seemed to be spinning, moving at a dizzying pace.

She pushed her toes into the sand, steadying herself. "Thank you, Max." He was the one true constant in her life. The person she relied on most, and if he was onboard, her quest seemed even more possible.

He kept smiling. "I loved watching you with him today. You were amazing the way you interacted with him."

She breathed in his praise. "I can't wait to see him again. But at least we've got the rest of the week."

Max's smile fell. "I can't believe how I screwed up, saying what I did about his drawings. I should have been aware of the hair thing before now."

"It's all right. When he gets adopted by his new mommy and daddy, he can add their hair and anything else that will identify them to him."

"He was certainly fascinated with your hair. But I figured he would be."

"That made me uncomfortable at first."

"I know. I could tell." His voice went a little rough. "It sure looks wild now."

"It's just the wind." She tried to sound casual. But it wasn't easy. Before they'd ventured out to the beach this evening, she'd removed her ponytail, and now her hair was long and loose and blowing past her shoulders, probably a lot like Lady Ari's in the painting he'd bought.

Before the moment turned unbearably awkward, she redirected his focus and hurriedly said, "We're going to have to talk to Losa about our plan, since she's the one who will be approving Tokoni's prospective parents."

"In a way, we will be, too, with the way we'll be searching for them." He stooped to pick up a shell at his feet and study its corkscrew shape. He returned it to the beach and asked, "Are we really going to know, Lizzie?"

"Who's right for him? I think we will. Besides, we have the guidelines his mother set."

A hard and fast frown appeared on his face, grooving lines into his forehead. "A young romantic couple, devoted as deeply to each other as they'll be to him? That's out of our league."

A heap of concern came over her. "You're starting to sound as if you don't want to do this. Are you having second thoughts?"

"No. But I don't want to choose the wrong people. Or send the wrong applicants to Losa or whatever."

"I agree, completely. We're not going to run right out and grab the first wannabe parents who come along. Besides, we haven't even figured out the best way to approach this yet."

"You're right. Once we research the possibilities and explore our options, I won't be as worried about it."

"Whoever his parents are going to be, they need to encourage his artwork. I think he's going to excel at art.

His cognitive skills blow me away, too, with the way he analyzes everything. I doubt many five-year-olds are as advanced as he is."

Max grinned. "That's exactly how I felt when I first met him. And with as happy as he is all the time, he makes everybody around him smile."

She laughed. "Gosh, do you think we're biased?"

He laughed, too. "With the way we're both singing his praises, you'd think he was our kid." His mood sobered, his handsome features going still. "But he's not."

"No, he definitely isn't." She couldn't get over the loss of her own mother, let alone become one herself. "But that isn't something we need to think about. No one is going to suggest that we adopt him."

"We couldn't even if we wanted to."

"No, we couldn't." They weren't married or in love or anything even remotely close to what Tokoni's mother had requested. "Not that you wouldn't make a great dad. It's being a husband that you would fail miserably at."

"You've got me there." He shrugged, reaffirming what they both already knew. "I definitely couldn't handle that, any more than you could cope with being a wife."

"That's for sure. I've never even dated anyone for more than three months, which is weird, when you think that someone could actually adopt Tokoni within three to six months." She added, "But that should help our cause with a couple who's eager and ready to adopt."

"You're right, Lizard." He turned playful, kicking a bit of sand at her ankles. "It should."

She kicked a bigger pile at him, some of the grains making it all the way to his knees. "Don't mess with me, Mad Max."

"Ooh, check you out," he teased her. "I should dunk your ass in the water for that."

She shot a glance at the ocean. Dusk was still closing in, painting the sky in mesmerizing hues. Bracing to get wet, to splash and frolic, she said, "If you do, I'm taking you down with me."

Yet when she turned back to gauge his reaction, a look of common sense had come into his eyes. He'd obviously thought better of it. Then again, why wouldn't he?

The only way for him to dunk her in the water would be to pick her up and carry her there, and that wouldn't be a good idea, not with how intimate it could get. Goofing around was one thing; creating intimacy was quite another.

Foolish as it was, she actually wished that he would lift her into his arms and haul her off to the sea. But that was just a side effect of the yearnings between them. Lizzie knew better than to want what she shouldn't have or push the boundaries of their attraction. But darned if he didn't affect her in ways she was struggling to control.

"You know what I could use about now?" He gestured in the direction of the resort's palm-thatch-roofed restaurant. "A pineapple smoothie at the bar. Do you want to join me?"

"They serve smoothies?"

He nodded. "Along with the usual spirits. But I'd rather skip the alcohol and have a smoothie."

"Then I'll have one, too." A sweet, frothy concoction that would go down easy—and help her forget about the troubling urges he incited.

The bar was dimly lit, with a tiki décor and a spectacular view of the ocean. Music played from an old-fashioned jukebox. Pop tunes, mostly, from eras gone by.

Max drank his smoothie in suffering silence. Being sexually attracted to his best friend was a hell of a burden to bear. But at least the feelings were mutual and Lizzie was suffering right along with him. They'd been dealing with this for years, so tonight was just more of the same—except for their pledge to find a family for Tokoni.

"Did you really mean what you said about me making a great dad?" he asked, breaking the silence with an emotional bang.

"Yes, I meant it." She stirred her smoothie with her straw. "You've always had a natural way with kids. It's a wonderful part of who you are."

"Thanks, but I've never actually considered being a father, not with the loner life I've chosen to lead. Now it seems sort of sad to think that I might never have kids." He glanced out the window at the darkness enveloping the sea. "But I guess being around Tokoni is making me feel that way."

"You could still have children someday if you wanted to."

"Yeah, right." He struggled to fathom the idea. "And who am I supposed to have these kids with?"

"You could adopt and become a single dad."

"I don't think that's very common."

"No, but it's still possible in this day and age, depending on the circumstances. Now, me…" She heaved a heavy sigh. "I'm not cut out to be a mom."

"You could've fooled me, with how beautifully you engaged with Tokoni."

"I'd be scared to death to be responsible for a child, to give him everything he needs."

He knew that she was referring to emotional needs. "You've always been there for me when I needed someone to lean on."

"I'm your friend. That isn't the same as being someone's mom."

"No, but it's still a testament to who you are. And so is your commitment to Tokoni. Truthfully, I'm starting to think you'd make an amazing mom."

"I don't know about that." She shook her head. Her hair was still windblown from the beach, as gorgeous as ever. "But thank you for saying it."

"I meant it." He honestly did. "Of course all that really matters is for Tokoni to have the parents he longs for."

"Does he know that you were once eligible for adoption?"

"No. I've never told him anything about my childhood, and thankfully he's never asked. But I was just one of many. About half the kids who enter the foster care system are eligible for adoption. Even now there are over a hundred thousand children in waiting." Max knew the numbers well. He helped run a foster children's charity that he and his brothers had founded. "Typically, foster kids are adopted by their foster parents. Or by extended family. That's the most common scenario."

She sighed. "Not for you, it wasn't."

Max nodded. His extended family had been as bad as his mother. He'd even had a bitter old grandmother back on the reservation who used to call him an *iyeska*, a breed, because she believed that he was half white, spawned by one of the Anglo men Mom used to mess around with in the border towns. Mom, however, had insisted that he was a full-blood and his daddy was a res boy. Till this day, he didn't have a clue who'd fathered him. He'd never been accepted by his grandmother, either. She'd died a long time ago.

"I never wanted to be adopted, anyway," he said.

"Not even by any of your foster parents?"

"I preferred being left alone. Besides, I got shifted

around so much in the beginning I never got close to any of them. Of course when I met Jake and Garrett, things got better." Two other misplaced foster boys, he thought, who'd become his brothers. "But you already know that story."

"Yes. I do." She relayed the tale. "Jake was leery of you at first because he thought you were a dork. Garrett, however, was your protector from the start and would fight off the kids who bullied you."

"Garrett saved my hide more times than I can count. But Jake came around, too, and accepted me."

"It's strange how I don't know them very well, even after all these years. I see them at fund-raisers and whatnot, but that's as far as it goes."

Max had never considered how superficial her relationship with his foster brothers was. Was that his fault for not bringing her together with them in a closer way? Probably, he thought. But he wasn't good at family-type ties. Sometimes he even shielded himself from his brothers. He'd cut everyone off during his sabbatical, including Lizzie.

"I missed you," he said, blurting out his feelings.

She blinked at him. "What are you talking about?"

"When I was gone. When I was traveling." Was that a stupid thing for him to admit? Or even think about now that she was here with him?

She gazed at him from across their rugged wood table. "I missed you, too. It was a long time for us to be apart."

"I needed to get away. It was just something I had to do."

"It's okay. I didn't feel abandoned by you. I knew you were coming back. And look how it turned out. You found Tokoni on that trip."

"And now we're going to work toward finding him the parents he dreams about," he said, confirming their plans once again.

And hoping they could actually make them come true.

Lizzie and Max's week of volunteering at the orphanage went well. And now, on their very last day, Lizzie was making banana pudding, Tokoni's favorite dessert, for all the children to enjoy. She was using a recipe that Losa's oldest daughter, Fai, had given her. Fai was the primary cook at the orphanage, but she was staying out of the kitchen today.

Nonetheless, Lizzie wasn't doing this alone. Max and Tokoni were helping her. She'd put Tokoni on banana duty, sitting him at a table where he could peel the 'nanas, as he called them. Max was seated across from him, slicing the fruit and dumping the pieces into a bowl. Later, they would be layered into casserole dishes.

"Come on, buddy." Max spoke gently but firmly to the boy. "If you keep doing that, there won't be anything left for me to cut."

Tokoni had already squished the banana that was in his hand. He could be quite the mischief maker when he wanted to be. Lizzie laughed as Tokoni stuffed a small glob of it into his mouth and ate it.

"Don't encourage him," Max said to her.

"Sorry. But after my mom was gone, my revolving-door nannies would bring me into the kitchen so I could observe our chefs preparing their masterpieces, except I always had to sit quietly and observe, like the proper little lady that I was." She glanced at the mess Tokoni was making. "It's nice to see a kid goofing around."

"Okay." Max smiled at her. "Then you're forgiven. You, too," he said to Tokoni. "Only maybe I better get you cleaned up a bit." Max got up and wet a towel at the sink. He returned and wiped the child's face and hands.

Afterward, Tokoni asked Lizzie, "What are 'volving-door nannies?"

Oh, goodness. She should have known better than to say that. Tokoni was a highly observant boy, picking up on just about everything around him.

"Nannies look after children, sort of like teachers and nurses. I had lots of them when I was young, so that's why I said revolving door. They never stayed at my house for very long."

"How come?"

"Because it wasn't a very fun place to work."

"How come?" he asked again. He was prone to do that, to keep asking until he got an answer that satisfied him.

Lizzie glanced at Max. He was silent, watching her, obviously waiting to see how she was going to handle this.

"I didn't smile and laugh all the time, like you do," she told Tokoni.

"Were you sad?"

She wasn't going to lie. "Sometimes, yes."

"'Cause your mommy was gone?"

Well, there you go. He'd picked up on that, too. "Yes."

"Is she gone like my mommy is gone? Is she in heaven?"

Lizzie turned down the heat on the mixture that she'd been stirring, letting it simmer on its own. Leaning against the counter, she said, "Yes, that's exactly where my mommy is." Only she couldn't tell him that her troubled Southern belle mother had chosen to be there.

"I don't 'member my mommy, but Mrs. Losa says that she loved me."

Lizzie fought back a glaze of tears. No way was she going to cry in front of this sweet, comforting child. "Losa told us about your mommy, too."

"I don't have any pictures of her. Do you have pictures of your mommy?"

"Yes, they're in an album at my house." Photos that Lizzie rarely looked at anymore.

He tilted his head. "Was her hair like yours?"

"No, it was blond. Yellow," she clarified, "and always all done up." She made an upswept motion. "She wore fancy clothes and lots of jewels, too." Lizzie had inherited her mother's diamonds and pearls. She lowered her hands. "My dad is a ginger, though, like me."

"Ginger?"

"That's what some people call redheads."

Tokoni peeled another banana, neatly this time. "Is Ginger the name of a goodness? I mean a goddess?" he corrected himself, peering at her with his big brown eyes.

Max was looking at her, too. He stood beside the table with the damp towel still in his hands.

She replied, "No. Ginger isn't a goddess. In some places, it's been used to make fun of redheads. But now lots of redheads are claiming it as their own and making it a good thing. Ginger is a spice that people cook with that gives food a reddish tinge. There was also a character on an old TV show named Ginger who had red hair. I've heard that it might have come from her, too, but I'm not sure."

"What was she like?" Tokoni asked.

"She was a movie star who got stranded on an island with some other people when the boat they were on was caught in a storm. It sounds serious, but it was a funny show."

Max was smiling now. "The island wasn't like this

one. It was uncharted, meaning that no one knew where it was. They built their own huts and ate lots of coconuts."

"We eat lots of coconuts here!" Tokoni got excited.

Lizzie replied, "Yes, you most certainly do." Losa's grandsons tended to the trees. They had a vegetable garden on the property, too. "But if we don't get back to the pudding we're making, it's never going to get done."

"We better hurry," the boy said to Max.

"You bet." Max returned to his seat and pretended to cut the bananas really fast.

Tokoni exaggerated peeling them, too. Then he said, "I wish this wasn't your last day."

"I know. Me, too." Max cleared his throat. "But we'll come back and see you again." He looked at Lizzie. "Won't we?"

"Yes, we definitely will." They couldn't tell Tokoni that they were going to try to find a family for him in the States. They discussed it with Losa, of course, and she was open to the idea, as long as they understood the challenges associated with it. Lizzie wasn't expecting it to be easy. But she wanted to stay as positive as she could.

Immersing herself in her task, she turned away to beat egg yolks in a bowl and add them to the mixture she was cooking. Lots of pudding for lots of kids, she thought. She couldn't imagine cooking regularly for this crowd.

"Is your mommy in heaven, too?" Tokoni asked Max suddenly.

Lizzie spun around. So far, Max had gotten away with not having to tell Tokoni about his childhood. But now he'd been put on the spot. He certainly couldn't claim that his mean-spirited mother had bypassed heaven and gone straight to hell, even if that was the answer buried deep in his eyes.

"Yes, she's gone," he said.

"Do you any have pictures of her?"

"No." He quickly added, "But I have pictures of my brothers on my phone that I can show you. I have two brothers, and they both have kids. Jake's daughter is a baby, and Garrett is adopting a little girl who belongs to his fiancée, the woman he's going to marry."

"He's 'dopting a kid?" Tokoni wiggled in his chair, gratification written all over his face. "He must be a nice guy."

"He is. Very nice. Both of my brothers are. After my mom went away, I became a foster kid. I lived in other people's homes because I didn't have anywhere else to go. Sort of like the foster children who stay here."

Tokoni nodded in understanding.

Max continued, "And that's where I met my brothers. Jake lost his parents, too, and Garrett's mommy was too sick to take care of him. But she got better. Or as well as she could."

"Better enough for him to go back to her?"

"Yes."

"Did you or your other brother ever get 'dopted?"

"No, neither of us ever did."

Max exchanged a glance with Lizzie, and she thought about how he hadn't wanted to be adopted. Of course he wasn't about to reveal that to Tokoni.

"I'm going to get 'dopted," the boy said. "I know I will."

Lizzie smiled, encouraging his dream. "I know you will, too."

Tokoni beamed, and her heart swelled, especially when he came over to her and wrapped his arms around her middle, giving her an impromptu hug. She reached down and smoothed his bangs, moving them out of his eyes, and for one crazy, beautiful moment, she believed what Max had said about her was true: that she would make an amazing mom.

But she shook off the feeling. This wasn't about her maternal stirrings, no matter how incredible they seemed. This was about uncovering the parents Tokoni was meant to have.

Five

Max and Lizzie were home, seated across from each other at a hectic little sandwich shop. They'd both gotten the same thing: turkey and Swiss clubs, side salads and lemonade. She looked tired, he thought. For the time being, he was exhausted, too.

They'd been back in LA for a month, working nonstop on their goal of finding Tokoni a family, using every resource they could think of. She'd written and posted her original blog article, along with a special feature on Tokoni. She'd also crafted tons of articles as a guest blogger on international adoption sites. Max had created a slew of social media accounts dedicated to their cause, and today, before stopping for this quickie lunch, they'd met with an adoption attorney to give him a packet about the orphanage in case he had any clients who might be interested in a boy Tokoni's age. This wasn't the first attorney they'd spoken to nor would it be their last. They had a checklist a mile long.

"You seem discouraged," Lizzie said. "But we knew this wasn't going to be easy."

"I'm not discouraged. I'm just—" he searched his befuddled mind for the right word and came up with "—worried."

She shifted in her chair. "About what?"

"The way I feel. How this is affecting me. How it's draining you. How it's making zombies out of us."

She furrowed her brow. "I'm doing fine."

"Are you? Are you really?" The late-afternoon light from a nearby window showcased the pale lavender circles beneath her eyes. "I think it's taking an emotional toll on you."

"So what are you saying? That you want us to slow down?" She frowned directly at him. "Or quit and leave that poor little boy in the orphanage? I can't do that. It'll break my heart not to try to give him the family he deserves."

"I'm not suggesting that we stop or slow down. I'm—" Once again, he faltered, struggling to say what he meant.

"You're what?" She picked at a corner of her sandwich, eating it like a bird.

"I've been thinking a lot about us lately. You and me. And how we would be better parents for Tokoni than these strangers we keep searching for. So far, no one else has even taken an interest in him. And even if someone does, are they going to care about him as much as we do?" *There.* He'd said it. He'd admitted the true reason for his exhaustion. Max wasn't physically tired. It was his heart that was working overtime.

"Oh, my God." She released a jittery breath. "Do you hear what you're saying?"

"That I wish we could adopt him? Yes, I'm hearing

it." From his own parched lips. He grabbed his drink and took a swig.

"It's impossible. You know Losa would never let us adopt him. We don't meet his mother's requirements. We aren't who she envisioned for him."

"I know, but it shouldn't matter that we're single. We'd still make the best parents he could ever have."

She picked at her food again. "Do you really believe that? Even about me? Am I really the best mom he could have?"

"Yes, you are. Look what you're going through to find him a family. There isn't another woman on earth who's fighting for his happiness the way you are." Max still hadn't taken a bite of his sandwich yet. But he was watching Lizzie, sweet, delicate, ladylike Lizzie, dissect hers.

"On our last day at the orphanage, when we were making the pudding, I was starting to feel like a mom." She tore at a slice of tomato. "But I knew better than to focus on it."

"It isn't fair that his mother set such strict requirements. Every other kid in that place is allowed to be adopted by a single parent. And in our case, Tokoni would be getting two single parents, a mom and a dad, who would raise him with as much love and care as he needs."

"Except that we would be parenting him from separate households," she pointed out.

"There's nothing wrong with that. Our friendship is stronger than most marriages, anyway."

"I agree, completely. But Losa is bound by their laws to follow his mother's instructions. She couldn't let us adopt him, even if she wanted to." Lizzie's voice rattled. "She already told us how imperative it was for him to be adopted by a married couple."

Max made a frustrated rebuttal. "Do you know how many people get divorced and fight over their kids or use them as pawns? What if that happens with Tokoni's future parents? What if their relationship turns bitter and he gets caught in the cross fire?"

"That's out of our control. Or Losa's or anyone's. All any of us can do is try to find him the parents his mother wanted him to have and pray for the best. I don't want to think the worst. It makes me too sad." She tore at her sandwich again, looking as if she might cry. "I need to believe that everything will work out."

"I'm sorry. I shouldn't have put such a negative spin on it. We'll just keep going, moving forward to find him a family." Even if it hurt, he thought. Even if he was convinced that he and Lizzie were the parents Tokoni needed. He went quiet for a moment, collecting his thoughts. "Speaking of adoption, Garrett called me this morning and said that Ivy's adoption was finalized today." Ivy was the toddler who belonged to Garrett's fiancée. The child he'd told Tokoni about. "He's officially her father now."

"Oh, that's wonderful. I'm happy for him. But do you think that's part of the reason you've been hit so hard about not being able to adopt Tokoni?"

"I don't know. Maybe." He hated to think that he was comparing his life to his brother's. "Garrett and Meagan are having a party to celebrate. A big bash they're planning for the Saturday after next. Do you want to come with me?"

"Yes. I'd love to go. I've never even met little Ivy."

"Then here's your chance."

"I haven't met Meagan yet, either."

Damn, he thought. He should have introduced her to Garrett's fiancée by now. But at least he was making up for lost time. "I think you'll like her."

"I can't help being curious about her, especially with her shaky past and how she stole from Garrett. And from you and Jake, too," she quickly added.

Max nodded. Meagan had embezzled from the three of them when she worked for their accountant. Her former boyfriend had talked her into committing the crime and then ditched her after she'd gotten caught. Meagan didn't even know she was pregnant until after she went to prison. "It's awful to think that she gave birth while she was incarcerated and that the father wanted nothing to do with her or Ivy."

Lizzie blew out a sigh. "It's sort of like what Tokoni's dad did."

"Only he can't try to come back into the picture." According to the adoption laws in Nulah, he'd relinquished his parental rights when he abandoned the boy and his mother. Even his name had been removed from the birth certificate. "Ivy's dad tried to make a claim on her."

"He did? When?"

"Soon after Garrett and Meagan got together. But he wasn't interested in his daughter. It was money he was after."

Lizzie made a tight face. "What a jerk."

"Totally. But you know what? Garrett paid him off, anyway. He just wanted to get rid of the guy so he could adopt Ivy."

"And now Garrett's her new daddy." She softened her expression. "I'm looking forward to the party. Thanks for inviting me to go with you."

"It's going to be a princess theme. Ivy was named after a princess in a children's book."

"Oh, that's cute."

"And just think, a princess theme is right up your alley, with you being a royal goddess and all."

She tossed a crumb of bread at him. "Smart aleck."

He smiled, trying to stay as upbeat as he possibly could. But that didn't change how troubled he felt inside or how much he wished that Tokoni could become their son.

The party was being held in one of the ballrooms at the luxurious beachfront hotel and resort Garrett owned. Lizzie was running a bit late, so she'd told Max that she would meet him there, and by the time she arrived, the festivities were well underway.

Everyone had the option of donning a complimentary crown. A table at the entrance of the ballroom was filled with them, in all sorts of shapes, colors and sizes. Lizzie chose a tiara decorated with green gems because it complemented her emerald gown. The attire was formal. Costumes were encouraged, too. Girls posing as Cinderella, Snow White and the Little Mermaid ran amok. Prince Charming and knights in shining armor were favorites among the boys.

Games, party favors, face painting, lessons on how to be a prince or a princess. You name it, this party had it. There was a magnificently crafted wooden castle/playhouse for the kids, which was also big enough for the adults. Even the food appeared to be fit for royalty, with a spectacular buffet.

Lizzie scanned the crowd for Max. She found him near the castle, holding a toy scepter. He wore a black velvet tuxedo with a tailcoat, and his big, bold medieval-style crown sat high atop his head, making a strong statement.

As she approached him, she noticed that he'd forgone the customary shirt and tie. Instead, he'd paired his tux with a Princess Leia T-shirt. Lizzie smiled to herself. Max was and always would be a *Star Wars* nerd.

"Look at you," she said.

"And you." He waved his scepter at her. "Your dress is hot."

"This old thing." She laughed. Along with the long silk gown, she'd draped herself in diamonds. "I see that you found a way to sneak in your favorite princess." She poked a finger at his T-shirt. "That was clever."

"I figured it would work. This is quite the kiddy soiree, isn't it?"

"I'll say. Where's the newly adopted girl?"

"In there." He motioned to the castle.

"Are you on guard duty?" A wonderfully offbeat king, she thought, behaving like a knight.

"For now I am. I told her parents that I would hold down the fort so they could grab a bite to eat. They'll be back from the buffet soon. You should have seen Ivy when she was first announced to her guests, under her new last name. We stood in a receiving line so she could greet us."

"I'm sorry I missed that. I can't wait to meet her."

"Hold on and I'll get her for you now." Max put the scepter on a gilded ledge of the castle exterior and went inside.

He returned with a dark-haired toddler dressed in a puffy pink dress, rife with taffeta and lace. Her face was painted with glitter, and multicolored gems embellished her sparkling gold tiara.

Max scooped up her up and said, "This is Ivy Ann Snow, the belle of the ball."

Ivy gazed at Lizzie and said, "Garry do this."

Garry, she assumed, was Garrett. And "this" was most likely a reference to the party, unless it meant the adoption.

Either way, Lizzie told her, "You look beautiful, like a princess should."

The child said, "Tank you," for "*Thank* you."

Lizzie smiled. Apparently Ivy had a bit of trouble with her pronunciation. But Tokoni mispronounced some of his words, too. "I know a five-year-old boy who would have liked to be here. But he lives too far away."

"What's him name?"

"Tokoni."

"Where him live?"

"In an island country called Nulah," Lizzie replied. Ever since Max had lamented that they should be the ones to adopt him, making her long for the impossible, she missed Tokoni even more.

"Do Maddy know him?"

Maddy? It took Lizzie a second to realize that Ivy was taking about Max. "Yes, he knows him."

"Maddy my uncle."

"Your favorite uncle," he said, tickling Ivy and making her laugh.

A few giggles later, she tried to wiggle out of his arms, her attention span waning. "I go now."

"Okay, Princess." He put her down, and she dashed off, back into the castle to play with her friends. Or her subjects. Or whoever she was holding court with.

"I didn't know she called you Maddy," Lizzie said.

"When I first met her, I told her my name was Mad Max, and she turned it into Maddy."

"I like it. Maybe I'll start calling you that, too, since I started the Mad Max handle to begin with."

"Go ahead, pretty Lizard. I don't mind." He reached out to touch one of her diamond drop earrings. "Are these new?"

"No, they're from my mother's collection." She went a little breathless, having him standing so close to her. "Vintage Harry Winston."

"And this?" He skimmed her necklace. "Was it your mom's, too?"

She nodded. "Yes, except it's early Cartier." She lifted her wrist to showcase her bracelet. "And here we have Tiffany and Company." Normally she kept her mother's jewelry in a safe-deposit box at the bank. "I got into the vault, so to speak."

"What made you decide to do that?"

"They remind me of when I was a little girl, so wearing them to a child's fancy party felt right somehow." She tempered her emotions, trying to keep her voice from cracking. "Mama used to let me play with her jewelry when I was young. She would dress me up and stand me in front of the mirror, giving me the history of each piece."

"I'll bet your mother would have loved this party."

"Yes, I'm sure she would have." She took a step back, away from him. But what she really wanted was to move straight into his arms and be held by him, soothing the ache of them not being able to become Tokoni's parents.

"Hey, you two," a masculine voice said from behind them.

Lizzie and Max turned simultaneously. The man who'd spoken to them was Garrett. He stood tall and trim and polished, his jet-black hair slicked straight back, his classic tuxedo sharp and crisp. He wasn't sporting a crown. But he'd probably removed it after the opening ceremony.

Next to him and holding his hand was his fiancée. Meagan was a lovely brunette with almond-shaped eyes and waist-length hair. She wore a powder-blue gown and a silver tiara.

Garrett introduced Lizzie to Meagan, and the women smiled and greeted each other.

Afterward, Lizzie said to Garrett, "Congratulations on the adoption. I met your new daughter. She's beautiful." To Meagan, she added, "She looks like you."

"Thank you." Meagan leaned toward Garrett. "She certainly adores her new daddy."

As if on cue, Ivy poked her head out of the castle, saw her parents and ran over to them. She grinned at everyone, her puffy dress askew. Then she said, "Come," to Garrett and tugged him toward the playhouse. With her other hand, she grabbed Max, pulling him in the same direction.

Meagan laughed. "Apparently the men have been summoned."

Lizzie laughed, too. "So it seems." She watched them disappear into the castle, with the toddler leading the way.

After a stretch of silence, Meagan said, "I saw you once before. It was at a fund-raiser at the park. But it was a while ago, before Garrett and I had gone public with our relationship. So no one introduced me to you. You were off in the distance, with a group of other women."

"Was Max there, too?"

"Yes. It was the first time I met him. Later that day, Garrett told me about you and how close you and Max were. I've wondered about the two of you ever since."

Lizzie's heart went bump. "What do you mean?"

"If you were more than friends—" The brunette stalled. "I hope it was all right that I just said that."

"You're not the first person who's been curious about us." And she wouldn't be the last, Lizzie thought. "It happens all the time."

"Then you must be used to it."

Was she? At the moment, she wasn't so sure.

Meagan said, "When Garrett and I first got together, we told everyone we were just friends, when we were actually having a secret affair. So I thought maybe that's what you and Max had been doing. That at some point, your friendship had turned into more. But Garrett insisted that wasn't the case. Still, I wondered how anyone, outside of you and Max, could know the absolute truth."

"The truth is that we're just friends." Friends who wanted each other, she thought. Being painfully honest, she added, "But I'm not denying that there's an attraction between us. That we…" That they what? Wished they could be lovers, but were afraid it would ruin their friendship?

"I'm sorry. I wasn't trying to pry." Meagan made a face. "Well, maybe I was. But only because of how fascinated I was by you and Max when I first saw you."

"I've been fascinated by you, too, and your history with Garrett. You've had a lot to overcome."

"That's why we kept our relationship a secret at first. I didn't want anyone to know that I was dating one of the men I embezzled from. But Garrett convinced me that we needed to come clean."

"He's a forthright guy."

"Yes, he is. I love him so much I could burst."

Lizzie couldn't relate. So far, her experience with love hurt something fierce: the loss of her mother, the pang of not being close to her father. And now she'd begun to love Tokoni, a child who wasn't even hers.

Determined to keep a rein on her emotions, she asked, "Did Garrett happen to mention the boy that Max and I are trying to find a home for?"

"Yes, he did. If there's anything I can do to help, just let me know."

"Thanks, I will." Lizzie gestured to their surroundings, her mother's Tiffany bracelet catching the light. "I told Ivy that Tokoni would have enjoyed coming to this party. It's hard not to think of him in a setting like this."

"Oh, I'm sorry that he couldn't be here." Meagan watched her with sympathy. "You must be really attached to him."

If she only knew how attached, Lizzie thought. "Max and I both are. He's a special kid."

"It's sad to think of kids living in orphanages and foster care. My brother, Tanner, raised Ivy when I was locked up, or else she would have been placed in the system. Tanner is here tonight, with his wife. My other brother and his wife and son are here, too. They flew in from Montana."

"Sounds like you have a wonderful support group."

"I couldn't have gotten through my struggles without them. Garrett's mom has been amazing, too. And of course, Garrett's brothers. Jake and Carol were here earlier with baby Nita, but they left already. Nita was getting fussy and needed to go home for her nap. Do you know Carol? Have you seen the baby?"

"I met Carol before Jake married her, when she was working for him as his personal assistant. But I don't know her very well. I haven't seen the baby yet. I sent a gift when she was born. But she must be about four or five months old by now."

"I didn't know Carol very well at first, either. But I'm becoming really close to her and the baby. Ivy adores them, too. She thinks her cousin Nita is the most wonderful being on earth."

"It's nice that you and Carol formed a bond and that your children will grow up together." Lizzie wanted Tokoni to have that type of family, too, the loving, caring kind every child should have.

"Maybe you could join us for lunch sometime."

"You and Carol?"

"Yes."

"Thank you. I'd like that." After they exchanged numbers, programming them into their phones, Lizzie asked, "Have you and Garrett set a wedding date?"

"Not yet. I want to complete my parole first. But Garrett didn't want to wait to adopt Ivy, so he started those proceedings months ago."

Lizzie smiled. "It sure seems to have worked out."

Meagan smiled, as well. "It definitely has."

Just as their conversation came to a close, Max and Garrett returned with Ivy in tow. Garrett was carrying her. He approached Meagan, and the child leaned forward to kiss her mommy.

Lizzie's heart ached from the sweet sight.

After the smooch ended, Garrett and Meagan took their leave, hauling their little princess over to the dance floor, where a kid-friendly band prepared to play Disney tunes.

In the moment that followed, Lizzie said to Max, "Meagan invited me to have lunch sometime with her and Carol."

"That's nice. I'm glad she included you in the girly stuff."

"She's easy to talk to. We discussed all sorts of things." She quickly added, "But I didn't tell her what you said about wishing that we could adopt Tokoni. There was no point in saying anything about that."

"I haven't told anyone that, either, not when there's no way to make it happen." He bumped her shoulder with his, his jacket grazing her arm. "Unless we suck it up and get married."

Her jaw nearly hit the floor. "Please tell me that you're kidding. That you didn't mean that."

"Of course I was kidding. You didn't really think…" He hesitated, frowned, blew out a choppy breath. "Besides, in order for something like that to work, we'd have to fake everyone out and pretend to be a real couple."

Lizzie's tiara was starting to feel uncomfortably heavy. "Meagan wondered if we were having a secret affair."

His voice turned grainy. "Yeah, people sometimes wonder about that. But in order for this to work, we would have to split up after the adoption with an amicable divorce. That way, we could co-parent Tokoni and still hang out as friends."

She couldn't believe what was coming out of his mouth. "Listen to yourself, Max. You're plotting the details. You're actually starting to think about it."

"I'm just thinking out loud."

"About us faking a marriage." Confused, she shook her head. "Do you know how crazy that sounds?"

"You're right." He cleared the roughness from his throat. "I shouldn't have mentioned it."

Lizzie shifted her gaze to the parents and kids and happy festivities. Everywhere she looked, she saw what she and Max were missing. But no matter how badly it hurt, entering into a phony marriage wasn't the answer.

Was it?

Six

At 1:45 a.m. Lizzie was still awake, alone in the dark, staring at the red digits on the clock.

She couldn't stop thinking about Ivy's party and the conversation she'd had with Max.

About marrying him.

Or not marrying him.

Or adopting Tokoni.

Or not adopting him.

She wasn't supposed to be letting that discussion spin around in her brain. Yet she couldn't seem to get it out of her mind.

Her only solution was to work even harder to find prospective parents for Tokoni. To sleep tonight and get up tomorrow, refreshed and ready to go. But that was easier said than done. She would probably be up for the rest of the night, fighting this battle.

And it was all Max's fault. If he hadn't tossed that

fake marriage idea out there, she wouldn't be in this insomnia mess.

Just as she cursed him, her cell phone rang.

She jumped to attention. Was it Max, having the same wide-awake struggle as her? God, she hoped not. He was the last person she wanted to talk to.

She reached for the blaring device, where it sat on her nightstand. Sure enough, it was him. His name flashed on the screen, way too bright in the dark. But instead of ignoring him, like she should've, she answered the damned call.

"What do you want?" she asked.

"I knew you would be up," he replied, undaunted by her frustration. "I can't sleep, either. Can I come over?"

She switched on the lamp beside her bed and shot a pissy glance at the clock. Three minutes had passed since she last looked at it. "Do you know what time it is?"

"Yeah, it's almost two. And I'm going to lose my freaking mind if you don't let me come over."

"All right. Fine." She gave in. If she didn't, she would only lie awake, even more embattled than before. "But you better bring some donuts. I need some comfort food."

"I'll stop by a convenience store on the way over and get a package of the powdered kind, the mini ones you used to eat when we were kids. Those always made you feel better."

"Get two packages." If she was going to pig out on itty-bitty donuts, she might as well do it right.

"Sure thing. I'll see you soon."

He ended the call, leaving her staring at the phone. What had she just gotten herself into, agreeing to entertain Max in the wee hours of the morning?

She got dressed, climbing into the nearest jeans and

T-shirt. She certainly wasn't going to answer the door in her short little satin chemise. Lizzie always wore fancy lingerie to bed. Her mom used to do that, too. But she shouldn't be likening herself to her mother right now. She'd already draped herself in Mama's diamonds earlier.

Hoping that a cup of tea would help soothe her nerves, she entered her bright white kitchen and filled an old-fashioned teakettle with water. She'd bought it at an antiques store, intending to use it as a flowerpot on her patio, but changed her mind and kept it on her stove top instead.

Anxious about seeing Max, she riffled through the tin container where she stored her tea bags and chose a fragrant herbal blend.

She sat at the chrome-and-glass dining table in the morning room, adjacent to the kitchen, and waited for the whistle.

Finally, when the kettle sang its song, she removed it from the flame and fixed her tea. She put an empty cup on the counter for Max, in case he wanted some, too.

He arrived with the donuts. He handed them to her, and she offered him the tea. He opted for orange juice, getting into her fridge and pouring it himself. He was attired in the same *Star Wars* T-shirt he'd worn to the party, only he was wearing it with plaid pajama bottoms instead of a velvet tuxedo.

"I can't believe you went out of the house like that," she said.

"What can I say? I'm still the same dork I always was." He grinned and toasted her with his juice.

"Stop that." It was bad enough that he was here, rumpled from bed; she didn't need him smiling like a sexy loon.

"Stop what?"

"Nothing. Never mind." She couldn't tell him how hot he looked. Better for him to assume that he looked like a dork.

He finally stopped grinning. "I can't quit thinking about us adopting Tokoni, Lizzie."

"I know. Me, too." She carried the donuts into the morning room, where she'd left her tea. She brought a stack of napkins, as well, certain she would need them.

Max followed her, and they sat across from each other. The blinds on the window that normally bathed the table in natural light were closed. Typically, Lizzie used this room for breakfast, not for middle-of-the-night snacks.

She tore into the donuts and ate the first package, right off the bat. They tasted like the processed junk they were, cheap and stale, but satisfying, too.

"Do you want one?" she asked him.

He shook his head. "Do you think we should just do it?"

"Do what? Adopt Tokoni?" She grabbed a napkin and wiped her mouth with shaky hands. "We can't."

"We could if we followed my plan."

"And get married?" Her hands shook even more. "Then divorced later? That's cheating."

"So you're suggesting that we should stay married instead? Cripes, Lizzie, that wouldn't work."

"No." Absolutely, positively no. "I'm saying that faking a marriage is cheating and that we shouldn't do it at all. It's not fair to Tokoni's mother."

"But we'd be good parents. The best we could be to her son."

"That still doesn't give us permission to bend the rules. And what about Losa? How are we supposed to convince her that our ruse is real?"

"We'll just tell her that our quest for finding Tokoni

a home created feelings for each other that we never knew we had."

She opened the second package of donuts. "Feelings?"

"Yeah, you know." He made a sour face. "We'll tell Losa that we've fallen head-over-stupid-heels in love."

"Gee, what a nice, romantic way to put it. And if your sickly expression is any indication of how in love you are, this story you cooked up is never going to fly."

"Stop giving me such a hard time. You look miserable, too."

"That's because I don't want to get married."

"I don't, either. But I want to be Tokoni's father, and I want you to be his mother. And I don't know how else to make that happen."

Heaven help them, Lizzie thought. He sounded so beautifully sincere, so deep and true, that a marriage based on a lie was beginning to seem like the right thing to do. "Do you really think we could pull this off?"

"Yes, I do. But we would have to fake it with everyone, even friends and family. We couldn't let it slip that we're only doing it for Tokoni or that we plan to get divorced later."

"Won't the divorce seem suspicious, so soon after the adoption?"

"Not if we say that we misunderstood our feelings for each other and mixed it up with our love for the boy. Besides, when people see how amicable our divorce is and how easily we've remained friends, there shouldn't be any cause for concern."

She imagined having Tokoni as her forever son, of sharing him with Max, of seeing this through. "I want to be his mom as much as you want to be his dad."

He leaned forward, lifting the hind legs of his chair off the floor. "Then let's go for it."

She looked into the vastness of his eyes. By now she could barely breathe. But she agreed, anyway.

"Okay," she said. "But what's our first step?" Besides sitting here, losing the last of their sanity? Her heart was pounding so fast she feared she might topple over.

He wasn't grounded, either, not with the way he was tipping his chair. "I think we should start by talking to Losa."

"Should we go see her?"

"Truthfully, I'd rather call her with the news." He dropped his chair back onto the floor with a thud. "In fact, we can do that later today."

Lizzie wasn't ready. "I need more time than that."

"What for?"

"To work on a script for us to follow."

"Winging it would be easier for me."

"I'd prefer to research what I'm going to say." She always prepared herself for proper speeches. "I can't just spout it off the top of my head."

"And I can't refer to something you drummed up. It'll sound canned."

She blew out a sigh. Already they were having problems, and they weren't even an official couple yet.

He glanced at the darkened window. "Maybe I should do it alone. It isn't necessary for both of us to call her, and it'll probably make me more nervous to have you there, anyway, with your handy-dandy script."

Lizzie considered his point. Lying to Losa was bad enough, but doing it together might make it worse, especially if they were out of sync. "All right, but you should go home now and try to get some rest. It won't help your cause if you're half asleep when you profess these phony feelings of ours."

"Okay, but you better not change your mind about marrying me between now and then."

"I won't." Because as afraid as she was of becoming Max's temporary wife, she was more afraid of losing the child they so desperately wanted.

Max did it. He'd talked to Losa. And now he was back at Lizzie's house, sitting on her artfully designed patio, with its built-in barbecue and portable bar, preparing to tell her how the discussion went. He glanced around and noticed that the greenery seemed far more tropical than he recalled it being in the past, as if she'd gotten inspired by their trip to Nulah and the private gardens at the resort where they'd stayed. But this wasn't the time to comment on her plants and flowers.

"I think Losa believed me," he said.

"You *think* she believed you?" Lizzie's blue eyes locked on to his. "What's that supposed to mean?"

"It means that I told her everything I was supposed to tell her, and it seems like she bought it. Of course I felt like I was going to have a panic attack when I got to the part about how we'd fallen in love during our search to find Tokoni a family. But I played up how long you and I have known each other and how close we've always been and all that. I tried to make it sound plausible." Even now his heart was roaring in his ears, the panic he'd endured still skirting through his blood. "Luckily, I didn't have to fake the part about how much we wanted Tokoni. That was easy to say."

Lizzie looked as nervous as he felt. "Is she going to let us adopt him?"

"She said that she can't make that determination until after we're married and start the process, like any other applicants would have to do. Legally, she can't promise him to us until we meet the requirements. But she did seem eager for us to come back after the wedding, so we can all meet in person again and discuss the specifics."

She appeared to relax, her shoulders not nearly as tense. "That seems like a positive sign."

"I thought so, too. I told her that we're planning on having a traditional ceremony. I didn't want her to think that we were going to elope or exclude our family and friends. To me, that didn't seem like what a happily engaged couple would do. I did stress, however, that we were eager to be together and bring Tokoni into our lives, so the wedding would be sooner than later."

"Sounds like you did a good job of presenting us as the type of parents Tokoni's mother wanted him to have."

He'd sure as hell tried. "Thanks. But now we really do need to hire a wedding planner and get this thing going."

"Maybe Garrett can recommend one of the events coordinators his hotel uses."

"I'll have to talk to him about it. But first I need to tell him and Jake the same story I told Losa." Only this time Max would be lying to his brothers, something he wasn't looking forward to.

"I need to tell my friends, too. And decide who is going to be part of my bridal party. I've been a bridesmaid before, so I have an inkling of what it entails."

Max nodded. He was also experienced in that regard. He and Garrett had shared the responsibility of being the best men in Jake's wedding.

She made a pained face. "What should I do about my dad? If we're having a traditional ceremony, should I adhere to protocol and ask him to walk me down the aisle?"

"I don't know, Lizzie. That's up to you." He couldn't make that determination for her. Nor did he want to.

"Damn, there's so much to think about, so much to do. I'm already getting overwhelmed."

"Me, too." She smoothed the front of her button-down blouse, fussing with the starched material, almost as if it were the lacy bodice of a wedding gown. "What about our living arrangements? Am I supposed to move in with you after we're married?"

"That makes the most sense. My house is bigger, and you can use one of the rooms in the guest wing, without anyone being the wiser."

"What about your maid service? Won't they notice that we're not staying together?"

"We can stage the master suite to give the impression that you're sleeping there. We can stage your room, too, so it appears as if we have a female visitor, a reclusive celebrity or someone that they're never going to see. They're not going to suspect it's you. Besides, it's a highly secure company, with housekeepers who are screened to work with wealthy clients and protect their privacy."

"If I move into your mansion, what should I do about this place?"

"You can say that you're going to rent it out for vacationers and whatnot, keeping it furnished the way it is. It would be an ideal condo for that."

"Except that I won't actually be renting it. I don't want out-of-towners staying in my home."

"That part doesn't matter. No one is going to delve that deeply into your business affairs." He considered another aspect of the plans. "If we're going to announce our engagement, then I need to hurry up and buy you a ring."

"You're right. Everyone will be asking to see it. Whenever one of my friends gets engaged, that's the first thing that comes up."

He didn't doubt it. "I'll arrange for a jeweler to bring

some rings by for you to choose from. We can meet at my house, maybe later in the week."

She frowned at her left hand, where the bauble was going to go. "I'll be sure to return it to you after the divorce."

He shook his head, refusing her offer. "I don't want it back."

"But you could resell it."

"I'd rather that you kept it. You can lock it away with the jewelry your mom gave you, as a keepsake or investment or whatever."

"What about a wedding band for you?"

"I'll have the jeweler bring those, too. We can do it in one fell swoop. And hopefully with the least amount of fanfare possible." But even as he said it, he knew it wasn't going to be a casual process, not when it involved a ritual created for people who were supposed to be in love.

Although Lizzie had been to Max's house more times than she could count, she'd never expected that she would be living there. Yet that was what would be happening, soon enough.

The three-story mansion had a spiral staircase in the center of the home that curved with an air of mystery. There was also a large entryway, a woodsy den, a formal drawing room and a screening room. On the third floor was a ballroom with a wraparound balcony, designed for glamorous parties. The original owner was the head of a movie studio, way back when.

The servants' quarters were located on the first level, directly off the kitchen, but Max didn't have a live-in staff. The maid service he used kept things tidy, and when he wasn't eating out, he cooked for himself. A chef wasn't necessary.

The mansion itself probably wasn't necessary, either, Lizzie thought. But Max had bought it to console the poor battered boy he'd once been, fascinated by its rich 1930s charm.

Today she and Max occupied the den, waiting for the jeweler to arrive. While she sat on an art deco settee, he stood beside the fireplace, with the painting of Lady Ari showcased above it. She couldn't deny how nicely the artwork complemented the spot he'd chosen for it.

Was this really happening? Was she actually going to become his bride?

"I'm getting stage fright," she said.

"About picking out rings?"

"About all of it. It's weird, but I wish my mom was here to help me through it. She loved big fancy occasions."

"I'm sorry you have to face this without her."

As much as her mother's suicide hurt, Lizzie couldn't bear to hate her for it. "She would have liked you, Max. This house would have impressed her, too."

"I've been thinking that we could have the wedding here, that we could do the ceremony outside, on the lawn, and then head up to the ballroom for the reception."

She studied him: his tall, trim physique, his shiny black hair falling just shy of his shoulders. He'd never had a picnic on his lawn, let alone a wedding. He'd never used his ballroom before, either. He wasn't keen on entertaining, even if his house was wonderfully suited for it. "Are you sure you're comfortable with that?"

He shrugged. "At this point, I'd rather do it here than somewhere else. Plus it'll be easier than trying to book another venue. I'd like to set the date for two months from now. I don't want to hold up the adoption any longer than that."

"Me, neither. But we'd better be prepared for a nonstop venture, if we're going to get everything done by then."

"We'll just have to find a wedding planner who's able to speed through it."

"I'll have to put a rush on finding a dress, too." But for now she didn't have a clue what type of gown she was going to wear. "Gosh, can you imagine how strange it's going to be, with you and me, reciting vows? Talk about being nervous."

He scowled, hard and deep. "They're just words, Lizzie."

"Words about love and commitment and things that don't pertain to us."

"We're committed to Tokoni, and that's all that matters."

"You're right. I need to try to relax and go with the phony-wedding flow."

"Yes, you do. And so do I." He pasted a smile on his face. "This is supposed to be a joyous occasion. We don't want the jeweler to think there's something wrong with us."

She smiled, as well, practicing her bride-to-be expression. "This will be a good test of how we're supposed to behave."

He glanced at a cuckoo clock on the wall, a quirky old timepiece from the same era as the house. "He should be here soon."

"I wish he would hurry." She was eager to get the ring thing over with. But thank goodness they had the luxury of the jeweler coming to them, instead of them having to go to him.

Max's gaze roamed over her. "You look pretty, by the way."

"Thank you." She was attired in a stylish tweed ensemble with her hair twisted into a neat chignon. "I tried to keep it classy."

"You always do."

"I noticed that you donned a jacket."

"Yeah." He smoothed the lapels of his sleek black sports coat. "I've got Batman on underneath, though." He opened his jacket and showed her his T-shirt.

"At least you didn't sleep in it." She gave him a double take. "Or did you?"

He laughed. "I'll never tell."

She laughed, too. "My fiancé is weird."

"Your fiancé, huh? Look who's trying out the lingo."

"After today, it will be official." Her ring would seal the deal. "So I better get used to calling you that."

"Until you have to start calling me your husband."

"Then my ex-husband." She turned serious. "Are you going to draw up a prenup for me to sign?"

"Why would I do that?"

"To protect your money. Typically, that's what rich people do when they're getting married, and you have a lot more to lose than I do."

"I don't need to protect my assets from you." He came over and sat beside her. "You're the person I trust most in this world."

"Me, too. With you." And that was precisely why they were adopting a child together. "We're going to be awesome parents."

"The best," he agreed. "And don't worry about the wedding expenses. I'm going to pay for everything."

"You don't have to do that."

"I want to." He touched her cheek, then lifted his hand away. "But what am I going to do during the part of the ceremony where I'm supposed to kiss my bride?"

She wet her lips, a bit too quickly. "You'll have to kiss her, I guess."

"She's going to have to kiss me back, too."

Her pulse fluttered at her neck, as soft as a butterfly, as sexy as a summer breeze. "Yes, she will."

As they both fell silent, she glanced away, trapped in feelings she couldn't seem to control. She didn't want to imagine what the wedding kiss was going to be like.

Still, she wondered how it would unfold. Would he whisper something soft and soothing before he leaned into her? Would their mouths be slightly open, their eyes completely closed? Would she sigh and melt against him, like a princess being awakened by the wrong prince? Just thinking about it made her feel forbidden.

Sucking in her breath, she shifted her gaze to his. She saw that he was studying her, as if he sensed what was going on in her head. Uncomfortable in her own skin, she clasped her hands on her lap. She'd been fighting these types of urges for what seemed like forever, and now the ache had gone warm and rogue.

Brrrrinng.

The security buzzer sounded, alerting them that the jeweler had arrived at the front gate.

What timing.

Max jumped off the settee and took his phone out of his pocket. He punched out a key code and opened the gate with an app he'd designed. When he glanced up, he studied her again. "You okay, Lizzie?"

She nodded, even if she wasn't. He'd certainly recovered much easier than she had. But he wasn't the one who'd drifted into la-la land. "I'm fine."

"All right, then. I better go." He headed for the door.

"I'll stay here." And collect her composure.

While he was gone, she opened her purse and removed

her compact, checking her lipstick. Nothing was out of place, of course. Max's mouth hadn't come anywhere near hers.

He returned with an older gentleman, formal in nature, who introduced himself as Timothy. The three of them gathered around a nineteenth-century mahogany card table, a focal point in the den, where Timothy could set up his portable cases. He started with the engagement rings, sweeping his hand across the impressive display once it was ready.

The diamonds were big and beautiful and dazzling. Enormous rubies, emeralds and sapphires dazzled the eye, too. But Lizzie struggled to focus. She was still stuck on that future kiss. She even bit down on her bottom lip, trying to inflict pain as a conditioned response to keep her mind off it.

Her method didn't work. Biting her lip just made her hungrier for the man she was going to marry.

"Wow. Check this out." Max lifted a ring from its slot. An oval ruby with two perfectly matched half-moon diamonds surrounding it. He said to Timothy, "This one is downright fiery." He glanced at Lizzie. "Like her hair."

His comment made her skin tingle. But she was already immersed in all kinds of heat.

Timothy glanced at her, too. Then back at Max. With a smile, he said, "Rubies are often associated with fire and passion. That particular stone is six carats and is a star ruby, a rare variety. See the starry points in the center? How they magically glide across the surface? It's an optical phenomenon known as asterism."

Lizzie finally spoke up. "It's stunning," she said about the ring. The ruby, the star, the diamonds, every glittering aspect of it.

"Try it on," Max said.

She placed it on her left hand and held it up to view. It felt right. Too right. Too beautiful. Too perfect.

Both men watched her, silent in their observations. She glanced at the painting of Lady Ari. And for a jarring instant, it almost seemed as if the goddess was watching her, too.

"That's the one, Lizzie." Max spoke up, pulling her attention back to him.

She nodded. "It is, isn't it?" She couldn't refuse the ring, no matter how much she wanted to.

Timothy suggested a petite pavé diamond band to go with it, and her bridal set was complete. Pavé was a French word, and in this context it meant that the ring was paved with diamonds, creating an unbroken circle of sparkle and light.

When Timothy presented the men's wedding bands, Max's demeanor changed. He wasn't as self-assured as when he'd been examining rings for her.

Lizzie took the liberty of choosing a design for him—a simply styled, highly masculine piece dotted with black diamonds. There was a ruby among the gems, too. Just one, she noticed, the same fiery color as hers.

When he put it on, he frowned.

"You don't like it?" she asked.

"No, I do. Very much."

Maybe too much? she wondered. Well, at least she wasn't suffering alone. They were in this torturous situation together.

And now they would both have bloodred rubies to prove it.

Seven

Max took his brothers out for a steak dinner and ordered a fancy gold bottle of Cristal. He did everything he could to make it a celebratory occasion and tell them his news, repeating the same tale he'd told Losa. At this stage of the lie, he had it memorized.

Jake accepted it easily, lifting his glass in an immediate toast. But that was Jake for you, with his half-cocked smile, fashionable wardrobe and stylishly messy hair. He'd probably never given Max's relationship with Lizzie more than a passing glance. Either that or he'd assumed the platonic part was bogus and they'd been sleeping together for years. Prior to settling down, Jake had been a playboy, dating actresses and models and whoever else caught his roving eye.

And then there was Garrett, with his protective personality and proper ways. He'd joined in on the toast, too, but now that it was over, he appeared to be analyzing Max. Was he questioning the validity of his story? Did he suspect the truth?

Max frowned. He didn't like being judged and especially not by a man who'd helped him fight his childhood battles. "Why are you looking at me like that?"

"Because I want you to say it one more time," Garrett replied.

"Say what?"

"That you're in love with Lizzie."

Shit, Max thought. *Shit.* He grabbed his champagne and took a swig, needing the buzz. "Why are you goading me to repeat myself?"

"I'm not goading you, little brother. I just want to hear you say it."

"I already did." And it had taken every ounce of strength inside him to rattle off those phony feelings. Topping it off, he was immersed in images of how Lizzie had looked when they talked about kissing at the wedding. Rubies and diamonds and dreamy musings. How was he supposed to deal with all that?

Jake put down his fork. He'd been enjoying his big old rib-eye steak, but now he watched Max and Garrett like a tennis match.

Garrett turned to Jake. "Does Max look like he's about ready to jump out that window to you?" He gestured to the view. The restaurant was on the tenth floor, overlooking the city.

"Actually, he does." A slow grin spread across Jake's face. "But I was like that, too, when I first realized how I felt about Carol."

"Ditto," Garrett said. "About Meagan."

Now Max wanted to wring both of their necks. Apparently, Garrett had only been kidding around, setting Max up and pulling Jake into it, too.

Max shook his head. Typically, Garrett wasn't a jokester. "When did you get to be such a wise guy?"

"Since you brought us here and told us you were getting married. But in all seriousness, I was surprised to hear it. I never thought you and Lizzie were anything more than friends." Garrett sat straight and tall in his chair, impeccable, as always. "But you already explained that the adoption brought you closer."

Just in case the lies weren't clear, Max reiterated, "We're not getting married because of the adoption. But it is part of the reason we scheduled the wedding so soon."

Jake interjected, "I had a short engagement, too. But that's what sometimes happens when children are involved."

Max managed a smile. "Oh, that's right. While I was on my sabbatical, searching for the meaning of life and volunteering at an orphanage, you were at a wild party in the Caribbean impregnating your assistant."

Jake chuckled. "It was just that one weekend. Speaking of which, are you and Lizzie planning a big family? Maybe more adoptions? Or a few seedlings of your own?"

Max all but blinked. They hadn't even gotten the first kid and already they were being prodded to have more? "We're just going to focus on Tokoni for now." It was as good an answer as any and certainly more diplomatic than admitting that they would be divorced long before the possibility of other children ever came up.

"I was panicked at first about becoming a dad." Jake returned to his steak, cutting into it again. "But not anymore. My wife and daughter are everything to me."

"I'm not scared of being a father." Max was thrilled about that. It was being Lizzie's husband that freaked him out. To combat those fears, he admitted, "I am a little anxious about the wedding." Before either of his brothers could question him, he chalked up his anxiety to being a rushed groom. "There's just so much to do in such a short amount of time. I'm glad you guys will be there, standing up for me." They'd already agreed to be his best men. He addressed Garrett. "Can you recommend a wedding planner? Maybe someone you use at the hotel or an associate of theirs?"

"Sure. I'll email you a list of names. And don't worry, it'll turn out great."

"It definitely will," Jake agreed. "But don't forget about the honeymoon, too."

Max quickly replied, "That's already been worked out. We'll be going back to Nulah to start the adoption proceedings. But we'll still get to hang out at the resort where we stayed before and enjoy the beach." Only on this trip, they would have to share a bungalow, like a husband and wife would be expected to do. And that was the part about being married that petrified him the most. Wanting Lizzie, he thought, more than he ever had before. But not being able to have her.

Within a week after getting engaged, Max and Lizzie hired a whirlwind of a planner who would be consulting with them at every turn. And if that wasn't enough to keep them busy, Max had decided to revamp his yard for the ceremony, with a custom gazebo surrounded by a garden. Lizzie already thought his yard made a stunning statement, with its parklike acreage, but now it was going to be even prettier. She walked beside him as he explained work that would soon be underway.

He said, "I told the landscaper I wanted something tropical. I showed him pictures of the private gardens at the resort in Nulah to give him a feel for what I'm after.

I assumed that you would approve, since you incorporated that style onto your patio."

"I only dabbled with a few extra plants." Nonetheless, she was impressed that he'd noticed her effort.

He gestured in the distance. "They're going to build a stone walkway from the back of the house that curves around to the gazebo and serves as part of the wedding aisle. Then all the way around that will be the garden, with a waterfall fountain and some intricate little pathways."

"So essentially, we'll be getting married in the middle of the garden?" She gazed at the lawn, imagining the changes in her mind. Clearly, the landscaper and his crew would be working around the clock to complete the job. "It sounds spectacular."

"I figured if we're going to do it, we might as well do it right. I also thought it would make a nice spot for Tokoni later, for when he plays out here. It's too bad that coconut trees don't grow in this environment or I would add some of those, too."

"To give Tokoni a sense of home? We're going to have to take him back to Nulah for vacations so he doesn't lose his connection to it."

"We'll definitely do that, as often as we can." Max smiled. "I can't wait until he's our son."

"Me, too. It makes all this wedding stuff worthwhile." She breathed in the late-spring air. It would be summer by the time the ceremony took place. "I haven't talked to my dad yet. I haven't even told him that I'm getting married."

"You're going to have to do that soon, Lizzie."

"I know. But I haven't been completely remiss. I called my friends. Not everyone I associate with, but the ones I asked to be my bridesmaids. I spent an entire day on the phone, chatting with my gal pals and pretending to be in love." But she knew Max had done the same thing when he'd dined with his brothers. "It was interesting, how mixed the reactions were. Some of my friends were surprised, but others claimed that they knew all along that something was going on between us."

He checked her out, softly, slowly. "Funny, how people can't tell lust from love."

Her skin turned warm, her blood tingling in her body. "At least it's working in our favor."

He didn't respond. Instead, his stare got bolder, hungrier, as if he couldn't seem to help himself.

Lizzie's mouth went dry. If they were a real couple, heading into a genuine marriage, would they pull each other to the ground right here and now, desperate to make love on their future wedding site?

Pushing those dangerous thoughts out of her mind, she glanced away from him, breaking his stare.

He walked closer to where the gazebo was going to be, and she fell into step with him, eager to get past the heat that warmed her blood. But nonetheless, an inferno ensued. Clearly, he was still feeling it, too.

Finally, she started a new conversation by saying, "I chose blue, green and purple for the colors, with shades ranging from turquoise to magenta."

He squinted. "Colors?"

"For the wedding. It's called a peacock palette." She envisioned it being deep and rich and vibrant. "I spent hours on the net, looking at color combinations and kept coming back to that one. I hope that's all right with you."

"Sure." He stopped walking. "It sounds beautiful. I wonder what peacock symbolism is. I'm always interested in the spiritual meaning connected to animals."

She noticed how the sun shone upon his hair, creating blue-black effects. "That's the Lakota in you."

"Yes, I suppose it is." He removed his phone from his pocket. "Why don't I look it up right now?"

Still studying him, she waited while he did an internet search.

He shared the results with her. "First off, they're birds in the pheasant family, and only the male is referred to as a peacock. The female is a peahen, and both are peafowl. In terms of spirituality, some of the peacock and peahen's gifts include beauty, integrity and the ability to see into the past, present and future."

Fascinated by it all, she said, "That's quite a résumé."

"It's the eye shape on the feathers that gives them the gift of sight." He kept reading, explaining the meanings. "In relation to human spirituality, beauty and integrity is achieved when someone shows his or her true colors, so that's where all those colors come into play."

Suddenly Lizzie took pause, concerned about what he was saying and how it related to them. "Maybe we shouldn't use the peacock palette."

He glanced up from his phone. "Why not?"

"Because we're not showing our true colors. This whole thing is a lie."

"No, it isn't. Not if you look at it on a deeper scale. What we feel for Tokoni is our truth, our true colors, and adopting him is what our wedding is about to us." He glanced at his phone again. "It also says that peacocks have an association to resurrection, like the phoenix that rises out of the ashes. And isn't that what we're doing? Rising out of the ashes of our pasts and creating new lives for ourselves by becoming Tokoni's parents?"

When he lifted his gaze, she got caught up in the feeling, looking deeply into his eyes. "I'm so glad I'm going to share a child with you."

"Me, too, with you." He fell silent for a moment, looking as intently at her as she was at him. Then he asked, "So you're keeping the peacock palette, right?"

"Yes." She broke eye contact, needing to free herself from his spell. "I'm going to keep it."

"Do you think you could add a bit of gold?"

"Gold?" she parroted.

"To the color scheme. It would be cool if your dress had some gold on it."

He was putting in a special wardrobe request? Then it hit her. Lady Ari was wearing a gold dress in the painting he'd bought. "Do you want me to wear my hair loose, too?" Long and free and wild, like the goddess's?

"It would certainly look pretty that way." He reached out as if he meant to run his fingers through her hair, but he lowered his hand without doing it. "But that's up to you."

"I'll talk to my stylist about it and decide when the time comes." She didn't want to sound too eager to please him, not with how romantic he was making her feel. "What do you think of Ivy and Nita as the flower girls?" she asked, moving the discussion away from her and onto the people who would be part of procession. "Meagan and Carol could walk down the aisle with them. Meagan could hold Ivy's hand, and Carol could carry Nita."

"That's a great idea, having them participate in the ceremony, especially since my brothers are going to be in it, too."

"I'm having lunch with Meagan and Carol tomorrow, so I'll talk to them about it then. Meagan invited us to her house." No men, she thought, only women and children. But Max and his brothers had already had their meeting.

"So, what should we do about a ring bearer?" he asked. "Who should we get to do that?"

"I wish it could be Tokoni." Her heart swelled just

thinking about him. "But Losa would never let us bring him to the States to be in our wedding." Tokoni didn't even know that she and Max planned to adopt him. He wouldn't be informed about his prospective parents until everything was approved.

"I wish it could be him, too," Max said.

"So maybe we'll just skip having a ring bearer?" She couldn't fathom having another boy in place of him.

Max agreed, then said, "We can have an adoption party for Tokoni later, like Garrett and Meagan did for Ivy. Also, I think in lieu of wedding gifts, we should ask our guests to donate to the orphanage."

"That's perfect." Exactly as it should be. Not only would their marriage serve as the catalyst for adopting Tokoni, it would benefit all the other children there, too.

Meagan, Carol and Lizzie gathered around a coffee table in the living room of the residence where Meagan lived with Garrett. The elegant beachfront home was located on a cliff that overlooked the hotel and resort he owned.

They'd already had lunch, a taco feast Meagan had cooked, and now Lizzie was analyzing her companions and thinking about what she'd learned about them so far.

Meagan looked soft and natural in a chambray shirt, faded jeans and pale beige cowboy boots. Her long silky hair was plaited into a single braid, hanging down the center of her back. Little Ivy was dressed in western wear, too, but her outfit was much fancier and in shades of pink.

Both mother and daughter loved horses. Garrett's resort offered horseback riding along the beach, making the activity easily accessible to them. In fact, Meagan still worked as a stable hand in the original job Garrett had given her when she was first released from prison, even though she was engaged to him now. She'd kept the job to pay back the restitution she owed and meet the requirements of her parole.

Lizzie glanced over at Carol, who was a lovely strawberry blonde with a curvy figure and sparkling green eyes. She still worked in her original job, too, as Jake's personal assistant. But nowadays, she and Jake had baby Nita to consider, so they took the infant with them to the office, where Jake had built an on-site nursery especially for their daughter. A nanny was also on hand to help. Lizzie thought it sounded like a wonderful setup.

Carol was a former foster kid who'd lost her family. In that sense, she and her husband shared tragic histories. But as youths, they'd handled their grief in opposing ways. While Jake was running wild, Carol compensated by being a bit too well behaved. Lizzie understood. She'd become an overly proper person herself.

She turned her attention to Carol's daughter. The baby was asleep in a carrier, with two-and-a-half-year-old Ivy sitting on the floor, watching her like a mother hen. Even if they weren't blood related, the children looked like cousins, with their dark hair, chubby cheeks and golden-brown skin.

Tokoni would fit right in, Lizzie thought. He was tailor-made for this group. She was certain that he was going to love being part of Max's foster family.

Even Lizzie was beginning to love it, with how warm and welcoming Meagan and Carol were being to her.

Would that change after the divorce, creating a divide between Lizzie and the other women, or wouldn't it matter, since she and Max intended to remain close once the marriage was over?

"Did Max take you shopping for your ring?" Carol

asked, drawing her into conversation. "Or did he choose it by himself?"

"We were together when he bought it," she replied. "But he picked it out."

"It's absolutely gorgeous." Carol leaned over to get a closer look. They were seated side by side on a comfy sofa, with a sweeping view of the ocean. "It's sexy for an engagement ring."

Fire and passion, Lizzie thought, burning deep within. "Max said it reminded him of my hair."

"I can see why." Carol smiled. "That ruby is perfect for you. I think all of our men did a great job of picking out our rings." She held out her hand. "Jake had mine made in the style of a Claddagh ring because my great-grandparents were from Ireland, and he wanted to honor my heritage. He gave it to me before I'd agreed to marry him because Claddagh rings can be worn if you're single, in a relationship, engaged or married. It depends which hand you wear it on and which way the crown at the top is facing. Mine is obviously in the married position now."

"What an interesting concept." Lizzie gazed at the ring. Along with the gold crown, it boasted a dazzling pink diamond in the shape of a heart being held by two engraved hands. The band itself was etched like a feather, a Native American detail that appeared to be woven into the Irish design. "It's very romantic."

Carol replied, "I didn't want to marry Jake at first because he was so opposed to falling in love. I loved him before he realized that he loved me."

"That happened to me, too," Meagan said. "I became aware of my feelings for Garrett before he recognized his for me. But with how complex our relationship was, we were both struggling with it."

Lizzie shifted on the sofa. According to the lie she

and Max had concocted, they'd embraced their feelings at the same time.

Meagan continued by saying, "Garrett gave me a blue diamond in my engagement ring because I'm fascinated with blue roses. I learned about them through my sister-in-law. She studied a Victorian practice called the language of flowers, where couples used to send each other messages by using plants and flowers. Blue roses aren't found in nature, so they aren't part of the Victorian practice, but they've been introduced into the modern language of flowers."

Lizzie asked, "How did the people in the Victorian era know what the plants and flowers meant?"

"There were dictionaries on the subject. But there were different versions, so it could get confusing if they weren't using the same one."

Lizzie remarked, "Max hired a landscaper to plant a big beautiful garden for the wedding. We're having the ceremony in his backyard and the reception in his ballroom."

Meagan said, "You should research the language of flowers and have the landscaper plant some flowers that have meanings that would be special to you and Max."

Lizzie thought about Tokoni. He was the most special thing between her and Max. "Do you think there are flowers or plants that represent parenthood?"

"Oh, I'm sure there are. I'll bet you can find the information online. It's so exciting that you'll be adopting that little boy." Meagan grinned. "And I was right about you and Max becoming more than just friends."

Lizzie, of course, nodded in agreement, protecting the lie. But even so, the lie was starting to seem real, with how badly she wanted to kiss him. And hold him. And feel his body pressed tightly to hers.

Before she delved too deeply into that, she said to Carol and Meagan, "I would love to have your children in my wedding." She explained her idea about having Ivy and Nita as flowers girls, with their mothers accompanying them.

Both women accepted with joyful reactions, excited about the upcoming nuptials.

Afterward, Meagan said, "This will be the second time Ivy will be a flower girl. She was in my brother Tanner's wedding. But she's going to love sharing this one with Nita."

Ivy didn't bat an eye. She continued watching the baby sleep, even tucking a fluffy yellow teddy bear close to the infant.

"Nita means bear in Jake's ancestral tongue," Carol interjected. "We picked it because of all the teddy bears we've been given as gifts for her."

"She's a beautiful baby," Lizzie said, turning to study the kids again. "And so is Ivy's connection to her." It was such a tender scene, so sweet and loving that she knew she'd made the right choice by including the children and their mothers in the ceremony.

But Lizzie wasn't out of the woods yet. She still had to marry Max and fight her touchy-feely urges for him.

Eight

Lizzie glanced around her condo. Everything was in order, neat as a pin. The decorative pillows on her sofa were plumped. The magazines on the end tables were angled just so. She had a platter of fresh-cut fruit and gourmet cheeses in the fridge, along with a liter bottle of her dad's favorite soda. She'd invited him over today.

"I hate seeing you like this," Max said.

She turned to look at him. He'd come by for moral support, but he wasn't staying. He would be leaving before her dad arrived. "I'll be all right."

"Are you sure you don't want me to hang around?" He stood in the middle of her living room, his thumbs hooked in his jeans pockets. "We can both tell him about the wedding. After all, I am the guy you're going to marry."

"I think it's better for me to do this alone." She couldn't handle sitting there, pretending to be Max's fiancée in front of her father, not with how uncomfortably romantic this wedding was beginning to make her feel. "Besides, what's the point of you expending the energy to try to become his son-in-law when we'll just be getting divorced later?"

"We've been expending that type of energy for everyone else. And at least he already knows me." He crinkled his forehead. "I'll never forget the first time I met him."

"And how awkward it was?" When they were teenagers, she'd invited Max to the house for Christmas dinner, and the three of them had stumbled through a stilted conversation, with a big professionally decorated tree in the background. After Mama died, Dad always hired someone to dress the tree. But for Lizzie that just made the glittery ornaments and twinkling lights seem fake and lonely.

Sometimes, even now, she brought Max with her on that dreaded holiday, just so she didn't have to suffer through it by herself. Last Christmas was particularly odd. Rather than going to the house, they'd dined on a catered meal at Dad's high-rise office, before he'd jetted off for an overseas business trip, leaving her and Max alone for the rest of the day.

"Yeah, it's always awkward with your dad," he said. "But how often do you see him? Once, maybe twice a year?"

"I wish I didn't feel obligated to spend every dang Christmas with him." But it had become a painful ritual neither of them had broken.

Max sent her a concerned look. "Have you decided what you're going to do?"

"If I'm going to ask him to give me away?" She released an audible breath. It was a loaded question, filled with jittery bullets. "I have mixed feelings about it."

Mixed and shaken. "I'm nervous about walking down the aisle by myself, so in that respect, it will be nice to have someone by my side. But with how distant my relationship is with him, will it even make a difference?"

"Whatever you choose to do, just remember that I'll be waiting for you at the altar."

Her temporary groom? Just thinking about kissing him at the wedding was already filling her with a flood of unwelcome warmth. She bit down on her bottom lip. This biting thing was becoming a habit.

Silent, he watched her.

She quickly said, "You'd better go. My dad will be here at two." And it was already one thirty. If anything, her father was highly punctual.

She walked Max outside, and when he leaned toward her, she panicked, her pulse pounding in her ears. He wasn't going to jump the gun and kiss her, was he? Now, like this?

She hurriedly asked, "What are you doing?"

"There's a ladybug behind you, and I want to see if it'll climb onto my finger. They're supposed to bring luck."

Good God. She glanced over her shoulder and saw the spotted beetle in question, perched on a shrub beside her door. "Sorry. I thought you were…"

"I was what?"

She turned back to face him, admitting the truth. "Going to kiss me."

"Today? While your dad is on his way over?" He glanced at her mouth, looking hot and restless and hungry. "Is that what you want me to do? Will that make it easier for you?"

She bit her lip again, chewing on her lipstick, struggling to contain her desire for him. "I think we should wait until the ceremony like we're supposed to."

He stepped back, away from the ladybug, away from her. "The gazebo. The garden. You in a long white gown."

The wedding that was messing with their heads, she thought. "I have an appointment later this week to try on dresses. It's at an exclusive bridal salon some of my friends have used. I told the owner that you want me to wear a dress with gold embellishments, so they've been gathering gowns from designers all over the world to fulfill your request."

"Really? That's awesome, Lizzie. But remember that I'm paying for everything, okay? So don't spare any expense."

And buy the best gown she could find? "I'm going to try to look the way you want me to look."

"You're always beautiful to me. I think about you all the time. In the morning when I wake up. When I'm in the shower. When I'm working. When I go to bed at night. It's frustrating, knowing you're going to be my bride."

He meant sexually frustrating, she thought. And she understood exactly how he felt. "I think about you all the time, too."

"The way I've been thinking about you?"

"Yes." She crossed her arms over her chest, trying to stop her heart from leaping into her throat.

He shifted his stance, the air between them getting thicker. "This is wrong, isn't it?"

To be torturing themselves this way? To be pushing the boundaries of their friendship? "We're supposed to know better."

He glanced toward his car, a luxury hybrid parked on the street. "I should leave now and let you get on with your day."

She nodded. They certainly couldn't remain where they were, saying intimate things to each other.

But instead of shutting him out of her thoughts, she watched him walk away, dazed by her appetite for him.

Forcing air into her lungs, Lizzie returned to the house to wait for her dad.

He arrived sharply at two. Stiff and formal, David McQueen was a tall, trim man with an impeccable posture. As always, his short graying red hair was neatly trimmed. He wore a conservative blue suit and pin-striped tie. She assumed that he'd just come from a business meeting. Even before Lizzie's mom died, he was a workaholic. But at least they'd been a family then. Sometimes he even waltzed around the parlor with Mama, bowing to her after each dance. Lizzie used to sneak down the stairs and watch her parents, fascinated by how good they looked together.

Clearing her mind, she placed the snack tray on the coffee table, with small serving plates and paper napkins. She offered him a glass of soda, over ice. He used a coaster for his drink. He always did. Dad wouldn't think of leaving damp marks on a table.

He thanked her and said, "You didn't have to go to all this trouble for me."

He put a few bite-size pieces of cheese on a plate. He took a handful of grapes, too, and some watermelon balls. A polite amount of food, she thought.

She sat across from him. Since he'd claimed the sofa, she went for a leather recliner. When she'd invited him to come over, she told him that she had something important to discuss with him. Most likely, he was waiting for her to get started. Dad wasn't one for small talk. Mama had been. She could chat about insignificant things for hours.

But at the very end, Mama's words were few. The only thing she'd written on the notepad beside her bed on that fateful day was *I'm sorry. Please be happy without me.*

Lizzie gazed across the coffee table at her dad. *Happy* wasn't part of his vocabulary. It hadn't been part of hers, either, not after she'd become a motherless child.

Their housekeeper had found the body and the note. Mama had done the deed while Dad was at work and Lizzie was at school.

"I'm getting married," she said, going right for her news.

Dad calmly replied, "I noticed the ruby on your finger when I first got here, but I didn't want to say anything in case it wasn't an engagement ring. But apparently it is." He paused. "Who's the lucky man?"

"It's Max."

"I'm glad to hear it."

"You are?" She hadn't expected him to express his opinion, least of all his approval. Normally, Dad remained neutral when it came to Lizzie's life. Then again, he'd said it in his usual cut-and-dried way.

"It never made sense to me that you weren't dating him. You two seem so suited. But it appears you both figured that out."

Lizzie nodded, playing her part as Max's fiancée. But still, she'd never suspected that her father had been analyzing her friendship with Max all this time. "It's going to be at his house, on the second Saturday in June. I'm sorry for the short notice, but we're anxious to make it happen. I hope the date isn't a problem for you, with your work schedule," she clarified.

He sat back in his seat. "Of course not. I wouldn't miss my daughter's wedding."

Well, okay, then. At least he'd confirmed that he would be there. Now on to the next phase, she thought, the next question. "Do you want to walk me down the aisle?"

"Certainly." He sipped his soda. "I'd be honored."

Did he mean that? Or was it merely the proper thing to say? With him, it was hard to tell. "Just so you know, Dad, there's a child who's part of this."

His eyes went wide. The most emotion he'd showed yet. "You're pregnant?"

"Oh, my goodness. No. I didn't mean…" Based on the fact that she'd never even slept with Max, she thought about how impossible that would have been. "We're adopting a child. A five-year-old boy from Nulah."

"The one you wrote about on your blog?"

She angled her head. "You read my blog?"

"Sometimes."

They barely communicated, but he took the time to read her work? Her father was full of surprises.

"So is he the one?" he asked again.

"Yes. It's the same child who was featured on my blog." She explained how Max had gotten close to Tokoni when he volunteered at the orphanage last year. "Then he brought me to meet Tokoni and I bonded with him, too. We're excited about making him our son." She backtracked a little. "We haven't started the adoption proceedings, but we're going to do that after the wedding."

He studied her, with eyes the same shade of blue as hers. "You'll be a good mother, Elizabeth." He quietly added, "A good wife to Max, too."

Her father was buying into her marriage, just as everyone else had done. But lying to him seemed worse. Was it because he was the only human connection she had to her mom?

I'm so sorry. Be happy without me.

Now wasn't the time to think about Mama's final farewell. But she couldn't seem to stop herself from feeling the brunt of it. "Max has always been there when I need him," she heard herself say.

Dad reached for a piece of fruit off his plate, lifting it slowly, methodically, before he ate it. "The man you marry should be there for you."

His words struck a chord. Was he blaming himself for not being there for Mama? She wanted to know what he was thinking and feeling, but she didn't have the strength to ask him. And especially not while she was sitting there, pretending that her marriage was going to be real.

Dad didn't stay long. Within no time, they wrapped things up and she walked him outside, just as she'd done with Max earlier.

"I'll keep in touch about the wedding," she said as they stood in her courtyard. "Your tuxedo, the rehearsal dinner, all that stuff."

"Tell Max how pleased I am that you two got together."

"I will." She forced a smile. "Take care."

"You, too." He gave her a pat-on-the-back hug, which was about as affectionate as he got.

After they parted ways, she returned to the house, steeped in the complications of becoming Max's wife.

Lizzie's appointment at the bridal salon was private. Being as upscale as it was, it catered to a high-end clientele and offered preferential treatment.

She'd asked Meagan and Carol to join her, and now the three of them gathered in the lavishly decorated salon, sipping Dom Pérignon from crystal flutes. They'd been offered caviar and crackers, too, but they'd declined the salty appetizer. Personally, Lizzie had never acquired a taste for it.

She glanced at her companions, glad they were here. She couldn't do this alone, not with how overwhelmed she was. She wanted them to accompany her because they were part of Max's family, and, today of all days, she needed a family connection, with as often as she'd been thinking about her mom. Her father saying that she would make a good wife triggered her emotions, too, making everything seem far too real.

The salon had arranged for a showing, with models wearing the gowns that had been selected for her. She'd already been given a keepsake pen and a printed program, so she could checkmark the styles that appealed to her.

She sat in a wingback chair, with Meagan and Carol by her side, and watched the models emerge.

Every dress was exquisite in its own way, but there was one that drew Lizzie into its long, flowing silk-and-lace allure. The creation offered a magical silhouette, embellished with crystal jewels and iridescent gold beads. A richly appliquéd bodice and chapel train with a French bustle lent the gown a sensual appeal.

Even Meagan and Carol gasped when they saw it.

Lizzie imagined it with a peacock-palette bouquet and her hair tumbling in thick red waves.

"Look how romantic that is," Carol said.

Yes, Lizzie thought. It was like something out of a wedding night fantasy. She even envisioned Max sweeping her into his arms and carrying her straight to his bed.

His bed?

She shivered from the forbidden thought. She wasn't supposed to be dwelling on her desire for Max. But she couldn't seem to control the ache it caused.

She drank more champagne, trying to cool off. But it didn't do any good. Daydreaming about the man she was going to marry swirled through her blood, heating her from the inside out.

"Are you going to mark that dress?" Meagan asked her.

Lizzie snapped to attention. "Yes." She was eager to

try it on, hoping it looked as enchanting on her as it did on the model.

She marked other gowns, as well. But her mind kept drifting back to the fantasy one.

Finally, after the show ended, she was escorted to a luxurious fitting room. Meagan and Carol came with her.

The fantasy gown was incredible. With the beautiful way the gold beads reflected the light, she looked like a princess.

Or a fire-tinged goddess, she surmised, like the painting of Lady Ari. But that was the point. The reason Max wanted her gown to be marked with gold.

"You look absolutely radiant," Meagan said. "Like a bride should."

A bride who was desperate for her groom. Lizzie squeezed her eyes shut, making her reflection disappear. But when she opened her eyes, the hungry woman in the glittering gown was still there.

Suddenly, she was afraid of how easily she'd found a dress, of how it seemed to be made just for her. "This is how it was when Max chose my ring for me."

Too right, she thought. Too perfect.

Meagan and Carol smiled, assuming she meant it in a good way. But there was nothing good about how badly she wanted to be with Max.

Two weeks before the wedding, Max awakened in a cold sweat. He sat up in bed and dragged a hand through his hair.

The closer he got to saying, "I do," the more restless he became. Hunger. Desire. Lust. He had it bad, so damned bad. Getting naked with Lizzie was all he thought about, dreamed about, fantasized about.

He blew out the breath in his lungs. He knew what she

looked like in a bikini, with her tantalizing cleavage and pierced navel. But he'd never seen her completely bare.

Were her nipples a soft shade of pink? Did they arouse easily? Would she sigh and moan if he rolled his tongue across them? He wondered all sorts of erotic things about her. Was she smooth between her legs or did she have a strip of fiery red hair? And what would she do if he kissed her there?

Right *there*, all warm and soft and wet.

He longed to kiss her everywhere, to hold her unbearably close, to feel the silkiness of her skin next to his.

He'd wanted her for years, and now that they were getting married, the wanting had taken on a new meaning.

The romance of making love with his wife.

Cripes, he thought. Since when did he care about romance? Max was out of his element, with the effect the impending marriage was having on him. But it would be over soon enough. After they adopted Tokoni, they would get happily divorced and everything would go back to normal.

But in the meantime…

He squinted at the light peeking through the blinds. It was the crack of dawn and he needed to get up and get moving. Lizzie was coming by later this morning to see the garden. The work was finished, the gazebo built and ready.

Was it any wonder he was stressed? A day hadn't passed where there wasn't something related to the wedding. Sure, the planner was doing a bang-up job of getting everything done. But it was still consuming Max's life.

And so was his yearning for Lizzie.

He climbed out of bed and put his running clothes on, anxious to hightail it out of his house.

And that was exactly what he did. He ran through the

canyons, taking in the crisp morning air. He worked up an even bigger sweat than the one that had drenched him during the night.

By the time he was done, he was ready for a long, water-pummeling, soap-sudsy shower. Of course, once he was naked, he thought about Lizzie again. But at least he didn't touch himself. That would have made the wanting so much worse.

After he got dressed and ate breakfast, he went out to the garden to wait for Lizzie. He'd already opened the security gate so she could let herself onto the property.

She arrived with her hair falling over her shoulders and a breezy blouse flowing over a pair of slim-fitting jeans. He wanted to ravish her right then and there.

"Look at this place," she said as she approached him. "It's absolutely gorgeous."

"Glad you like it."

"Like it? I love it. It's like the Garden of Eden."

The last thing he wanted to think about was a biblical paradise, where temptation ran amok. If Lizzie presented him with an apple, he would devour every luscious bite.

"Max?"

He blinked at her. "What?"

"Are we going to walk through it so I can see everything up close?"

"Yes, of course." The design was lush and dense, surrounded by stately palms and giant birds of paradise. Vertical layers of plants and flowers created a jungle-like appearance within a bold, brightly colored interior.

They wandered the variegated pathways, then stopped to admire the fountain, listening to the rainlike sound it made.

Next, they headed for the gazebo and stood inside the

custom-built structure. It wasn't decorated for the wedding yet, but when the time came, it would be adorned with flowers and sheer linen drapes.

"This is where it's going to happen," she said.

Yeah, he thought. Where he would marry the woman he longed to bed. But at least he would get to kiss her.

"So, how are things going on your end?" he asked, trying to shake the anticipated kiss from his mind. "Do all the women in the bridal party have their dresses and whatnot?"

"Yes, they do. I decided on mismatched dresses, with each of them choosing what looked best on them. I wanted them to express their individuality instead of putting everyone in the same style. My only stipulation was that they remained within the color theme."

"Are you pleased with the dress you got for yourself?" With as much time as they'd spent talking about it, he was eager to see her in it.

"Truthfully, it makes me feel a little strange."

He angled his head. "Strange?"

She winced. "Just sort of wedding nightish, with how soft and pretty it is."

Damn, he thought. *Damn.* "I guess it's too late to trade it in for an ugly one, huh?"

She smiled, laughed a little. "Now, why didn't I think of that?"

He doubted that it would make a difference. He slid his gaze over her and asked, "Did you have to get special lingerie to go with it?" He didn't have a clue what brides wore under their gowns.

She flushed in the sunlight, her fair skin going far too pink. "We're doing it again, Max."

He frowned. "Doing what?"

"Saying things to each other we shouldn't say." She

fussed with the buttons on her blouse, as if they might accidentally come undone. "We need to change the subject."

His brain went blank. "To what?"

"I don't know."

He hurriedly thought of something. He gestured to a small section of the garden. "See that area over there?"

She glanced in the direction of where he pointed. "Yes."

"Those are the plants that were added for the language of flowers you told me about. I asked the landscaper to research it and he worked up a collection of flowers that pertain to joy and parenthood and welcoming a new son."

"Oh." She made a soft sound. "That's wonderful. Thank you."

"You're welcome. We'll have to tell Tokoni about it when he comes here."

"He's going to love this garden." She gasped. "Oh, my goodness, look. It's a ladybug." She showed him where the little creature was crawling on a railing of the gazebo. "Do you want to see if it'll come to you?"

"Sure." He went over to the ladybug and held his hand close to it. Sure enough, it crawled onto his finger.

She watched the exchange. "I wondered if they bring a specific type of luck or if it's general goodwill."

"I don't know. I'll look it up after it flies away."

Just then the ladybug winged its way toward Lizzie and landed on the back of her hand.

She smiled and glanced down at it. "This has to be a good omen, right?"

Finally the beetle took off, disappearing into the garden. Curious, Max got on his phone to research the luck they'd just been given.

"What does it say?" she asked.

"There's lots of information. They mean different

things in different cultures. But get this—in one of the old myths, if a ladybug lands on a woman's hand, it means she is going to be married soon."

"Oh, wow. Imagine that? Does it say anything about a ladybug landing on a man's hand?"

He scanned the material. "There is something here about…" Oh, shit, he thought, as he read the contents. "Never mind. It doesn't matter."

She scrunched up her face. "It's not something about the wedding night, is it?"

"No." He frowned at his phone. "It's about love. It says, 'The direction in which a ladybug flies away from a man's hand is where his true love will be.'"

He glanced up, and they gazed at each other with disturbed expressions. The ladybug hadn't just flown in Lizzie's direction. It had gone right to her, making her his supposed true love.

But Max refused to believe a message like that, especially when there were other ways to analyze it.

"I'll bet the ladybug is part of our lie," he said. "That it's aware of the reason we've been pretending to be in love and is playing along with us."

A strand of hair blew across her cheek. She batted it away without saying anything. She still seemed a little dazed.

He prodded her for a response. "Don't you think my theory sounds logical, Lizzie?"

"Yes." She walked out of the gazebo, her hair still blowing. "That has to be it. It's the only thing that makes sense."

"Definitely," he said as they left the garden. They both knew that neither of them had the capacity to fall in love for real.

Nine

On the day of the wedding, Lizzie clutched her father's arm. Within a matter of minutes, she would be walking down the garden-path aisle, heading toward her groom.

Max Marquez. Her best friend. The man with whom she would be adopting a child.

She glanced over at her dad. Surprisingly, his strong and silent presence helped keep her limbs from shaking. But the storm that raged through her mind was a whole other matter.

Ever since the ladybug incident, she'd been struggling with the dangling, tangling heartstrings of love. Max's explanation that the ladybug's message was part of their lie should have satisfied her. But instead she'd begun worrying about love, fearful that it could happen to her.

Anxious, Lizzie looked down at her bouquet. At the moment, she was wearing blue, green and purple diamond earrings that complemented the colors of the flowers. Max had given the earrings to her as a wedding gift. They'd been specially made for this occasion.

She'd given him a jewelry gift, too: antique gold cuff links to wear with his tuxedo. Of course, once the ceremony was underway, she would be placing the band she'd chosen for him on his finger.

As for her rings, her engagement ruby and diamond pavé band had been soldered together to create one shimmering piece, and that was what Max would be marrying her with today.

She shifted her gaze to the elegantly decorated gazebo, where he waited for her. Soon, so very soon, she would be his legally wedded wife. She'd never believed herself capable of love, and now she was fretting over it. But given how long she'd known Max and as close as they'd always been, weren't those types of feelings possible?

As the opening notes of "Here Comes the Bride" began to play, signaling her entrance, she lifted her chin, determined to stay strong.

Her father glanced over and said, "It's time."

She nodded. Everyone, including Max, turned to watch her come down the aisle. But she doubted that he was worried about love. He seemed fixated on how she looked, his appreciative gaze sweeping the long, silky, white-and-gold length of her.

She shouldn't have told him that her dress made her feel "wedding nightish." But she couldn't take those words back. She couldn't take any of this back. She was marrying Max and afraid that she might fall hopelessly in love with him.

Would she know the moment it occurred? Would it pierce her like a warrior's arrow? Or would it be a gradual wound, a slow bleeding with an eventual loss of consciousness?

Lizzie held her breath, praying that her heart remained intact. Because nothing would tear her apart more than loving a man she was destined to divorce.

As her dad turned her over to Max, she wished that she'd worn a veil to cover her face. She felt terribly exposed, with the passion-steeped way Max was looking at her.

She gazed longingly at him, too, mesmerized by his tall, dark beauty. He wore his hair in its usual style, as thick and shiny and straight as it naturally was. His designer tuxedo featured satin details and notched lapels, and his boutonniere was attached on the left side, above his heart, where it was supposed to be.

He recited his vows first, as instructed to do. As he promised to love and honor her for all eternity, a soft rattle sounded in his voice. She recited hers just as quietly, just as shakily. Only her vows were rife with fear.

They exchanged rings, and when the time came for him to kiss her, Lizzie refrained from running her tongue across her lips. But that didn't ease the romantic restlessness that baited her soul. She was wearing red lipstick, as hot and fiery as the rubies in their rings.

"Are you ready?" he whispered.

"Yes," she said. She was more than ready.

He leaned forward and put his hands in her hair. His lips touched hers, and her eyes fluttered closed. This was the kiss she'd been thinking about, fantasizing about, waiting for. He pulled her closer, and the elements flowed through her.

The sun. The wind. The bloom of flowers.

Was she becoming part of her surroundings? Or did she feel this way because she was becoming part of him?

Lizzie couldn't think clearly, not while she was in the dreamy midst of wanting him. He didn't use his tongue and neither did she, but it still felt beautifully forbidden.

It ended far too soon, with him separating himself from her. She opened her eyes. His were open now, too.

Her mind went hazy. Was her lipstick smeared? Max didn't have any on him, so it must be okay. It was supposed to be the long-lasting, non-smudge kind. For infinite kisses, she thought.

The ceremony came to a close, with the man officiating it introducing them as husband and wife.

"We did it," Max said to her, his voice seductively quiet.

"Yes, we did," she murmured back. They were married now, first kiss and all.

As they descended the aisle, they were celebrated with cheers and the fragrant tossing of dried lavender. It dusted them like confetti, purple buds sprinkling the air. The wedding planner had recommended it, providing little mesh bags to their guests. Lizzie hadn't thought to check on what lavender meant in the language of flowers until last night, discovering that, among other things, it was said to soothe passions of the heart.

But as Max held her hand, his fingers threaded through hers, she wasn't the least bit soothed.

His touch only heightened her fears about falling in love.

The chandeliers in the ballroom had been altered, the original crystals replaced to reflect the colors of the wedding. Also enriching the décor were fancy linens, glittering candles and big, bold flower arrangements trimmed in peacock feathers.

The cake was outstanding, too. Max could see it from where he sat, displayed on a dessert cart, the four-tiered creation a frothily iced masterpiece. But for now he and Lizzie and their guests dined on their meals, prepared by a renowned chef and served on shiny gold plates.

Their table consisted of the wedding party. The best men and maid of honor had already made their toasts, and the flower girls and their mothers looked exceptional in their feminine finery. Baby Nita's nanny was part of the group, ready to whisk her off to a makeshift nursery that had been provided, in case the wee one needed a nap. A playroom for the older kids was also available, with child-care attendants standing by.

Lizzie's father fit naturally into the high-society gathering. He didn't seem as detached as he normally was, and for that Max was grateful. He wanted Lizzie to feel protected by her one and only parent, especially today. Watching her come down the aisle with her dad had left Max with a lump in his throat.

Becoming Lizzie's husband was confusing. The weight of the ring on his finger. The fake vows. The bachelorhood he'd lost. The make-believe wife he'd gained.

Earlier someone had imposed a "kiss and clink" ritual, where the bride and groom had to kiss whenever glasses were clinked together. So far, at the reception, Max and Lizzie had locked lips at least ten times. But he could have kissed her a thousand times and not gotten enough.

He leaned over and said to her, "Is it okay if I tell you again how beautiful you look?" He'd already told her how breathtaking she was, but he thought it bore repeating.

She softly replied, "You can say whatever you want, as often as you want."

"Then I'm going to say it every chance I get." With her sparkling gown and wild red hair, she was a seductive sight to behold. He wanted to haul her off to bed tonight, to strip her bare and relish every part of her. But that wasn't part of the arrangement.

In the next alluring moment, a whole bunch of glasses clinked in the background. Max hastily obliged. He cupped Lizzie's face and slanted his mouth over hers.

He'd yet to use his tongue. He wanted to, but it didn't seem appropriate with everyone watching. Still, he made sure that his lips were parted, just enough to entice a sigh from Lizzie.

No one would ever suspect that they weren't lovers. But Max knew. He craved her with every breath in his body.

Later, they engaged in their first husband-and-wife dance, with a well-known DJ spinning records. They'd chosen Queen's "You're my Best Friend," a classic soft rock ballad, for the opening song. Some of the lyrics included professions of love. But this was a wedding, and they were supposed to be projecting that type of sentiment, even if it wasn't true. Mostly, though, the song made sense, with how deep their friendship was.

As they swayed to the beat, holding each other close, Max ran his hand along the back of her gown, where it laced like an old-fashioned corset.

"Was it hard getting into your dress?" he asked.

She shook her head. "Sheila helped me."

Of course, he thought, her maid of honor, who was one of her old sorority sisters, a high-society girl, much like Lizzie. "She's probably used to dealing with these types of events."

"Yes, she is. But I had a team of assistants, too, a hairdresser, a makeup artist, a manicurist."

Max had gotten ready by himself. He hadn't wanted anyone, not even his brothers, straightening his tie or pinning his boutonniere to his lapel. He'd needed to spend his last few hours of being single alone. "Who's going to help you get out of your dress?"

"I can do it myself." She spoke quietly, with the colors from the chandeliers raining down on her. "I just have to be careful not to damage it."

He looked into her eyes, curious about what she had on under it—the mysterious lingerie that kept invading his mind. "You can come to me if the laces give you any trouble."

She nearly stumbled against him. "Do you think that's a good idea?"

"I don't know." He steadied her in his arms, wondering what the hell he was doing. He'd just invited her to his room, crossing a line that wasn't meant to be crossed. "I honestly don't." He couldn't be sure what would happen if they gave in to the temptation of being together. Would they regret it afterward, would they survive the heat? They'd been so careful not to jeopardize their friendship, and now they were drowning in a sea of unholy matrimony. "Maybe we should both forget that I ever suggested it."

"Yes," she agreed. "We should block it out."

He was trying. But the back of her dress kept getting in the way. He couldn't seem to stop from touching it.

The reception continued, with dancing and drinking and party merriment. During the removal of the garter, Max knelt beside Lizzie's chair, asking the Creator to give him the strength to endure it.

He'd been obsessing about her lingerie, and now he was getting to cop a husbandly feel of her sheer white stockings. They were the kind that stayed up all by themselves.

No hooks, no fasteners.

While he was still on the floor, with his hand lingering

on her thigh, Jake called out, "Hey, Max, did you know that in earlier, bawdier times, wedding guests used to follow the couple to their bedchamber and wait for them to undress so they could steal the bride's stockings and toss them at her and the groom until they hit one of them in the head?"

"That's not funny," Max called back, even if he and Lizzie laughed right along with everyone else.

"It was for luck," Jake assured him.

Yeah, Max thought, because at least the old-time groom had been lucky enough to bed his bride, even if one of them had gotten softly pelted in the head.

As he looked up to meet Lizzie's gaze, preparing to slide the garter down, a group of jovial guests clinked glasses, daring him to kiss the graceful sweep of her leg.

Accepting the challenge, he pressed his lips to her ankle, being as gentlemanly as the moment would allow. But damned if he still didn't want to peel off every jeweled-and-beaded stitch of fabric she wore.

By the time Max and Lizzie cut the cake, the sexy tone had already been set. He fed her a piece of the frothy white dessert, and when some banana-cream filling stuck lusciously to her lips, he leaned forward and kissed it right off her mouth.

Holy. Mercy. Hell.

She returned his salacious kiss, with camera phones flashing and recording every detail. For better or worse, Max felt wildly, sinfully married, their tongues meeting and mating.

Logic flew straight out the door. Desperate to have her, he whispered hotly in her ear, "Come to my room later and let me undo your dress," repeating his earlier offer and meaning every word of it.

Although Lizzie went beautifully breathy, she didn't

respond, leaving Max waiting and wondering if his wife would succumb to his request.

Or leave him hanging.

The mansion was empty, the guests and staff gone. There was no one left, except Max and Lizzie. They stood on the second-floor landing, silence between them. In one direction was the master suite and in the other were her accommodations. She stalled, not knowing which way to go.

He watched her through pitch-dark eyes. In the low-level light, they looked as black as his licorice-toned hair.

So deep. So intense.

She struggled to tame her desire. "Sleeping with you wasn't supposed to be an option."

His gaze didn't waver. "It doesn't have to affect our friendship, not if we don't let it."

"How?" she asked. "By only doing it this one time and never again?"

"That seems like the safest way to handle it." He moved a little closer. "But it's up to you, Lizzie."

There was nothing safe about how much she wanted him. Or about the fear of love that kept burrowing its way into her thoughts. If she told him what was going on in her mind, would he still be willing to go through with it?

"I can't," she said, fighting the feeling. "No matter how much I want to."

"Are you sure?" Roughness edged his voice: loss, disappointment.

She nodded, trying her darnedest to be certain.

He said, "Then sleep well and think of me, and I'll think of you, too."

She imagined him, alone in his bed, fantasizing about her. "I better go." Before she crawled all over him. She could still taste the cake they'd kissed from each other's lips.

The sweet creaminess.

Lizzie turned away, but he didn't. She sensed him, standing in the same spot, tall and sharp in his tuxedo.

She headed toward the guest wing. Again, there was no movement behind her, no masculine footsteps, echoing in her ears. He remained as motionless as a statue.

She stopped to breathe, and when she glanced over her shoulder, she lost her reason.

He was still there.

Lizzie ran to him, her dress swishing with every beat of her bride-in-jeopardy heart. He pulled her tight against him, lifted her up and carried her the rest of the way to his room.

She kept her arms looped around his neck, hoping she survived the night without falling in love with him.

He took her into his suite, past a royal blue sitting room and into the area where a big brass bed took precedence. This was the place where he slept each night, she thought, where he dreamed, where they would be together.

"Just this once," she said, stating the rules, making sure she repeated them. "Then never again."

"Yes," he replied, putting her on her feet. "This is the only time it's going to happen." He moved to stand behind her. "On our wedding night."

She felt his hands on the back of her dress, working the ties. Wonderfully dizzy, her vision nearly blurred.

He loosened more of the fabric. "It's so soft and pretty."

"The material between my skin and the dress is called a modesty panel." But she wasn't feeling very modest. Soon she would be half-naked. The only garments she had on underneath were lace panties and the thigh-high stockings he'd run his hands over earlier. Her gown had been structured so she didn't need a bra.

Still standing behind her, he helped her remove the dress, allowing her to step out of it. She didn't turn around, and he didn't ask her to. But she heard his sharp intake of breath as he closed in on her. Lizzie shivered, immersed in his nearness, while he skimmed his fingers along her spine.

"Look how bare you are," he said, following the line of her tailbone.

Yes, she thought. With her upper half clothes-free and only a wisp of lower lingerie, she was mostly bare.

Remaining where he was, directly behind her, Max circled her waist and reach around to the front of her panties. When he slipped a hand inside to cup her mound, she gasped on contact.

"You're smooth," he said, his voice raspy against her ear. "I've thought a lot about…"

The style of bikini wax she favored? She leaned back against him, stunned by how detailed his curiosity was. "You wondered about that?"

"All the time." He kept touching her, moving farther down, until he spread her open with the tips of his fingers.

Lizzie nearly came on the spot.

He rubbed her, teasing her, making her warm and slick and wet. He used his other arm to hold her in place, pressing it firmly across her breasts. Her nipples went unbearably hard.

There was something dominantly provocative about what he was doing and how he was doing it. He had all the power.

Her groom. Her husband.

She couldn't see his expression or the flashes of heat that she suspected were in his eyes. But she felt every insistent touch.

"Are you going to come for me, Lizzie?"

She gulped her next breath. "I almost did."

"Yes, but are you going to do it for real?"

She nodded, as he continued his intimate quest, using her as his bridal plaything.

"This is just the beginning," he said.

"Of what?" she asked, feeling deliciously dazed.

"Of how many times tonight I'm going to make you come."

Her heart raced, spinning through her body like a top. "When am I going to get to do things to you?"

"You already are." He bumped his fly against her rear, showing her how aroused he was. "But I'm not anywhere near being done with you, so that will have to wait."

She closed her eyes. Every second of his stimulation brought her closer to the countless times he promised to invoke pleasure.

Lizzie moaned. Was the arm around her breasts getting tighter? Were his fingers strumming harder and faster? He kept his hand inside her panties, creating massive amounts of friction.

Her dress was on the floor beside their feet, so close they could have stepped on it. But neither of them did, not even when she came.

She convulsed in a flood of carnal bliss, shimmering and shaking, the back of her body banded against the front of his.

He nuzzled her neck and said, "Let's take these off now, shall we?"

She wondered what he meant, until she realized that

he was talking about her panties. Blinking through the haze, she did her shaky best to recover.

He divested her of what remained: the panties in question, her shoes, her stockings, even the colorful diamond earrings he'd given her. He did all that while he was still standing behind her.

After there was nothing left to remove, he turned her around so he could view her nakedness.

"Damn," he said. "You're even more gorgeous than I imagined."

She couldn't think of a response, at least not one that wouldn't leave her mewling like a kitten at his feet. He was still fully clothed. If this was strip poker, she would have lost the moment he'd unlaced her gown.

He spoke once again. "I want you to turn down the covers and get into bed."

So he could finish what he started? She was eager to do his bidding, but nervous about it, too. He was looking at her as if he meant to hold her captive for the rest of her life.

But she knew that wasn't the case. Tonight was their only night. The only time they'd agreed to be together.

Wondering what it would be like to stay with him, to be his forever wife, she fought her fears, reminding herself that this was just sex—hot, dreamy sex—where love had nothing to do with it.

Ten

Max gazed at Lizzie, gloriously naked in his bed, with her hair tumbling over her shoulders and the soldered ring set that sealed their union glinting on her finger. She looked as much like a bride now as when she'd walked down the aisle. Wilder, he thought, more sensual, but a bride just the same.

He picked up her dress and placed it on a nearby chair, along with her panties and stockings and earrings. The only item left on the floor was her shoes. They weren't glass slippers, but they had a fairy-tale quality nonetheless. The entire wedding had seemed that way. Which was part of its allure, part of how it had been designed, he thought, fooling their guests into believing it was going to last forever.

And now he and Lizzie were alone, immersed in one married night of romance. The anticipation in her eyes excited him. And so did her ladylike moments of shyness.

"Don't cover up," he told her, when she began to pull the sheet over her body.

She released it, giving him an unobstructed view once again. Mesmerized, he stood where he was, drinking in every beautifully bare part of her. Her nipples were as pink and pretty as he'd imagined, and his fingers were still warm from where he'd touched her.

Finally, Max removed his tux and draped it over the back of the same chair where he'd placed her dress.

"I never knew you were so meticulous," she said.

"Normally, I'm not." By tomorrow, the careful placement of their clothes wouldn't matter. But for now it did.

Once he was naked, he joined her in bed and took her in his arms. He kissed her with gentle passion, and she roamed her hands over him, her glitter-polished nails skimming the ridged planes and sinewy muscles that formed his body.

She paused when she came to a scar, a cigarette burn—a pale circular mark of childhood torture. Although the majority of them had disappeared, some of the deeper ones, mostly on his chest, remained visible.

"Max?" Still lingering over the scar, she lifted her gaze to his, her voice soft and compassionate. "Have other women asked you about these?"

"Yes." Other women, other lovers. "But I've never told them what they are. I just tell them what I tell everyone who is curious enough to question me about them. That I had a bad case of measles when I was a kid that left me scarred."

"Oh, yes, of course. Your measles tale. I always thought that seemed like a believable story, even if I knew the truth."

Max nodded. Lizzie was privy to the pain his mother

had inflicted on him because he'd shared those gut-wrenching secrets with her.

"I'm so sorry for what she did to you," she said.

"I know you are." She'd told him that many times before. But hearing her say it now distressed him. He didn't want to be reminded of the abuse, not while they were being intimate. He moved her hand away from his scar, imploring her to stop touching it, letting her know it was off-limits.

A wounded look came into her eyes. Clearly, she wanted to comfort him, to do what she'd always done before. But Max couldn't bear to accept what she was offering.

When he turned down the bedside lamp, trying to shift gears and create a softer ambience, she asked, "Are you sure that being together like this isn't going to affect our friendship?"

"We can't let it," he said, even if a change was happening already. A discomfort he couldn't deny. But there was more at stake, he thought, than just the two of them. "We're going to co-parent a child. He's going to need us to stay close."

"But not this close," she said.

He climbed on top of her, preparing to kiss his way down her body, to turn their troubled closeness into mindless pleasure. "Everything will be okay, Lizzie."

"Promise?"

"Yes." Max licked her nipples, going back and forth, exploring each one. After tonight, they would do whatever was necessary to resume friendship.

But for now...

For now...

He moved languidly, enjoying the taste of her skin. He flicked his tongue over the delicate gold piercing in her navel. She'd gotten it while they were still in high school. It was the only rebellious thing she'd ever done, other than becoming friends with a nerdy kid like him.

He said, "I should buy you a ruby for here. Or a colored diamond, like what's in the earrings I gave you."

"No, you shouldn't."

"Why not?"

"Because it will only remind us of what we did tonight."

Damn, he thought. She was right. Giving her another jewel would be a mistake. "I won't do it. I won't buy you anything else." He thought about the cuff links she'd given him and the groomlike way they'd made him feel. "You can't buy me anything else, either."

She played with the ends of his hair. "I don't intend to."

"Good." He pushed her legs open and went down on her, kissing and licking and swirling his tongue.

She gasped and arched her hips, watching him through the misty light, telling him how much she liked it.

How good it felt.

How she never wanted it to end.

But it did end, with her shaking and shivering and coming all over his mouth.

She insisted on doing it to him, too, on giving him the same kind of lethal pleasure he'd just given her. She let her work her magic, his body responding in thick, hard greed.

But when it became too much for him to handle, he grabbed a condom, anxious to thrust inside.

He entered her, and they kissed warmly and fully, the sweetness of her lips drawing him deeper.

Locked together, they rolled over the sheets, and within no time, Lizzie was straddling him, her hair falling forward and framing her face. He gripped her waist as she traveled up and down, riding him quickly, fiercely.

They shifted again, bending and moving. He was behind her now, nibbling her neck and pumping like a stallion.

It didn't stop there. They swiveled onto their sides, kissed like crazy, then returned to where they'd begun, with Max braced above her.

Driving her toward a skyrocketing orgasm, he pushed her to the limit, making sure she came again.

And finally, *finally*, when she was in the throes of making primal sounds and clawing his back, he let himself fall.

Into the hot, hammering thrill of his wedding night.

In the morning, Lizzie awakened next to her husband. He was still asleep, the sheet bunched around his hips.

Should she gather her things and tiptoe off to her room? No, she thought. That would make her feel cheap, dashing down the hall, clutching her wedding gown.

The least she could do was find something to wear. She climbed out of bed and put on her panties. From there, she went to Max's giant walk-in closet, where his dresser was, and rummaged through the drawers.

The only belongings Lizzie had brought with her were in a suitcase that she'd left in her room. Later today, they were leaving on their honeymoon, jetting off to Nulah to start the adoption proceedings, and she wasn't moving into Max's mansion, not officially, until they got back.

She kept digging through his dresser, trying to decide what to borrow. Keeping it simple, she went for a black T-shirt and gray sweat shorts. She had to roll the waistband of the shorts down to her hips to make them fit, but it was better than just being in her panties. Rather than leave the hem of the T-shirt hanging, she twisted the material into a center knot and tied it below her bust.

Lizzie gazed at her reflection in the closet mirror, enjoying the way his clothes felt against her skin.

She frowned at her seductively smudged eye makeup and sleep-tousled hair. Nothing had changed in the light of day. She was still afraid of falling in love with him.

Determined to sneak off as quickly as she could, she exited his closet, hoping he remained asleep. But he was awake and was sitting up in bed.

He squinted at her. "What are you doing, pretty Lizard?"

"I borrowed some of your clothes." She stated the obvious, wishing her nickname didn't sound so endearing on his lips.

"So I see." He swept his gaze over her. "And how stylish you look in them, too."

While he studied her, she glanced at the scars on his chest, trapped in the memory of the well-intentioned touch he'd rebuffed. The solace he'd refused. She forced herself to look away from the scars, not wanting him to catch her doing it.

Would he rebuff her love, too? She hoped that she never had to find out.

He said, "I could use some breakfast. How about you?"

She wasn't the least bit hungry, but she replied, "Sure. I can fix it while you shower or whatever." She needed to bathe, too, but she wasn't ready to strip off her clothes. Or his clothes, as it were. She wanted to wear them a little longer.

"I'll shower after we eat." He got out of bed and took his tuxedo pants from the chair where he'd left them. Same chair where her dress was. "I can help you make the food."

He climbed into the pants, sans underwear. Of all things he could have worn this morning, he'd chosen to go commando in his wedding attire? He threw on the formal shirt, too, leaving it unbuttoned with the tails loose.

"No point in wasting a perfectly good suit," he said. "After all, I did buy the dang thing."

"Yes, you did." But most men wouldn't treat a pricey tuxedo as if it was casual gear. But Max wasn't most men.

He glanced toward his bathroom. "I'm going to brush my teeth before we go downstairs."

She tried for a smile. "So you can be minty fresh before breakfast? I should do that, too."

He smiled, as well. "I'll meet you in the kitchen."

When he was gone, Lizzie scooped up her gown, wrapping her shoes and stockings and jewelry inside it.

Once she was in her room, she deposited the bundle on her bed and went into her bathroom to brush her teeth. She washed her face, too, removing the remnants of her makeup. She also tamed her hair, taking a few minutes to get her emotional bearing.

Still wearing Max's clothes, she ventured downstairs and entered the kitchen. He was already there, removing pots and pans from cabinets. He had a carafe of coffee going, too.

She pitched in, and with minimal conversation they fixed ham, eggs and steel-cut oatmeal.

They sat across from each other at the main dining table, and Max drizzled honey over his cereal. Lizzie preferred hers with milk. But what struck her was how intently they were watching each other eat.

"Are you ready for our trip?" he asked.

Their big, fat, fake honeymoon, she thought. "Yes," she replied. "Are you?"

He nodded, but he didn't look any more ready than she was.

* * *

Since Nulah was twenty hours ahead of Los Angeles, Max and Lizzie arrived in time to hang out on the beach and swim in the crystal-blue sea. They tried to behave like newlyweds whenever other people were around. But mostly they kept to themselves, so they didn't have to make it harder than it already was. But either way, being in each other's company was absolute torture.

And so were their accommodations, Max thought.

Their bungalow was similar to the ones they'd stayed in before, with wonderful island amenities. The only difference this time was that they were sharing the same space.

Bedtime rolled around far too soon. Lizzie changed in the bathroom, putting on a long cotton nightgown. Max suspected it was the most modest thing she owned. But that didn't stop him from noticing how gracefully it flowed over her body.

"I can sleep on the couch," he said.

The couch was adjacent to the bed, as the main area of the bungalow was basically one big room. Even if he wasn't sleeping with her, he would be within tempting distance. But there was nothing either of them could do about that.

"All I need is a sheet," he said. "Sometimes I get hot when I sleep." He didn't mean "hot" in a sexual way, but it triggered sweet, slick memories of their wedding night.

Apparently for her, too. She shot him a dicey look.

A second later, she composed herself and removed the top sheet from the bed, gathering it for him. He took it from her, and she handed him a pillow, as well.

"We've got a big day ahead of us tomorrow," she said.

Max nodded. In the morning they would be going to the orphanage. "I hope Losa lets us see Tokoni. When I spoke with her earlier she said that she wasn't sure if we should see him on this trip."

Lizzie frowned. "Why not?"

"Typically she waits until the process is further along before she lets applicants spend more time with the child they are trying to adopt. She says it can get too emotional later if something goes wrong or if the applicants change their minds."

"We would never change our minds." She got into bed, but she didn't lie down. She sat forward and pulled the covers over her legs.

"I know. But that's just how she does it."

He settled onto the couch, plumping the pillow behind him. Neither of them turned out the light. They gazed at each other from across the room. The windows were open, with a tropical breeze stirring the curtains.

"Why didn't you tell me this before now?" Lizzie asked.

"I didn't want to disappoint you. I know how badly you want to see Tokoni. How you were looking forward to his big, bright smile and giving him a hug. I want to do that, too."

Concern etched her brow, signaling another frown. "I hope she lets us see him. We've been waiting all this time."

"Yeah, planning a wedding, getting married. We've been to hell and back to become his parents." He made a tight face. "Sorry, that didn't sound very nice."

"I knew what you meant. It would have been so much easier if we could have stayed single and still adopted him."

"But that isn't how it worked out." He glanced down at his hand. "It's strange wearing a ring."

"You think you've got troubles?" She waggled her

fingers, showing off her ruby. "Look at me, hauling this gigantic bauble around."

He laughed a little. "I'm surprised you didn't sink to the bottom of the ocean today."

A laugh erupted from her, too. "Good thing I didn't or you would've had to rescue me."

"Me performing CPR on you would have been a disaster." He smiled, winked, made another joke. "Mouth-to-mouth and all that."

She shook her head, and in the next uncomfortable instant, they both went silent. No more smiles. No more laughter. Their silly banter wasn't helping.

"We should try to sleep now," she said. "I just hope that I don't keep you awake, with the way I might be tossing and turning."

"I'm probably going to be restless, too." Being in the same room with her, knowing she was just a forbidden kiss away. But in the morning, they would get past it. Because all that mattered was doing what they'd come here to do.

To make Tokoni their son.

Lizzie and Max sat across from Losa in her office, but their meeting wasn't going well. Something didn't feel right, Lizzie thought. Even though she and Max had been prattling on about their wedding and how excited they were to adopt Tokoni, Losa seemed cautious of them.

In fact, she watched their every move, as if she were analyzing their body language. By now, Lizzie was so nervous that she kept glancing out the window, avoiding eye contact. Max seemed anxious, too. He shifted in his seat, like a kid who'd gotten called into the principal's office for committing a schoolyard crime.

Did Losa suspect that their marriage was a ruse? And

if she did, why hadn't she said something before now? Why had she allowed them to continue the charade, letting them believe that they were being considered for the adoption?

Losa asked Lizzie, "Do you remember what I told you when you first interviewed me for your blog?"

"You told me a lot of things," she responded, getting more nervous by the minute. "I used a lot of it in the articles I wrote."

"Yes, you did. But what did I say about our guidelines and what's the most important character trait we look for in prospective parents?"

Lizzie's heart dropped to her stomach. "That they must be honorable people."

Max spoke up. "Are you questioning our character, Losa?"

The older woman turned toward him. "Yes, unfortunately, I am. When you first called me and said that you'd fallen in love and were getting married, I was concerned about the speed in which it seemed to be happening. But I gave you the benefit of the doubt, wanting to believe that your feelings were genuine and you weren't just playacting so you could adopt Tokoni."

Max's dark skin paled a little. But he said, "We're going to be the best parents we can be. We intend to devote the rest of our lives to Tokoni."

"Yes, but you don't intend to devote the rest of your lives to each other, do you?" She turned her attention to Lizzie. "I could tell from the moment you walked into my office today that you weren't a true bride. I know the difference between a happily married woman and one who is finding it difficult. You can barely look at your husband without having shadows in your eyes."

Lizzie gripped the edge of the desk. Not only were

she and Max on the verge of losing Tokoni, but Losa was calling her out, baiting her to admit that the marriage wasn't real. But she couldn't do it. She couldn't say it out loud, not when she was so painfully afraid of falling in love with Max. "Please don't take Tokoni away from us."

"How can I allow you to adopt him," Losa replied, "when your actions haven't been honorable?"

Max interjected. "It isn't fair of you to say that."

"Isn't it?" Losa asked, challenging him to come clean. "Tell me, what were you going to do once the adoption was approved? Were you going to divorce your wife and create a broken home for your son? I want to know the truth, Max, and I want it now."

"All right," he said. "We are going to split up. But we aren't creating a broken home, not in the way you're implying. After the divorce, Lizzie and I planned to raise Tokoni in separate households, but we also planned to co-parent him with love and devotion. Both of us, together, as friends."

Losa blew out a heavy sigh. "That's not what Tokoni's mother wanted for him."

"I know." Max continued to defend their position. "But we couldn't bear to lose him, so we devised a way to make him our son. We can make the divorce work and still give Tokoni everything he needs."

Losa asked Lizzie, "Are you as certain about the divorce as Max is?"

Lizzie's grip on the desk tightened. She'd been wondering what it would be like to stay with her husband, to be the only woman in his life, and now she was being asked if dismantling their marriage was the right thing to do. She couldn't think, couldn't rationalize, not with him watching her from the corner of his eye. When he reached over, drawing her hand away from the desk and encouraging her to support the divorce, she knew that her worst fear had just come true.

That she loved him.

Absolutely, positively loved him.

What an awful time to figure it out, to see through the veil of her own heart. But she couldn't admit how she felt, not without destroying what was left of their friendship, so she lied and said, "Yes, I'm as certain about the divorce as he is."

Losa measured her. "So you honestly believe that it won't cause any problems later?"

"Yes," Lizzie lied again.

The older woman shook her head. "I'm sorry, but I disagree." She then told Max, "Neither of you is ready to be a parent."

His expression all but splintered. But in spite of his distress, Lizzie could tell that he wasn't giving up without a fight.

He said to Losa, "I understand how upset you are about our deception, and I apologize for leading you on. But we are ready to be Tokoni's parents. We love him and believe that he's meant to be our son."

Losa adjusted her glasses. "I'm not denying that either of you loves the boy. I know you do." She spoke with strength and careful diction. "I wish things could be different, but I won't go against his mother's wishes or subject him to a broken home. There's another couple who's interested in him, and I'm going to consider their application in place of yours."

Oh, God. Lizzie pitched forward in her chair. Losa wasn't just denying their application. She was thinking of giving Tokoni to someone else.

"Who are they?" Max asked, firing a round of questions at her. "And how long ago did they apply? Do we know them? Are they someone who contacted you through our efforts to find Tokoni a home? Or are they a local couple?"

"I can't discuss them with you," Losa said. She sounded weary now, troubled that she was hurting Max and Lizzie, but determined to abide by her decision.

"Whoever they are, they won't be us," he said. He looked at Lizzie, his voice quaking. "They'll never be us."

She could see that his heart was breaking. Hers was, too. Everything inside her was shattering, cutting her in two.

Lizzie got up and ran out of the orphanage. Once she was outside, she burst into tears.

No child. No husband to keep. Only fractured love.

Max soon followed her. He wasn't crying. But he was shaking, his chest heaving through ragged breaths. He reached for her, and she collapsed in his arms.

More lost than she'd ever been.

Eleven

Feeling horribly, sickeningly numb, Max stared at the beach, where the sky met the sea, where peace and beauty were supposed to reign. But all he saw was emptiness.

He glanced over at Lizzie. She sat beside him on their bungalow deck, curled up in her chair, her knees drawn to her chest. After they'd left the orphanage, she'd dried her tears, but her eyes were still swollen, her mascara still softly smudged.

"We got married for nothing," he said, the hope of becoming a father crushed beneath the weight of his heart.

Her voice hitched. "Our wedding night didn't seem like nothing."

"No, but it was something we shouldn't have done." The glittering warmth, the romance, the sex. Even now he longed to do it all over again, even if he knew it would only make matters worse. Taking fulfillment in Lizzie's body, holding her close, burying his face in her hair—

none of those things was the answer. "We messed up." Mired in his grief, he kept looking at her. "If we hadn't slept together, we wouldn't have been so uncomfortable around each other, and then Losa wouldn't have figured us out."

Lizzie's voice hitched again. "She said that she was suspicious of us from the beginning."

"I know, but with the way we were acting, we gave ourselves away. We didn't seem like a real couple to her."

Still wrapped in the fetal position, she rocked in her chair. "We aren't a real couple."

"Everyone else believed that we were. Everyone except Losa." The person who had the power to take Tokoni away from them. "I can't believe that she turned us down. That Tokoni is never going to be ours. I wish she would have told us who the other applicants are. At least then—"

"We'd know who we're losing him to? How is that going to help?"

"I don't know. But they must be happily married or she wouldn't be considering them." He analyzed the strangers who might become Tokoni's parents. "What if their marriage breaks apart at some point? What if they end up divorced, too? It isn't fair that she's blaming us for not being in love. Who even knows what it means, anyway?"

A choked sound escaped from Lizzie's lips. "I don't want to talk about the definition of love."

"I'm just saying that—"

"Please, I can't do this…" She unfolded her arms and put her feet on the ground. Then, as quick as that, she ran toward the beach, on the verge of crying again.

Max's gut wrenched. Should he leave her alone? Or should he chase after her? He knew how fiercely she was hurting. He hurt, too, so damned badly.

He took a chance and headed toward her. She looked so lost, facing the water, the hem of her pale summer dress fluttering in the breeze. Was she blaming herself because Losa had put the initial burden on her? Did she think that she'd botched their phony presentation of love more than he had?

He came up behind her. The air smelled of salt and sea and sand, of tropical flowers and leafy foliage, of everything that reminded him of this trip they'd taken together. Their phony honeymoon, he thought.

"Lizzie?" He said her name, letting her know he was there.

She turned around, drew a breath. "Yes?"

He gently asked, "Do you think it's your fault because of what Losa said to you about not seeming like a true bride?"

She nodded. "Yes, but it's more than that, so much more."

"Tell me."

"I can't." Behind her, the ocean turned a foamy shade of blue, rolling its way onto the picture-perfect shore.

"Yes, you can. I'm your BFF, remember? You can tell me anything."

"You won't understand."

"Yes, I will. You can confide in me." If not him, then who would she reveal herself to? "That's what we do, Lizzie. Tell each other our secrets."

"Then here it is. I want to be what Losa said I wasn't."

Too confused to make the connection, to let it sink in, he blinked at her. "That doesn't make sense."

"Yes, it does," she said, in a ghost of a whisper. "I want to be your true bride."

He shook his head, shook it so hard his brain rattled.

"You don't know what you're saying. You're sad, you're agonizing over Tokoni, you're—"

"I'm in love with you, Max."

Recoiling from her words, he flinched. His mother used to tell him that she loved him after every beating, every cigarette burn, every painful punishment.

Trapped in his memories, he pushed his feet into the sand. Beneath the surface of the thick white grains, something pierced his skin. The edges of a broken shell, maybe. Or a tiny shard of glass or something else that didn't belong in a beach environment.

"I knew it was going to freak you out." Lizzie spoke quietly, cautiously. "It freaks me out, too. I was so afraid I was going to fall in love with you, and I did."

He snapped back into the conversation. "You've been afraid of this? For how long?"

"Since the day when you first showed me the garden."

Her deception punched him straight in the gut. "You've been stressing about this since before we got married, before you slept with me?"

"Yes. But I've been fighting my fears. On the night we were together, I prayed to survive it."

Max wasn't surviving it. Already he could feel the monsters coming to get him. The two-faced creatures lurking in the closet with the door barred shut.

"I think my fear of loving you is what Losa was seeing in my eyes," Lizzie said. "The shadows she mentioned. I doubt she knew that's why I didn't seem like a true bride, but she still sensed that something wasn't right."

Shadows, he thought. Monsters. He glanced up at the sun, then back at Lizzie. "My mother could have been her. *Anog Ite.*"

She squinted at him. "Double-Faced Woman?"

He nodded. The being who was condemned to wear

two faces for seducing the *Wi*, the sun. He gestured to the sky. The setting sun was turning red, as if it was fused with fire, as bright as Lizzie's hair. "My mother had two faces. She was beautiful like *Anog Ite*, but ugly, too. Some people say that *Anog Ite* isn't evil. That she's just a figure of disharmony. But to me, she'll always be evil, like my mother, like the love she used against me."

"Love isn't evil, Max."

"No, but it makes people hurt." He reached out to touch Lizzie's hair. The beautiful redness. The fire. "Look what happened with Tokoni. We lost him, even though we loved him." He lowered his hand. "But maybe it's all just a smokescreen, this love that you think you feel for me. Maybe it isn't even real."

"It's real." Her voice broke. "What I feel is real."

"I don't think it is." He didn't want to believe it, couldn't let himself believe it. "You just think you love me because you got caught up in the fantasy of being a wife. But that's not you. You aren't the wifely type."

"My dad said that I was going to make a good wife."

"Your dad? He barely knows you. But I know you, Lizzie." He thumped a hand against his chest. "I know who you are."

"You don't know me anymore." She argued with him, defending the person she claimed to be. "I'm different. I'm changed."

He fought the urge to grab her, to shake her until she admitted that she didn't love him. But he wanted to hold her and kiss her, too. Max was a mess, more emotionally wrought than he'd ever been. "You were supposed to be my friend, my partner in parenthood. I trusted you."

"But you don't trust me now?"

"I don't know." He didn't know anything anymore.

"You can do whatever you want," she said. "But I'm

going to pack my bags and catch the last boat to the mainland, before it gets dark."

He tried to stop her. "You don't have to do that."

"Yes, I do. I'll get a room on the mainland and take a commercial flight back to the States in the morning or whenever I can arrange it."

"I understand that you want to go back early. I do, too." The pretense of being on a honeymoon was over. "But we can take my jet and return together."

"What for? So you can keep trying to convince me that I don't love you? I need for you to believe me, to trust me." She turned and walked away, leaving him alone.

As he watched her go, he knew it was just a matter of time before the monsters reappeared.

Smothering him in the dark.

It took Lizzie three days to get a flight, and by then she suspected that Max was already home.

While riding in an airport limo, en route to her condo, she thought about the wedding dress she'd left in the guest room at his house. She couldn't bear for it to be in his possession.

So what was she going to do? Text him and ask him if she could come and get it? Oh, sure, she thought, just pop over to his mansion to collect her gown, as if there was nothing weird or painful or foolish about that.

Nonetheless, she did it. She fired off a text. Deep down, she knew this was just an excuse to see him. She could have sent a delivery service for the dress.

Max replied quickly, accepting her excuse and agreeing it was okay for her to stop by. But they didn't keep texting. Their communication was brief and choppy.

She gave the driver Max's address, and he plugged it into his GPS and headed for their new destination.

When they reached the security gate, Lizzie squeezed the handles on her purse, clutching the leather between her fingers, her nerves skittering beneath her skin.

After they were admitted onto the property, the car glided up the circular driveway and parked out front.

The chauffeur opened her door, and she said, "I won't be long. I just have to pick something up."

"Take all the time you need," he said.

What she needed was her husband to accept that she loved him. But she couldn't say that to the stranger who'd brought her here. So she merely smiled and thanked him. He was an older man, probably around her dad's age.

He returned to the limo, and she took the courtyard path to the front door. Lizzie rang the bell, trapped in a situation that she'd created. Was coming here a mistake? Or would it make things easier?

Max opened the door, and they gazed awkwardly at each other. He wore a pair of faded jeans with one of his prized *Star Wars* T-shirts. She almost smiled in spite of herself, but then she noticed the depiction was of Luke Skywalker battling Darth Vader, the latter with a blood-like redness behind his black-helmeted eyes.

Good versus evil. Love versus pain.

"Come in," Max said.

Silent, she entered the mansion. She wanted to take him in her arms and make his pain go away. But she couldn't mend his ache, any more than she could cure her own.

She noticed that he was still wearing his wedding band. But she suspected that he was keeping up appearances and protecting his privacy, rather than face the questions people were going to throw at him if they saw him without his ring. He'd probably even told his pilot a phony story about why he'd returned from their honeymoon without her, citing a business emergency or something.

Lizzie hadn't taken off her ring yet, either. But she wanted to stay married. Her reason was better than his.

"I'll just go get my dress," she said, crossing the foyer and heading for the staircase.

He fell into step with her. "I'll go with you."

They made their way to the second floor, and once they reached the landing, she glanced in both directions, remembering the choice she'd made on their wedding night.

He appeared to be thinking the same thing. But neither of them said anything. They continued to the guest wing.

They entered the room where she'd left her dress. Her gown was on the bed, with the accessories that went with it, including the earrings Max had given her.

He stood off to the side, looking dark and brooding.

"It's as pretty as the day you wore it," he said, about her dress. "With all its silk and lace and shiny beads." After a long pause, he added, "If everything hadn't gotten so messed up, you would have been moving into my house instead of dashing over here to grab your gown."

She wasn't running out the door yet. For now she was having a painful discussion with him. "Even if the adoption would have gone through, I would have left eventually with us getting divorced."

"That's what we agreed on."

"Until I bent the rules and fell in love with you?"

"It's not love, Lizzie. You just think it is."

"I can't see you again after this." It hurt too much to be near him, to keep hearing him deny her. "I shouldn't have even come here today." It was definitely a mistake.

He pulled a restless hand through his hair. "I know

that we need to stay away from each other. But damn it, I'm going to miss you."

She couldn't begin to express how much she was going to miss him. She sat on the edge of the bed and touched a lace panel of her dress. "Nothing is ever going to be the same again."

He came forward and lifted one of the earrings, turning it toward the light. "Love was never supposed to be part of the deal. That's why our marriage and divorce was supposed to work."

But none of it had worked, not even the adoption. "When are you going to tell your family and friends about us?" Eventually he would have to remove his ring and face the music.

"I don't know. I just need a bit more time for now."

"Me, too." To hole up in her condo and cry. "When you're ready to deal with it, you can file for the divorce." She couldn't bring herself to end their marriage. They'd already lost the child who was supposed to be their son, and now they were losing each other, too. Just thinking about it made her want to crumble.

Turning away from him, she headed for the closet to retrieve the garment bag that had come with her wedding dress.

While he stood silently by, she placed everything inside the bag, zipping it up, shutting out the memory. The broken dream, she thought, of a marriage that never really was.

Max walked through his garden. He'd been spending countless hours here. He'd been going to the gym every night, too, but he always increased his workouts when he was stressed. Of course, immersing himself in plants and flowers was a whole other form of therapy. Or torture or whatever the hell it was.

Two weeks had passed since he saw Lizzie, since she collected her wedding dress, and he couldn't get her out of his mind. This was the worst era of his life, the absolute worst. And he'd been through some horrendous stuff when he was younger.

Yeah, he thought wryly, like the time his mom had abandoned him in their rathole of an apartment for three excruciating days. He'd survived on a half-empty box of cereal. No milk. No juice. No loving, caring parent. The TV had kept him company: cartoons in the morning, game shows in the afternoon, sitcoms and whatever else he could find that didn't scare him at night. Being alone was scary enough. And now he lived in a gigantic mansion, all by himself.

Hoorah for the nerd. The rich, single bachelor.

The monsters were back with a vengeance, just as he'd suspected they would be, keeping him awake at night, creeping and crawling into his brain. Hideous shadows in the dark. He couldn't shake them, no matter how hard he tried.

He kept walking through the garden, and as he approached the foliage that had been planted in honor of Tokoni, he stopped in midtrack. Mired in his loss, he wanted to pull every damned one of those plants out by their roots. But he would let them thrive instead, hoping and praying that Tokoni thrived in his new life, too. But it still tore him to shreds that the Creator had taken the boy away from him and Lizzie.

Lizzie. Elizabeth McQueen, his beautiful, faded friend. Even her name suggested her station in her life. She'd always been royalty, even before she'd become a high school homecoming queen or a grown-up likeness to Lady Ari.

Why did she have to misconstrue her feelings into what she thought was love? Why did she have to fall into that kind of trap?

He strode over to the gazebo and went inside, thinking about the moment they'd first kissed. He envisioned her with that luscious red lipstick, her mouth warm and pliant against his.

He missed her beyond reason. But why wouldn't he? Normally when Max needed someone to ease him out of an emotional jam, he called her. She was his go-to, his dearest, closest friend, his comrade in arms. Sure, he had his brothers, but he always chose Lizzie first. He'd shared his secrets with her, things he'd never even talked to his brothers about. Garrett and Jake knew that Max had been abused as a kid, but he'd never opened up to them about it, not like he had with Lizzie. He'd told her everything, how it felt to be beaten and burned and scorned by his mother, how he used to cower in the closet, how he'd cried himself to sleep, but most of all, how his mother had insisted that she loved him.

Sharp, jagged, bloodthirsty love.

Lizzie knew that he'd never wanted to hear another woman say those words to him again. And now she claimed to love him, feeding the monsters and making his heart hurt from it.

Max twisted the ring on his finger, warning himself to remove it, to let Lizzie go, to divorce his wife, as soon as he could summon the willpower to do it.

Twelve

Lizzie couldn't stop thinking about Max, every minute of the day, every hour of the night.

She glanced at the microwave clock and saw that it was almost 7:00 p.m. On a Wednesday, she noted to herself. But that didn't matter because one day blurred into the next.

God, she was lonely without him.

She prepared a cup of hot tea and carried it into the living room. She hadn't been out of the house since they broke apart. But being a recluse wasn't all that tough. For food, she ordered groceries online and had them delivered. She'd had a few take-out meals brought over, too. But mostly, she didn't feel like eating.

Her dad, of all people, had texted her this morning. He'd wanted to know if she was back from her honeymoon and how the adoption proceedings had gone. Since she couldn't get away with another lie, she'd typed out the truth. Not in detail, but enough to convey that the adoption had fallen through, triggering a painful separation between her and Max.

She'd also told her father that she wanted to be alone. Not that he'd offered to rush over and comfort her. But she'd made it clear that she needed her space.

So far, there was no word from Max about the divorce. But she figured it was only a matter of time before he took legal action. Lizzie still hadn't removed the ruby and diamonds from her finger. For now she was still emotionally attached to being Max's wife, even if it was killing her inside.

She contemplated where he was at this early evening hour. She suspected that he was at the rough-and-tumble gym he frequented, letting off some steam. He took his workouts seriously, especially his boxing routines.

Her doorbell rang, and she nearly knocked over her tea. Was this the final countdown? Was it someone delivering the divorce papers? Was she being served?

She didn't want to answer it, but that would only prolong the inevitable. She opened the door, preparing for the worst.

Lizzie started. The person on the other side was her dad. What part of her needing to be alone didn't he understand?

"I just wanted to check on you," he said. He wore a dark gray business suit and a concerned expression.

She glanced away. "I'm okay. I'm handling it."

"You don't look okay."

If she broke down, would he know what to do or how to comfort her? She almost pitched forward, just to see if he would catch her. But she maintained her composure.

"This isn't necessary, Dad."

"Please, let me visit with you."

Lizzie gave in to his persistence, hoping it was going to be quick. Like a bullet to the head, she thought. The last thing she wanted was to feel like a sad and lonely child, longing for her daddy's affection.

"May I get you some tea?" she asked, playing the hostess, doing what came naturally. "I already brewed a cup for myself. Or I can make you coffee or something stronger, if you prefer." She knew that he sometimes enjoyed a martini after work.

"I'm fine, Elizabeth. I don't want anything."

"Then have a seat." She gestured to the sofa. He never called her Lizzie. That name had come from Mama.

They settled into the living room, and she clutched the armrests of her chair.

He asked, "What happened to cause all this? Why did the adoption fall through and why is it keeping you and Max apart?"

She'd already given him a condensed version in her texts, but that wasn't going to suffice, not face-to-face. So Lizzie took a deep breath and explained why she and Max had gotten married, how they'd lost Tokoni and why they were separated now, including the achy part about her falling in love with Max.

"I'm so sorry," her father said. "I never would have guessed that you weren't a true couple."

"Losa certainly figured it out."

"That's her job, I suppose, to be more observant than the rest of us. Maybe I didn't see through your charade because I always thought you were meant for each other."

She fought the threat of tears, forcing herself to keep her eyes clear and dry. "I'm never going to stop loving him."

"I never stopped loving your mother, either, even after

she was gone." He paused, frowned, straightened his tie. "I just couldn't get over the loss."

"Mama dying was my loss, too."

"I know. And I should have been a better parent to you."

Yes, she thought. He should have. "Is that what you're trying to do now, Dad? Be an attentive parent?"

He nodded, making one last pull at the knot in his tie. "How I am doing so far?"

She managed a smile. Suddenly she was grateful that he was here, attempting to be the kind of father she'd always longed to have. "Pretty good, actually."

He blew out a relieved sigh. "Really?"

"Yes, really."

He finally smiled, too. "Did your mother ever tell you how she and I met?"

Curious, she shook her head. "No. No one ever told me."

"It was at a charity ball, a big, stuffy Savannah soiree. It was the first function of that type that I'd ever been to. My family was new money, nouveau riche, as they say, and this was an old-money crowd."

Lizzie leaned forward in her chair. "When was this? How old were you?"

"It was the summer before I left for university. Your mother was still in high school then, in her senior year at an all-girls' academy. That's who was hosting the ball. I was invited by a buddy of mine. He was dating one of the students and asked me to come along to meet her friend."

"And that friend was Mama?"

He nodded. "She was such a strange delight, the most eccentric person I'd ever known. We dated that summer, and even after I left for university, we stayed in touch. She used to write me the most fascinating letters. Later she went off to college, too, but we continued to correspond and see each other when we came home on breaks."

"When did you get engaged?"

"A year after she graduated. And two years later we were married. I wanted to wait until I was more established in my career. Her parents accepted me, but I still felt the new money stigma. They were such old-world people, so refined in their breeding. To me, they were like royalty."

"I wish I could have known them. And your parents, too."

"It was a tragedy that your mother and I shared, with both of us being only children and both of our families passing on so early in our lives—my father with heart failure when you were a baby, my mother with cancer when you were a toddler, and her parents in a helicopter crash, before you were even born. You'd think we were cursed."

Maybe they were, Lizzie thought. Being rich hadn't saved them, not old or new money.

He said, "Your mother never quite recovered from losing her parents. But she was already having bouts of depression before they died. It was always a part of who she was, being happy, then sad, then happy again. She had dramatic impulses, too, to do over-the-top things."

"Did you ever encourage her to seek help?"

"No. I thought that if I loved her enough, she would be okay. I didn't understand how depression worked. She might have been bipolar. Or maybe she had another type of disorder. I don't know. She never saw a doctor about it, so she was never diagnosed with anything."

Lizzie had to ask, "You never suspected that she was suicidal?"

His features tightened. "Sometimes she said odd things about death, about how freeing she thought it was going to be. But I didn't attribute that to her being suicidal." Another tight look came over him. "Even with as much as I loved her, sometimes she was just too much to handle. The moodier she got, the more time I spent at work." He lowered his head. "But I should have been there. I should have saved her."

Her heart went out to him, the father she'd barely known until now, the man struggling with his guilt. "You couldn't have, not without knowing how truly ill she was."

He glanced up. "If I'd gotten her the help she needed, she might be alive today."

"You can't go back and change it. You can only move forward."

"I'd like to do that, with you." He met her gaze. "But I have to admit that when you were a teenager and you brought Max home for the first time, I was impressed with how close you two seemed. I didn't know how to be a father to you, but he knew how to be your friend, just as you knew how to be his. It made me feel better, with him being part of your life."

Her emotions whirled, her breath lodging in her throat. "He went through some horrible things when he was a kid. Things he shared only with me, and now he's probably alone with his turmoil. He doesn't confide in people very easily, not even his brothers."

"If that's the case, then don't you think he needs you? More than he's ever needed you before?"

Yes, she thought. Heavens, yes. This wasn't the time to give up on Max. Even if he refused to believe that she loved him, she could still do what she'd always done.

Be his friend.

* * *

Max had been at the gym for hours, trying to knock the crap out of his past, throwing power punches at a heavy bag.

Why couldn't he let go of what his mother had done to him? Why did those memories have to be there, lurking in the dark? He should be better than that; he should be stronger than the monsters.

As he threw another punch, a warm, hazy feeling came over him. He sensed a presence behind him.

An immortal, he thought, a spirit helper. The Lakota called them *Tunkasila*. Although it translated to Grandfather, it applied to all guardians. In that regard, the term was genderless. Sprit helpers came in many forms, and he could tell that his guardian was female. He could feel her whisper-soft energy.

Max had never seen one before. None had ever appeared to him. But now a guardian was here, offering to help him banish the monsters, to get rid of them for good.

He turned around, startled by what he saw. His guardian looked just like Lizzie: bright blue eyes, long, fiery red hair.

Confused, he shook his head. Had a spirit helper borrowed her form? Or was it Lady Ari dressed in street clothes? Had *Tunkasila* called upon her to intervene?

He felt as if he were in the middle of a dream. Maybe he was. Maybe he wasn't even at the gym at all.

She moved a little closer, this beautiful, oddly alluring spirit who mimicked Lizzie.

"I'm sorry I didn't call," she said. "But I figured you'd be here, so I came on over."

He blinked, told himself to get a grip. The female standing before him wasn't an immortal. She was flesh and blood. She was human. She *was* Lizzie.

Tunkasila help him, he thought. He longed to pull her into his arms, to tell her how miserable he'd been without her. But he stood motionless instead, dripping with sweat, still wearing his boxing gloves. What if he touched her, what if he held her and the monsters still didn't go away?

He glanced down, taking a quick inventory of her hand. She was wearing her wedding ring. So was he, under his left glove.

"My dad came to see me," she told him.

Max finally spoke. "He did? When?"

"Today. This evening. We had a meaningful conversation, mostly about my mother. But he stopped by to make sure I was all right. He knows that you and I aren't together anymore." Her gaze lingered on him. "I'm sorry for taking my friendship away from you."

"Are you offering to be my friend again?"

She nodded. "Yes."

"Even if we get divorced?"

She nodded again, tender, determined, true. "I'll be your friend, no matter what."

He glanced at her ring again and noticed that her nail polish was chipped. He'd never seen her without a flawless manicure before. It made her seem fragile, but somehow powerful, too. "You'd do that to yourself? You'd deliberately put yourself in a painful situation for me?"

"I can't turn my back on you. I love you too much to do that."

His heart thumped in his chest. She wasn't *Tunkasila*. But she was still his guardian, his helper. He removed his gloves, setting them aside.

He held out his hand to show her his ring. "I couldn't bear to take it off. I haven't filed the papers yet, either. I kept telling myself that I should, but I just couldn't bring myself to do it." He studied her, with her gauzy blouse and long, floral-printed skirt. He appreciated how it looked on her. Flowers were becoming her signature to him. He imagined them raining down from the ceiling like petals from the gods. "Since we split up, I must have walked through the garden at my house a hundred times, going into the gazebo and thinking about our wedding. It's been torture, Lizzie, not having you in my life."

She reached for him. "I'm here now."

As soon as he hugged her, her blouse stuck to his bare skin. "I'm getting you all sweaty."

"I don't care." She held him tighter. "It feels good."

"I'm sorry for punishing you for loving me, for turning a deaf ear to it. But you know how badly it scared me."

She stepped back to look at him. "I'm not trying to push you into more than you're ready for."

"I know. But I want to be ready. I want to stop being afraid of love, to accept that I'm worthy of it." He explained the feelings rattling around inside him. "Whenever my mother used those words, they diminished me, as if I didn't deserve to be loved. They made me feel small and insignificant. A shell of the boy I was, of the man I was going to be. But that's not what you're doing. That's not what love is."

She touched his cheek, skimming her fingers along the hollowed area beneath the bone. "This is a huge step for you. For both of us." Tears welled in her eyes. "I love you, Max."

For the first time in his life, he wanted to hear a woman say those words to him. But in this case, she wasn't just any woman. She was his wife. "I love you, too," he said. He knew now that he did. That maybe somewhere in the depths of his angst-ridden soul, he always had loved her.

She kissed him, creating a fusion of warmth and comfort and strength. If the monsters tried to come back, Max would slay them. He would slice them to bits, with his guardian by his side.

Lizzie wasn't an immortal, but *Tunkasila* had sent her to him just the same. She'd been there all these years. The friend he needed, the lover he craved, the fiery-haired, tender, loving, supportive partner who'd turned his heart around.

When the kiss ended, he took both of her hands and held them in his. "There's something we need to do, besides resume our marriage."

"We have to try to get Tokoni back," she replied, clearly aware of where his mind was at.

He nodded. "Even if Losa already started processing the other couple's application, we have to try. It's only been a few weeks. There's still time for her to change her mind."

"What if she won't budge?"

"Then we'll have to keep trying. We can't give up, Lizzie. Tokoni is a part of us. He belongs to us as much as we belong to each other."

"Yes, he does." She put her head against his shoulder. "We're supposed to be a family, the three of us."

"I'll call Losa and make the arrangements for us to go to Nulah as soon as we can." He wrapped his arms around her. "But for now I want to take you home with me." And be together, he thought, as husband and wife.

Lizzie stripped off her clothes, her heart reeling. Max loved her the way she loved him. He'd said it openly, with a truth she'd seen in his eyes. And now they were in the master bath at his house. He hadn't showered at the gym. But she was glad that he'd waited, so they could get cleaned up together.

Clean and naked and wet.

He adjusted the water temperature, and she joined him in the clear glass enclosure. There was plenty of room for two people. But to her, it felt warm and cozy.

He took her in his arms, and they stood that way for the longest time, just holding each other, letting the water rain over them.

As steam fogged up the glass, Lizzie turned to face the enclosure door and drew a Valentine-type heart on it, using the tip of her finger. With a look of fascination, Max added their initials.

$M + L$, in his masculine script.

She smiled, laughed a little, felt her own heart go bump. "How wonderfully teenage of us."

"We're making up for lost time. Or I am, anyway. I still can't believe you had a crush on me when we were kids."

"Just like you had trouble believing that my love was real?"

"I believe it now." He kissed her, strong and deep, his tongue making its way into her mouth.

Her body flexed, her mind swirled. She pulled him closer, the taste of passion between them. The kiss went on and on.

And on some more.

Finally, when they came up for air, she realized that her eyes were still closed. She opened them, water dotting her lashes.

Max pumped liquid soap into his hands and began washing her breasts. He thumbed her nipples, making them peak from his warm, slick, sudsy touch.

Sweet love. Sweet marriage.

Lizzie relished every wondrous thing he was doing to her. "I like the scent of your soap." The sandalwood that often lingered on him.

"And I like touching you this way."

He bathed her entire body, front to back. He washed her hair, too, with his shampoo. Everything in the shower belonged to him, including her.

He massaged her scalp, his fingers kneading her skin. She'd always enjoyed going to the salon, but this, this...

He used a conditioner, then moved out of the way, encouraging her to step under the spray so she could rinse, completing the task herself. But it didn't end there. He watched her, like a voyeur taking forbidden thrills.

Within a heartbeat, he came forward, kissing her again. She nearly lost her breath, especially when he dropped to his knees. She gazed down at him, and he glanced up at her, a carnal warning in his eyes.

Lizzie didn't know if she was going to make it out of this situation alive. He used his mouth in wicked ways, relentless in his pursuit—an intense journey, hot and thorough.

The orgasm that rocked her body sent her into a state of erotic shock. She moaned in the midst of it.

"Max... Max... Maxwell..."

She rarely used his full name, but she was doing it now, slipping into the sound of it. She gripped his shoulders to keep from falling over, her knees going weak, her pulse thumping in intimate places.

In the afterglow, he stood and smiled, obviously pleased by what he'd done to her. Then, leaving her staring after him, he lathered his own body and washed his own hair.

As the steam thickened, she blinked through the haze. Her husband looked like a modern-day god, a contemporary warrior, every muscle in its place.

Needing him more than ever, she approached him. As she moved into his arms, he obliged her, pulling her tight against him. She wedged a hand between their bodies. He was already half-hard.

Lizzie took it all the way, giving him a full-blown erection with a rhythm that rippled through both of them.

He grabbed the condom that he'd brought into the shower and tore into it. She was just as eager, just as wanting.

Having sex while standing up wasn't an easy feat, but they managed just fine—in lip-biting, nail-clawing, body-twisting ways.

He rasped, "If we weren't already married, I would ask you to marry me, right now, just like this."

"And I would say yes." A thousand, hard-driving, hip-thrusting times yes.

They feasted on each other, mating like animals. Max came in a burst of male heat, and Lizzie held him while he shuddered, held him until she lost the battle and exploded into a soul-shattering orgasm, too.

Seconds passed before either of them had the stamina to move. When they did, it was to put their foreheads together and glance over at the mist-drawn heart.

Although it was melting, dripping down the glass, the sentiment remained.

M + L. Forever.

Thirteen

Three days later, Max and Lizzie arrived in Nulah, ready to fight for the adoption. Losa agreed to see them and hear what they had to say, but, as usual, she wasn't making any promises.

On this summer afternoon, they gathered in the picnic area of the orphanage. The sun was shining, with a fresh, clean, grassy scent in the air.

None of the kids were outside. Max wished they were. He was desperate for a glimpse of Tokoni. He knew Lizzie was, too.

She sat next to him, with Losa seated across from them, a wooden tabletop between them.

Max decided to start the conversation with an emotional tone since that's how he was feeling. "I love my wife," he told Losa. "And she loves me. She loved me on the day you denied our application, but she was struggling with her feelings then."

The older woman squinted beneath her glasses, narrowing her gaze at him. "This better not be another fake attempt at trying to make me think you're a couple."

"It's real." He reached for Lizzie's hand and held it, threading his fingers through hers. "We're not pretending to be together. We *are* together. On the day our application was denied, we returned to the resort where we were staying and had a breakdown. But it was worse for Lizzie because she admitted that she loved me, and I turned her away."

Lizzie didn't interject. She remained silent, listening to him recount their story. Losa was listening, too.

Max continued. "I was afraid of being loved by Lizzie, afraid of hearing her say those words. It relates back to my childhood and the terrible things my mother did to me."

Losa didn't reply. But she was no longer squinting at Max. Her expression had softened. Of course she already knew that he'd come from an abusive environment. He'd mentioned it when he first volunteered at the orphanage, but not to the degree he was speaking of it now.

He went on to say, "I accepted being loved by other people. My foster brothers love me, and I love them. I love Tokoni, too. That kid has been part of me since the moment I met him." He glanced at his wife, and she squeezed his hand, giving him her support. "But it was different with Lizzie because she knew all my secrets. When we were teenagers, I told her every painful detail, things I never told anyone else. That brought us together as friends. But now that I'm able to look back on it, I think it created a wall between us, too. I built that wall around other women, as well, insisting that I was incapable of falling in love. Yet all along, I think I was having those types of feelings for Lizzie, even though I was too mixed up to recognize them." He paused, giving himself a second to breathe. "I'm sorry if this sounds like psychobabble, but it's the only way I know how to describe it."

"I understand," Losa said. "We have children here who've been abused. I know how it can affect them. But we do everything in our power to get them the help they need."

"That didn't happen for me. I got lost in the foster care system, with social workers who were overwrought with work, with caseloads they couldn't handle. But I was glad that they left me alone. I didn't want to be singled out. Once my brothers took me under their protective wings, I felt a little better. But I was still guarded. I've always been that way." He turned toward the beautiful redhead by his side. "But not anymore."

Lizzie scooted even closer to him. "Max isn't the only one who's been working through his issues. I was just as afraid of loving him as he was of loving me. Those are the shadows you saw in my eyes the last time we were here." She softly added, "But I'm stronger now, and I'm ready to be a wife and mother."

Max quickly added, "You were right when you told us before that we weren't ready to be Tokoni's parents. We deceived you and ourselves in our effort to adopt him, but now we want to do it in the right way. We love Tokoni, and we want the opportunity to make him our son, to devote ourselves to him and each other." He implored her. "Will you consider our application in place of the other couple you told us about? Will you give us a chance?"

Losa didn't reply. She only shifted in her seat.

Max hurriedly said, "I guarantee that everything we just told you is true. But if you want us to sign an affidavit to attest to our feelings, we will. We'll sign it in blood if we have to."

"You don't need to go that far." Losa removed her glasses, cleaning them on the hem of her blouse. She put them back on and sighed. "I have a confession to make." A beat later, she said, "I lied to you about the other couple. They aren't real. They don't exist."

Max jerked his head in surprise. Lizzie did, too.

Losa explained, "I was concerned that if you thought Tokoni was still available, it would be harder for you to move on with your lives. I didn't want you holding on to false hope. Also, it was easier to deceive you once I surmised that you were deceiving me." She frowned. "I'm not prone to lies. That isn't my nature, and I'm sorry I used that tactic on you. You deserved the truth from me, just as I deserved it from you."

Max's thoughts spun inside his head: relief, confusion, new hope. Beside him, Lizzie's hand began to tremble. Their fingers were still interlocked.

He asked Losa, "Is this your way of telling us that you're reconsidering us for the adoption, that we have a chance? Or are you just making amends for deceiving us?"

"Both," she replied, her frown morphing into a smile. "You told me everything I needed to hear, and now I'm able to look past your former lies and see the love and care and devotion between you. The kind of devotion Tokoni's mother wanted his adoptive parents to have."

Lizzie burst into a grateful sob, and Max thanked Losa and drew his wife into his arms, inhaling the sweet scent of her skin, this beautiful, perfect woman who was going to be the mother of his child.

He turned back to Losa. "May we see Tokoni? Just for a minute or so? You don't have to tell him that we're going to adopt him. You can wait until we've been approved." Max knew that he and Lizzie still had a ton of paperwork ahead of them. "But it would be wonderful if we could at least visit with him."

Losa smiled again. "I think that would be all right. I'm certain that he's going to be as thrilled to see you as you are to see him." Short and stout, she came to her feet and moved away from the bench. "Stay here, and I'll bring him to you."

Max and Lizzie waited together, holding hands, anxious to see their boy. Nearly three months had passed since the last time they saw him, but it seemed like an eternity.

When they spotted him crossing the lawn with Losa, they stood and exchanged a smile. He was just as they remembered him, with his bangs flopping across his forehead and a wide grin splitting across his face. The older woman let Tokoni go, and he raced through the grass, heading for Max and Lizzie.

They knelt to greet him, and Tokoni barreled straight into them. The three of them toppled to the ground, arms and legs akimbo. Peals of laughter ensued, rumbling into breathless, mindless joy.

Max helped Lizzie up and pulled Tokoni toward them for a group hug: this crazy, beautiful family in the making.

After leaving the orphanage and returning to the island where they'd stayed before, Lizzie enjoyed a cozy evening with her husband. This was the trip of a lifetime and the original honeymoon they should've had.

For dinner, they ordered room service. And now that they'd finished their meals, they shared a dessert designed for two: a fruit tart, smothered in vanilla cream and laden with kiwis, bananas, berries and figs. They ate from the same plate, both with their own fork.

Lizzie gazed admiringly at her man. He sat cross-legged on the bed, wearing nothing but a pair of boxer-briefs. She was in her underwear, too. It just seemed like the thing to do on this warm summer night.

"What an amazing day," he said.

She nodded her agreement. "Yes, it was. But I can't wait until the day comes when we can bring Tokoni back to the States with us. Can you imagine how excited he's going to be?"

Max smiled and dipped in to the tart. "He'll be able to finish the drawings in his booklet, filling in the color of his parents' hair. His mother is going to be a beautiful redhead, and his father is going to have black hair."

"His gorgeous father, you mean."

He smiled again. "If you say so."

"I do." She took a creamy, fruity bite and moaned. Then she laughed and covered her mouth. "This is so darned good. I probably have it all over my face."

"You don't, actually. But it kind of reminds me of feeding you our wedding cake and kissing it off your lips. That was the sexiest thing I've ever done in a room full of people."

She suspected that this dessert session was headed in a sexy direction, too. That once they finished pigging out on the tart, they would be kissing like mad. But for now she asked, "What happened to the top tier of our cake?"

"I don't know. What's supposed to happen to it?"

"There's a tradition where brides and grooms freeze it and then eat it on their first anniversary."

"If that's the case, then the chef or someone in the catering staff probably kept it for us, putting it in the freezer in the ballroom kitchen."

She hoped they did. "We'll have to check when we

get home. It would be fun celebrating with you next year with our cake."

As Max speared his next bite, some of the crust crumbled onto his lap. He grinned, shrugged it off. "You know what I love, besides you?"

"What?" she asked, mesmerized by him.

"I love hearing you refer to the mansion as home. I love that my place is your home now, too."

She leaned over and nabbed another forkful. "I wonder what Tokoni is going to think of it. I'll bet he's going to be overwhelmed with how big it is."

"Once we're able to tell him about the adoption, we should show him pictures of it so he knows ahead of time where he'll be living."

"I hope the adoption goes quickly." Lizzie was anxious for them to become Tokoni's parents, to make that dream come true.

"It could happen as quickly as three months. We could have him home by Halloween. That could be our first official holiday, with the three of us together."

She glanced toward the window, where an ocean breeze was stirring. "Do they celebrate Halloween here?"

"I don't think so. But once we take the online classes that are required for the adoption, we'll know a lot more about how to blend Tokoni's traditions with ours." He shifted his legs, keeping them crossed, but moving his knees a little. "Remember when we talked about bringing Tokoni back for vacations so he can visit his homeland? I was thinking we should take it a step further and buy a summer house in Nulah."

"I love that idea. Maybe we can find a home near the orphanage, so Tokoni can play with the other kids and we can volunteer our time."

"That sounds good to me." He polished off his section of the tart. "Maybe, at some point, we could even adopt more kids."

Oh, wow. Lizzie widened her eyes. "You want more children?"

"Sure. Why not? If we're going to be a family, then we might as well share the love. We could adopt them from here and from the States, too, from foster care. Is that okay with you, to have more kids?"

"I hadn't thought about it until now. But yes, I would love to have a big family with you." She imagined them with a house full. "I think it would thrill Tokoni, too, to have siblings to call his own, to be part of something so meaningful."

"Then it's a deal. A future plan." He watched her take the last bite of the tart.

As she licked a dollop of the cream filling off her lips, he took the empty plate away, along with their forks. Was he preparing for the fast, mad kissing?

Once the area was clear, Max nudged her onto the bed. But he didn't rush her into it. He took his time, kissing her languidly, making her sigh like the dreamy new bride that she was.

He was warm and giving, gentle and passionate. There was no reason to hurry, she realized. No reason to get frantic on this soft, sweet island day. They had all the time in the world to be together.

She ran her hands over his body, over his scars, over the pain from his past. He looked into her eyes without the slightest flinch.

He caressed her, peeling off her bra and panties. Naked, with her heart fluttering, she moaned from the pleasure. The foreplay was as light and breezy as the ocean air.

He ditched his underwear and climbed on top of her. She felt the beats of his heart, tapping against her own.

He used protection, and they made love in a stream of consciousness, of tender awareness, with him being deep inside her. Deep, deep inside, just where she wanted him.

They moved in unison, her body becoming part of his, rolling over the bed, kissing as they tumbled. Lizzie had never had sex this magical before. But she was with Max, her husband, her dearest friend, the man she'd known for nearly half of her life.

He rocked his hips, filling her up, sliding back down, creating a motion that took her to the edge—and beyond.

Lizzie came, shuddering in silky warmth. And so did Max. She felt him, falling, drifting, spilling into her.

At the very same time.

The adoption was final in mid-October, and now it was Halloween, the holiday Lizzie and Max had talked about.

With the joy of motherhood in her heart, Lizzie studied the people that surrounded her. Jake and Carol were here with their daughter and Garrett and Meagan with theirs. Everyone gathered in the living room of the mansion, preparing to take the kids trick-or-treating.

Tokoni was dressed as a superhero, and he looked darned fine in his red-and-blue outfit and fly-through-the-air cape. Lizzie's mind drifted back to the first day she'd met him in the library of the orphanage. She'd told him that she was writing an article about the kids there, and he'd asked her then if he could be a superhero in her story.

And now he was. Lizzie had her very own superhero son.

She smiled at him, then glanced at her husband. He was as excited as she was. Tokoni had transitioned beautifully into their lives. He loved being their child and living in his big, fancy home in America. Halloween was new and exciting for him, too. Already, he adored sharing the spotlight with his cousins.

Ivy was costumed as a fairy, with glitter and sequins and colorful prettiness. Only she called herself an "Ella" instead of a "fairy." Meagan explained that it was because Ivy had a toy fairy, a tiny statue, named Ella, which also meant fairy. But it meant more than that to Meagan. When she was a child, she'd had a baby sister named Ella who'd died of SIDS. An angel in heaven.

Speaking of angels...

Nita was dressed as an angel, in a frilly white dress with gossamer wings. She was ten months old now and holding on to tables to walk. She babbled, too, in pretoddler speak, saying things that no one understood except her. She was a darling child, a combination of her mother and father.

"I guess it'll be my sworn chocolate duty to eat her candy," Jake said as he caught Lizzie admiring his little angel. "Since she's too young for it."

"Yeah," Garrett chimed in. "That's probably just what the devil himself would do."

Jake flashed a mischievous grin. He sported a shiny red tuxedo and a set of pointy horns. He was the only parent out of the bunch who'd gotten dressed up. "Nita likes my costume."

Carol laughed. "That's just because she knows her daddy has always been a bit of a demon."

Lizzie couldn't ask for a nicer group of people. She loved Max's family. They were her family now, too, hers and Tokoni's.

She walked over to Max. "My dad is coming by later," she told him. "After we get back from trick-or-treating."

"Really? That's great." He leaned into her. "I'm glad he's taking the time to get to know Tokoni."

"I think he wants to learn to be a grandpa."

"He's welcome to see Tokoni anytime. Besides, we're going to keep him busy with the brood we're going to adopt. Just think of how many superheroes there will be around here in the future. And whatever else they decide to be."

Lizzie nodded, turning to look at the kids who were here today, pleased with how happy all of them were. They sat in a circle on the floor, all with their own plastic jack-o'-lantern candy bucket. Halloween was fast becoming her favorite holiday. But Christmas was going to be spectacular, too. She couldn't wait for it to arrive.

Jake adjusted his horns and asked, "So, is it time to get this show on the road?"

"Definitely." Max dashed over to Tokoni and picked him up. He spun him around, making him fly. "We're ready."

Yes, they were, Lizzie thought, as their son squealed in delight. They were ready.

For everything.

* * * * *

GETTING LUCKY

AVRIL TREMAYNE

For my wonderful, supportive, honourable husband,
without whom there would be no books.

CHAPTER ONE

ROMY RANG THE DOORBELL, and a few seconds later, heard a "Coooomiiiing," from somewhere inside.

It was hard to believe that this house—or was *mansion* the correct word for Russian Hill?—was Matt's. To say it was a departure from his usual student-like accommodation was a whopping understatement.

An inside door slammed. A closer "Gotta find the keys" was called out, followed by an even closer, much louder "Fuck!"

Okay, it was *definitely* Matt's place.

She ran a neatening hand over her hair while she waited for him. Unbuttoned her overcoat. Brushed at the flared skirt of her new red dress.

Stupid, really. Matt never noticed what her hair looked like or what she was wearing. He saved such observations for women he wanted to have sex with—and Romy had come to terms with not being one of those women ten years ago.

Still, her natural inclination was to look immaculate-but-fashionable for business discussions, and the deal she'd made with Matt on the phone two weeks ago was definitely in that category, despite the chaos of that crazy call. Serious enough to warrant a flight from London to San Francisco to dot every i and cross every t.

Footsteps on floorboards. A fumble at the lock. Another "Fuck" that had her battling a giggle, because it was so typical of Matt to be impatient with a door that didn't open fast enough. A click, a swoosh…and there he was.

Six feet three of lean, hard muscle looking rebelliously casual in just-snug-enough jeans and a just-tight-enough T-shirt; hold the footwear because he never wore shoes unless he had to. Good-looking in a boy-next-door-meets-fallen-angel way. Thick waves of red-blond hair, sharply alert green eyes, incongruously olive skin. Tick, tick, tick, tick and tick—Matthew Carter was a prime genetic specimen.

"Good evening, Mr. Carter," Romy said, tamping down another giggle at the absurdity of assessing Matt's attributes like he was breeding stock. "I'm here to discuss your sperm."

Matt gave her a censorious tsk-tsk at odds with the twinkle in his eyes. "I hope you don't say that to *all* the boys, Ms. Allen!"

"Only the ones with a really big— Matt!"—as he yanked her over the threshold and into a fierce hug.

"A really big what?" he asked, digging his chin into the top of her head. "Go on, I dare you to say it."

"Cup, you pervert," she said, dissolving into laughter even though her bottom lip was suddenly trembling from the emotional toll of being on the cusp of something momentous with him. "A really big *cup!*"

"Cup?" he scoffed. "More like a bucket! We're talking serious size and don't you forget it!" He released her, looking down at her with a grin that promptly faded.

"Uh-oh, do *not* cry! You know you look like a troll when you cry!"

"Trying not to," she said shakily. "It's just…you're just…you're going to hate me for saying it again, but you really are my— Hey!" as he dragged her in for another hug.

"If you call me your fucking hero one more fucking time I'll squeeze you hard enough to crack a fucking rib!"

"Okay, *okay*!" Watery chuckle. "Enough fucking!"

"There's never enough fucking to suit me, you know that." And as she chuckled again, "But I mean it, Romy. It's one hybrid kid. Not like we're spawning a dynasty of Targaryens to rule the Seven Kingdoms."

"Except I feel like I'm carrying the iron throne in my briefcase," she said, wrapping her arms around his waist. "Weighs a ton."

"Briefcase?" He half and half laugh/groaned. "Tonight is going to suck sooo badly."

"A briefcase *which you made me drop*. Serve you right if it gouged a hole in your floorboards. And you're squeezing me hard enough to crack *two* fucking ribs, by the way."

He dug his chin into the crown of her head again. "Keep complaining and I'll bench-press you!"

"You'll give yourself a hernia."

"I've been working out—I can take you."

"You haven't seen my backside lately! It's expanded. Way bigger than anything you're used to."

"I'll look at it if you want me to, but as an expert in all things posterior I usually start by copping a feel," he said.

"Hmm, well, I've eaten enough to feed an army in

the past two days and I'm fit to burst out of my clothes, so maybe just take my word for it. I wouldn't want to shock you."

"You always eat enough for an army, so don't try using that as an excuse for your butt—*or* for not cooking the paella you promised me, if that's where you're heading."

She choked up again, because paella was a pathetically inadequate thank-you for what he was doing. She searched for words to express her gratitude more eloquently, but she knew he wouldn't let her say them—he *never* let his friends thank him, always brushed them off, said it was easy, he was doing it for himself, no big deal, anything to shut them up—so she simply rested her cheek against his chest and...ahhh...breathed. In, then out, in, out.

"It'll be all right, Romy, I promise," he murmured into her hair.

"You always say that," she said huskily.

"Because it's true."

Romy smiled against his chest. Matt's *It'll be all right, I promise* had become a group slogan in their Capitol University days. He'd said those words to her, Rafael, Veronica, Artie when he couldn't run away fast enough, and even the older and more rational Teague, whenever he was trying to convince them to do something off-the-wall. Skydiving, bungee jumping, that outrageous sex-in-a-public-place challenge, the horrendous pub crawl during a near blizzard, flying all the way to Sydney, Australia, for a *weekend* to support Frankie the Aussie barmaid when her bastard ex got married, skateboarding down Lombard Street the time they'd all come to San Francisco to hear Matt speak at that tech conference and he needed to release some energy. An endless stream of dares that had them following Matt like lemmings off a cliff because whenever he said *It'll be all right, I promise*, they believed him. And even though such adventures mostly *didn't* end up all right in the end, they'd lemminged after him the next time anyway, because Matt was invincible.

But this time, *this* dare, the consequences were forever. And while Romy wasn't so much willing to embrace those consequences as desperate to do so now the carrot had been dangled in front of her, she couldn't bear the thought that this might be the one time Matt wound up regretting something.

Already, though, she was ready to believe things would be as all right as Matt promised. That was the effect he had on her, probably because he was always picking up her pieces, whether they were fully broken, slightly chipped or just a little bit scratched.

She closed her eyes, blocking out everything except the smell of the arctic pine soap he always used, the feel of his chest rising and falling with his breaths, the well-washed texture of his T-shirt beneath her cheek, his hand pressing between her shoulder blades, bringing her closer. So close her heart felt bruised against his hardness. No…not bruised, squeezed. Squeezed until it was pounding. Pounding until she was dizzy.

And then she realized Matt's heart was pounding, too, and the world tilted. A rush, a swirl, a blaze of heat, and she was in territory that was both familiar and *un*familiar—like she'd been pitched into a color-saturated virtual reality. A picture darted into her head. The two of them chest to chest and hip to hip against the wall, Matt's mouth on hers, his hand fumbling her skirt up out of the way, his fingers tugging at her underwear, and then… Oh God, *God*, he was big and hard and sliding into her until she was full of him, stretched and throbbing and wildly wanting. *You want my sperm, then take it, Romy, as much as you need, take it all, but take it like this.* Her legs wrapping around him, jerking in time with his thrusts. *Yes, please, Matt, please.*

"Matt, please!" she whispered, tilting her hips into his as though what she saw in her head was hers for the asking, for the *taking*.

Matt went perfectly still, and so did she as reality clubbed her back to her senses.

Long moment of nothing but hectic heartbeats and held breaths. And then he let her go so suddenly she stumbled back and almost fell over her briefcase. He grabbed her arm, righted her, released her abruptly again.

Romy, frantically replaying that fantasy in her head, knew how that breathy *Matt, please* must have sounded—like a woman on heat. Nothing new for Matt, who'd been beating women off with the proverbial stick ever since she'd known him, but definitely new between the two of them. And Matt's holy-fuck-help-me expression was telling her their status quo wasn't about to change.

"Sorry, jet lag," she said—the first excuse she could think of. "It kicked in last night, and I barely slept so I've been feeling light-headed all day. I guess when you squeezed me like that, it made me a little…a little woozy. A little…breathless…?"

Okaaay, best case scenario would be for Matt to grab her in a headlock, rub his knuckles against her scalp and tell her to stop bullshitting him, because she'd been flying between the UK and the USA for ten years without suffering from jet lag, so she should just confess—ha-ha-ha—

that she'd thrust her hips at him like a nymphomaniac because she wanted his body. To which she'd respond—ha-ha-ha—that being part of a harem wasn't her style and he should stop wanking over himself. The same comedy routine they'd been doing since the night they'd met to ward off any vaguely sexual frisson that might oscillate between them.

Worst case scenario would be... Hmm, well, that would be what he was doing now. Closing his eyes, then bolt-opening them as though he'd seen something horrific behind his eyelids. Smiling like he was trying not to throw up. *Agreeing* with her, "Yeah, jet lag's a bitch." And then reaching past her to close the door with the air of a guy who'd dislocate his own arm if necessary to avoid contact with her.

About the only good thing to be said for such a response was that he was obviously intent on ignoring her momentary lapse into oversexed insanity—praise the Lord!

She bent to fiddle with the clasp on her briefcase, buying herself a minute to recover, reassuring herself that all she really had to do to get past this episode of utter mortification was not thrust her hips at him like a nymphomaniac *again*. Should be easy enough: she'd had ten years' practice pretending not to lust after him.

Fixing a smile on her face, she took her briefcase by the handle and straightened—and if she was daunted to find that Matt had taken himself out of touching range, presumably for his own safety, at least she had enough self-control to keep smiling.

"We'll talk in the library," Matt said, looking at her right eyebrow. "Through here." And he opened a door to the left of the entrance hall and fled.

Romy dropped her briefcase again—and her smile with it—covering her face with her hands to trap the groan she just couldn't keep inside. She wasn't sure she'd cope if he started addressing all his remarks to her eyebrows. Deep breaths. More deep breaths. Phew. She slowly lowered her hands—and then drew in a few *more* deep breaths as she finally noticed the grandeur of her surroundings, which were definitely in the mansion-not-a-house category.

The floors were a chocolatey-dark wood, the walls painted low-sheen gold. Two impressive staircases curved their way to an upper floor. Behind and between the staircases were two massively proportioned doors, closing off what she presumed was the living area. To the right was a door matching the one Matt had gone through to get to the library.

She tilted back her head, expecting to find a chandelier hanging from the ceiling, and even when that was exactly what she found, she couldn't quite believe it. All that was missing was a gigantic vase of exotic flowers on a marble table and Matt's entrance hall would rival the lobby of the five-star hotel she was staying in. Her entire flat, with its jammed-together living, dining and kitchen areas, would fit into this one space.

She tried to imagine the library, using this as an example, and decided she couldn't actually get past the fact that Matt *had* a library. He only read ebooks! How did an e-reader require an entire room?

Of course, Matt had only moved in a week ago; the first she'd heard he was even looking for a place was when he'd emailed her three days after her fateful phone call, asking what he'd need to set up his new kitchen. So the library was probably just an empty room waiting to be repurposed. Or maybe it was nothing but a grandly named study housing a desk, a couple of chairs and his computer paraphernalia. Because *libraries* weren't Matt's style. *Libraries* were what the Teague Hamiltons and Veronica Johnsons of the world had in their homes. And not because Teague and Veronica were any more loaded than Matt—by his twenty-seventh birthday last year Matt had made a fortune selling the online payment software he and Artie (his partner in all things geek) had built while still at college. It was more that where Teague and Veronica carried the suggestion of the bred-in-the-bone wealth that went with stately homes, self-made Matt was just Matt. He still drove a beaten-up Toyota, still wore Levi's, T-shirts and Vans when barefoot wasn't an option, still drank Sam Adams.

A curse floated out to her through the doorway on the left, followed by a thud.

Ha! And he still swore like a sailor and had the patience of a gnat.

She reached up a hand to pat at her hair. Took off her overcoat and gave her dress a more thorough brush down. Adjusted the silicon-lined band at the top of one of her thick black thigh-high socks, which had slid down half an inch. Re-pasted her smile. Picked up her briefcase.

Showtime.

CHAPTER TWO

Fuck, fuck, *fuck*.

It had seemed so easy two weeks ago. A favor to a friend. On par with what he'd done for Romy back in their Capitol U days, when they'd all lived on top of each other in Veronica's town house and there'd been no hiding the fact that menstruation was more a feat of endurance for Romy than a normal bodily function.

He, Veronica and Rafael had taken turns refilling her hot water bottle, making her cup after cup of Lapsang Souchong, breaking the megawatt-but-useless painkillers out of their blister packs, restocking her why-are-they-disappearing-so-fast sanitary items. Even Teague had taken a few turns, despite not living with them—during *and* after his brief stint as Romy's boyfriend.

So when Romy had called two weeks ago to update him on where she was at with getting her whack job of a uterus fixed, it was pretty much a case of business as usual.

Or it *would* have been, if Camilla hadn't answered his phone.

Women he was fucking always seemed to need to do that when Romy's name flashed up, so it wasn't the act of answering the phone that bothered him so much as the way she'd said, *Oh, it's your Romy,* before swiping to accept the call.

His Romy? Fuck that! Romy was just Romy.

And then Camilla had told Romy that Matt would call her back, and that was a step too far in the proprietary stakes so he'd pulled the phone out of her hand fast enough to give her whiplash of the wrist and taken it into another room.

Camilla had looked mightily displeased, but it was poor form for a guy to ask a girl about her menstrual cycle in front of someone she'd never met, so he'd left Camilla to it and launched straight into it with Romy via a short, sharp opener: *Enough of this bullshit, how do we fix it?*

We can have an ablation, she'd said.

Then have one, was his response.

She *couldn't* if she wanted a kid one day—which she definitely *did*, she'd explained—because there'd be no having one afterward.

So have a baby now, he'd said, what was stopping her?

Little problem of no man in her LIFE! And yes, she'd screamed the last word, because a cramp had ripped her in half at that exact moment.

He'd paced the floor while she'd breathed through the pain, and then said, fuck it, *he'd* give her a baby—why not?

And she'd said, *Why not?* Because it was a big deal requiring more than the *one minute's* reflection he usually afforded life-and-death decisions.

And he'd told her it sure as hell didn't require her usual *one thousand years'* reflection, *and* that it would make the top ten list of easiest things he'd ever fucking contemplated: a quick ejaculation on his side of the

Atlantic, a turkey baster on hers, a courier in between, a baby at the end and Yippie-Kai-Yay motherfucker to the problem.

She'd laughed so hard at the *Yippie-Kai-Yay motherfucker* she'd snorted, but she was crying at the same time, and then she'd said he was the next best thing to Captain America to offer, even if she couldn't accept.

And *he'd* snort-laughed then, insisting that Captain America was a *virgin* as well as not being the masturbatory type, whereas Matt had shot out so many gallons of semen over the years—with and without the assistance of a second party—he could have his own page in *Guinness World Records* so where was the comparison?

And somehow during the ensuing argument over Captain America's sexual expertise—or lack thereof—which they'd been having forever—Matt's sperm offer had been accepted and general terms for proceeding agreed to, and he'd felt pretty damn happy with himself because hey, he was going to be a father, which he'd *never* thought he'd be.

Correction: godfather.

Because *obviously* he couldn't be a *real* father.

By that stage Camilla had left, presumably in a huff since he hadn't heard from her since, and Matt had figured that was just as well since she probably wouldn't appreciate his commitment to impregnating another woman even if he wasn't actually coming within spurting distance of Romy's fallopian tubes.

And now here they were, and he felt pretty sure Camilla had jinxed him with the *his Romy* bullshit because *his Romy* wasn't the Romy he'd opened the door to.

His Romy had obviously been kidnapped by aliens and replaced with a metamorphosed porn star version who looked exactly like *his Romy*—neat and chic, clean and bright—but was on a mission to drive him out of his fucking mind with the need to get his hands on her. Which he *could not do*, because *his Romy*, his *real* Romy, was off-limits.

He wasn't *allowed* to imagine taking *his Romy* against the wall energetically enough to shake the crystals off that god-awful chandelier. He would never have flung *his Romy* halfway across the hall for fear of what he might otherwise do to her! Because he would never have mistaken *his Romy's* breathless *Matt, please* as an invitation to enact that shameful scene in his head when it was really nothing more than a plea to stop his rampaging dick from stabbing her in the stomach—and thank God she hadn't called him on that but had taken pity on him by blaming a mythical case of jet lag for the whole damn disaster.

And okay, taking the blame for him was something *his Romy would* do, which meant she really *was his Romy* and his alien abduction theory therefore was a bust.

The only other explanation for this whole phenomenon was that it was an aberration brought on by his two-week sexual hiatus—and the fact he'd lasted two weeks without sex, ever since Romy's phone call, was the equivalent of *him* being abducted by aliens and replaced with a *choirboy* version of himself!

Matthew Carter a choirboy? Now, *that* was an aberration.

As he'd hurried into the library and manhandled his chair into the best position for hiding the beast in his jeans under the desk—not without a certain amount of cursing and desk-related violence—he'd decided it probably wasn't unusual for sex addicts to crave the first available person they saw during periods of deprivation. Didn't mean he was going to act on it, though. He'd been keeping Romy safe from his perversions for ten whole fucking years and that's how things were going to stay if he had to lock a chastity belt onto her himself!

What the hell was keeping her, anyway? They should be halfway through her first document by now. The tedium of paperwork would put a stop to any weird-ass sexual cravings, so he wanted those damn documents stat! Bring them *all* on, the whole fucking briefcase full!

He checked the time on his cell phone. She couldn't be lost between the entrance hall and the library—only one door in the corridor was open and she'd have to see not only the glow of the lights but feel the heat from the monstrous fucking fireplace that was slowly stewing him in his own juice.

Maybe he should go and find her.

Take her by the hand…lead her upstairs…into his bedroom…strip her…lie her across the bed. Ash-brown hair tangled on his pillow…eyes a glitter of hazel from beneath those heavy, tilted lids that made her look perpetually, deceptively sleepy…mouth slightly open as she panted for him…tongue darting to lick her top lip… breasts round and heavy…beige nipples jutting proudly… thighs opening to reveal her pink, juicy core…waiting for his fingers…his tongue…his cock. A whimper, a moan, as he slid inside her…clenching around him… hips rising to meet his thrusts…

Oh God, he wanted to come…needed to come.

His heart was thudding the way it had in the entrance hall when he'd had his arms around her, his shoulders tightening, thighs clamping, his dick straining for release. And then the hairs on the back of his neck vibrated themselves upright as though a lover's finger were trailing down his spine, and he realized he was no longer on his own in the room.

He focused his eyes on his cell phone, counting out the seconds, willing himself to get it together before turning to confirm Romy's presence behind him... aaand go...

He swiveled his chair, and lust rushed at him like a bullet. He wanted to suck the breath out of her, rip the clothes off her, lick the scent from her skin.

What the fuck was happening to him?

"Sorry to make you wait," she said, her trying-but-not-quite-making-it smile telling him she felt his tension. "I had to call Lennie to report on last night's restaurant."

She'd taken off her overcoat, and when she paused on her way to the desk to drape it over a chair he saw what she meant about bursting out of her clothes—her bodice was skintight, and she looked ripe as a ready-to-eat-immediately peach. He really didn't think he was going to survive tonight.

"It's two in the morning in London," he said, the snap in his voice a symptom of his overwrought edginess.

"So?"

"So don't try telling me you called Lennie." Not that it was anything to *him* if she called Lennie at two in the fucking morning.

"I...I did," she said, and blushed, defensive. "Chef's hours. I couldn't have called him any earlier."

"Yeah, well, Lennie's an asshole, expecting you to report in after every meal," he grumbled, and swiveled his chair back to the desk, because the blush pissed him off and he didn't want to see it. Not that it was anything to him who she blushed over, but she shouldn't be blush-ing over Lennie of all people. "You're a restaurant con-sultant not a slave."

She'd reached the desk and took her seat, holding her briefcase on her lap as though it were that chastity belt he'd told himself she needed. "You know I have to jump when he says jump."

"I know you can't trust a guy who fricassees garden snails," Matt said, because *he* didn't trust Lennie. Len-nie thought he owned her.

She gave an agitated little huff that told him he was being a dick. "And here I was thinking you might have given up burgers for escargot."

"Why would I do that?"

"The house...this room." She looked around. "Your tastes have changed."

"It's just a library."

"Yes, and it's very *library*-like," she said, looking around again. "Hmm. It reminds me of the library in Teague's family's place in the Hamptons. All those shelves full of...of books."

"Hel-lo! Library!"

"Yes but the chairs, tables, Persian rugs, velvet cur-tains. That fireplace! Big enough to incinerate an ele-phant!" She laughed, but it sounded forced. "Remember that time we were all invited to the Hamptons for the Hamiltons' Fourth of July ball? Even Veronica was wowed by the library!"

"You went into raptures over it, too, so what's the problem here?"

She grimaced—*grimaced!* What the fuck!

"I just...wondered if you'd bought the place already furnished, that's all," she said.

"Why? Because I don't have Teague's good taste?"

"Well, you *don't*, actually. Nobody does! But what I meant was that not even *you* could get all this done in a week."

"Oh." He shrugged, suddenly self-conscious that it *hadn't* been furnished, that he'd hired people to do it, that he'd told them to copy Teague's style and to get it ready in a week in time for Romy's visit. The library, the kitchen, two bedrooms—his and a spare in case she decided to stay—and an outdoor table, two chairs and a patio heater so they could eat breakfast on the deck tomorrow, because the deck wasn't as oppressive as the rest of this fucking ginormous house. And now it felt all wrong. "Look, are we going to spend the night talking about decor or can we get on with the business at hand?"

"Okay!" She huffed a breath in and out as she pulled a sheaf of pages out of her briefcase and put the briefcase on the floor beside her chair. And then she frowned at him. "You know all this paperwork is only to help you make an informed decision, right? I'm not here to torment you with red tape."

"I'm not tormented."

"You sound tormented. You look tormented. You—"

"I'm not tormented!"

Pause. "Let me put it a different way."

"Fuck!"

"If you're having second thoughts about giving me your sperm, I'll let you off the hook, no questions asked."

He almost laughed at that! "Romy, I'm having so many thoughts about giving you my sperm I can barely keep up with them—but not one of them involves being let off the hook."

"I just want us to be…you know…normal."

"So we make that a nonnegotiable condition, okay? We stay normal or it's off."

"Yes, but—"

"Jesus, Romy, move things the fuck along or I'll think *you're* having second thoughts!"

She opened her mouth, closed it, opened it, closed it, opened it, and all that drawing attention to her mouth was not helping because it made him want to kiss her! And then, "Fine!" she said. "Fine. If you're sure." She sorted agitatedly through her paperwork. "Here," selecting a page and holding it out to him as she placed the rest on the desk in front of her.

He took the page. "What is it?"

"A waiver my lawyer drew up for your protection."

"Protection from what?"

"From me. Think of it as the prenup you have when you're not getting married."

"You've got to be kidding me!"

"I'm not going to have people say I baby-trapped America's favorite dot-com billionaire."

He stared at her for one long, fraught moment. And then, "Okay," he said, and read the document. "Right." Looking up. "Got it."

"Read it again."

"I don't need to read it again, Romy."

"Yes, Matt, you do. You make decisions too quickly. And this is important. Important enough that you might want to have your lawyer read it. In fact, you *should* get your lawyer to read it."

"I don't need my lawyer to read it, because I'm not signing it."

"Well, of course I'm not expecting you to sign it right this minute."

"I'm not signing it, period."

"What?"

"Will this make it easier to understand?" he asked—and ripped the page in half, dropping the two pieces back onto the desk.

"Why did you do that?"

"Because if you think I'm going to sit here on a fortune while my kid lives on a budget on the other side of the world, you've got rocks in your head. I may know fuck-all about being a father, and we both know I'd be a shitty role model for a kid—"

"You would not!"

"—but one thing I *can* do, and do easily, is money."

"I don't want your money, Matt."

"The money's not for you, so get over it. You're getting just about everything you want out of this deal, Romy, and that's fine. That's great. I'm cool with it. But for the love of God, stop rubbing in the whole I-don't-need-you-Matt thing."

"Rubbing—? Need—? I don't—!" She peered at him as though trying to dive into his brain. "I don't understand. All I'm trying to do is protect you!"

"I don't *want* to be protected. I just..." He stopped, dragged in a slow breath. "I just...want to do this."

"You *are* doing this. You're providing half the chromosomes."

"Yeah, anyone with a dick can do that."

"But I want *your* dick," she said.

They looked at each other in shock—and then they both burst out laughing. And God it felt good. Back to normal. Almost.

"Is that a Freudian slip?" he asked. "Because hey, come on over to my side of the desk."

"Oh, shut up."

"Look," he said, "seriously, what difference is it going to make if I fling you a few dollars? I could support a hundred kids and not notice the outlay."

"It's not supposed to be about buying a baby."

"I'm not selling one."

"It's not *fair* to you. Not when you'll have a real family one day."

"You *are* my real family. You, Rafael, Veronica, Teague, crazy Artie."

"You know what I mean. What happens when you get married?"

"I'm not getting married. No other kids. This is it for me. My one chance. So don't take it away from me over something stupid like money."

"Are you blackmailing me?"

"I'm appealing to your kind heart."

"You are so full of it!"

"Okay, I'll switch to blackmail if you're going to be mean about it. I'm making it a nonnegotiable condition of my participation. No money, no kid." He picked up the pieces of paper. "Now, are we starting negotiations on the same torn page, or not?"

"Blackmail isn't a negotiation."

"Ticktock, time's a-marchin'."

"Yes, but it's my clock that's ticking, not yours. You have all the time in the world to have other kids."

"Don't want others. I'm good with clocks. Might as well synchronize my alarm with yours. Are we on? Decide."

"I don't— I can't— I'm not…not *like* that. I don't make decisions on the fly."

"But I *do*, Romy. And things work out just fine for me. So decide. Now."

Long, long moment. And then, "Okay," she said, the word sounding as though it had been dragged out against its will. "I'll take the money, but I want it tied up in a trust. I mean it, Matt. No sneaky stuff. No saving me from imaginary destitution on the sly. I'm getting my lawyer involved—I'm warning you."

He dropped the paper pieces. "Just so you know, I've already got my lawyer on the case, and I'll bet she's scarier than yours. If I want to sneak money to you on the sly, it'll be done before you know it's happening and there'll be nothing you can do about it."

"Now you see, that's your inner superhero waving his flag. You think you're saving a damsel in distress, but I promise you, I'm not in distress."

"Have you thought that maybe this isn't about you, it's about me? How do you know I'm not the one buying a baby?"

"What? No!"

"And if I told you straight out that I am?"

"I guess I'd ask why you chose me."

Their eyes met. Held. Something flashed inside him. Hot. Vivid. "And I'd answer…*because* it's you," he said. And the instant the words were out, he knew they were true. He was doing this not only *for* her, but because it *was* her. Because she was the one pure thing in his life and he needed her and if they shared a child he'd always have her. And his child…? Well, of course he had more to offer his child than money: he had *her*. Her light, to cancel out his darkness.

"Oh!" she said, blinking furiously.

Shit! "Don't go troll on me," he warned.

"I won't. I promise. It's just…nice. To hear that."

"Yeah, well, don't get sentimental about it. It's to my benefit to give my kid a good mother. Less chance it'll want to come and live with me one day."

"Oh!" she said again, and gave a tiny sniff that freaked him out.

"Jesus, Romy! Get a grip. Are you on hormones or something?"

"No. No, no, that's just nice to hear, too. In a…a twisted kind of way."

"That's me—twisted."

She gave him that peer-into-your-brain look again. "Why do you always do that, Matt?"

"What?"

"Make yourself something…less."

He hunched a shoulder. "I'm not doing anything except reminding you there's something in this for both of us. Right, we still have a hundred documents to get through and I'll be ripping up any that have a tear splotch on them, so get it together."

She wiped a finger under each eye. "It's not a hundred, it's fifteen."

"That's my girl! Precision document preparer." He laughed. "We'll get through a paltry fifteen like a hot knife through butter."

He hoped she'd laugh, too, but she didn't. She was watching him, her forehead creased as though she wasn't sure whether or not she should be frowning, and Matt felt panic edge its way up his spine because maybe she was about to call things off—and suddenly, unexpectedly, he knew he'd move heaven and hell to keep the deal alive. "Are we good, Romy?" he asked.

She bit her lip, and he did his best to make himself

look nonthreatening. If he could have willed the right response out of her, he would have—he certainly directed every synapse in his brain at her as he silently urged: *Say yes...say yes...say yes, damn you.*

"Yes," she said, and his limbs went weak with relief. "Yes, we're good."

"So," he said, as nonchalantly as he could manage. "What's next?"

She flipped a page, another, another, muttering something under her breath. He knew what she was doing. Sorting the documents, easiest to hardest, building her case. The muttering thing usually made him want to get her in a headlock, rub his knuckles against her scalp and warn her she was talking out loud, not in her head. But not tonight. Tonight, for reasons he *did not want to face*, it made him want to take her on his lap like he used to do at college when something was worrying her. But this was different from college. Because he didn't just want to reassure her, he wanted to kiss her.

He forced his eyes away from her mouth to her hands, and the platinum signet ring on her right pinky finger caught his eye. She'd worn it every day since Teague had given it to her for her twenty-first birthday seven years ago, and he barely noticed it anymore. But now he wanted to rip it off her finger and throw it into the fire. What a fucking crazy upended night this was turning out to be.

"This one," she said, and picked out a page.

The ring caught the overhead light, distracting him. "Huh?"

She held the page out to him. "Timing."

He ignored the page. He wanted this done. Wrapped

up. Settled, before she could change her mind. "Choose any time you want—I'll fit in with you. Next."

Flip. Shuffle. She held out another page. "Clinic options in San Francisco."

He ignored that document, too. "Mark your preferred one and I'll make an appointment. Next."

New page—held out. "The process."

"Fuck, Romy. I grab a girlie magazine and jack off. Do you really think I need instructions? Next."

She chose a new page, held it out to him, then pulled it back and put it on top of the pile. "You know what?" she said, neatening the edges of her documents as that fucking ring flash-flash-flashed at him. "Let's stop pretending you're interested in the paperwork. Just point me in the direction of the kitchen so I can make your *fucking* paella! And *then*, since your mind is clearly on what time Camilla's arriving and not on me, set the table for the two of you, *not* all three of us, and I'll go back to my hotel, and that way—"

She broke off as his hand shot across the desk and latched itself around her right wrist, shocking the bejesus out of both of them. He watched her fingers curl, then flex, then curl again—but she didn't break his hold the way she should have if she had any sense. He imagined her feeling the tremor that was shimmering through him and working out what it meant, then blushing for him the way she had for Lennie. Her slumberous eyes half closing as she offered herself to him. He could see her on the desktop, raising the skirt of her cherry-red dress…see himself taking off her black stockings, sliding her panties down her legs. One lick, to taste her. *Do that again, Matt…lick me… I want you to do everything to me…anything you want…*

"Matt," she said, in that same breathy whisper she'd used when he'd hugged her too hard in the entrance hall, and he released her just as suddenly as he had then. He had to get his shit together. Stop the Jekyll and Hyde fuckery.

He put his hands palm down on the desk, ordered them to stay there. Splayed his fingers, then brought them in again, splayed…and back. Breathing, breathing, breathing through the moment of holy-hell panic and trying to remember the last thing she'd said and how he was supposed to respond. Something about the documents…kitchen…paella…Camilla…

"Why would you think Camilla was coming for dinner?"

"Because your girlfriends always do."

"Point of clarification, Romy—I haven't had a 'girlfriend' since I was seventeen."

"Well, *whatever* you call them, they're always joining us for dinner or lunch or drinks or something."

"I *call* them by their name."

"You know what I mean."

"Hookups, then. I call them hookups."

"I'm talking about women who are *more* than casual hookups."

"They're *all* casual hookups."

"Um…no! You met Camilla a week before Thanksgiving, and I called you two weeks ago—five weeks *after* Thanksgiving—and you were still with her. That length of time with someone does *not* equal a casual hookup."

"What would you call it?"

"An affair, maybe?"

"Affair? Fuck!"

"What's wrong with *affair*?"

"*Affair* is so *bourgeois*," he said, and immediately recognized *bourgeois* as one of his father's words. *Why be bourgeois, Matthew, when you can be bohemian?* How many times had he heard variations on that theme? And now he was parroting his father to Romy! What the hell was wrong with him tonight?

"Well, how '*bourgeois*' is it to answer a guy's phone for him?" Romy asked. "Casual hookups don't answer your phone."

"Yeah, well, she was on top, it was easier for her to reach it," he said, goaded by who-knew-what into yet more assholery.

Her eyes went wide. "You spoke to me in the middle of having *sex* with her? You—you—"

"Bastard? Is that the word you're looking for? Because *that's* bourgeois." Her eyes were still wide, and her naïveté provoked him into wanting to shock her further. Shock her...show her who she was dealing with here. "It's just sex, Romy, and nonexclusive at that. *Hookup* fits better than *affair*, trust me on this. And since Camilla hasn't called me since that night, whatever she *was*, she's not *it* anymore."

"Not exclusive?" Pause. "You mean exclusive as in—"

"Monogamous."

"You were hooking up with other women simultaneously?"

"Not at *exactly* the same time, if you know what I mean."

"Well, that's...something. I guess."

"Although I have in the past. There's nothing quite like a threesome."

"Oh," she said faintly, "I see. But…but not with Camilla. But doesn't that mean—?"

"Camilla, of course, was hooking up with other men—she's not at all bourgeois."

"I see."

"Good," he said. "Now you know."

"I just thought…"

"What? That I was an innocent, clean-cut boy?"

"I thought…at least you used to be… I was *sure* you were…monogamous."

"Still am, on request. You want monogamy, you got it. That tends to get the cardinal rule broken a little faster, though, and that's always the end," he said, threading his voice with amusement.

"Cardinal rule? How do I not know about a cardinal rule after ten years?"

"You don't know because you don't break it, Romy. You don't *say* it."

"Say *what*, Matthew?"

"That you love me."

Romy had this thing she did when she was trying to make sense of something that did not compute: a raised-eyebrow blink in slow motion, which he called her blink of insanity. She did it now. "A woman tells you she loves you, your instant reaction is to *dump* her?"

"I don't like the word *dump*. It's more what I'd call a withdrawal of interest."

"Now, you see, I think a woman might still regard that as being dumped."

"Then she'd be wrong, because dumping implies there was a relationship. And, like I said, I haven't had one of those since I was—"

"Seventeen? She must have been some girl, the one you were with at seventeen, to be so hard to replace."

"Oh, yes, Gail was some girl, all right," Matt said, and although his voice was steady, the old sick rage he thought he was done with welled up in him.

Romy saw it, too. Or sensed it. He could tell. Ah shit. He braced for follow-on questions, holding his breath as she did the open-shut mouth routine…

But she must have decided that was one story too many, because with a slight shake of her head, she changed tack. "So when you *are* monogamous," she said, "they fall in love…when? Are we talking days? Weeks? Months?"

He managed an almost-natural laugh. "You think I keep track?"

"Too many to keep track of? Maybe you and Artie could invent a track-keeping app."

"Smart-ass."

Pause. "So…how long does it take *you* to fall in love, Matt?"

"What is this? The Spanish Inquisition?" He tried out another laugh, but this one missed natural by a mile.

"Just a simple question."

"Then here's a simple answer—I don't."

"Not since you were seventeen, I suppose."

Back to that. He pushed his chair back from the desk, then pulled it straight back in. Restless. Agitated. "It's like this: both people in a…a…"

"Relationship?"

"…*situation* need to want the same thing or someone's going to get hurt."

"Are you saying you never want the same thing they do?"

"No, sometimes we want *exactly* the same thing, and that's great."

"But it's never love?"

"Search your memory for a contradictory example, Romy. You won't find one."

"Well, that's a shame, because you've gone out with a lot of wonderful women." She sighed. "I hope you at least warn them up front what to expect."

"Oh, I make it clear, what's in it for both of us."

"Sex."

"*Good* sex. And fun. And respect. I'm not jealous or possessive, which means they can leave whenever they like, no questions asked. No stalking or bad-mouthing or revenge porn when it's over. Friendship if they're up for that at the end, although very few are and that's okay, too. I just...don't want them to love me."

"And yet they *do* love you, Matt. I've talked enough of them off the ledge at the end to know it."

He shook his head, dismissive. "They don't stay on the ledge for long. And that's because although they *say* they love me, they really don't."

"You can't know that."

"I know they almost invariably speak those magic words at the peak of an orgasm, which tells me it's about sex. And if they think sex is the way to my heart, they sure as fuck don't know me well enough to love me. In fact, I'll let you in on a deep dark secret about the way to my heart, Romy." He leaned across the desk, confidante-style, and lowered his voice. "There *is* no way, because I don't *have* a heart."

"If that were true I wouldn't have trusted you all these years and I wouldn't be here now. I trust you, Matt. I trust you absolutely."

"Trust in anything you like except my heart. Or my soul, come to think of it. I definitely don't have one of those. It's the Carter curse, inherited along with the hair. So don't look into my eyes for too long or I'll steal yours." He leaned back in his chair and smiled mockingly. "Have you thought what'll happen if you have a red-haired, soul-stealing kid? Will you reject the baby?"

She looked directly into his eyes. "I like your red hair. I want the baby to have it."

That look, so serious and compelling, was like a blow to the chest, and it took Matt a moment to absorb the impact. Trust, she'd said she trusted him. And it was in her eyes. Even after everything he'd just told her. She was a babe in the woods, wandering through the forest in her red dress with no idea wolves were lurking behind the trees. She needed to be protected from the likes of him.

"Yeah well, I suggest you look past the red hair," he said, "and understand that the only thing I have to offer is a very big cock."

She surprised him by not flinching, by looking at him just as steadily, as seriously, as trustingly. "And if I were to say that I *love* your red hair? That I love *everything* about you? What would you do, Matthew? Would you dump me? And…and Veronica and Rafael and Artie and Teague? Would you dump them, too? Because I—they—*we*—all love you! How could we not, when you push and pull us to do things we never would otherwise? The baby you're giving me, for starters."

"I told you—that's for me."

"Then what about the time I couldn't afford the airfare to Sydney for Frankie's wedding, and lo and behold, a ticket materialized."

"Air miles—it cost me nothing!"

"And Artie—the software that would have stayed in your heads if not for you. You made him rich."

"Made me rich, too, and it wouldn't have happened without his brain."

"Then what about the Silicon Valley tech hub you set up and dragged him into."

"That's a partnership, benefiting me, too."

"You pushed Rafael into entering that international writing competition, which he won."

"He didn't take much pushing."

"You got Veronica the gig with the university's Student Healthcare Outreach program because she needed a good deed on her CV."

"Stop!"

"And Teague only snagged a spot crewing in the Sydney Hobart Yacht Race because of you."

"Teague almost drowned!"

"He loved every minute of it! And he loves *you*. Like a brother. He's told me so."

"Goddammit, Romy." He looked away from her, because that shook him. Teague. *Teague*, who'd seen more than the others, who'd guessed it all, who fucking *knew*. Teague might be the closest anyone had come to sainthood, but he wasn't stupid enough to want a brother like Matt. Romy was deluding herself. He brought his eyes back to her. "You're wrong. All those things…they're nothing. I've done other stuff you wouldn't congratulate me for, believe me."

"What stuff?"

He had to force himself not to look away again; to do so once was barely acceptable; twice would give too much away. "Stuff you don't need to know."

"Why can't I know?"

"Because you'd back out of this deal if you did."

For a long moment she just looked at him. And then she sighed. "How am I supposed to understand why it's so hard to accept that people love you if you won't tell me?"

"You don't have to understand, you only have to accept that to me, love is nothing but an overused word," he said. "I love ice cream, oysters, pizza. I love cooking, sailing, camping. How's anyone supposed to take that word seriously when it's thrown out about anything and everything? So I'm asking you not to say it, the way you haven't said it for ten years."

"I *must* have said it before."

"Not to me. And I figure if you were ever going to say it, you'd have said it by now. I don't *want* to hear it, Romy, so don't say it now." He stopped to take a calming breath. "There are other words for what we have. More meaningful words. Words that can't be desecrated. Words like *friendship*, *camaraderie*, *affection*. Be as creative as you want. Just don't call it love."

"Okay." She held up her hands, palms out, surrender. "This is me not calling it love."

"Good."

"I hereby promise not to love you."

"Great."

"I refuse to love you."

"Okay, I get it, Romy, give it a rest."

"It's not like I was going to propose marriage."

"Fucking fantastic. Go you. Now, moving *on*!"

She snatched up the page on top of her pile. "Visitation," she announced. "My lawyer thinks—"

"Not interested in anything your lawyer says," Matt

interrupted irritably. "I'll just tell you what I want—access without restrictions when I'm in London."

"I'm sure we can come up with a form of words to that effect," she said, all business now. "You're only in London for one week a year, so give me advance notice and I'll make sure I'm not out of town."

"It'll be more than once a year. I'll be over in four months' time to look at premises, and then again two months after that to sort out tenancy agreements."

"Premises? What have I missed?"

"Artie and I are opening a tech start-up hub in London similar to the Silicon Valley one. He's taking the lead so he's already over there, but once it's up and running, I'll be there on and off for the first year at least."

"Okay. No problem. Like I said, advance notice, and I'll make it easy for you to see the baby." She shot him a curious look. "If that's really what you want."

"Why wouldn't I want it?"

"You indicated on the phone you were looking for a no-strings godfather role. It's a little…confusing, I guess, to hear you talk about unrestricted access. And I…I just think it's a good idea to start as you mean to go on."

"What does *that* mean?"

"That you don't keep changing your mind—like, one year you decide to come every month, the next year you come once in the whole year. Children need certainty."

"Okay then, how about we leave it at once a year, scheduled, and you decide whether or not to allow other visits on a rolling basis."

"Fine. Then let's move on to—"

"I'm not finished."

She waited, watching him warily.

"The kid's going to be half-American," he went on,

"so if I'm only going to be guaranteed one visit a year, you need to bring it out here once a year. For...I don't know...heritage purposes."

"Easy! I'm already here once a year—and I'll be over more often if I land Suzanne Plieu as a client. She's keen to open a fine dining restaurant in New York and we've had a preliminary chat about what I can do to help her find a partner."

"New York is Teague's territory, not mine."

"Well, yeees." That same curious look, as though she were trying to work him out. "And if Suzanne needs a lawyer, he'd be—"

"I'm not talking about Suzanne's restaurants or legal needs. I'm talking about you being needed in San Francisco with me, the kid's father, not in New York with Teague."

"It's going to depend on whether I can afford it."

"*I* can afford it."

"My clients pay for my travel here and you're not my client."

"Then start working on your aversion to staying with me. No accommodation costs, and I won't *feel* like your client when you sashay in with your briefcase."

"I can't stay with you, Matt."

"Why not? You stay with Teague when you're in New York."

"Only when my work is finished."

"Should I point out that you're not working tonight?"

Pause. He knew that slight twist to her mouth. She was working out what to say. "Teague's apartment is... spacious. It's easier there."

"And I now have a large house. So when you come

with the kid, you stay. As long as your 'form of words' contains that, we're good."

"We're not good in that case."

"Why not?"

And she was up, out of her chair, walking over to the fireplace, dragging her hands through her hair—which she never, ever did.

"Why not?" he asked again, when she just stood there looking into the flames.

"It won't work."

"Asking again—why not?"

Shake of her head.

"Romy, what's going on? Why did I buy a house with a million rooms if you and the kid are going to stay in a hotel?"

She turned to face him then. "But th-that's not why you bought the house!"

"Isn't it?"

He saw the breath she took, and prepared himself for an argument.

"Okay then, Matthew," she said, "in the spirit of ne-gotiation—"

"It's not negotiable."

"—I'll *agree* to stay here, on the condition that I know in advance who else will be here and I can opt out if I'm uncomfortable."

"Uncomfortable?"

"I don't want to impinge on your lifestyle."

"My 'lifestyle'?"

"There'll be times it won't be appropriate for me to stay, depending on…on who…"

He shot to his feet. "Who I'm *fucking*? Is that what

you mean?" He realized he'd yelled that, but couldn't get the anger under control enough to care.

"If you'd let me expl—"

"You think I'm going to have someone stashed in my bedroom for after I've finished reading my kid a bed-time story?" Yelled again.

"I wouldn't put it quite like—"

"Will I have to fill out a form? Name, age, occupa-tion, social security number? Nominate what nights of the week I intend to fuck them?"

"Oh, for God's sake!" she said, firing up at last and yelling back at him. "I already *know* what nights of the week! *Every* damn night of *every* damn week! That's the problem!"

"I'm glad you appreciate my stamina!"

"That place we shared back in the day had paper-thin walls! We *all* appreciated your stamina! Veronica and I used to joke about buying shares in Durex, you went through so many jumbo boxes of condoms!"

"So you counted my condoms and listened in? In-teresting."

"Sadly, the pillow I jammed over my head to filter out the moans, grunts and squeals didn't quite block everything."

"What can I say? I do a good job. A better job than Teague, now I think of it, since he didn't ever stay with you overnight."

"This isn't about Teague."

"No, it isn't, is it, or maybe *I* would have heard some-thing."

"Not over the racket going on in *your* room!"

"Jealous?"

She raised her chin. "Just over it! Okay? I'm over it!

I don't *want* to hear you anymore! I've had *enough* of hearing you!" And she was on the move again, storming over to the drapes, trying to drag them open as though their very existence was cutting off her oxygen supply.

He stalked across the room, reached her, spun her. "Then how about you stay tonight and test the sound-proofing? In the absence of my usual fuck noises you can listen for the loud howl of sexual frustration that'll be coming out of my room because I haven't had sex for two fucking *weeks*! Does that scare you, Romy?"

"Why should it scare me?"

"Because you're here alone with me and I...I... Arrrggh! It's dangerous, can't you see that?"

"Dangerous how?"

"Jesus, Romy, how naive *are* you?" Matt said. The room was hot, stifling, claustrophobic. He needed air, needed...*something*! "Fuck this!" He reached past her, grabbed a handful of velvet, yanked on it, heard a satis-fying rip, and then the drapes dropped to the floor. He kicked them for good measure. "When are you going to accept that I'm not your damn hero, Romy? I'm not like Teague. I don't *do* chastity, and yet I've just told you I *have* done it, for *two weeks*."

"So *what*?"

"So I'm a *sex addict*. And you're *here*."

"A sex addict would have made a move on me the night we met! God knows I gave you the chance! So don't talk to me about not 'doing' chastity when you've been nothing *but* chaste with me for ten years!"

"You're not like the others!"

"Well, that just goes to show that you're an *idiot*! Be-cause I *am* like the others. I'm *exactly* like the others. I want what *they* want, damn you!"

Sudden, charged silence.

Matt's skin prickled, his senses going on high alert. "Tell me what you mean," he said, breathing the words. "What you want."

She closed her eyes. Heartbeat. Opened them. "You know what I mean. You of all men *know* what women mean!" And it was as though the angry energy drained out of her, even though her hands had clenched into fists by her sides. "What I want is you. I want…you."

CHAPTER THREE

TEN YEARS OF not saying the words, and now they were out, hanging between them.

Romy's heart was beating hard enough to leap out of her body. And Matt looked rigid enough to bounce the poor thing off his chest. Like a stone column. Or... or petrified wood.

Petrified being the operative word.

She choked down a rising bubble of hysterical laughter at the notion that big, bad Matt could be scared of her. *She* was the one who should be scared. Scared he'd tell her no and leave her with nothing: friendship in tatters, no baby and still no clue about what it was like to...to *be* with him like all those other women.

"You don't know what you're saying," Matt said.

And on the spot, she consigned any last vestige of caution to hell. For ten long years she'd been subjugating her lust for him. That was long enough! "Yes, Matt, I do," she said. "Exactly what I *did* say. I want you. But you can call it Plan B if that's easier for you to deal with."

"Plan B?"

"I need to get pregnant. You offered to provide the sperm. We've discussed the turkey baster method—

Plan A—but there's no reason it can't be done the old-fashioned way—Plan B."

"Old-fashioned way."

"We have a window of opportunity here. It's almost like fate stepped in."

"Window of opportunity," he said, like he was having trouble keeping up.

"Neither of us has someone in our lives—a minor miracle in your case. You said you were sexually frustrated, so you need a release valve, and here I am offering to be it."

"Release valve."

"From my perspective, it's cheaper than IVF. It's certainly more *efficient*. Like a direct deposit, cutting out the middleman."

"Direct deposit."

"Oh, for God's sake, stop repeating everything I say," she semiexploded as her resolve frayed around the edges. "It's easy to understand, isn't it? It's just a one-night stand! We've already been through your ground rules about not mistaking sex for anything more, so don't worry that I'll be expecting a bourgeois romance. And you're not the only one who knows what it is to be sexually frustrated, because it's been a while for me, let me tell you, and I daresay it'll be a much *longer* while once I'm pregnant."

"One-night stand."

"Yes, one night. No encore required. If it doesn't work, we simply revert to the turkey baster/courier option and…and…and aren't you going to say something?"

"No encore."

"Something that's *not* a stupid repeat of what I've already said."

She waited; he stared.

Romy couldn't recall an instance in which Matt had taken this long to make a decision. She wondered if she should shorthand the argument by taking off her dress.

"Matt…" she said, reaching for the zipper at her left side—but before she could touch it, a log fell in the fireplace, jolting the momentum out of her so that she lost her nerve. "Forget it. It was just a suggestion. If you can't bring yourself to do it, there's nothing more to be said. Plan A it is."

"I'm pretty sure I can bring myself to do it," he said, and then he started laughing as though she'd told the funniest joke on the world.

She drew herself up, glaring at him. "I'm glad I've managed to amuse you."

She tried to push past him, but he blocked her. "Wait!" he said.

"We've wasted enough time. We need to go back to the paperwork."

Again he blocked her. "I said wait. Let's at least *talk* about Plan B."

"I'm no longer interested in Plan B."

"Why not?"

"Because you've just reminded me how it ends."

"How can that be when it hasn't happened yet?"

"It'll be a carbon copy of the time I told you Jeff Blewett kissed like his mouth was an octopus suction cup and you dared me to let you demonstrate the way you imagined that to be. I was stupid enough to say yes because I thought…I thought…never mind what I thought, it doesn't *matter* what I thought, because at the last minute you changed direction and gave me a hickey right here…" jabbing at the center of her forehead "…and no amount of makeup would cover it up so I went around for two days looking like I'd been hit by a cricket ball and you thought it was all hilarious."

"So how about I try it now?"

"I don't need another forehead hickey, thank you."

"I mean I could kiss you for real. And then...well, then you could decide if we go ahead with Plan B."

"It'd serve you right if I said yes."

"So say it."

Romy licked her lips nervously. "Be careful, Matt, or I really will call your bluff."

"Call it. I dare you to."

"After the forehead hickey, you're going to have to convince me you'll be able to get it up at the crucial moment before I go any further," she said.

He took a step back from her, which she didn't consider promising. "One look at me will tell you that's not going to be a problem. So go on and look."

She examined his face, trying to gauge his seriousness. She was so keyed up, she'd rip his throat out if she saw so much as a glint of humor in his eye.

"Lower," he instructed.

Her eyes dropped to his chest.

"Jesus, Romy, are you doing this on purpose? Lower!"

To his jeans. "Oh."

"Bingo," he said.

She raised her eyes to his face again. "I've heard that's always there."

"Are you fucking nuts? I'd never function as a human being if that were the case." He reached for her then. "But it's been there since you walked in tonight." Folded her into his arms. "So if you're telling me you didn't feel it in the entrance hall, I'm going to think I've shrunk.

And I know I'm ten years past my sexual peak, but it seemed to work very…*sizably*, shall we say, two weeks ago."

She choked on a laugh. "Your ego is gargantuan."

"My ego isn't the thing that's gargantuan. Although if you really didn't notice the size of my cock when you first arrived, it's going to need some stroking."

"I hope you mean your ego."

"Actually, I really do mean my cock. So stay riiight… theeere, ahhhhh, that feels good." Nudging his cock against her. "Think about what it means vis-à-vis your question about whether or not I can bring myself to do it."

"What it means…" she breathed out, fairly sure she could orgasm just from what he was doing here and now.

"It means yes I can, and when I do it's going to be amazing. I'll make it amazing for you, Romy. The moment you say yes."

Same man she'd been friends with for ten years, same man who'd hugged her, tousled her hair, dragged her onto his lap, forced her earrings through her ill-pierced left earlobe. But this was different. *He* was different. And she had a premonition that he would always be different, from this moment.

The fear of losing him if she said the "yes" he was asking for was real, because women in whom Matt had a sexual interest were never around for long. The only women who lasted in his life were those who dated his friends—like Veronica, whom he treated like a sister even after her split from Rafael. And wasn't that at least one reason Romy had transferred her starry eyes from Matt to Teague in their freshman year? Not only because Teague really was perfect but because Matt had *brought* him to her, thereby marking her place in Matt's life while she got her head around consigning Matt to the friend zone?

How long would she last if she stepped out of that zone? Matt had said friendship at the end was possible with women he'd had sex with but that most didn't want it. Why would she be any different from all those other women?

The baby, of course. The baby made her different. But the baby made her vulnerable, too, because it was precious not only for its own sake but because it would be a part of Matt that would always belong to her, a part she was allowed to love. She so wanted to believe Matt would come to love the baby, which would be like loving a part of her, even if he didn't call it love.

Impossible to risk all that for one night...and yet just as impossible *not* to after wanting him for so long. Oh, how she wished she could blur the line between sex and friendship instead of stepping over it, keeping everything in its proper place.

If the sex was awful, she probably could. They'd laughingly accept that they'd given it the old college try and there was no harm done whether she was pregnant—experiment concluded successfully—or not—back to Plan A.

If it was awful...

But Romy knew it wouldn't be awful.

The tightness of her skin told her that. Her racing heart, too. The way the smell of his pine-tree-scented soap made her want to lick him.

Those were the feelings lovers had, not friends.

Lovers.

Love.

Don't call it love. Call it anything *except* love. Friendship, camaraderie, affection. A window of opportunity. A cheaper, faster, more efficient method of sperm insertion. Release valve. Direct deposit. Plan B. Sex, just sex.

If she kept all those descriptions in mind, surely she could do this. She could blur the line, she *would* blur the line, and she'd survive the end.

"All right, yes," she breathed, both brave and terrified.

He pulled her in even more tightly. "Then I suggest we go upstairs immediately because it's not your forehead I want to suck right now, and if we don't move, I'm afraid I'll drag you down to the floor and have my evil way with you right here."

She huffed out a desperate laugh. "Evil is fine by me."

He rubbed his cheek across the top of her head, and she felt him sigh even though she didn't hear it. "Careful what you say, Romy."

CHAPTER FOUR

ROMY MADE IT to the entrance hall—and stopped.

"The stairs on the left." Matt, behind her.

She hesitated. "Do you really think we can be friends at the end of this?" she asked.

"That's the idea."

"It didn't work out that way for Veronica and Rafael. They haven't spoken to each other since graduation."

"Those two weren't friends to start with, Romy. They were a Molotov cocktail from the night we all met, hell-bent on being in love. But you and I are a whole different ball game. We've got our plan straight."

"Plan B," she said. What a time to realize that for once in her life she didn't *really* have a plan—not for the mechanics of what would happen next. She was far from having an encyclopedic knowledge of the *Kama Sutra*—whereas Matt, whose sexual prowess was the stuff of legend, probably had his own annotated version.

"What is it?" he asked.

"Nothing," she said in a small voice.

Pause. "Do you want to stop?"

"No." Same tiny voice.

"Because if you've changed your mind, this would be a good time to tell me."

"I haven't changed my mind," she said, and made it to the base of the stairs before stopping again. Oh God, what if she couldn't even get him to have an orgasm and he ended up just as sexually frustrated at the end as he'd been at the beginning?

Matt's hands landed on her hips. She expected him to urge her to go up, but instead he pulled her back against him as though they had all the time in the world. She swallowed a mouthful of saliva as she felt his erection prodding against her back. He'd said he had a very big cock and he wasn't kidding. If its size really was illustrative of Matt being ten years past his sexual peak, he must have had the penis of a freaking giant at eighteen.

"Romy?" he said, with a tingle-inducing nudge at her ear. "Be certain you want this, because there'll come a point when I'll stop asking and you'll have to *tell* me if something's bothering you."

"There's no problem," she lied—because she wasn't going to ask him if he'd ever been bored enough to fall asleep halfway through sex—and headed up the stairs, only to stop again at the top.

Matt must have reached that point where he stopped asking, because all he said was, "To the left, fourth door, the open one."

Inhale, step, exhale, step, inhale, step, exhale.

Just the feel of his hands on her hips was making her lust for him in a way she'd never thought possible. What would she do for him when his hands were on her naked flesh? Anything, she suspected. Anything at all. Everything he asked.

Now breathe. Because they'd reached the bedroom. The final frontier.

She stepped over the threshold. Dark floorboards,

white walls, a night view of San Francisco Bay in the distance, through curtains opened wide. There was an inner door she assumed led through to a bathroom. Aside from a built-in wardrobe, the only furniture was a gigantic bed and one armchair—a scarcity that amplified the room's size.

"It's big," she said.

"So all the girls say."

And somehow, that made her laugh as she turned to face him, despite her anxiety. "Are you obsessed with size?"

"Only with what I can do with it."

"Don't overpromise, Matthew."

"Not an overpromise," he said huskily, and ran his hand over her hair—a sensual stroke that made her breath catch in her throat. "Are you nervous, Romy?"

"No," she said—but a tic jumped to life at the side of her mouth and gave the lie to that. "Not…really."

Matt pressed his thumb over the tic. "We'll take it as slowly as we need to. I'm not going to do anything I think you won't like, I promise. Stop me anytime. I won't be angry. I won't argue. I won't pressure you. We'll just find another way."

She gestured to the bed, so nervous she could barely stand. "Why don't you tell me what position you want me in so we can get started?"

"Romy! We're not even naked yet."

"I'd rather have it worked out in my head before we take our clothes off so we don't get…you know… distracted."

"Getting…you know…distracted is kind of the aim. So why don't we just play it by ear?"

"By ear?" She reached up and touched her left earlobe, the one he'd nudged with his nose, feeling a residual tingle. "No, that won't work."

He looked at her for a long, quiet moment. "If you don't want to touch me, Romy, there's no point to this."

"I do want to. But I…I just know I could prepare myself better if I knew where we were headed."

"You're overthinking it."

"But what if I suck?"

"Then that'll be perfect."

"Oh!" She laughed. "You know what I mean."

He sighed. "I want you, Romy. I *want* you, *however* this unfolds. I'm telling you that straight. And you know how important you are to me outside this room, which means I have to know this is what you really want. So tell me. Tell me you want me."

"I already t-told you."

"Tell me again. Make me believe it. Or this stops now."

Her pulse leaped—fear, excitement. "I want you."

"Tell me you want me to not only make you pregnant, but to make you come."

Another leap. "Oh God."

"Tell me."

"Fine. I want you to make me come, and come, and come." She rolled her eyes at him. "There. I said it. Now can we get on with it?"

"Come and come and *come*," he repeated.

"Well…yes."

He smiled. "Pfft."

"Pfft?"

"Three orgasms is for amateurs. Let's make it four." He turned her to face the bed. "You want to talk positions? This is how I want you. Go and lie facedown across the bed with your hips at the edge."

Her hands went to her zipper. "Should I—?"

"Leave your clothes on. We'll do this first orgasm fast so you can relax."

Romy went to the bed and took up the position Matt had instructed her to take, her heartbeat now at a gallop. Oh God. Oh God, oh God, oh God, this was going to happen, it really, really was. She was about to find out why all those girls had followed him all over campus, why so many women since had put their lives on hold waiting for him to come back to them even though history told them he'd never do it. She'd know the secret to being the one for him, and she didn't *care* that it was only for one night, she *wouldn't* care, wouldn't stop to think, wouldn't stop at all. She'd waited too long for this.

"And don't worry, you don't have to prepare yourself," he said, coming up behind her, "because *I'm* going to prepare you."

Next second, he was easing her slightly backward and opening her legs. She felt a rush of moisture between her thighs, readying her for what would come next.

"Good," Matt said, as though he'd seen that gush, and Romy *wanted* him to see it, wanted him to *feel* it, wanted him to taste it. The anticipation was already better than anything she'd actually experienced.

He raised the skirt of her dress, hissed in a breath, slid his hands around the bands of those black socks that suddenly seemed erotic rather than fashionable. "These stay on," he said huskily.

"Whatever you want."

"You have no idea how much I wish…"

"You wish…?" she breathed, doing some wishing of her own—that he'd finish what he'd been about to say so she could tell him yes, do it, do anything, do everything; it was one night and she wanted it all.

But he didn't complete the sentence. Instead he moved his hands to the bare flesh of her upper thighs above her socks, and Romy lost interest in anything but his stroking fingers.

"You are so absolutely perfect," he said, his voice a raw note off an actual throb. "Now open your legs a little more." She obeyed, only to be told, "Wider, I need room to kneel behind you so I can get my tongue in."

Tongue. She started to tremble, and bit at her bottom lip, determined not to moan. *Tongue.* God help her, she was going to come the moment he touched it to her. She gripped two handfuls of his duvet in preparation.

"Ordinarily I'd suck you through your panties before taking them off," he said, causing another gush. It was a reflex action, to close her legs and contain it, but he laughed, low and strained, and said, "Oh no, you don't," and pushed her thighs wider apart. "But I want my tongue right on you, so I think…yes, I think I'll leave those snug panties of yours on and just move them…" sliding his fingers under the crotch "…so I can see them as I lick you. Win-win for me."

He grazed her with his fingers, only *just* touching her, making her gasp before she could catch it back. Then one quick tug, and Matt hissed in another breath, groaned this one back out. How did she look from back there, with the soaking-wet crotch of her lilac panties shoved aside? What was he thinking, seeing her like that—half on display, half hidden, swollen with need? Ah God, who cared what she looked like or what he thought, as long as he touched her.

"So pretty—more than I could have imagined," Matt

said, and next second he was kneeling between her open thighs. "Better than I deserve." That was added so softly, her heart thumping so strongly, Romy wasn't sure she'd heard him correctly. It didn't make sense, that he could not deserve her. Not when she was so sure she didn't deserve *him*, when she'd somehow tricked him into this.

"Wh-what?" she asked, but his answer was to tug the crotch of her panties still farther aside.

His answer was to lick all the way along her sex with the flat of his tongue so that she jerked and cried out, her hands twisting in the duvet, her leg muscles quivering, and she cared about nothing except that he keep going. He licked her again, and again and again, until she was pushing herself against his mouth. *Harder, harder.* She screamed it only in her head, but it was as though Matt heard her, because he settled into a rhythm, directing his assault at her clitoris now, alternating the flat of his tongue with the tip. Strokes and flicks, changing the pressure from hard to soft and back, increasing speed. Faster, faster, faster. It was coming, she could feel it, she didn't even have to reach for it, didn't have to will it. She had no control. One, two, three harder licks, and he sucked her clit into his mouth. He kept sucking until she was ready to bang her head on the mattress, so great was the effort it took not to humiliate herself by begging him to finish it. Her breaths were ragged, hips thrusting convulsively back and forth as though he were actually fucking her and she was meeting each lunge of his cock, but his mouth stayed with her, winding her tight like a key in a toy. *His* toy.

Something had to give. Something had to break. Something had to—

"OooohhhhhmyyyyyGooooooood." The cry wailed

out of her as the orgasm slammed into her, crashed over her, zigzagged through her like burning, bright, hot lightning.

Matt had to know she was coming, she was rigid with it, pulsing under his mouth, but he didn't stop. He kept tonguing her, going at her until her twitching body went limp. She was still gasping for air as he slowed and finished with one opulent lick. And then...hold, hold, hold, his fingers still on the panties he'd dragged out of his way. He was looking at her, she knew he was, and she had neither the strength nor the desire to stop him. His labored breathing, rough and fast, made her long to know what he was thinking.

But one more lick, a quick kiss, and his thinking was over. He turned brisk, repositioning the crotch of her panties, pulling her dress down to cover her, standing.

"Two minutes and twenty seconds," he said. "Was that fast enough for you, Romy?"

His words settled into her fried brain. Lodged there, stuck there...*stung* there.

She got off the bed, brushed at her dress with an unsteady hand. Saw that he was...smirking? Oh no. No, no, *no*! No smirking allowed. This wasn't going to turn into an octopus hickey moment.

"Yes, that was fast enough," she said briskly, "but that wasn't the deal."

Up went Matt's eyebrows. "I said we'd make the first one fast. You didn't complain."

"About the orgasm, no. But there was no semen, therefore no sperm inserted. So although it was good in terms of elapsed time, it was also a *waste* of time."

"Elapsed time? Wow! How...technical. Okay so I'll be technical back and tell you that happy though I am to oblige your demand for multiple orgasms, men have to pace themselves through four orgasms when they'll only get to two or three for themselves."

"Yes, but in this instance it's not like you need to re-charge since that was all about me."

"Nooo, but think about it like...well, like a restaurant meal. Appetizer, main course, dessert, petits fours. Cun-nilingus is the appetizer. Good to start with, not going to fill me up."

"But what you just did could have been the petits fours—not everyone gets to them, and they're hardly essential to a satisfying meal."

"Er...you know, I'll try almost anything once, but there's one thing I won't do: drink my own semen. Not going to happen. Hence...appetizer. Gotta get the order right when you're not wearing a condom."

A laugh exploded out of her before she could stop it.

Matt grinned. "I see you understand."

"I'd offer to drink it for you, but it would be a—"

"Waste of sperm. Sad but true. For now, though, you can taste yourself." And he stepped right up to her and cupped her face in his hands.

Why hadn't she ever noticed how big Matt's hands were? How big *he* was, compared to her. She was a woman who liked food and she was no twig—so why did she suddenly *feel* like a twig? Small and snappable. She wanted to fold into him but at the same time pull back, run away, protect herself. Because she was already in danger of wanting more than he was willing to give, and it was hard to remember that whatever was happening now wasn't real. Reality would come roaring back later. Outside this room, outside this moment. When this night out of time was over and they were just friends again.

He tilted her head back so she was looking into his eyes, which had gone dark, the pupils having taken over almost all the green. One of his thumbs moved to her mouth, dragged roughly across her bottom lip. He was going to kiss her. She stiffened, afraid to risk the intimacy of a kiss, wanting to hold herself back from it. She tried to form a phrase with the word *no* in it, one that wouldn't betray her confused sense of truth. But all she could find to say was, "Kissing isn't required." A stupid, mood-shattering thing to say.

"I thought we had a dare going."

"D-dare?"

"Octopus kiss."

"You said you weren't interested in my forehead."

"I'm interested in every part of you."

"If that were true you would have kissed me back then."

"Ah, but if I'd kissed you back then, where would we be now?"

"I think…" she whispered. "I think we'd be nowhere."

"Nowhere…" he repeated, and the way he looked at her was as melancholy as a goodbye, even though they'd barely begun. "I don't like that thought, Romy."

"Neither do I, so let's not think," she said, wanting to take away that look. "Go ahead and kiss me. Do it."

"Forgive me for it first."

"For what?"

"Just…say that you do."

"I'll forgive you anything, always, you know that."

She looked into his eyes as he smoothed his thumbs across her cheeks. And then he gently rested his mouth on hers, and even though he went no further, the moment felt more serious than anything he'd said or done so far. She was balanced on the knife edge of that line she *could not blur*, and one wrong move would slice her in two. Friend…lover. Which was more important to her? Which would Matt choose to be if he couldn't be both? Which would she *want* him to choose?

"Romy," he breathed against her mouth, and she wound her arms around him, held on to him, as though she'd save him from whatever it was that was chasing him. She wished she could pour herself through his skin and comfort him from the inside out, but all she could do was let him take whatever it was he needed from her, the forgiveness she didn't understand.

She knew then there was no choice to be made. She might not know what she'd end up being to him after tonight, but at this moment she would be whatever he wanted her to be.

He tightened his hands on her face and rubbed his mouth across hers, side to side to side, and she catapulted over that damn line into something that was more than friendship and way more than sex.

She parted her lips, inviting him in, expecting a swoop of tongue, a conquest. Instead, he licked at her top lip, then sucked it into his mouth. She opened wider, desperate now for his tongue against hers, and at last he fitted his mouth on hers, tight as a seal. And there it was, his tongue, inside her. Heady, heady moment, the taste of him at last. Unfamiliar—and yet as right as though she'd been expecting exactly this forever. He made a sweep of her mouth, and while her senses were still absorbing the feel of that, he came in hard, his tongue demanding a response from her so that she clung to him and kissed him back, wanting the moment to go on and on.

When he eased away from her and looked down at

her, any hint of gentleness was gone. Something in his eyes she couldn't decipher made her skin prickle all over with heat.

"Orgasm number two coming up, Romy," he said, and there was the promise of something wild in his voice. "And this time, by God, you'll get the sperm."

CHAPTER FIVE

"THAT'S...GOOD," Romy said, and she sounded so breathily gorgeous, Matt wanted to kiss her again.

And maybe he would have, if he didn't have so much more he wanted to do to her.

It had been so damn *hot* to take her mouth like that, with the salty, lemony butter from between her thighs still on his tongue. How had he overlooked the blatant sensuality of her mouth for so long? He figured it was because her lips were almost colorless so there was a hide-in-plain-sight thing going on, but that seemed a piss-poor excuse now he'd kissed her. Everything about her mouth was sexy as hell. Wide bottom lip, top lip almost unnaturally heavy. Lickable. Suckable. If he'd known how it would be, he'd have kissed her ten years ago, fuck his good intentions.

And then, of course, they'd be exactly where she said they'd be: nowhere. Because he'd barely known her, and he would have turned her into a hookup and it would have been over within days and he wouldn't have had the past ten years of having her look at him the way she always did, like he could slay dragons.

Of course, she had no idea that the biggest dragon in her life was him. Which was why his conscience kept tap-tap-tapping at him, telling him that even one night had consequences.

But it was too late to listen to his conscience and so he told himself that since it *was* only one night, the risk was limited. And if he fucked things up…well, hadn't Romy just said she'd forgive him? If she could forgive him anything, surely he could forgive himself for taking this one night. Anyway, he *couldn't* stop now. Not after the way she'd kissed him, like she was making up for those ten lost years. Enticing him to give more, to take more, to devour her mouth, until it was pink and swollen and wet.

Pink, swollen, wet. Like the luscious place between her legs—mysterious, like a dewy flower, its petals closed, peeking out from around the barrier of her panties.

Burrowing his tongue between the petals, searching out every fold, had been an adventure in eroticism. Hidden secrets, buried treasures. And he would use his one night to find every last concealment and plunder it.

How he wished he'd plunged his tongue inside her, but she'd come before he'd had the chance. She was so effortlessly sensitive, it had taken almost no time to get her there. It was like she was made for his mouth. For his cock, too, judging by the way it had throbbed all the way through, demanding its turn. It was a miracle the poor thing hadn't exploded, depositing a gallon of semen through his jeans.

Wasted sperm, Romy would have called that. And so would he. He wanted to be buried all the way inside her when he lost it the first time. And maybe if he was lucky—really, really lucky—the time after that, she might take him into her mouth before she remembered *that* would be a waste of sperm, too. But hell, one suck, one lick, even the briefest kiss, would get him ready to do whatever she wanted. Just the *thought* of seeing her lips wrapped around him was enough to make him wild. It was going to take some willpower to not fall on her like an unrestrained caveman when her clothes came off.

He sent a quick message to his dick: *control yourself.* His dick twitched in response, which Matt interpreted as the penile equivalent of being flipped the bird.

"So…what do you want me to do?" Romy prompted, making him wonder how long he'd been standing there arguing with himself. "Do I take off my clothes now?"

Matt shook his head, closing the small distance between them. "I'll do it," he said, because he needed his first touch to be controlled and once she stripped, all bets would be off. He reached for her zipper. "All you have to do is kick off your shoes."

She kicked. And waited.

He unzipped. And hovered.

Stop, breathe, swallow, control yourself. "Lift your arms," he said.

She did as he asked, and he drew her dress slowly up and off, tossing it in the direction of the chair without taking his eyes from her. He was going to need every ounce of self-restraint he could muster, because he'd never seen a hotter sight than Romy in her underwear. The contrast of the opaque black of her stockings against the matte cream of her upper thighs and the translucent lilac of her panties was pin-up-girl sexy. The neat little patch of brown hair he could see through her panties had his fingers twitching with the need to touch it. Her bra was ivory lace, her full breasts pushing against the cups as though craving both release and his hands, the pastel-pink areolae showing through the material longing to be licked.

"Shall I...?" she asked, reaching behind her for the clasp of her bra.

"No!" Too harsh. *Stop, breathe, control yourself.* "I'll do it." Better. Just.

She nodded, her hands falling to her sides—a simple movement that told him she was ceding herself to him. He liked the idea of her giving her body wholly into his care a little too much for it to be healthy, but he was in thrall to the idea of it nonetheless.

He circled her, drinking in the sight of curves delectably full and lush. He wished he could ravish her a thousand times all at once, in her underwear and out of it. He unclipped her bra, drew the straps down her arms, let it fall to the floor. One long look at her milk-pale back before allowing his eyes to dip lower. When he reached her generous bottom, which was stretching out the lace of her underwear to the limit, he wanted to sink his teeth into her. His hands were shaking as he reached for her panties to push them past her hips, down her legs.

He was glad she wasn't repeating her earlier question about what position he wanted her in; he wasn't sure how he'd frame an answer that included every position known to man. On her back, on her knees, on her side, on top, underneath him, straddling him, sucking him off, on his tongue, in his mouth, hanging from the fucking chandelier. He was past desire; what he felt for her was darker, like a craving—and he knew it was that darkness he had to control at all costs. He *would not* tarnish his bright and brilliant girl.

She stepped out of her panties and he picked them up, sifting them through his eager fingers before throwing

them who-the-fuck-knew-where because it struck him
that he might savage a hole through the lace—a dead
giveaway that he wasn't in control.

He came around in front of her. If she felt uncomfortable wearing nothing but those black stay-ups in front
of him, she didn't show it. She looked like she belonged
exactly like that, waiting for his touch. Like she trusted
him—exactly as she'd said she did—to take care of her.

She reached out a hand, fingertips on his chest, frus-
tratingly tentative. "What about *your* clothes?"

He'd intended to strip off pretty damn quick, but
when he looked for outward signs that Romy was as
aroused as he was, he got such a shock his hands stopped
midaction. Her face was appropriately flushed and her
breathing was revealingly fast and shallow—but her
nipples were steadfastly flat.

He'd been so busy imagining her breasts with nipples
jutting out as per his steamy daydreams in the library,
it took him a moment to process that there was no jut.
No jut *at all*.

Romy gave a sigh that could only be described as
long-suffering. "They're inverted," she explained. "And
I'm guessing you haven't seen their like before, despite
your revolving bedroom door."

"Inverted. Does that mean…? What does that mean? I
mean, I know what *inverted* means but does it…mean…"
Oooooh, shit. "Does it mean you don't like them to be
touched?"

"No! I mean…no."

Thank you, God.

"They're actually super sensitive," she continued, blush-
ing. "It's just not easy to guess how I'm…you know…"

"I know?"

"How I'm...*feeling*, okay?"

God, did she think that was a problem? Because he fucking *loved* the idea of having to work hard to make her show herself. He wanted to work over every inch of her until there was nothing he didn't know. One night. He wanted it all.

He leaned in for a groan of a kiss. "I guess that means I'll have to check how you're *feeling* by doing this..." Sliding his fingers between her thighs to swirl them around her clitoris before slipping them inside her. "Mmm. I think you're almost ready, Romy."

"Not almost. I am. I am ready...I am...I am... ooooh..." she said between pants, and clenched around his fingers as they pulled out of her, as though to keep them inside her. "Oh, please!"

Much as it thrilled Matt that she wanted him to stay there, though, that wasn't the game now. "I *will* please you, Romy, I promise. But first, I want to play with these." His hands went to her breasts, thumbs rubbing over their mysteriously hidden nipples. "Do they ever come out?" he asked, intrigued.

"Sometimes," she said, and arched her back, thrusting her breasts into his hands. "Depending..."

"Depending on what?"

"What you do."

No way was he going to turn down that invitation to experiment!

He pinched around her areolae. "Do you like that?" he asked, and when she groaned and nodded, he said, "Me, too." Only it came out more like a growl, like something feral, so he paused for a moment to rein it all back.

And then he started pinching again, feeling what he couldn't see, the hardness secreted inside. Another buried treasure, waiting to be coaxed out of hiding. Irresistible.

He lowered his head to lick over the top of one nipple, then the other. Her gasping breaths told him she liked that, too, so he kept going. One then the other, back and forth, over and over. She leaned into him, enticing him to more. Her hands were on his hips, gripping hard as he kept licking, experimenting with his tongue. Flat, pointed, lines, circles, hard, soft. What did she like?

The answer was everything, judging by the way she kept shifting from foot to foot, pressing her thighs together, then releasing, then pressing. When he put a hand around each breast and squeezed, narrowing his focal point so he could intensify the pressure of his tongue, she actually moaned. It was hot, hot, *hot*, to hear her. Hot, hot, hot to taste her. He *liked* wanting her like this. The insistent kick of lust, the anticipation of what was to come without knowing quite what path they'd take to reach the cliff, taking her with him every step.

He raised his head, stared into her heavy eyes. "Shall I test again?" he asked, and without waiting for an answer, released one breast, sliding that hand down her body, slipping his fingers between her thighs again. Her clit felt like a small oiled pearl, and as he rolled it between finger and thumb he imagined dropping to his knees to suck her there. But before he could turn the thought to action, she tensed, gasped and—bang!—she came in a clenching rush, the act of it, the *force* of it, taking Matt completely by surprise.

As she collapsed against him, Matt couldn't think past the ease with which he'd gotten her there. Either she was the most responsive woman he'd ever had or he was a fucking magnificent foreplayer. Whichever, he was euphoric. He loved that her sleepy eyelids were even sleepier, loved the way her breaths were still more like pants, loved the way her nails were digging into his hips. And then she topped it all by nestling her face into his chest and biting him through his T-shirt, and his dick leaped like an animal.

"Two down," he said—no, *snarled*, like a beast. "Two to go."

One more twirl of the fingers that were still between her thighs because he simply couldn't resist. And then he started stripping with a vengeance. Thank God he was barefoot; if he'd had to bend down to take off shoes, he was pretty sure his dick would see it as an opportunity to wrap itself around his neck and strangle him—revenge for making it wait.

His T-shirt was wrenched up and off. Jeans and underwear shoved down, kicked aside. A glance showed a damp patch on his boxer briefs. He'd been leaking precum for so long his poor imprisoned penis had had just about enough. He reached for her, but she stepped back. Prime position to be tumbled on her back on the bed, exactly where he needed her. He reached again.

"No," she said.

Freeze. "No?" It came out disbelievingly.

"Not *that* no," she said. "I mean no as in wait." Her eyes dropped to his dick, which all but lunged at her. He needed a leash for it, that was becoming obvious. "Wait because I want to look at you. First time, you know?"

Jesus God yes, he knew. He took a deep breath to curb the rush in his veins. He could wait while she looked him over. He fucking *loved* that she was looking him over. Another deep breath to calm his body, which had broken out in a sweat.

"Can you make it fast? The looking?" he half asked/
half pleaded. "Because I'd like to move on to some mutual touching."

Her eyes raced over him as he started counting in his
head. *One, two, breathe, breathe*, as her eyes snagged on
his lower abdominals and she licked her lips. He went
taut as a bowstring as he pictured her licking her way
up and down the V framing them. *Three—God-help-
me—four*. She reached out a finger, touched the top of
his dick where more liquid was leaking. *Holy-Mary-
mother-of-God—five—six*. She raised her finger to her
mouth and sucked it inside.

"Mmm," she said.

And the bowstring twanged, whip-fast, sending his
arrow flying. "Fuck this," he said, and launched himself at her.

She landed on her back on the bed, Matt on top of her.
A keening moan—hers. A ground-out curse—his. She
tried to put her arms around him but he stopped her, forcing them over her head so that her big, beautiful breasts
were thrust up at him. He leaned in for one more lick of
each nipple, shuddering as her back curved up off the
bed, offering him more. His thighs settled between hers,
knees splaying to open her, spreading her wide. His hips
were pistoning even before his cock was in position. He
was so hard he knew he wouldn't need to guide it in. It
knew where it had to be and was in a fever to go there.
One thrust, and he was inside her, her legs wrapping
around him. On his third stroke he felt her heels digging
into him, encouraging him to go harder.

He tried to kiss her, but he was too far gone to manage anything except a riotous assault of lips and tongue,
goaded on by the fact she was attacking him right back.

He was sweating enough to make sliding off her a real possibility, so he let go of the hands he still had pinioned above her head and wrapped his arms around her, burying his head between her neck and her shoulder, dragging her in so close they were plastered together tightly enough that a tornado wouldn't separate them. Pulse thundering in his ears. Romy almost sobbing as she spurred him on—heels *and* words. "Matt, I'm going to come. Make me, make me, make me come."

And as he felt her internal muscles start to contract around his cock, he unleashed himself, hands moving beneath her bottom, angling her hips, surging into her, aiming for the spot he knew would tip her over.

"Yes, there," she gasped, grinding against him. "God, right *there*."

Thrust, thrust, fucking thrust, and he felt his own orgasm zap through him. She spasmed around him, crying out his name, and it was as though she'd set a torch to him, so sudden was his eruption, like a gush of lava bursting from a volcano. Gush…then scorching flow. An endless stream, endless pour from him to her. Hot, wet, tight. Delirium.

He stayed, hips bowing into her, as the almost painful tension finally started to drain out of him. He realized he was shivering, but he was still so hot. He had no control over his body, even in the aftermath. Distance. He needed distance. But when he tried to roll off her, she tightened her arms and her legs around him and clung.

"I'm too heavy," he said.

"One minute," she said, her voice muffled because she'd buried her face against his chest. "Just one."

And so Matt stayed on top of her, caught between helplessness and dread at the terrible, aching, never-

before closeness. He was relieved when she finally relaxed beneath him, unhooking herself, freeing him.

"I'm fine now," she said, and he eased off her to lie
beside her, staring up at the ceiling, not knowing what
came next.

She propped herself up on an elbow. "How long do
you need to recharge, Matt?"

He angled his head toward her, uncomprehending.

"I'm flying out in the morning, remember, so I need
to get back to my hotel soon," she explained. "I need to
check my notes for Lennie, and pack, and…and double-
check the time of my transfer to the airport. All the
things an overthinker does. So if we're going to do it
again…" She offered him a tremulous smile. "Well,
we're up to petits fours, right?"

Flying out in the morning. Flying. Out. "I thought—"
He stopped himself. One night, she'd said. That didn't
have to mean *all* night.

But…but he'd thought she'd stay.

Stop! He didn't care if she stayed. It was better if she
didn't stay.

Safer.

How many goes did it take to get pregnant, anyway?
Okay, stupid question. He knew it only took one. It was
just a matter of *which* one. A matter of what point in
the cycle she was at, and whether the stars were align-
ing and shit like that.

He thought back to her phone call two weeks ago,
when she'd been on day three of her period. If he used
that as a guide, they were damn close to target. And
when you combined that timing with the fact that he'd
shot off inside her like a NASA-grade rocket, she was
probably already pregnant. He'd probably given her *trip-*

lets to match the three orgasms. She didn't even have to stay for her fourth…fourth orgasm…if she didn't… want…oooohhhh.

Brain slowing down. Blood, heart, nerves, seizing up. *Back up a step. Back* up.

She was probably already pregnant. Already…pregnant. Already…

Matt reached out a trembling hand, laid it low on her belly.

Romy stopped breathing, stopped everything, looking at Matt's hand on her.

She knew what he was thinking, and now that he was thinking it, she was thinking it, too: she might already be pregnant.

Way to change the dynamic! A few minutes ago, it was all about sex. Now it was about more.

She put her hand over his. "So?" she asked softly, searching his face.

He kept his eyes on their hands. He said nothing but she felt the shiver that ran through him all the way to her bone marrow, as though he'd become a part of her. She wanted to warm him, to rub away the crease between his eyebrows, tell him everything would be okay.

Except that everything wouldn't be okay. His silence told her that, and the look on his face—a look she'd never seen on him before. Haunted. Hunted.

They hadn't blurred the line, and they hadn't crossed it; they'd drawn a new one. And it wasn't a situation that could be withdrawn from. It was real, and it was forever. He'd become hers in a way that was different from before, and she had a sudden insight that he always would be hers, whether she was pregnant or not, no matter what happened in her life, or who else he slept with. And that was more than he'd bargained on and *way* more than he wanted.

"So," Matt said, and took a deep breath as he eased his hand out from beneath hers. "I'm recharged—let's go for broke this time."

Fast, practiced, blank-faced, he stripped off her socks, and even *that* seemed portentous. Because it felt as though they were no longer erotic—they were just something in his way.

CHAPTER SIX

MATT ENJOYED MORNINGS AFTER. When he was alone, sated, relaxed and a little nostalgic for the previous night's experience even though the details were already hazy.

But this morning, standing in the kitchen Romy hadn't seen even though he'd kitted it out especially for her, he was neither sated nor relaxed. And the details weren't hazy—each one was crystal clear.

Romy, so hesitant going up the stairs.

Romy, diffident and wanting to get it over with once they'd reached the bedroom.

Romy, talking about returning to her hotel room after he'd gone at her like a battering ram.

What did that fucking *tell* him? That she wasn't his speed!

Why hadn't he fucking *listened*? Because he was a fucking monster!

What had he done about it? He'd forged ahead and done her again! Shoving himself into her deep and hard and relentless, wringing a double orgasm out of her, making her beg for it!

And his reward for that brutality was for her to jump out of bed even before she'd stopped gasping his name, grab her clothes as though he'd steal them if she wasn't fast enough, and run for the shower like she couldn't wait to wash him off her skin.

That's when he'd seen the purple marks on her hips, and he'd thanked God she wasn't staying the night after all because he'd have marked her black-and-blue and scraped her raw all over by morning.

He'd pulled on his clothes and waited impatiently for her to reappear from the bathroom, rehearsing apologies, explanations. But when she'd resurfaced, scrubbed and dressed, paper white and jittery, he'd known there was no excuse that would make it right.

"Well, that's that, then," she'd said. And the look on her face as she'd said it had ripped a hole in him. Like she was going to cry, like she was going to *break*.

And so Matt had called her a cab, and trailed after her like a stray dog all the way down that overwrought staircase, and fetched her overcoat and briefcase from the overstuffed library while she waited in the pretentious entrance hall of his mausoleum of a house. And then they'd stood by the door and stared past each other for a million fucking years until the taxi arrived. Then she'd said, "I'll know one way or the other in two weeks, so I'll be in touch then." And with a restrained, chicken-like peck on his cheek, whoosh! She was gone, the door had closed, the taxi was driving away.

Matt had stayed at the door, and it wasn't until three minutes had passed that he'd realized he was waiting for her to come back. Because she *never* left him without hugging him like a maniac and ruffling his hair. He'd actually rested his hand on the door handle, preparing to wrench open the door the moment he heard the cab pull up.

Another minute—no cab.

His knuckles had turned white as it registered that she wasn't coming back. That the peck on the cheek was all he was going to get. That it might be the last thing he ever got from her. And he'd raced up to strip his bed, as though by doing so he could rip the experience out of his room, out of his house, out of his exploding head.

That was when he'd spied the tiny ball of lilac, scrunched up behind the armchair. She'd been so eager to leave, she hadn't even looked for her panties; she'd gone commando—something *his Romy* would never, ever have done because she'd have been all, *What if I get hit by a bus?*

And even knowing that that meant she had to have been in a panic to escape him, he couldn't stop himself from picking up those panties and sniffing them like a sexual deviant, which triggered a leap in his cock that *infuriated* him because those were *Romy's* panties! *His Romy's* panties that he hadn't let himself near for ten fucking years!

He'd grabbed the sheets, screwed them and the panties up together, strode into the bathroom and shoved the lot into the laundry hamper so hard he pushed his hand right through the wickerwork, giving new meaning to the term *basket case*—which he clearly still was the morning after a sleep-deprived night because here he was standing in *her* kitchen, his dick throbbing like the devil, willing her to come back even though he knew she was already in the goddamn air.

"Fuuuuuuuuuuck!" he yelled, and when that didn't release enough pressure, banged his fist on the counter. "Fuck." Bang. "Fuck." Bang. *"Fuck* this!" And he swept an arm across the kitchen counter, knocking the coffee he'd made for himself but hadn't drunk into the sink.

Fuck the coffee, too! Why was he drinking coffee? He needed an anesthetic, not a stimulant. He wrenched a beer from the fridge—and he was beyond fucking *caring* that Romy always tsk-tsked him out of drinking beer in the morning—and made his way out onto the deck because it was past time for his dick to start behaving like a regular body part and not a Viagra-fueled nightmare and he hoped the frigid wind would knock an inch or two off his erection.

Throwing himself into a seat at his purpose-bought-for-Romy outdoor setting, he took a vicious swig of his beer and forced himself to look out toward San Francisco Bay, where he was going to keep looking until he calmed the fuck down.

An intention that lasted forty seconds, when he experienced an overpowering need to check his cell phone just in case he'd missed a text message from Romy.

Aaaand nope. Moron. If he hadn't gotten a text by now he wasn't going to get one, because she was *already-in-the-goddamn-air*-how-long-did-it-take-to-get-that-through-his-head!

He tossed his phone onto the table, only to pick it up again immediately to call up the message Romy had sent him after their phone call two weeks ago—the selfie, in which she was blowing him a kiss. "My hero" was the text that accompanied it. He'd rolled his eyes at that, but he'd laughed, too, because her mouth was too wide for that expression to be anything other than comical. Maybe seeing it now would give him hope that the two of them might laugh about last night in due course.

But when he pulled up the photo, instead of laughing at her duckbill lips, he found himself running his fingertip over them while his breathing went haywire and his heartbeat went bump-bump-thump and he could almost…taste her.

He snatched his hand away from the phone, picked up his beer, took another swig. But swilling the beer around his mouth did nothing to disperse the taste of her, which seemed to have drenched him at some cellular level.

She should be here, telling him he was still her hero even though he knew he was an asshole. She should be here, forgiving him the way she said she always would. She should be here, easing his rage the way being around her always did—that bitter strangle of fury he'd been carrying inside forever, forever, for ever, at what his parents had turned him into. This…*thing*, dark and twisted and disgusting, that made him not good enough for her.

"Fuuuuuuuuuuuck!" Another gut-wrenching yell. Because he wanted her here…and yet he should be glad she wasn't. He'd spent ten careful years keeping her away, blocking every sexual thought of her, trying not to ruin what he'd felt that first night he'd met her, that glimmering sense of comfort she gave him.

It was ever-after stuff, what he'd felt that night. And what he'd felt for her had stayed in the realm of ever-after through three and a half years' living in the same house, through six and a half years' living on different continents, through the past two weeks of knowing the baby was his gateway to a permanent link with her because she'd have only one child and that child would be his and whoever came after him could therefore *never* take his place in her life.

If he were a decent human being, he would have told her everything about himself and given her the chance to find better sperm. But he could live with not being a decent human being. He'd lived with it a hell of a long time now.

He reached for his beer, saw that his hand was shaking and took a long, painful breath.

If he'd succeeded in accomplishing the ultimate betrayal and impregnating her, would she hate the thought of having his child, after last night? And if she *wasn't* pregnant, would she write him off and look elsewhere?

Two weeks, and he'd know. Two weeks—that's when she'd said she'd be in touch.

Although he could contact her, couldn't he? He could text her now, if he wanted to.

He picked up his phone again, racking his brain for something funny to say. Maybe something about preparing the kid for a lifetime of dealing with redhead jokes…?

But…no. She might get all serious and tell him again that she loved his red hair. Loved his hair…loved everything about him…loved…him…?

No!

No, she couldn't tell him that. He wouldn't let her tell him that.

The text would have to be something simple like checking she got home all right. He always sent that text when she was flying home. And it never mattered that he sent it while she was in the air, because she got it when she landed and she always responded straightaway and that way it would be only hours—not two weeks—before he heard from her.

He tapped out the message…and then froze.

What the fuck was he doing?

She'd said two weeks. The inference being she didn't *want* to be in touch until then.

Was he going to start hounding her when she didn't want to be hounded? After he'd *told* her he didn't do that stalking shit? Why make her more uncomfortable with him than she already was?

Nope. Delete. Delete that message. Delete, delete, DELETE, GODDAMMIT!

He realized he was about to crack the case on his cell phone, and forced himself to ease his grip. He threw the phone down, got up and strode over to the edge of the deck. The view was the only thing he liked about this house. He should be out on that damn bay, kayaking. It would be worth freezing his ass off to get out of the house.

He strode back to the table, scooped up his phone—in case a message came through—shoved it in his pocket—because he knew it wouldn't—and headed inside to the library to find his kayaking map because no way was he taking his cell phone with him; odds were instead of using it to check his coordinates he'd obsess about text messages he wasn't getting and didn't want to *think* about getting.

But once in the library he was drawn to the desk, where Romy's paperwork was, and he lost interest in looking for the map. He could see her, even with his eyes open, muttering to herself as she flicked through pages. And when he closed his eyes… Oh God, the images. Furtive flashes of naked bodies, eager thrusts, cries and tongues and fevered flesh.

His eyes bolted open. "Jesus Christ, stop!" he cried.

And as if in answer to a prayer, his cell phone pinged with an incoming text.

Bump-bump-thump went his heart.

Romy!

So she hadn't caught her flight. She was still in San Francisco.

He put his hand over the phone in his pocket and smiled. She'd forgiven him.

Call or text back?

Call, he decided. He'd suggest she come over and hang out here, strictly friend zone now their one-night stand was over. He'd remind her about the paella she owed him and then help her make it, and they could eat it while watching a movie—there was a TV behind a panel in this godforsaken library and it didn't get more innocent than watching a movie; they always watched movies together when she was over. He fumbled the phone out. He'd get her new flight details, drive her to the airport at the appointed time the way he usually did, when she wasn't running for her life. And if she didn't hug him goodbye he'd headlock her!

He swiped his cell on. It would all be back to norm—

"Shit." As he saw who the message was from.

Not Romy, Camilla.

Coffee? Can meet you in ten.

Coffee. Camilla's daytime euphemism for sex. Nighttime was margarita.

Well, obviously *that* wasn't going to happen. A guy who'd offered to impregnate a friend didn't fuck his way around town until the job was done. Still…hmm…any red-blooded man would get a libidinous spark at the thought of sex with Camilla—so why wasn't he?

He tried picturing Camilla. Honey-blond hair; aquamarine eyes; sharp, high cheekbones; pouty mouth; curved in all the right places and perfectly proportioned. A very beautiful woman. She was fun, too. She laughed a lot; she ate like a normal person and drank beer. She was even clued up on tech talk, unlike Romy, who thought the only Java that existed was an island in Indonesia. He *liked* Camilla. They were good together. They thought alike. And she was the type to flay the flesh off a guy—literally, not metaphorically—which was exactly what he needed at that moment, a physical pain to replace the other kind.

He tried to coax some hot blood into his veins, some rigidity into his cock. But it was no use. His veins remained disinterested. His penis positively *un*interested—in fact, it was...deflating...? Oh God, he really was deflating!

He sighed, and sent back a simple text to Camilla of the sorry-no-can-do-some-other-time variety. Then he stared at the phone some more, but no matter how long he stared, no text from Romy materialized.

He shoved the phone into his pocket. He was going to go back to his bedroom. He was going to take the sheets out of the hamper and rip the fuckers in half.

He was three strides to the door when he recalled that there was a pair of lilac panties in with the sheets and—whooshka—up came his dick, like an amphetamine-loaded cobra from a snake charmer's basket. Un-fucking-*bearable*.

He whirled again, returned to the windows, desperate to calm down, but there was no calm to be had out there. Swollen gray clouds were gathering over the bay, like they were building apace with his turbulent mood. The weather wouldn't stop him taking out the kayak— in fact, he relished the idea of carving through the water in a storm.

He watched until the first raindrops dotted the window…gathered power…started pelting. He turned into the room, strode to the desk, looked down at those motherfucking pages. Their only saving grace was that Teague hadn't drawn them up; he'd hate to have to beat the crap out of Teague for getting between him and Romy.

Not that the documents really mattered. The crux of the deal was that Matt's name wouldn't be on the birth certificate. He didn't need fifteen documents to confirm he wasn't going to be a real father.

He picked up a three-page document at random and ripped it in half. An action that reminded him of what he wanted to do to his sheets, so he ripped it again. Again. Again. He hated those fucking pages. Rip, rip, fucking rip. To the next document. Rip. Rip. Over and over and over, page after page.

He was breathing heavily by the time he'd finished his harried tearing and looked at the pieces scattered across the desktop. What a mess. An all-round fucking mess. On the desk, and in his head.

It wasn't meant to be like this. It was meant to be easy. A carefree donation of easily produced body fluid. So why had it felt like something else, something more, last night?

Oh God, why could he *see* her so clearly? His red-haired, hazel-eyed daughter, looking at him with the same quiet trust he'd seen in Romy's eyes last night.

He didn't know how to banish that image; he didn't know how to fix him and Romy; he didn't know how to stop wanting forever; he didn't know how to reconcile all those things into a way of existing that didn't feel like he was being ripped into pieces, like those fucking pages on the desk.

He rubbed his fingertips up and down his forehead, trying to ease the ache that was building in his head. His sinuses felt swollen. The back of his nose was stinging. He blinked hard and swallowed against a sudden lump in his throat. Swallowed again, but the lump remained.

He imagined getting Romy's regular parcel of photos, and that in with the shots of her parents, a guy she might be dating, restaurant dishes she was about to consume and shoes she needed a second opinion on before purchase, were photos of his daughter. The birth. The home-from-the-hospital shot. First tooth. First crawl. First birthday. First walk. First day at school. First French fucking snail being eaten. Photos of a normal kid, who had a normal mother and normal grandparents. A normal, innocent childhood.

He spun away from the desk, strode to the window, kicked aside the ruined curtains, stared out. The rain was pelting down now. "If only..." he said, conscious of a horrible, clawing, push-pull need in his life for less... and yet more. He placed the palms of his hands on the glass, wishing he could feel the storm. "If only..." But he blocked the thought before he could finish it. No point in going there.

The back of his nose was stinging again, and there was a crushing ache in his chest.

There was no use pretending he didn't know what it was.

It was grief.

And it was out of his control.

CHAPTER SEVEN

NOT PREGNANT.

Not.

A month had passed since San Francisco, and Romy, sitting at her computer with her email account open, knew she could no longer put off telling Matt.

She should have done it the instant she'd gotten her period two weeks ago, but she'd had a minimeltdown in the bathroom and bawled her eyes out instead.

And then the cramps had hit, the pain going all-out to completely incapacitate her as though punishing her for daring to do what she'd done with Matt—and surely agony was a valid excuse for delaying the call.

Disbelief had come next. With all Matt's potency, delivered at the right time of the month, it was *inconceivable* that she wasn't pregnant. So maybe her uterus was playing a last, loathsome trick on her and she *wasn't* not-pregnant after all.

That had bought her a week.

But today, when Lennie had called to ask her to return to San Francisco because he'd finally made a decision and needed her to scout out a definite location for his restaurant, it was a case of time's up. Within two minutes of peeing on the stick of her home pregnancy kit, she'd burst into tears again.

And now, sitting at her computer, she knew there'd only ever been one honest reason for not telling Matt two weeks ago: fear that the instant he knew, she'd lose him.

Okay, that wasn't quite true. It was more that the instant he knew, she'd have to accept that she'd *already* lost him. She could even pinpoint the exact moment it had happened: when he'd put his hand where their baby might have been and what he'd done had become real.

The mind-blowing sex he'd almost immediately launched into made no sense after that...but Romy had a nagging feeling that if she figured out what had motivated him to "go for broke" following that club to the head, she'd have the key to the tower Matt kept himself barricaded in.

Not that she'd had time to test any locks! The vortex into which he'd hurled her had been so wild, she hadn't been able to so much as catch her breath from start to finish. No words, no instruction, no invitation—just his touch driving her inexorably on until her eyes rolled back in her head and her toes curled. The crescendo? Two soaring, thrilling orgasms, the last one adroitly, effortlessly, synchronized to his own.

And yet despite his almost slavish attention to her pleasure, and despite that careful synchronization she though may well have curled his toes, too, she'd felt... alone. Flung away, like an electric guitar that had been played for maximum flash and drama before being pounded onto the stage and obliterated.

Her self-preservation instincts had kicked in, and she was up, preparing to leave, desperate not to face being Matt's first-ever regret.

She'd reached for her mobile phone so many times that night, wanting to jump back over that crossed line and at least open the door to reclaiming their friendship, but every time she'd started a text, she'd lost her nerve. There'd been no adequate words for what she was feeling. Or at least, none he'd want to hear. *Don't call it love*, he'd said, and she hadn't, she wouldn't. But she had no other words, either.

So here she was, still with no words, effectively in limbo, with Matt's email address staring accusingly at her from the To box above the blank message space.

She scrubbed her hands over her face. Had it really been only six weeks since that phone call, when Matt had assured her having a baby would be the easiest thing in the world?

She closed her eyes, steeling herself to call up the image of his face after he'd come inside her that first time—the bleakness of it. To remember the way his expression had changed to something cool and calculating as he'd said, *I'm recharged—let's go for broke this time.* The silence as he'd walked her downstairs. The desolation in his eyes when she'd kissed his cheek—as though in going for broke, he'd broken *himself.*

And she knew what she had to do was formally, officially, let him go.

She opened her eyes, and started typing.

Hi, Matt
The big news is I'm not pregnant, so no Yippie-Kai-Yay motherfucker just yet.

Been thinking that with you there and me here and all that paperwork we never got to the end of, a donor closer to home makes more sense. So consider this an official notification that Plan A is extinct—in other words you're off the hook, services no longer required.

She paused there, not sure how to sign off.

Would these be her last words to Matt? If so, she knew what she'd want them to be. She'd broken the cardinal rule before she'd known it existed and said them in her heart ten years ago. She may not have said the words aloud but she wanted to. She was *tired* of keeping them inside. So tired, her fingers trembled on the keyboard with the need to type them…

I love you

Almost by magic the words were there on the screen. Her heart raced as she read them; she knew if she sent them it really would be over.

In which case, wouldn't the words be useless?

If she wanted to get him back into her life she had to be more strategic. She had to let him know there was a cleared path back to their old friendship…but only if he chose to tread it. And so she deleted those three words and tapped out a new closer. Light and bright and cool and unthreatening:

But I owe you a favor of your choice for giving it the old college try. If you're still hankering for paella, I've got a new twist on the old recipe so give me a shout when you're next in London if you'd like to collect.
Romy
X

And then she hit Send, closed her laptop and burst into tears.

CHAPTER EIGHT

"I NEVER PRETENDED to be a computer whiz," Romy said, bringing Teague's fourth cup of coffee over to him.

"Neither did I," Teague said, "so say a prayer that between us we haven't lost everything while you *open that damn door*! With any luck it'll be Matt, come to save us."

She checked, but only for an instant, at hearing Matt's name. "It won't be him." She plonked Teague's coffee on the dining table beside her laptop, within reach of his hand. "So keep going. And remember, you can lose anything you like as long as you find the—"

"Romy—the door—I beg you."

"—Lennie_SanFrancisco file," she finished, before heading for the door, calling out an en route "Keep your shirt on!" to whoever was outside.

She swung the door open...and her mouth snap-froze in a gape.

Her heart jolted, then hammered, as Matt—it really, astoundingly, unbelievably, *was* Matt!—lowered the clenched fist he'd raised as though preparing to pound a hole through the wood.

When had she sent her email? She counted back, lightning fast. Less than twenty-four hours ago. If her email was responsible for rocketing Matt across the Atlantic, was that a positive, negative or neutral development? She didn't know, couldn't work it out because her thoughts were flying past each other, refusing to land.

"Keep my shirt on?" Matt asked, sounding oddly breathless, and when one corner of his mouth quirked up in a rueful smile, her thoughts stopped flying and stuttered to a halt. "You sure about that?"

Shirt. On. Here. London. Matt! Gorgeous.

Her brain was too mangled to form actual sentences and her mouth was too dry to say them. She was reduced to stepping back and vaguely beckoning with her hand, a mute version of *Come in*.

Matt stepped over the threshold, and ever-careless of his possessions, ignored the coat stand to drop his overcoat on the floor along with his duffel bag. For a hopeful moment, Romy thought he was going to pull her into his arms, but a sound behind her—Teague's chair scraping against the floor—distracted him.

"Yay! The hero arrives!" Teague said.

Shock sparked in Matt's eyes as he looked past her, but when Romy turned to uncover the problem all she found was Teague looking at them over the top of her laptop screen.

"Uh-oh," Teague said.

Uh-oh? Romy's eyes went from Teague to a now-expressionless Matt.

"Just to be clear, Matt," Teague said, "all I was doing was reinstalling Windows for her."

"I'll finish it," Matt said.

"It's finished. But by all means check what I did."

Romy looked from Matt to Teague this time. Something was wrong.

Teague closed her laptop and made his way over to them.

"But…are you leaving?" she asked him as he retrieved his overcoat from the stand.

"Yes, Romy, I am."

"Where are you going?"

Shrugging into his coat. "Back to my hotel."

"Why?"

Grabbing his scarf. "Because dinner appears to be canceled."

"It's *not* canceled!" Romy said, and turned to Matt. "Tell him to stay." Getting nothing from that quarter, she tennis-balled back to Teague. "Teague!"

Teague laugh-winced. "Are you trying to get me killed, Romes?"

"What? No! I mean— What?"

Teague's response was to look squarely at Matt as he draped his scarf around his neck. "Just one thing," he said. "Prove to her I've recovered the Lennie_SanFrancisco file or you'll have a meltdown on your hands. She's got a meeting with him tomorrow."

"Fuck Lennie!" Matt said with extreme loathing.

Teague grinned. "He *wishes* she would, anyway!" He knotted his scarf. "But it's your job to rescue her if Lennie steps out of line, isn't it?"

Matt's eyes narrowed. "What's that supposed to mean?"

"It means you'll swoop in to save Romy's day, as usual."

In the hanging moment that followed, Romy found herself holding her breath. She could feel tension rolling off Matt in thick waves, but his voice was calm when he asked, "Do *you* want the job, Teague?" Almost *too* calm.

"Oh, I can't do *that* job," Teague said. "Lennie's not scared of me."

"What makes you think he's scared of *me*?"

Teague kept his gaze steady on Matt. "Intuition."

Matt made an infinitesimal adjustment to his stance. "Are *you* scared of me, Teague?"

"No," Teague said. "Because *I* know *you* know I'm not a threat."

On the verge of passing out from oxygen deprivation, Romy took in a tiny breath, then held it again when Matt made a sound like a cut-off growl as Teague pulled her into his arms for a hug.

"Call me if you need me, Romes, okay?" Teague said in a stage whisper, before letting her go. "But now, if you'll excuse me…"

"Wait!" Romy cried, and caught Teague's hand. "You don't have to leave!"

Teague squeezed then released her fingers. "Yes, Romy, I do."

"Then…then at least let me walk with you to the train station and…and explain," she urged—even though she didn't know what the explanation *was*.

Teague touched her cheek briefly. "I don't need an explanation. And I'd prefer it if you stayed to soothe the savage beast." He flashed her a whiter-than-snow smile. "For *all* our sakes, hmm?"

And then he clapped a hand briefly on Matt's shoulder, said, "Play nice with my girl," and left.

Romy stared at the door after it clicked shut behind Teague, trying to figure out what had just happened.

She sensed Matt moving, heard him settling into Teague's chair at the dining table. *Play nice with my girl*, Teague had adjured him. But Matt didn't appear to be in a "nice" mood.

Or maybe…thinking back to Matt's smile as she'd

opened the door…maybe seeing Teague had *changed* Matt's mood. It had certainly upped the testosterone quotient. But that would mean Matt was jealous, wouldn't it? And he was *never* jealous. He didn't *care* enough to be jealous. Or maybe…maybe he did…?

She turned, intrigued by that notion, to find Matt tapping away at her computer, and cleared her throat to get his attention.

Matt ignored her. And that was interesting, because he'd never ignored her before and she was *p-r-e-t-t-y* sure he hadn't flown all the way from San Francisco just to do so now.

So why *was* he here? Question of the day.

She took two steps, and cleared her throat again. "Are you going to tell me why you're here, Matt?"

He stilled, eyes on her keyboard. "Are you going to tell me why *Teague* was here?" And then he raised his eyes, pinning her in place. "Because fixing your computer is *my* job, isn't it?"

Okay, that definitely smacked of *some* kind of jealousy, and it made her heart flutter like a leaf in a storm. "You were in San Francisco."

"I've installed updates on your computer remotely before."

"It's just…he was here."

"So I noticed."

"For dinner."

"So I gathered."

"He's working on a big corporate merger, and one of the parties is British so he's here for a couple of weeks and he called me and I offered to cook—just like I do for *you* when you're here. And when he arrived, I mentioned my computer problems, and…" She stopped, threw up her hands. "Why am I explaining this? I've done nothing wrong."

"Why *are* you explaining, if you've done nothing wrong?"

"Probably because you're glaring at me, making me *think* I've done something wrong. He came—he saw—he fixed. The end. Unless you want to know the dinner menu, in which case it was supposed to be steak and ale pie."

Matt leaned back in his chair. "Let me ask a different question. When did he arrive in London? Could it possibly have been *yesterday*?"

"Yes, so what?"

"So that gives me some context for that 'closer to home' reference in your email."

"You mean…? No, you *can't* mean—! *Teague?* Teague lives in *Manhattan*. How's that close to London?"

"He's here now. Ergo, close."

"As are you—so *what*?"

"So it finally makes sense why you took so long to contact me."

"You mean…?" But she shook her head. "*What* do you mean?"

"I mean I hear nothing from you for a month, but then Teague arrives and—wham!—notice to terminate my services comes flying through cyberspace."

She stared at him while that sifted through her foggy brain. And then, "Oh. My God!" she said. "You cannot be serious."

"And yet I am."

She came storming over to the table as four weeks of pent-up emotion ruptured. "You *dare* to tick me off for not contacting you? You didn't send me one text! One email! I didn't get a phone call, a Facebook message, nothing! I had to fill the void by overthinking every damn thing that had happened in San Francisco until I thought I'd go crazy!"

"I've been hanging on the edge of my fucking seat waiting for two fucking words from you—not pregnant. A few seconds is all it would have taken!"

"Oh! Oh! You were *not* hanging on the edge of your seat! You made it crystal clear you'd lost interest in the whole thing even before I left your house! I saw your face, Matt, when it hit you—it hit you like a ton of bricks—what you'd let yourself in for, that maybe, just maybe, that boring paperwork I wanted to go through with you was worth reading after all!"

"I tore up that paperwork!"

"You—you—"

"*Bastard* is the word I think we agreed on in San Francisco."

"You bastard!" she rapped out.

He set his jaw. "Which doesn't change the fact that *you* were supposed to contact *me*, goddammit!"

"And I *did*!"

He banged his hand on the table. "Two weeks *late*!"

"Well, excuse me for not being buoyed with optimism by your last words to me. 'Let's go for broke this time'! It took me the whole month to get over that!"

He pushed his chair back from the table, jumped to his feet. "I told you to stop me if you didn't like what I did!"

"It wasn't that *I* didn't like it, it was that *you* didn't. That last time was a performance—a bravura performance but definitely a performance, even if you didn't really want to give it."

"That wasn't a performance, Romy, that was me. What I *am*. What I *like*."

"You didn't like *anything* after you realized I might be pregnant. You couldn't even muster up a goodbye when I left!"

"You didn't give me *time* to say goodbye. You ran out on me like your ass was on fire."

"You could have stopped me!"

"I don't stop women from leaving me, remember? You want to leave, you leave!"

"If you believe that, why are you here?"

Split second while he stared at her. And then, "Good question!" he snarled, and strode for the door.

She hurried after him. "What are you doing?"

"Figure it out," he said, and reefed his overcoat up off the floor, one-handed.

"Matt!"

Up came his bag. Flung over his shoulder.

She grabbed his arm. "You're not leaving until we talk this through."

He jerked away from her. "Read your own fucking email. You talked it through for both of us."

"What is the problem? If you want to try again, we'll just…try again!"

"No, Romy, we won't. It's too dangerous. *I'm* too dangerous." And he turned to the door again.

"No!" she cried, and dragged his overcoat from him, threw it back on the floor. "What are you talking about?"

"I saw the bruises, okay?"

"They were nothing!" Romy cried.

He reached for his coat again—she blocked him. "If that's really what's bothering you—a few love bites—I'll put some on you right now and we'll be even."

"That's not funny."

"No, it's not funny, if you think I'm some delicate flower who can't handle some enthusiastic sex! So read my lips: You. Didn't. Hurt me. You didn't. And you're not going to leave me like this after keeping me hanging for a month."

"You left *me*, Romy," he said to her.

"Only because you *wanted* me to go."

"Bullshit. I asked you to stay the night."

"That was *before*."

"Before *what*? Before you moved the goalposts? Before you replaced ten years with one night on a fucking *whim*? Plan B! Jesus! What made you think that was going to work with someone like me?"

"Someone like you? What does that even mean?"

"It means your email hit the nail on the head—I'm *not* the man for the job. I don't *want* the job. So…so sign Teague up! I don't care."

"What *is* it about Teague tonight? It's just Teague—same old Teague! But it's like you're suddenly jealous of him!"

He recoiled. "I'm not jealous of Teague."

"Then what was all that about when you arrived?"

"Not jealousy. Not…what you think."

She rolled her eyes. "Okay."

"I mean it!"

"Okay!"

"I *mean* it, Romy! I'm the opposite of jealous! I *want* him to have you. I *always* wanted him to have you. That's why I introduced him to you in the first place. He's a fucking saint! There's no one better for you."

She blinked at him—once, twice, slowly—and she finally understood why Matt called it the blink of insanity when she did that: because she was blinking at a stark, staring madman. "Oh my God," she said. "You want him to *have* me? What am I? A reward for good behavior?"

"You've got it ass-end around, Romy, I want *you* to have *him*."

"And what about what I want for myself?"

"We're *talking* about what you want—a clean-cut, solid-gold hero."

"No, Matt. If we were talking about what I want, we'd be talking about you."

"Romy, you only *think*—"

"*Don't* tell me what I think! If I wanted to have sex with Teague I'd have done it when we were dating!"

"But this is about more than sex. It's about sharing a baby, raising a baby, providing the best for a baby."

"And if I'd wanted to have a *baby* with Teague, I'd have turned down your offer and called him straight up to ask him!"

"So ask him! Go on! You know it'll be better with him."

"And if I asked him, what do you think he'd say?"

"He'd say yes." He tore his hands through his hair. "Ah Jesus, he'd say yes."

"He'd say *Let's wait, Romy*, that's what he'd say. He'd say *Let's think it through. Let's do the* math. *Let's get the fucking* paperwork *in order. And meanwhile, Romy, why don't you get your own lawyer to look into precedents, even though I'm a lawyer myself, because two lawyers are better than one, and maybe go back to the doctor for some stronger painkillers and bleed your goddamn life out while I think it through, and then when you're* sure *you're sure and I'm* sure, *we'll get married and then* we'll start trying."

"And that's what you wanted—due process."

"No! No! I don't want another version of myself! I want what *you* did! What *you* offered is what I want. Fast and brave and unthinking and…and fuck-it-all, let's just do it. That's what I want. And you! I wanted *you*! I want you still."

"Stop, Romy!"

"No, I won't stop. You turn up here, all but scare Teague out of the flat for what reason I have *no fucking idea* since you're *not fucking jealous*, and then you tell me I'm supposed to fall into Teague's arms because you think that'll work better for me? Well, the answer is no! I'm not doing it. I remember very well that you got me and Teague together in college. I also remember you never asked why we split up."

"Because it didn't matter why."

"Of course it mattered! But I think you *knew* why we split up. And I think you didn't want to face it. Well, I want you to face it. So in case you *don't* know, I'm going to tell you—it's because I couldn't love him. And the reason I couldn't love him is because I already loved—"

"No!" he said, cutting her off.

"Why *not*?"

"Because it'll be the end. Don't. Say it. Don't, Romy."

"Not saying it out loud won't change the truth."

He grabbed her right hand, lifted it. "Wanna know about love? It's *this*. He gave you his dead sister's ring even though you'd been broken up for two and a half years. What does that tell you?"

"That he knew I'd cherish it."

"The way he cherishes *you*."

"No!" she said.

"Not saying it out loud won't change the truth," he

said, throwing her own words back at her. "You want love—he'll give it to you. I won't."

"We're friends. Teague and I are *friends*."

"What do you think you and I are?"

"I don't... I want... I don't know anymore."

"Having sex didn't make us more than friends, Romy—all it made us is friends with *benefits*. Benefits that were supposed to accrue to *you*. And who knows? If you'd stayed the night those benefits may have had more of a chance to accrue. Well, spilt milk, water under the bridge, whatever—you cut things short. So stand by that decision, because your instinct was right—I'm not the best man for this. And if the friend dynamic is what's bothering you about Teague, let me tell you that I've had sex with friends before and I will again. So I suggest you accept that you *can* have sex with friends, take another look at Teague and the next time he gives you a ring it'll have a whopping big diamond in it."

"I don't want a diamond."

"Yeah, well, even without the diamond, compare his platinum ring to what I gave you for your twenty-first birthday. A computer game. I mean, seriously! There's the difference between him and me right there on your finger."

"You gave me *shares*, Matt, not a computer game. Shares in Artie's start-up gaming company. Shares he wanted to be *yours*, not mine."

"They were worthless."

"And now they're not."

"Yeah, well, as I've said before, money's an easy thing for me to give."

"Those shares weren't money to you. They came from that soul you say you don't have."

He flung her hand away. "Oh, for fuck's sake! Don't worry about my soul, Romy—protect your own. Or I may yet give in to my baser urgings and steal it."

"Oh, Matt, can't you see? You don't *have* to steal my soul. I'll give it to you willingly. I'll *gift wrap* it for you. I'll change it to suit you, twist into any shape you want, paint it any color you like."

He grabbed her by the upper arms and pulled her in close, looking down at her with such an intense mix of fury and fuck me, a sliver of almost-pleasurable fear shimmied down her spine. "Make it pitch-black and we might have a deal," he said.

"I said any color—I meant it."

"I've told you before, Romy, be careful what you say. What you open the door to. There are wolves out there—wolves like me."

"Then teach me to be a wolf."

"A kitten can't become a wolf."

"What can I do to convince you?"

"Nothing."

"What about if I…if I bite you?"

He laughed.

"I mean it. It's what I've always wanted to do. Bite a man through the skin until I draw blood. There. That's my deepest, darkest fantasy. What do you think about that?"

He released her, stepped back, tilted his head to one side and dragged at his sweater, the T-shirt beneath, to expose his neck to her. "Go ahead, Vampira."

She swallowed. "I…"

He laughed again. Released his sweater. "You're *not. My. Speed.*"

Her eyes flickered downward, to the front of his jeans. "I don't believe you."

"As you said—that's always there."

"As you said—you wouldn't be able to function like a human if it was."

"I'm not much of a human. And my services are no longer required, remember?"

"And yet, knowing that…here you are."

"I came because we had unfinished business."

"Then finish it!"

"It was finished the minute I walked in the door and saw him."

"Prove it's finished. Kiss me."

"No."

"Then don't kiss me. Fuck me."

CHAPTER NINE

"ASKING TO BE fucked isn't enough to bring you down to my level," he said, but although his voice carried the right amount of sneer, desire raced through him so fast he trembled with it.

She straightened her spine, and it made his heart lurch. God, she'd always been a straight arrow. The straightest. "Then tell me what will," she said.

He retook her right hand, brought it to his mouth, licked the problematic platinum band, then sucked her pinky finger into his mouth. He watched her as he sucked, as he kept sucking. *Stop me, stop me, Romy*, he pleaded silently, because he hated himself for what he was about to ask.

But she didn't stop him. She did nothing except close her eyes, and then open them as though she wouldn't allow herself that weakness. He slipped his mouth from her finger, slowly, insolently, but kept hold of her hand. "Taking off his ring will be a start. Do that and I'll fuck you."

He saw her eyes go wide, the swallow she took. But she tipped up her chin and threw his challenge back at him. "I won't make what's between us about Teague. It has *nothing* to do with him."

"It has everything to do with him. I'm the bit of rough you have on the side—he's the one you go home to. You don't take off the ring of the man you go home to."

"I came home to *you*, Matt. For three and a half years I came home to you. After every man, I came home to you. And you…you came home to me."

"Oh, Romy." He had to touch her. Had to. Just once. So he cupped her cheek, even though he knew she'd feel the fine quivering in his fingers. "I could count your men on one hand. And there's the difference. Do you have any idea how many sex partners I've had?"

She brought her hand up to cover his, keeping it there. "I only care that it took ten years to make me one of them."

"But you were only one of them for a night," he said. "And you won't be again unless you take off his ring."

"If it's so important to you, *you* take it off. Take it to Teague. Tell him everything. Tell him the reason I always wear it is because I feel guilty for not…not loving him the way you seem to think I should. But do it *after*, not before, so I know this is about me, not him."

"And if I insist on doing it now?"

"You won't. I know you won't. You stopped me so many times in San Francisco, making sure I was okay, making sure I hadn't changed my mind. You said you wouldn't do anything I didn't like—and you didn't. I know you won't do anything I don't want you to do now, either. You're not the man you're trying so hard to tell me you are."

And that was when he lost it, as though he could hear a snap in his brain, and he crushed her against his chest. How could he want to be her hero and yet simultaneously need to show her that he'd be her downfall? He was confused, and crazy with lust for her, and so damn tired of not having her.

"So be my type all the way now. *Mine*, not his," he said, and ground his cock against her to let her know exactly what his type was.

And *God*, she felt good. Plump and fragrant and perfect. A delicious tremble ran through her and he loved the feel of it so much he ground his cock against her again.

"Do you like that?" he asked.

"Yes," she gasped.

"My cock?"

"Yes."

"You can't even say the word, can you?"

"Cock. Your cock."

"And if I said I wanted to see you on your knees for me, with my cock in your mouth, sucking?"

"I'd do it."

"Say it, Romy."

"I want to suck your cock."

"Would you do anything I ask?"

"Anything!" she moaned, her hips arching helplessly into him as he rubbed himself against her again. "Oh God, it isn't fair to torment me like this."

His mouth hovered over hers. "You want fair? Then hear me. I don't care about your heart, or your soul. I care about your body, for a limited time only. And all that's of interest to me right now is if…" grind "you're…" grind "wet!"

A whimper reached past the whoosh of his pulse in his ears, but no words. He wished he could see her eyes, but they were tightly closed now. It was hard to see her so lost in passion, knowing he wanted to be more for her, to be better for her, and yet be unable to convince himself that was possible. But he was helpless. He would take her, lost or found, his or Teague's or anyone else's, any way at all, even though he didn't deserve her, and pray that this time he'd get her out of his burning blood so he could leave her alone.

He ground himself against her again, more urgently now, and she edged her thighs slightly apart. "Tell me, Romy. Hurry. Tell me you're ready, you're wet and ready enough for me."

Her eyes bolted open. "I'm not telling you—you'll have to find out for yours—"

It was as far as she got, because Matt found he couldn't wait another second to put his mouth on hers. Not gently. He couldn't be gentle. He wanted her too much. No more words. No taunts. No dares. No time. He needed her on his tongue, needed her limbs and her breaths tangled with his. He needed to be closer, surrounding her, inside her.

For the longest moment she stayed with him, and then she moaned against his mouth and it seemed to snap her back to reality. She bolted against him and struggled free, and then stared up at him, her breaths coming in sharp bursts, her magnificent chest heaving.

Had he scared her off already? "Romy," he said. Just her name, but there was a plea in it—a plea both to stop him and to not stop him.

She gave a cry of surrender, flung herself into his arms again, kissed him so hard their teeth crashed together and he fucking exulted in it. It wasn't anything soft that she was offering, nothing comfortable. No more stopping. No backing out. So when she eased slightly away, a murmur of apology for hurting him on her lips, he used his hand on the back of her head to jam her mouth against his and instantly she gave herself up to him. A drench of heat, back and forth between them. He shoved one thigh roughly between her legs, and she surged against him. A drugging, sucking kiss. A wanton, blazing kiss.

When he broke to breathe, he kept his mouth close enough to taste her. "Tell me it's me you want, that I'm the only one."

"Yes!" she said, surging against him. "You, I want *you*, any way you want to be."

"Only me."

"Only you." She shoved his chest. "There." Another shove. "Satisfied? Now do it!"

God, the triumph of it! He didn't care if she shoved him through the nearest wall as long as she meant those words. It was wrong to want to hear them, worse to *ask* to hear them, but he needed them. A kind of forgiveness, permission to be exactly who he was, to be only what he could.

"Am I satisfied?" he asked, and framing her face with his hands, he kissed her harder still. "I won't be satisfied until I'm buried inside you."

Another rough kiss, hot and wet. Her hands were at the front of his jeans, unbuttoning, unzipping him, and he wondered how long he'd last when he'd been starving for her for so long. Mouths crushing, bruising, a clash of teeth and tongue, his heartbeat going crazy, excitement fizzing in his blood.

He kept kissing her, couldn't seem to stop, as he dragged her jeans halfway down her legs. Unable to wait another inch, he ripped off her panties. He wanted to tear every stitch of her clothing and rend from her life everything that had kept her from him for four unfathomable weeks, for ten clueless years.

Romy's hands were under his sweater, under his T-shirt, skating up his chest. He wished she'd rake him with her nails and make him bleed for her. And as if answering that need in him, she dug her fingernails in. He drew back, not to stop her but to see her as she marked him, and the ferociousness in her face made him kiss her again. Wanting him made her angry. Well, he was with her there, furious at how much he wanted this with her. So if a bit of fierce would bring them to terms with what was between them, then he'd *give* her fierce.

He untethered the last of his restraint, hauling her to the floor and under him, his cock lunging even though her legs weren't open to him. He was going to take her here, now. He was going to pretend there was no choice, even though he knew the choice would be waiting at the end of whatever they did.

Her jeans were manacling her legs, but he couldn't bear to let her go long enough to release her from the bind. His cock wasn't going to wait; it was weeping for her already. He'd have to take her as she was, even though she'd be so tight in that position he'd likely explode the moment he was inside her. He tore his mouth free and dragged in a tortured breath.

"Hurry, hurry," she pleaded, struggling against the stubborn jeans that wouldn't let her open her legs for him. "Oh God, hurry!"

She craned upward to lick his lips, and he kissed her again, easing a hand between their bodies, sliding it down, down, tangling his fingers in her pubic hair. She sobbed out a breath, raised her hips in encouragement and he delved lower, pushing between thighs that were almost clamped together. She started to shudder, her hands pulling at the hip band of his jeans, trying to free him.

"Make me come," she said. "Do it."

"I will," as he plunged his fingers into her.

"More, I need more."

But he stayed there for a maddening moment, loving the silky moisture against his fingertips, playing in her heat, absorbing the little shivers of her body.

"Matt!" she cried.

He eased off her, barely enough to free himself while one hand continued to play in her wetness. He jolted as his naked cock nudged at her opening, so eager for her he fumbled uncharacteristically as he slid his fingers out, pushed his cock inside. The fit was so snug he thought he wouldn't make it all the way in. But one thrust and he was there. *Fuuuuuuuck.* He stopped to absorb the dizzying sensation of being one with her as she whimpered and gasped and gripped him. A blinding, heaven-hell moment. It was tight, so tight, having her thighs almost closed.

"God, you feel good," he gasp-groaned.

"So do you. Right there. Exactly there, exactly like that. Stay there. Fill me."

He tried, he really did, despite his cock demanding that he move into the age-old rhythm. He dropped his head to her shoulder, panting through the need. But it was no use. "Romy, I have to move. Just…oh God… once. Just once."

"Then do it, but hard, I want it hard. Fill me up, and up, and up." So he withdrew all the way, then pushed all the way in again. Stop. Counting in his head to try to control the animal urge. "That's sooo good," she moaned out, and he withdrew again but try though he did to regulate himself, when he plunged into her again he went so violently she shifted a foot along the floor. He stopped again, fearful that he'd been too rough but she didn't flinch and she didn't let go of him and he sure as hell wasn't letting go of her.

And then it was on. Ruthless. This was more than wanting her. He was claiming her as his so that whoever came after him could never own all of her. One, two, three, five, ten thrusts. Stuffing himself inside despite the constriction of her almost-closed legs, thankful for her drenching moisture but for which he could never have found his way. Whatever was happening, it was tighter, hotter, wilder than anything he'd ever experienced.

Missionary position. As vanilla as you could get, but this was *hot* vanilla. Hot and intense, like a secret flavor, hidden away for only him to taste.

All too soon the rush was there. He threw back his head, a "Gaaaaah" tearing from his throat as he tried to stop himself from coming and then he felt her inner muscles clamp. Another cry ripped out of him, like an endless death, in sync with her own, and he was coming and coming and didn't want to stop, never, ever stop. Didn't want to leave her heat. Never…ever…leave.

CHAPTER TEN

ROMY FLOATED BACK to earth slowly, breaths settling inhalation by exhalation, heart rate decelerating beat by beat.

She wanted the world to stop so she could keep savoring the feeling of Matt still inside her, his head nuzzled between her neck and her shoulder.

Her limbs felt heavy, her eyelids, too; she was warm and drowsy and replete.

She almost couldn't believe the things she'd said, telling him to go deeper, to stay there, to fill her. Unfiltered demands she couldn't imagine making of any other man. She felt a laugh burble up, because the moisture coating the inside of her thighs told her he'd taken her at her word and filled her all right.

He raised his head and looked down at her, and for a moment his eyes told her he could belong to her, and only her, forever. His eyes told her that he loved her.

She held her right hand to his face, and he turned his mouth to it, kissing her palm.

"Take it off," she said.

"Hmm?"

"The ring, take it off."

And in the time it took her to blink, the poignant tenderness she was so sure she'd seen in his eyes was gone and in its place was that other look, the one full of despair at what he'd done, what it meant. But that was just as fleeting, replaced by an emptiness so icy it made her shiver.

Funny how the springlike warmth their friendship had basked in for so long had transitioned so quickly into a season of extremes—the sear of summer, the frost of winter, no temperate zone.

Matt removed her hand from his face, withdrew from her body swift and hard, and stood. One hand hitched his underwear and jeans back into place. And it seemed they were back to square one: she may or may not be pregnant; he may or may not be interested; and sex was definitely not love.

Unutterably depressed, Romy moved more slowly—getting up off the floor, refastening her jeans, plucking the destruction that was her blue silk underwear off the floor and stuffing it out of sight in her back pocket because she didn't think he needed the reminder.

And then she fixed her eyes on him. "If you didn't really want me to take off the ring, what was the point of demanding that I tell you I want you, only you?"

He hunched a shoulder. "They're just…words."

"Just words," she repeated. "I see. Like love. And saying them during sex makes them meaningless?"

He took a step toward her. "Romy, I just—"

"No!" Pulling back.

"I wasn't going to— Ah, Jesus! I just— I want you to know that whatever applied before still applies, that's all."

"What does that mean?"

"Arrangements. The trust fund."

She took a slow, do-not-punch-him breath. "You know what? Go ahead and set up the trust fund—or not. I don't care. See your lawyer—or not. I don't care. I don't even care if you've been with fifteen women in the past month, as long as you give me a shout if you discover you've caught something nasty."

"I haven't."

"Caught anything? Good to know."

"*Been* with anyone. I'm monogamous on request, remember."

"I didn't request it."

"It was implied."

"Well, good for you, but like I said, I don't care."

"It's the truth."

"How many ways can I say I don't care?"

His jaw had tightened. "Just so you know, Romy, *I'll* care."

"You'll—?"

"If you're not monogamous, I'll fucking care."

"My, my, how *bourgeois*! But I suppose you have to have some guarantee that valuable trust fund won't be supporting another man's child, right?"

"I don't give a fuck about the trust fund."

"For someone who doesn't give a fuck about it, you talk about it a lot. But anyway, back to the new plan."

"We don't need a new plan."

"Sure we do, Matt, because whatever we've been doing for the past ten years isn't working for me anymore. For ten years, I've wanted you. And you've known it, and ignored it, because I guess you wanted me just as much as I wanted you but in a different *way*."

"Romy—"

"Please, just…let me say this. Think of us as actors in a movie, filming a scene that goes on way too long because nobody's prepared to call 'Cut.' You, our hero, are walled up in a castle tower surrounded by a moat. One by one, the best and strongest women in the kingdom have been diving into the moat and swimming across to the tower hoping to scale your impregnable wall, yet not one of them has made it inside.

"Enter the heroine of the piece—that's me, in case you're wondering. I've been assessing the structure of your tower for ten years, learning the makeup of the stone and waiting for the perfect moment to make my own attempt. And a window of opportunity opens, and I can see you framed in that window. So I jump into the moat and swim like crazy, but the water is murkier than I expected, choked with weeds, so it's hard work— so hard, I'm exhausted by the time I get to the tower. I don't care, though, because I've found a gap in the stonework at last, and even if it's not quite big enough to slip through, it's there, and I figure if I scrape and claw and gouge and dig, I'll find my way in. But it takes me a while to realize I've torn open my flesh trying to reach you, and my heart…my h-heart is on display. But when I look up to the window in that tower to ask you to open the drawbridge, because my heart needs you, and I know you can see me, clinging to the wall with my heart *bleeding*, Matt, bleeding for you…you turn away, even though you know I'll drown if I fall back into that moat."

"Stop, Romy."

But she wouldn't stop. She couldn't. "So I think we need to recut that scene, change it from a heart-wrenching drama into a fun comedy. Which is what we've done for the past ten years so it should be easy— all we really have to do is go back to being just friends. We even have a new window of opportunity, because you're here and I'm here, but this time, we need to stay

here, as in *together*, so as to avoid any unfair accusa-
tions about who hasn't contacted whom in two weeks'
time when I find out if I'm pregnant. My plan—let's
call it Plan C—has two possible outcomes. One—I'm
pregnant: we draw up new paperwork according to the
level of friend zone success we've achieved. Two—I'm
not pregnant: you go home and keep the hell out of my
life." She offered him a wintry smile. "Deal?"

"No," he said, and picked up his duffel bag. "Con-
trary to what you seem to believe, I don't enjoy seeing
you bleed, and whatever happens, Romy, you *will be
in my life.*"

"I won't be in your life if you walk out that door, because I will never see you or speak to you again."

"That's not fair."

"Your definition of fair doesn't suit me. I've spent too
long waiting for you to see me."

"I *do* see you, Romy."

"You see what you want to see, but I dare you to look
harder. I *dare* you, Matt. Stay and play it out."

"Jesus!" he said, and picked up his overcoat.

Romy said nothing, did nothing. Even though she
knew it would half kill her if he left.

And then he yelled, "Fuck." He glared at her. "FUCK!"
He threw his overcoat and duffel bag across the room.
"Fuck this, and fuck you for doing this to me."

Up went her chin. "You won't be fucking me, Matt,
but other than that, I'll take your response as a yes."

CHAPTER ELEVEN

PLAN FUCKING C.

Matt gave his duffel bag, sitting innocently on the floor of the spare room to which he'd been relegated, a savage kick.

Fun comedy—so why wasn't he laughing?

Just friends—when it was fucking obvious that things had changed and he'd just made it fucking obvious to both of them the only way he could keep his hands off her was to do it from the other side of the fucking Atlantic!

He didn't know how to describe the way he was feeling. Like he desperately wanted to get away from her… yet he was terrified of not being with her. Like he was a wolf baying for a mate…but strangling himself to silence.

Excruciating. Agonizing. Confusing. Bewildering. All of those things together. With an overlay of panic that in two weeks' time she'd be pregnant…but maybe she wouldn't. That he couldn't control what happened, and couldn't even blame her for taking control out of his hands because he'd made a fucking mess of things in two countries!

Ha. To think he was in this latest mess all because of an *X* in an email. That pathetic *X* of a kiss, which was the way Romy signed off her emails to everyone—even that prick Lennie—and to which Matt had taken exception on the basis he wasn't going to start being an "everyone" to Romy after ten years' being number one with her!

And then to get to her apartment, and see Teague and…and resent him, in part because Teague was so damn perfect he *hadn't* slept with her when he'd had the chance?

Up came his hands, fingers rubbing at his forehead.

It was going to be a struggle to live with Romy in this tiny place for two weeks. She'd complained about noises through their old thin walls, but she'd hear his *thoughts* ticking in this apartment—and his thoughts were far from celibate. God help him if she came into this room, because there was barely room for the two of them to stand. He could probably cross it in three strides.

He took one long step past the single bed to test that theory, another, stretched his arms out and up and… stopped, mid-third-stride, because his hand had hit something.

He looked up and saw the mobile hanging from the ceiling—silver-and-white stars.

With a sense of foreboding, he turned a slow circle, taking in the freshly painted walls—a silvery gray with a scatter of white stars on one wall, the small rug on the floor with the same white stars on a gray background, a new white bureau against one wall.

Bump-bump-thump went his heart.

Because he was standing in the nursery.

He'd be *sleeping* in his baby's room.

He looked around the room again, soaking in the details. Typical of Romy to have the interior decorating under way before she was pregnant. Not that there was a lot to see other than the paint scheme and the star/moon theme. A lamp sitting on his bedside table—a full moon— was clearly intended for the baby. And the bureau, in white—that had baby clothes written all over it.

Curious, he went over to it and opened the top drawer. "Oh!" he breathed, as he saw the cache of tiny garments.

He lifted out a minuscule white cardigan, raised it to his face, rubbed the wool against his cheek. Soft as a cloud.

One by one, he opened the drawers, taking out all the other perfect things, holding them to his face, inhaling their pure scent. Three sleeper suits. Two pairs of knitted booties. A cap in white wool that matched the cardigan. Baby vests and leggings and tops. Wraps and rugs, a small fluffy towel. The tininess of each item as he carefully placed each item back in its spot squeezed his heart until he felt like it had been pushed up into his throat.

When only the little white cardigan remained, held against his chest, Romy knocked on the door. "Matt?" she asked. "Dinner will be ready in twenty minutes if you want to grab a shower."

He couldn't speak.

"Matthew?"

He took a moment to reel everything back in, hand rubbing his throat to ease the choking sensation there, and then forced out a "Got it."

Pause. "Are you okay?"

"I'm fine," he said. Because he *was* fine. Just fine.

If you didn't count that stinging at the back of his nose and the longing to tuck that tiny white cardigan under his T-shirt, right against his still-throbbing heart.

CHAPTER TWELVE

DINNER WAS…NOT GOOD.

Oh, not the steak and ale pie, which was as it always was, but the general atmosphere of *What the hell are we doing?* that had pervaded the flat.

Or perhaps the more accurate question was *What the hell am I doing?* because Romy knew very well she was the one who'd pitched them into this awkward hell. *She'd* wanted to have sex; *she'd* blackmailed him into staying; *she'd* positioned her heart ready for a trampling at the end of the two weeks when Matt left—as he would do, no matter which of her two scenarios came to pass.

She might have enticed him into having sex with her—twice, now—but the scalding truth was that she loved Matt and he didn't love her.

Love? Ha! He didn't even *like* her anymore, judging by his nonexistent dinner conversation. Her own dogged attempts at it—questions about Matt's flight, the chaos of Heathrow, the weather in San Francisco, his new business venture with Artie—were met with such headache-inducing vagueness, Romy almost wished for a return to the rage that had had her fearing he'd spontaneously combust before she'd shown him to the spare room and left him to froth at the mouth in peace.

When Matt opted to work in his room straight after dinner, Romy was relieved but also apprehensive. From tomorrow, she'd be at work during the days so the after-dinner hours would become important harbingers of the direction their relationship would take. Two weeks suddenly seemed a very short time to navigate their future as potential parents—it would be even shorter if they spent every possible minute of that time avoiding each other.

Romy didn't expect to fall into an easy sleep—and she didn't. Dreams of Matt had haunted her ever since she'd left San Francisco, and his presence in the flat acted on those dreams like an injection of steroids, supersizing them. The taste of his mouth, the feel of his hands, the way he fit inside her—they were all there. Right along with the things he'd said to her that night, which played in her head over and over... *If I said I wanted to see you on your knees for me, with my cock in your mouth, sucking... All that's of interest to me right now is if you're wet... I won't be satisfied until I'm buried inside you...*

No romance, not love words, but dear God, so indescribably, feverishly arousing she had to struggle not to go to him and tell him she was ready to suck anything he wanted her to suck.

Such a night left her ill prepared for seeing him in her kitchen the next morning. He'd gone for a run—as he always did—and looked so sweatily, deliciously scruffy as he scrambled eggs, she didn't trust herself not to lick him so she mumbled an apology about being late and left the flat without eating.

And despite lecturing herself half the day about Plan C's restrictions, when she arrived home that night all it took was one look at Matt sitting on her couch with a beer in his hand to knock her straight into the same state of salivating hunger in which she'd left that morning.

Matt's eyes locked with hers, the beer he'd been raising to his lips stalling halfway to its destination. He got to his feet as though hypnotized and the air thickened so that it would have taken a chain saw to cut through it— and Romy's briefcase slipped from her now-nerveless fingers and hit the floor, jarring them out of a trance that had nothing of friendship about it and everything about sex. Saved by the briefcase!

Romy blurted out something about chicken curry, Matt said he'd set the table, and they proceeded to keep out of each other's way until dinner was served.

They set the pattern that night for the rest of the week. A stilted conversation over dinner, followed by watching a movie on TV while occupying uncomfortably opposite-end-of-the-couch positions so as to avoid accidentally touching. Not exactly a return to their old friendship.

Matt gave up halfway through the movie, citing the need to check in with the manager he'd left in charge of his San Francisco hub, and Romy surrendered to a tension headache and went in search of painkillers and a restless night's sleep.

The next morning, when Romy cried upon waking at the prospect of seeing Matt in his running gear and actually touched the walls in the shower as she imagined soaping Matt's naked body, she knew she wasn't going to survive two weeks of living this way.

It was with considerable trepidation that she ventured out to the kitchen, where she found Matt looking hotter than sin. He plonked a plate of scrambled eggs and a mug of steaming coffee on the counter for her, giving her a rusty "Good morning" that melted her insides. Thankfully he then promptly took himself off for his turn in the bathroom, leaving her to choke down her breakfast around a mouthful of drool.

As she paused outside the flat and laid her palm on the wood of the door like she was trying to feel Matt through it, she knew a storm was brewing between them and it was going to either break or suffocate them.

Something was going to have to give, and give soon. The only question about it was which of them would be the catalyst.

Matt had no idea how he was going to reclaim his position in the friend zone when he was fucking Romy all night in his sleep and thinking about fucking her every moment of the day.

His solution was to distract himself by invading Artie's Wimbledon house. Annoyingly, he could think of only two business matters for them to discuss, and both were finalized by 11:20 a.m. on Matt's first day.

At that point, Matt decided he had no option but to confess to Artie that impending fatherhood was responsible for his earlier-than-expected arrival in London. He felt a surge of energy after getting that off his chest, and urged Artie to join him in some steam-releasing activities. But he was doomed to disappointment. Artie, never the most intrepid of adventurers, was uninterested in abseiling down the ArcelorMittal Orbit, rap jumping down a tower or kayaking on the Thames, and informed Matt that he got all the daredevilry he needed from his DIY obsession: in fact, his only recent hair-raising stunt had been making a birdhouse in his mantuary—a.k.a. backyard shed—during which he'd narrowly avoided slicing off an arm with a circular saw.

Which was when Matt had the brilliant idea of making his baby a crib. What better way of a) keeping himself from going stir-crazy in that Romy-saturated apartment, and b) demonstrating to Romy that he didn't *really* think fatherhood was all about slinging money at the kid?

By one o'clock, he and Artie had downloaded a design for a crib in a half-moon shape with cutout stars on the sides to match Romy's nursery decor, ordered wood and paint, familiarized themselves with the necessary tools and were ready to blaze a home handyman trail starting Tuesday morning.

And thus, the pattern of Matt's temporary life with Romy was set.

He'd go for his morning run, then make and eat his own breakfast. When Romy headed for the shower, he'd scramble her eggs the way she always made them, with mayonnaise, Parmesan and basil. She'd come to the kitchen counter, they'd exchange a subdued "Good morning" and he'd leave her to eat while he took his turn in the bathroom. By the time he was done Romy would have left for her Islington office and he'd be ready to head to Artie's to get macho with the power tools. He'd then be back at the apartment showering off man-cave grime before Romy left her office at six o'clock for the trip home.

When she arrived, Matt would be reduced to farcical TV Sitcom Land, making use of anything readily available to hide his exhibitionist dick—his laptop, Romy's *London AZ* guide, a cushion. If she'd had a damn pot plant in the place he may even have snapped off a frond and tied it around his groin! He'd get a reprieve while she cooked dinner, because she'd banned him from helping her in the kitchen on the—correct—grounds there wasn't enough room for the two of them.

They'd eat dinner while making inane conversation, then watch TV until the rigidity of perching as far away from her as possible without falling off the damn couch gave him an actual pain in the neck. At that point, he'd excuse himself to catch up on his San Francisco projects while the time zones were favorable, after which he'd dream about Romy all night and wonder if she was dreaming about him.

In other words, it was Hell. On. Earth.

And then, on Friday night, everything changed.

CHAPTER THIRTEEN

THE CRADLE WAS finished on Friday afternoon.

Artie was jubilant that they'd completed it with only one trip to the emergency room to get his forearm stitched.

Matt *had* been jubilant because he'd thought it looked fucking amazing…until he saw it in situ and by comparison to Romy's pristine paint job on the walls, realized it was in fact fucking crap.

He pictured Romy coming into the room in all her chic neatness and zeroing in on that drip of silver paint that he'd thought was unnoticeable but could now see would be visible from Jupiter using nothing but the naked eye. He envisioned her comparing his amateurish jigsaw-cut stars to the perfection of the ones painted on the wall. He imagined her waiting impatiently for Matt to leave London before she threw it out.

And then it sank in that he probably wouldn't *know* what she did with the damn cradle, because given the way things were going between them the chances of her inviting him anywhere near her for the rest of their lives seemed remote.

He thought back to what he'd said to her when she'd put Plan C to him—that whatever outcomes her Plan C covered, she'd be in his life no matter what. The truth was he needed that guarantee; it was what had driven all his decisions about Romy from the night he'd met her. Her, in his life somewhere.

And not the way they were at the moment. That wasn't having her in his life; that was *losing* her from his life—piece by piece, a little more every day. And it was going to have to stop.

He was going to fix whatever was wrong. Change the dynamic between them. There could be no more meaningless conversations over dinner. No struggling to keep their limbs separated on the couch. No more scheduling of morning showers to avoid contact. They had to have contact! They'd *always* had contact. Except for those four weeks after she'd flown home from San Francisco when he'd heard nothing from her, and he couldn't take another month like that. Nor could he wait another nine days to find out what sort of contact they'd have in the future. He had to know now, tonight.

Babies needed certainty, she'd told him. And he was ready to do his bit to guarantee their baby had it, via parents who would never give up on each other! If his gruesome parents could stay together for thirty years, he and Romy had to be able to manage some kind of longevity, didn't they?

Restless, he gave the cradle a gentle push with his fingertip to check the way it rocked on the nursery floor. Another push. Another. Picturing his tiny daughter in it.

He wondered if Romy had any names picked out. He kinda liked the name Rose… Similar to Romy, and yet…different. Pretty. Sweet. A little serious. He liked the idea of a serious kid.

Okay, it was a little crazy to be thinking so far ahead. The kid was still only a blastocyst, if she was here at all!

Still, he wondered what Romy would look like pregnant. As chic as ever. Beautiful.

He hoped she wouldn't get morning sickness. That would suck after all the pain she'd already been through. Morning sickness could be serious if you got it bad— like that type the Duchess of Cambridge got. She'd have to move in with her mother if she got that kind because it would be impossible to live alone and suffer like that. Or she could go into the hospital.

He'd better check out the hospital she'd chosen for the birth, now he thought of it. In case other serious shit happened. Blood pressure problems. Gestational diabetes…

Miscarriage. Twenty percent of women had miscarriages.

Or—hang on—did women still die in childbirth?

Jesus, he hadn't researched that one! He was going to have to look into it.

Because fuck.

Like…fuck.

No. Just no. Not going to happen.

He realized he'd stopped rocking the cradle and looked down at the sweaty palm he'd been gripping it with. He swallowed, breathed deeply, but the questions wouldn't leave him. Pregnancy, childbirth, the things that could go wrong. He was going to have a stroke thinking about this stuff when he was back in San Francisco.

Which…meant…ooooh. Holy shit! He was going to have to *not be* in San Francisco—he was going to have to be *here* for the next nine months to make sure nothing went wrong.

For a moment, he felt disorientated, and had to sit on the edge of the bed and breathe through it. Ha! Anyone would think he was having sympathy contractions nine months early!

Nine months. Living with Romy for nine months... Was it possible?

Well, yeah! Perspective! He'd lived with her for three and a half years, hadn't he?

And all right, that was different. He hadn't even caught an accidental bathroom flash of Romy's body in all that time, and now he'd had sex with her twice and could visualize every damn inch of her skin. That made it a little harder to maintain a hands-off friendship.

Also, he was having a kid with her, for Christ's sake, so...so...ooooh. He was sleeping in the nursery, and he'd have to *get out* of the nursery so he and Romy could get the nursery finished, which meant there was only one place to sleep and that was with her.

He stared around the room, seeing nothing, as he assembled thoughts and then disassembled them. He wasn't flavor of the month with Romy—she'd told him sex was out of the question and she looked a lot like she wasn't intending to back down on that anytime soon. And he had no intention of backing down on it, either.

But...but...would it be so bad? If they put strict rules in place? It was only nine months, just until the baby arrived, and she could put together whatever legal documents she wanted to regulate the arrangement, couldn't she?

He had to shake his hands at that point to release some tension, then rub them on his jeans because his palms were sweaty again. Oh God. God! Whichever way you sliced it, this was a big deal. Huge! This was *not* a hookup. This was an affair. A real, bourgeois affair. He had to think this through. Maybe…maybe set the arguments out the way Romy did and try them on her tonight, easiest to hardest, no rushing his fences the way he usually did. He'd call it a Plan D.

He got up, went over to the cradle, set it rocking again, picturing a little tuft of red hair, a mini version of Romy's pursed duckbill lips.

He smiled. That kid was going to be *cute*!

CHAPTER FOURTEEN

MATT FIRED HIS opening salvo over their evening meal of spaghetti with ricotta, prosciutto and arugula pesto— "You look tired."

And okay, that statement wasn't going to set any woman's heart aflutter, but it was harder than he'd anticipated to think of something scintillating to say after five days of cold shoulder.

Romy didn't even look up from twirling a piece of spaghetti around her fork. "That's because I am."

Matt waited for her to finish eating that forkful, and tried again. "Tiredness is common when you're pregnant."

She paused, another forkful halfway to her mouth.

He gave her a weak smile. "I...er...read up on the symptoms, that month in San Francisco. Just...just in case."

The fork continued its journey in silence.

He cleared his throat. "So? Do you think you're... you know...*tired*?"

Aaand she laid down her fork. "I have no idea if I'm pregnant. If you're impatient for an answer because you're ready to call it quits and go home, however, I can grab a no out of the air for you. Or you could just *go*!"

"I'm not leaving, Romy," he said, which of course was exactly the point he'd been intending to work up to, but before he could elaborate she tossed her napkin on the table and stomped off to her bedroom.

Okay, that hadn't gone exactly as he'd planned. But he had a Plan E.

He cleared the table, stacked the dishwasher, sat at the dining table with his laptop, pretending to work in case she came out but in reality checking what was on TV because he knew Romy would be out eventually to watch it with him—she'd been making a point of *not* running away from him as though it were a badge of honor to suffer his company.

Sure enough, twenty minutes later she emerged in sweatpants and a loose T-shirt that screamed *I am in the friend zone* but which nevertheless set him on fire.

Out of the corner of his eye he watched her hesitate at the couch, then take up her usual position on the extreme right end, pick up the remote, turn on the TV and start changing channels at a rate of knots.

He took a couple of deep-but-silent breaths, adjusting his dick for the millionth time to try to give it a little extra room in his jeans, then he grabbed a beer for himself and a glass of water for Romy and made his way over to the couch. He deposited the drinks on the coffee table and took his allocated place on the extreme left.

Immediately, his penis eased out of the position he'd forced it into, making him squirm.

Romy looked at him, frowning. "What is it?"

"Just a twinge. In my…hip," he said, and grabbed the nearest cushion to thrust over his lap with a telepathic order to his dick to behave because he was *not* going to rush his fences!

"I've got some Deep Heat in the bathroom if you need something for it."

He almost burst out laughing at that. Deep Heat on his cock? That'd serve the bastard right. "No, I'll be... fine," he said, and he let himself look at her, really look at her, in a way he hadn't allowed himself for five days.

Every cell in his body seemed to vibrate with the need to touch her immediately. The idea of never touching her again was unendurable. And he didn't want to build an argument rationally—he just wanted her. Fast-tracked.

Okay, he was going to rush a fucking fence.

He threw his lap-covering cushion over the back of the couch. "Romy?"

She turned to him, her hand tightening on the remote. "Yes?"

"Stick a fork in me—I'm done."

CHAPTER FIFTEEN

"A WHAT?" Romy asked.

"A big, sharp fork. Or your teeth if you prefer."

She choked on the breath she'd been taking, coughed, wheezed, grabbed for the glass of water on the coffee table and took a massive gulp. *What* had he just said?

He grinned at her. "I can do kink, you know."

And she choked again, this time on the water, and coughed up half a lung.

"You okay?" Matt asked. "Maybe you need some of that Deep Heat."

Deep Heat? Yes! *Yes*, she needed deep heat. The deeper the better.

"But if you're trying to change my channel," he said, with a half laugh, "it's too late. It's preprogrammed."

"Wh-what?"

He gestured to the remote, and she looked down at it as though she'd never seen it before.

"Here," he said, taking it from her and pointing it at the TV. "Let's agree that the next channel switch we stick with no matter what."

But when he jabbed his finger on the remote and somehow found *The Proposal*, she wanted to snatch the remote off him and try again.

She and Matt had watched *The Proposal* together the night she and Teague had broken up. February 14, nine years ago to the day. Not that Matt would remember that. But it was etched in her mind as the date she finally accepted Matt didn't know she was equipped with boobs and a vagina.

"What is it about this movie and Valentine's Day?" Matt asked.

Blink of utter, *utter* insanity. "You *remember* watching this?"

"Well, yeah! *I* wasn't the one who drank a whole bottle of red wine on my own—my memory is unblotted. Now shh, we've already missed half of it." And he fixed his eyes on the screen while simultaneously reaching out a hand and yanking her close to him.

What the *hell* was going oooon—dear God, he'd put a hand on her thigh.

She waited for him to move it. One…two…five…ten seconds… But his hand stayed where it was.

What was she supposed to do? Leave it there? She tried to think if she'd felt this hot and bothered in the old days when they'd watched a movie and he'd casually touched her, but her body had gone into free fall and there was only now. A deep, painful longing for him suffused her. She'd sit through anything as long as he kept his hand there—golf tournament, snooker, home shopping channel, even *The Proposal*.

"So," he said, his eyes still on the TV screen.

"Yes?" she breathed.

"Back to that fork…"

The fork. Ha! Stick a fork in *him*? Stick a fork in *her*! She was so done she was like a slab of overcooked pork crackling!

Matt hooted out a laugh as though he'd heard her thoughts, then gestured to the TV. "Do you remember this bit?"

She forced herself to focus on the screen. Ugh. "Unfortunately, yes. You made me get up and chant to the universe and dance around the living room."

"You didn't take much persuading."

"Red wine."

"Wanna have another go—without tripping over the coffee table this time?"

"Thank you, no."

"Then shh," he said, and as he refocused on the TV, he released his grip on her thigh and pulled her under his arm instead.

Romy kept watching the screen, conscious of the need to appear like she was just…well, breathing. Like a normal woman would breathe when she was jammed under the arm of a guy she was gagging for!

But she was struggling to take in anything, because she was seeing instead Valentine's Day evening nine years ago…

Matt and his date *du jour*, Kelsey, were going to a brasserie. Rafael and Veronica were at a diner because Rafael was broke and his pride wouldn't bend by so much as a quarter inch when it came to Veronica contributing funds toward their date nights. Romy, who'd been dating Teague for two chaste months, didn't know where Teague was taking her because it was a surprise, but she knew if she was ever going to sleep with him this was the night. She might have actually gone through with it, too, if he'd booked any old restaurant. But the moment she'd seen it was the exclusive, expensive Catch of the Day—which she'd been dying to try but couldn't afford—she'd had a crisis of conscience. Going to bed with Teague after such a meal would feel like a dinner-for-sex trade, and she liked him too much to go through with it. So she'd put her hand on his arm to stop him from entering the restaurant, and he'd given her his gentle, crooked smile and said, "It's okay, Romes. Apparently Valentine's Day breakups are almost as common as Valentine's Day engagements."

And they'd hugged, and she'd tearily rejected his what-the-hell-it's-Valentine's-Day offer of as much lobster and champagne as she could consume, and thirty minutes later Romy was back in the town house with a take-out pizza.

She'd been about to indulge in her first bite when Matt walked in, looked at the pizza in its box on the coffee table, at the glass of red wine beside it, and asked, "What's with the pizza?"

"Can't a girl order a pizza every now and then?"

"Not when the girl is you."

"I don't cook *every* night."

"Yes, Romy, you do. You're *obsessed* with cooking." And he'd swiped a slice, sampled it, grimaced, picked up the pizza and taken it to the kitchen, where he threw it in the garbage.

"I haven't eaten dinner!" she complained.

"If you want pizza, I'll take you to Vendetta's."

"It took so long to get into this dress I can't be bothered getting out of it just to go for pizza. The whole point of takeout was that I didn't *have* to."

"Yeah, I guess you do look overly trussed for a pizzeria."

"A real man wouldn't be deterred by a few buttons."

"*Any* man would be deterred by three million of the

things, so to save us both the effort…" dragging her off the couch "…I'll make you something to eat instead."

He'd tugged her to the kitchen counter, got a beer for himself, poured her a fresh glass of red, tapped the neck of his bottle to her glass, taken a quick swig and started gathering ingredients.

Recognizing the makings of Matt's infamous cheese, bell pepper, chili and Henry's Hot Sauce omelet, Romy had spared a mournful thought for her trashed pizza capricciosa. But she knew Matt only made this particular omelet when someone was miserable—there was something about hot sauce and egg that helped take your mind off your troubles, he insisted, to everyone else's disbelief—and so she'd said, "What happened?" preparing to take one for the team and help him eat the damn thing.

"Huh?" As he roughly chopped the pepper.

"Tonight. What happened with you and Kelsey?"

"Nothing." Shaking out a ton of chili flakes.

"Nothing as in…nothing?"

"What?" he said, distracted by cracking eggs into a bowl and whisking enthusiastically. And then he paused and looked at her. "Oh no, I don't mean *nothing* nothing. I mean nothing *interesting*."

He mixed the cheese, chili and pepper chunks into the egg, tipped the mixture into the pan and pushed it around with a spatula. A couple of minutes later he scraped what looked like a lumpy red-and-beige splotch onto a plate. Without ceremony, he poured the hot sauce over it, threw a knife and fork on top and slid the plate across the kitchen counter to her.

"Where's yours?" she asked, dismayed at the gargantuan size of the thing.

"Shit, *I* don't need to eat." He grabbed for his beer and took an enthusiastic swallow. "I had to eat Kelsey's dinner *and* mine because she's on a diet." Another slug of beer. "Fuuuucking hell, Romy—a diet!"

"She's a *cheerleader*, Matthew," Romy said, and shoved a valiant forkful into her mouth. She swallowed with some difficulty, then grabbed his beer off him, needing a sip to extinguish the flame in her throat. "She has to wear skimpy outfits, and people have to toss her in the air and…and things. You're the American—you know this stuff better than I do."

"So what?"

"Sooooo she can't eat like the rest of us—she has to keep her weight down."

"Oh. Yeah. I guess."

"And come on, you *know* girls don't look as good as Kelsey without a little self-deprivation."

"Who cares about looks?"

Romy choked on the bite of omelet she'd just taken. Took another sip of Matt's beer. "Name one nongorgeous girl you've been out with."

He grabbed his beer bottle back off her. "Names aren't important. And neither are looks."

"Ha ha."

"I'll qualify that—looks are a drawcard, but not if the rest of the person is annoying."

"Yeah, well, your problem is you're spoilt for choice. You get the pretty ones and the creative ones and the smart ones—all the ones."

"At least I don't get the nasty ones like you! Don't make me regret wasting the Omelet of Compassion on you, Romy."

Romy slowly lowered the laden fork that was halfway to her mouth. "What makes you think I'm in need of compassion?"

"Er...the pizza? Obvs!"

"Try again."

He ran a hand behind his neck. "Well, you're here, and Teague's not."

"How did you know I'd be here?"

Another rub of his neck. "I saw Teague at Flick's."

"Flick's? *Teague?*"

A look of annoyance crossed Matt's face. "It's not a den of iniquity you know, it's just a bar that happens to show films on Wednesday nights. They went anti-Valentine tonight with some godawful indie horror film. *Lots* of people were there."

"Yes, but Teague?"

"Why not Teague? At twenty-one he doesn't even need a fake ID, even if they could be bothered carding us, so—"

"It's not that! It's just... I don't know. It doesn't *seem* like him. It has a bit of a reputation."

"Oh, so Flick's is good enough for me but not for him? Yeah, well, he *was* there, halo and all! So I asked him why you weren't with him and he told me you two had called it quits."

"And you assumed I'd be in need of an omelet! Well, let me assure you the split was amicable." She pushed her plate away. "I promise you it wasn't worth leaving Kelsey unsatisfied."

"As it happens, smart-ass, we'd already done the satisfying stuff before dinner." He grinned. "*And* after. We were just out for a postcoital drink and the movie, and to be honest I was looking for an excuse to skip the film because there's a scene with an eyeball being chewed in *close-up*. Blech."

"I'm glad I didn't *completely* ruin your evening," she said drily.

"You don't *look* glad."

"Because you threw out my pizza!"

"Hey, I was going to take you out!"

"Oh, great—me eating and you watching!"

"Well, I... Sorry. I got a little ahead of myself with the pizza."

"That's because you always act first and think later. But since I don't need a babysitter, please take yourself back to Flick's."

"Don't make me go back there, Romy! I've got a DVD of *The Proposal* for us to watch instead—much better than a chewed eyeball. Kelsey said you'd like it and she's a film major so she'd know. She says it's perfect for V-Day."

"*Kelsey* suggested it?" Romy didn't know how to feel about not being considered a threat; she was *living* with Matt, after all!

"Come on, Romy, you know how squeamish I am. I can't take the eyeball. Don't make me go back there."

And so she'd laughed—of course!—and let him pour her more wine and put on the movie and tuck them both under a blanket on the couch. And then he'd poured her *more* wine, and made her do the chant-dance, followed by more wine...

And then came the scene with the ivory satin wedding dress and Romy had started to cry, and as though Matt had been waiting for exactly that, he'd scooped her up and sat her on his lap and patted her back and she'd snuggled against him.

Matt made stupid *It's all right, I've got you, You've still got me* murmurs into her hair, and even stupider than what he was saying was that she'd fallen asleep. Cradled on Matt's lap *she'd fallen asleep*! What a waste!

When she woke up, she was sprawled on Matt on the couch, and for the longest time she'd watched him sleep. Awake, he was always so sure of himself, and yet asleep there was something defenseless about him that made her want to hug him.

She'd felt an insane desire to take his face between her hands and rub her lips against his to see what it was that he gave to other women that he wouldn't give to her. It had shocked her, how much she wanted to do it, not only because it felt wrong to break up with one guy and kiss another all in the one night but because she hadn't allowed herself to think about Matt like that since that first night they'd met, when they'd *almost* kissed.

Whatever the reason, she'd sucked in a breath and the small noise woke him. For a moment, he'd stared at her, and then his eyes heated, and hooded. The hands that had been loosely crossed over her back tightened and he'd pulled her in close and she'd felt his erection.

Time stopped. She'd sensed rather than felt his heart-beat, steady and strong. Or maybe it was her own she was in tune with: it was telling her to kiss him, kiss him now because she might never get another chance.

"One thing I noticed last night..." he'd said, and she'd held her breath, dying to know. And then he'd grinned. "You look kind of like a troll when you cry."

"Oh, you...you bastard!" she'd exploded, whacking him in the chest and oofing her way off him.

"Hey, it's cute," he'd insisted, laughing at her disap-pearing back as she stomped to her room, where she told herself that she was to Matthew Carter what Teague Hamilton was to her. A friend you liked too much to love. A friend you needed in your life but not your bed. A friend, nothing more.

And now, so many years later, nothing had changed... and she still wanted him anyway...

"Hey—remember this bit?" Matt, giving her a nudge and bringing her back to the present. "Betty White trying to find Sandra Bullock's boobs in that dress. You started crying and said your boobs were too big, so you were going on a diet like Kelsey to shrink them."

"Yep, got it, thank you."

"And I had to lift you onto my lap and cuddle you."

"Aaaand you can shut up now."

"And I said I'd take a look at your boobs for you and give you an honest appraisal."

"Shut *up*, Matthew!"

"And you started undoing those three million buttons on your dress."

"Yes, I *remember*," she said, exasperated. "I also remember that you stopped me."

He looked at her, eyes heating. "I was a moron. How about I check your boobs now?"

Oh God, oh God, what did that mean? Fork. Done. No! If she asked about it, it would probably turn out to be something about barbecued steak! "Very funny."

"Except that I'm not laughing, Romy."

For one perilous minute, she vacillated...but then she remembered that her buttons *hadn't* been unbuttoned that Valentine's Day nine years ago, and she turned back to the television.

"I can hear you sniffling, Romy," Matt said. "Just saying."

"I'm not sniffling."

"Are you, you know, hormonal?"

She looked up at him. "Am I *what*?"

"When women fall pregnant, they get sort of emotional."

"Oh, they do, do they?"

"Apparently."

"Shut up, Matt. And stop reading up on pregnancy. You won't be here, so you don't need to know."

"I could be here. If you needed me. If you...wanted me."

She swallowed, letting that sink in. "You can barely fit in this flat *before* I'm fat."

"I fit better if I do this," he said, and lifted her onto his lap. "Just like old times, huh?"

Old times? Not quite, Romy thought.

"And yet not like old times, is it?" Matt said, as though reading her mind.

"No, not like old times," she said.

"You see, Romy," he said, "I have a feeling the old times aren't coming back. Which leaves us with a choice of either no times or new times. And I...I don't want no times."

Breathless. Wanting. "So what do new times look like?"

"That's something we'd need to work out."

"How do we do that?"

"I don't know yet. What I *do* know is I still want you. I know, also, that if you didn't want me, too, you'd be down the other end of the couch. So I have a suggestion, if you're interested in hearing it."

Could this be real? Oh God, she didn't know what to think.

"Romy?"

"What's the suggestion?"

"That I give myself to you for the night, and you do whatever you want to me and we see how we feel at the end. And if it's good…I stay. But I stay in your room with you."

"Do you mean that?"

"Cross my heart, hope to die."

"Just so you know, I'll help you with the dying part if this turns out to be a joke," she said, and tilted her head, closed her eyes, waiting for the kiss.

Long moment of…nothing. And then Matt spoke. "Er, Romy…? I think you've got the wrong idea."

CHAPTER SIXTEEN

HER EYES BOLTED OPEN. "I knew it! I'm going to get the carving knife!" she said, as she started pushing off his lap—but he held her tight.

"You don't need a knife if you want to kill me," he said. "All you need to do is say no. Because I'll drop dead if you don't take me within the next two minutes."

"Take...you? Oh, take *you*! You mean I'm in control."

"That's what I mean."

"But why?"

"Because you said no sex, therefore you have to be the one to reverse that order. Because I like the idea of being your slave. And because...I trust you with my body, like I've never trusted anyone before."

She felt tears prickle, as they always did when he said something that moved her.

He groaned. "Hey! Cut that out. Tears aren't sexy."

"But big tough guys who turn to putty when they see them are."

"I'm scared of trolls, that's all," he said.

"I don't think you're scared of anything, Matt."

He cupped her cheek in one hand and looked at her, very seriously. "I'm scared of *you*, Romy, and that's the truth," he said. And then he gave a shaky laugh. "But here's a hot tip to help you with my seduction—I'm an easy lay—it won't take much to make me come. So the floor is yours. Or the couch. Too bad there's not a chandelier or you could—"

"Shut up and kiss me," she said, leaping straight into the fray before anything could snatch the chance from her—and almost before she finished saying it his mouth was on hers, his tongue in her mouth.

One, two, three seconds—and he sat back, took her hand, put it over his heart. "Feel that?"

"Yes," she said. "It's banging like a drum."

"I am going to come so hard for you," he said.

Oh God, just hearing him say that! "I'm going to make you," she said. "But first, I'm going to kiss you and you're not going to kiss me back—this is just for me."

He kept himself still as she brought her mouth to his. First she kissed one corner, then the other.

When she pulled back to look at him, he touched her mouth and breathed out slowly. "That's just the start, right?" he said.

Instead of answering him, she leaned into him again, trailing tiny kisses between those two corners, sometimes letting her tongue slide between his lips, sometimes not.

She pulled back again, watching for his reaction. "Well?"

"Well," he said, and licked his lips. "Am I allowed to ask for more? Because I want more, Romy. I want you to kiss me all night."

And with a little cry of surrender, she planted her mouth over his. "Open," she said against his mouth. "Now you can kiss me back."

And obediently, he did, his tongue gliding deep and

wet into her mouth, seeming to touch everywhere at once. She swiveled on his lap to straddle him, her arms twining around his neck, knees digging into the back of the couch either side of his hips as she brought her body snugly against his. Her hips moved back and forth, and so did his, as if their bodies were already planning to take over the show. He felt so good there, *her* toy now, and the thought that she could do whatever she wanted to him was an exhilarating one, even if all she really wanted to do was strip off their clothes and impale herself on him.

But she remembered how in San Francisco, when she was climbing the stairs, she'd wished she could be memorable for him, and so she forced herself to slow down, to throttle back. She would tell him what to do to her, because he wanted her to do that, he *trusted* her to do that—and being the one he trusted was already something memorable.

Her hands went to the hem of her T-shirt. "Do you know what I want you to do to me when I take this T-shirt off?" she asked.

"Tell me."

"I want your hands on my breasts. And then your mouth. I want you to coax my nipples out, to not stop until you do."

"Oh Jesus," he groaned. "I am so up for that."

She laughed, low and soft, and scooting back as far as she could on his lap, lifted her T-shirt up and off. Lowering her arms to her sides, she lifted her chin. Displaying the wares. Watching his eyes drop to her chest. Seeing him swallow hard. Her breasts seemed to swell from the heat in his eyes, begging to be released from the confines of her bra.

"Well?" she said.

"Well," Matt said fervently. "I could drool a fucking river looking at you."

"Hands. On me."

And as he raised his hands, placed them gently over her covered breasts and her heart gave a savage leap. He raising smiling eyes to hers and she knew he'd felt it.

He started to move his hands in circles over the white mesh of her bra, and her nipples tingled as though getting ready for him. One firm squeeze, and he pulled his hands back but only far enough for his fingertips to take over the work, drawing the lightest of circles around her areolae, which were on clear display through the mesh of her bra.

She huffed out a shuddering breath, so hot for him she thought she might scream. One more circle, another, another, each one infinitesimally smaller than the last, heading inward to his twin targets.

She squirmed on his lap, frustrated, and the way he laughed low in his throat told her he knew exactly what he was doing to her. Well, of course he knew!

But she wasn't entirely clueless, either, and when she made a little figure eight on his lap with her backside, using her hips to propel her, he actually gasped, his cock doing an involuntary lunge upward against her heat. "Ride me if you want, Romy. Do anything to me. Ask anything of me."

"Then…then I want your fingers on my nipples, right on them, right now, rubbing," she said.

"Your wish…my command," he breathed out, and used two fingers to rub each nipple through the white mesh. "Tell me when I can use my mouth."

A deep, drawn-out moan of a "Now" had him going

straight to the job, holding her breasts in his hands and bending forward to lick around one areola, then the other, moving back and forth, back and forth again and again, before shifting to her nipples and using the flat of his tongue to lick her like an ice cream, then the tip to stab into the centers.

"Soooo gooood," she sighed.

"Don't I know it," he groaned, and gave each nipple a lightly sucking kiss.

"Take off my bra," she said. "I need you to touch me properly."

"How about I do it like this?" he said, and peeled the cups of her bra down. He leaned back to look at them, licking his lips as though he could taste her. "Ahhhh, God, it's a crime, how sexy you are."

She slipped her hands under his T-shirt, ran the palms up his chest. "You feel so hot."

"I am hot. Hot for you. Hot and hungry and ready."

She pulled her hands free, sat back to give him room. "Then take off your T-shirt."

He pulled it up and off lightning fast. "Romy, please touch me," he said. "Please."

She put her hands over his pecs, rested them there for long seconds, absorbing the thud of his heart and then moving her hands in the slow circles he'd used on her. "Are your nipples as sensitive as mine?" she asked.

"Find out," he said, and she moved her hands, softly, delicately circling them with her fingertips.

"Yes," she said. "They're hard. Oh, I wish you could feel mine."

"Say the word and I'll get back to work."

"First, I want to do this," she said, and leaned in so

that her breasts were only just touching his chest. She closed her eyes, lost in the moment. "Oh, I like that."

He bucked against her, as though jolted by a burst of uncontainable energy.

"Don't," she ordered, even though she loved it. "Stay still and let me do this. It feels so wonderful." And it did, her skin against his, the crunch of his hair against her nipples, the graze of his own small nipples against her.

"Are you trying to torture me, Romy?"

"What do you mean?"

"Do you know how hard it is for me to wait?"

"Yes, because I've waited ten years for you, wanting this."

"So you're punishing me?"

"No," she said. "No, never. I would never hurt you. I want to give you everything." For an instant, she sensed a withdrawal in him, and the next moment his hands were in her hair, his forehead pressed to hers.

"Not those words tonight," he said.

"Why not, when I mean them?"

He released her, eased back, not answering. "Come on, get rough with me. I want you to fuck my brains out and make me beg."

Her hips moved, her core sliding over him, back and forth. "Does it feel good to have me do that?"

"Yes, you know it does—you can feel how hard I am."

"So say the words. Tell me exactly. I like it when you say the words to me."

He smiled again, a sexy curve of mouth. "It feels so good when you ride my cock. You make me so big and hard, I can't wait to be in you. I want to make you wet. I want to fill you up. I want to do you fast and slow and make you come all night."

"Yes," she panted, restless, seeking.

"So can I?"

"Not until you make my nipples come out. Undo my bra."

Swiftly, he undid the back clasp of her bra and stripped it from her.

"Get to work," she commanded.

He recupped her breasts with his hands, going straight for the nipples now, thumbing them gently, then harder, then pinching them between thumb and forefinger.

The air was full of small sounds. Sighs and moans and gasped-out breaths and tiny sucking sounds, rasps from his jeans against her as she writhed on his lap.

"Now your mouth," she said. "Lick them. Suck them. Say again you'll do anything, but this time I want to know it's only for me, no other woman."

"Only for you, Romy. Only ever for you will I do what I'm told, always you, only you, forever."

She closed her eyes, surprised that the words brought her pain, and he seemed to take that as his cue to increase the pressure because he went hard at her now, hands squeezing her breasts, settling in to suck on her, focused on only one, going hard, hard, hard, as though he were starving for her, so that she was arching her back and dragging his head closer and tighter. The intensity hovered just short of pain.

She let out a low, keening cry, and he went crazy, his sucking almost frenzied. And unbelievably, with one last, long, luxurious suck, her nipple popped out into his mouth.

He pulled back, looked at it and she felt herself flame.

"I am so horny," he said, low and hoarse, as his fingers went to where his mouth had been, pinching and rolling. "I'm scared I might actually come." And he shuddered as though to underscore the truth of it.

"Suck me again," she said, and he bent his head and kept sucking, this time using his fingers on the other nipple as though to prepare it. And then with one final light bite, he switched sides, using the same technique, the same firm suction, the same concentration, and it happened fast his time, the nipple suckled into his mouth, eager and ready.

"Now," she said. "Now. I need you inside me now."

"Not yet," he begged, as he continued to lash one nipple with his tongue, twirl the other with his fingers, pinching, rolling, squeezing.

"Now," she said again.

"One minute more," he begged, and latched onto her nipple, sucking and sucking until she was shifting on his lap, whimpering, panting.

"I'm going to come if you keep going!" she cried.

"Good."

"No!" she said, and pushed against him so that she tumbled backward and would have fallen to the floor if he hadn't caught her hips, pulled her up, held her steady.

"You are driving me fucking wild, Romy," he said.

Their eyes clashed, warred. She undulated on his lap and a look of triumph came into her face. "Then kiss me, show me," she said, and he dragged her in, lunging his cock so high and tight against her she almost wished he'd take over, roll her under him and jam his cock into her. His mouth landed on hers, his tongue thrusting as though he were fucking her mouth, and she lost all sense of time and space until there was only heat and lust and musk.

Her slave. He really was her slave.

"Let me have you, Romy," he said against her mouth, between deep, drugging kisses. "Let me have you now."

And she was off his lap, dragging him up after her, kissing him again as her hands went for his jeans. Unzipping, hands diving, gripping him, squeezing him. "I want to see you naked," she said, and stepping back, she flicked a hand at his jeans. "Get them the fuck off."

"You bet," he said, and while he kicked his way free of his jeans and all but tore off his boxer briefs, she stripped off her sweatpants, her underwear.

And then she stopped to breathe before lowering herself onto the couch, where she laid herself out like a feast, and when he looked at her she felt a surge of power that this man, of all the men in the world, would want to be hers even for a fleeting moment.

As Matt looked at her, so confident on the couch, tenderness almost blinded him. She'd asked him to tell her he'd do anything only for her, no other woman.

To him it seemed so obvious, it didn't need to be said. Ten years of running only to her, ten years of doing whatever she asked. Even the fact that she'd asked him to take her, that night in San Francisco, the first time she'd ever outright asked, was proof. Because he'd held himself so rigidly back from her for so long—and yet he'd obeyed her. *Of course* he had. Here in London, too. It wasn't in him to deny her what she wanted. She'd always belonged to him, in every way but this—and now she was claiming this, too. Did she not see that he always would have done this for her if she'd asked? That he'd already done everything he could think of to keep her with him, even when the only way he could think of was to deny himself this final piece?

His body one giant throb straining toward her, held back only because he'd put himself at her command and she was reveling in her power over him.

Her silky light brown hair was spread out above her head. One arm was crooked beneath her head, the other stretching up the back of the couch, her hand flopping over the back of it. Creamy skin. Sleepy eyes. Mouth swollen from his kisses. Those small pink nipples, hard and impudent and all the more amazing because he'd had to work for them, and because she'd demanded he work hard. The tiny tangle of hair at the apex of her thighs, which made him want to fall to his knees and beg her to open her legs for him.

As though she'd divined that unspoken need, she spread her legs so that one foot was on the couch, the other on the floor. Like she was saying: yours.

"Ah, Romy," he said looking down at her. The moment felt too big for words, the air heavy with the promise of something special.

"Come," she said.

And slowly, he lowered himself on top of her, waiting for her arms to enclose him, folding his own tightly around her at the same time as he closed his eyes—the better to sharpen the moment. He stayed like that, quiet and still, for the longest time, absorbing her.

When he opened his eyes, it was to find her waiting for him. She strained up to kiss his mouth, deep and soft, and she kept kissing him as he slowly, so very slowly, entered her.

He stopped when he was all the way in, wanting to remember this moment because surely sex could never be so blissfully perfect again. And then he moved. Out, in, out, keeping it slow and rhythmic so she knew exactly what to expect.

Over and over he entered her, and she kept her mouth on his all the while. He wanted to take forever, wanted to immerse himself in the sound of sex, the arousing smell of her, the taste of her mouth, the pant of her quickened breaths, the feel of those delicious little nipples poking against his chest, the strength of her inner thighs gripping the outside of his as though she'd never let him go. But his cock was trying to slip the leash, desperate for the finale, and his orgasm was building, grabbing at him despite his efforts to slow it down.

Not yet, not...yet. He ground out the words in his head, but he knew it was a stroke or two only away. His breaths were heaving so much, he had to move his mouth off hers, gulping in air as his hips rubbed against hers. *Oh God, not yet, I want more.*

And then Romy's whole body went stiff. A gasp, and cry, her wet heat tightening around him as he sucked against her neck, then licked, then sucked, then licked.

"Let me say it, Matt," she said.

Oh God, he knew. Knew what she wanted. He shook his head, no. *No! Let me just have this.*

"I have to say it, Matt."

Panic. "No!" Aloud? In his head? "No, no, no, please no, just let me, let me, Romy."

But it was out of his control. Push, push, push, push, his body inside hers, owned. Her heart was thumping in time with his, the smell of her wrapping around him as surely as her arms. *Oh, please, no.*

"I love you, Matt," she cried, and the words pushed him over the edge so that he abandoned himself to the waves. "I love you, Matt. I love you, love you, love you. Ahhhhhhhh, I love you. Love."

Silence.

Full. Heavy. Lost.

His arms unwrapping, his mind unraveling, his body shivering.

He eased himself up over her, hands on either side of her, looked down into her face and all he could think was, *No, please don't say it*, even though it was too late.

She watched him. Boldly, unwavering, unapologetic.

Was she expecting him to say something? Because he had nothing to say.

He moved off her, stood, located his jeans and put them on. Found his T-shirt, dragged it over his head. He was covered, but he still felt exposed.

Romy sat up without taking her eyes off him. "What is it, Matt?"

"You know."

"Just words. Three little words."

"You promised not to say them, that night in San Francisco. You told me you refused to love me."

"And yet you knew I did."

"But you didn't tell me, you didn't say it. And then… Ah Jesus. You said them like that. At that…that moment. That's not love, Romy."

"So if I'd said them over dinner, that'd be different? You'd have *welcomed* them over dinner?"

He shifted his shoulders. He felt worn out. Exhausted. "Well, doesn't matter, does it, because now I've heard them. So…thanks. I guess." He gave a throat-clearing cough, wanting his voice to be steady. "I'm going to catch up with Teague tonight, have a few beers."

More silence. Stretching, as she watched him.

Another clear of his throat. "You know, Teague…"

"Yes, I know Teague," she said. "Your friend. The man I'm supposed to be with. *That* Teague."

"He and I…" Pause. "We're going to…" Pause. "I'm… due there soon."

"And is it going to be an all-nighter with Teague?"

"Maybe."

"You asked me for tonight, Matt. All night."

Again, his shoulders shifted. "Plans change."

She sighed as at last she got off the couch. "Okay then, we understand each other," she said, and put on her sweatpants, her T-shirt—not hurrying.

"The whole…whole friend thing. We all need to get back to that. You. Me. Teague."

She sighed again. "You don't have to explain yourself to me, Matt. We…you and I… I guess we sorted out those 'new times' we were curious about, so we're good. On the same page."

"Are we?"

"Well, maybe the same book, different chapters. You gave yourself to me to do with what I wanted, I did what I wanted and now we both know what's what, how we feel."

"Romy—"

"I love you and want to have sex with you because of that. You want to have sex with me, but don't want to love me because of that. I guess that translates into you being at chapter five while I'm up to chapter twenty-five. But whereas I know I want to finish the book, you're bored with it and want to move on to a different story."

"That's not— I mean—"

"What? Did I misinterpret something?"

Matt tried to figure out how to say his feelings were

more complicated than that, but when he thought of all the plans he'd made for himself just a few hours ago, all he could come up with was: "I need you, Romy."

She sucked in a breath, like he'd hurt her. "Yes, I think I know that. But I need you all the way, no secrets, no fears. And that's different from the way you need me." She smiled, with a roll of her eyes that managed to be both dismissive and defensively dramatic. "I shouldn't have called it love, I know, when you can't feel it, when you don't...don't know the...the *agony* of it. And it *is* agony, it really is. But I'm running out of nouns and adjectives, so you might have to give me some help there. I mean, we're not friends anymore, are we? I haven't been feeling much of a sense of camaraderie this week. I don't think what we just did was affectionate. We're not really having a casual fling because you're not using a condom the way you always do. So if you don't want it to be love, I don't know... Fuck buddies perhaps? Except that I've broken the cardinal rule so that's obsolete. How about ex-hookup?" She ran her hand over her hair, smoothing a tangle. "How strange that I thought I was different, being the only female you weren't interested in fucking...and now I'm just like all the others. Right down to telling you I love you at the peak of an orgasm, like the worst cliché. But I understand it now, Matt. I understand all those women who choose that moment to do it. It's that gap in the tower wall, you see. We can't help saying it at that moment because you make us feel so close to you, like we really could slip inside and find you. I even know why they don't want to be your friend at the end—because it hurts to see you and not have you. And you know what? I'm glad I'm not different. I never *wanted* to be different. I *want* to love you. And *I* don't want to be your friend at the end, either."

She picked up her underwear and headed for her bedroom, saying over her shoulder, "Better get your skates on or you won't make it to Park Lane by eleven."

Ten minutes later, Matt found himself outside Romy's flat, leaning against the wall like a drunk, one hand over his eyes. The agony of love. She'd called it agony, what she felt for him. He stood there for a full five minutes, battling the stinging at the back of his nose he was starting to get used to.

And then he took a deep breath, and headed out into the night.

CHAPTER SEVENTEEN

ROMY SPENT THE first half of the night lying in bed, reliving Matt's reaction to her grand declaration of love—which was to look at her as though she'd stabbed him straight through the heart he professed not to have.

The second half of the night she spent pacing through the flat, wondering what she could expect from Matt when he eventually returned.

When there was no sign of him by nine o'clock, she switched to wondering *if* he'd return.

By eleven o'clock, she was convinced he wouldn't.

She'd gone to his room many times, hesitating outside, knowing one quick peek would tell her if he'd taken his duffel bag. But she hadn't been able to bring herself to open the door, instead hurrying to the kitchen to distract herself by making coffee—and for her to make coffee instead of tea was a true indicator that her state of mind was unsound.

By noon she'd drunk so much coffee she was totally wired—which she figured explained the sudden grip of terror that convinced her Matt was lying dead in an alley.

At one o'clock, she pulled up his number, ready to call him despite the fact that last night she'd told him he didn't have to explain himself to her...and then made more coffee instead.

At two o'clock, she had the brilliant idea of calling Teague to find out what he knew, and when he answered on the third ring she almost collapsed with relief.

"T-Teague?" she stammered.

"Romes!" he said. "Let me guess—you're calling to tell me all is well in the land of the lovers so I can stop worrying about you."

"You'd know more about that than me."

"Er...not following."

"Is Matt—? Did Matt—? Oh!"

"Still not following."

"Matt said he was spending the night with you, but... he didn't. Of course he didn't."

"Oh. Er..."

"Don't," she said. "Please don't cover for him. There's no need. It's none of my business where he spends his nights. I'm not his girlfriend. And that...that's not what's worrying me. It's just...you know how reckless he is, and I keep expecting to hear he's BASE jumped off The Shard and broken his neck or something, so—"

"Hang on, hang *on*! He's lying to you about where he's going, you're checking up on him and you're telling me you're not his girlfriend?"

"He doesn't have those."

"Well, you're not just friends if that's how you're both carrying on."

"We're not friends at all anymore, it seems."

"Oh, Romy, you two were never friends. Look, much as it pains me to do this, let me give you some advice— stop giving him so much rope, because he'll keep hanging himself with it."

"Rope?"

"Stop letting him come and go in your life as he pleases, see any woman he wants, do anything he likes. He doesn't want that freedom—not from you. Deep down, he wants you to give him boundaries."

"I don't...understand."

"Matt's problem is nobody ever reins him in. Not his friends, because we like him exactly the way he is—fast and brilliant. Not the women he attracts just by breathing, because they'd give him anything he asks for—which sucks, by the way, for guys like me who don't get a look-in when he's around. As for his parents—well, they don't want to rein *themselves* in let alone anyone else, and I don't think they'll be happy until they corrupt him absolutely."

"I don't—? His parents? I've never met them."

"Now you see, that's interesting. Ask him why. And while you're at it, *tell him* what you want from him, how you feel, lay it on the line—"

"Oh, Teague, I already told him how I feel." She closed her eyes as the heat of humiliation flooded her. "Last night I told him I loved him."

"Aaand it all makes sense. You told him—he ran away."

"What am I going to do?"

"Tell him again. Keep telling him. Keep showing him, too, but you've been showing him forever, so I have a feeling it's the telling that's going to get him."

"He doesn't like being told. I knew that, and I told him anyway."

"He'll hear it, from you he'll hear it, but you'll have to make him hear it, and hear it, and hear it, because he won't believe it."

"And if I lose him for good?"

"Then at least it'll be an outcome, won't it? For you, if not for him. You can't keep limping around the edges of a relationship with him, Romy. If he really won't step up to the plate, it's time he let you go so you can find someone else. Someone who…who wants all of you, not just the parts Matt will spare."

"He'll say no—he won't step up."

"Then let him say no, and let him go. Look, just… think about it, okay?"

"Okay, I'll think about it…I think."

Teague laugh/sighed. "Okay, but while you're thinking about thinking about it, consider that every time you've needed him he's come running—and when I say running, I mean sprinting. You know, the night you and I broke up and I saw him at Flick's and told him we were through, he was out the door faster than a speeding bullet—"

"He hates being compared to superheroes."

"Then he should stop trying to save you. The point is, I was sure he was off to get the girl that night—but here you are, ten years later, still limping along the edges."

"Don't you think that means it's not supposed to be that way for us?"

"No, I think it means he's terrified. You're *different* for him, Romy."

"That's just it—I'm not different. I'm like everyone else who wants him but can't have him."

"I'm not talking about sex, except insofar as it took him ten years to get around to it with you—which *is*, in fact, the difference. He's scared to death of you, scared a wrong move will lose you, scared of his…his need for you to see him the way you see him. Because I'm telling you, he may not like you supersizing his heroism but he also kind of lives for it. He wants to be a hero for you, but deep down he won't believe he can be. He's scared—but don't you be scared, too, or you'll both still be limping around those edges when you're ninety. Anyway, enough Truth or Dare." He took a breath. "I'll tell you what I'll do. I'll text him, make sure he's alive, and then I'll text you so you can use your brain for more productive things than worrying about the idiot."

Romy received the "all clear" text from Teague half an hour later, but by four o'clock there was still no sign of Matt.

The time had come to make sure he hadn't moved out. Without hesitation this time, she opened the door to his room, walked boldly in...and her jaw dropped at the sight of a silver cradle in the shape of a half-moon.

She walked over to it, not quite believing it was real even though its slightly mangled cutout stars smacked of a DIY project so it was hardly a celestial gift beamed out of nowhere.

This was what Matt had been doing all week while she was at work? Not plotting a tech takeover of the world, but making his baby a cradle?

She blinked in disbelief as she ran her fingertips over the wood. As she gave it a little rock. And then she couldn't seem to stop blinking—not in disbelief anymore, but because tears had formed in her eyes. Everything about the wonky cradle moved her unbearably. Because she knew in that blinding, wrenching, heartshattering moment that she'd gotten something very wrong about Matt and his motivations. He'd suggested giving her his sperm not as a favor to her, not to be a godfather, but because he wanted a baby. He'd wanted, specifically, *her* baby. He'd flown to London to stop her from finding a different donor because he *loved* their baby. He'd loved it then, when it didn't exist, and he loved it now when it *still* might not exist. He loved it even though he'd probably never be able to say the words.

And *she* loved *him*—so much in that moment she would have gladly cut out her heart and given it to him on a plate made of her own soul, painted not black but silver and white, to match the priceless, utterly wonderful gift he'd made for their child.

She put both her hands over her belly. "Please be there, my little one," she whispered. "For your daddy, if not for me, because whether or not he knows it, he needs you."

CHAPTER EIGHTEEN

THERE WAS NO sign of Romy when Matt opened the door at 7 p.m.—not even a wisp of aromatic steam coming out of the kitchen, which was where she'd normally be at this time of night.

He experienced a short burst of relief, followed almost immediately by a surge of panic.

But then he heard his name, "Matt?" called out like a question from her bedroom and the panic receded... and then surged right back, because he had no idea what he was going to do.

He'd had a turbulent night and a torturous day wandering the city, trying to work out why Romy's *I love you* was different from every other *I love you* he'd ever heard even though it *wasn't* different, why it made him want to stay instead of leave, why leaving therefore was exactly what he should do and why he needed to stay anyway.

Yeah, like any of *that* made sense.

"Matt?" she called again.

He opened his mouth to say yes, it was him, but when no sound emerged, he closed it.

And then she was there, in the room with him, smiling as though nothing had happened last night. "I'm glad you're back. I need you," she said, and walked over to him holding out something he accepted by reflex.

"Can you put that in for me?" she asked, and when he looked down at his hand he saw it was an earring. "The left ear is always tricky, as you know."

Of all the openings Romy could have given him after last night, this was about as far from his imaginings as it was possible to get.

"Matt?" she prompted when he stood there like his own mummified remains, and she moved closer so that their bodies were almost touching. And God, how he wanted to touch her, even if it was only her ear. He wanted to beg her not to hate him. He needed her to put her arms around him and hold on to him. He felt so lonely for her, which didn't make sense when she was standing in front of him.

She tilted her head as trustingly as ever, moving her hair out of the way. He started to put the spike of the earring through her lobe, but his fingers were trembling so much it took three attempts. "You need to get it re-pierced," he said—an excuse for his clumsiness.

She offered him a tremulous smile. "I'll get you a needle and you can do it for me."

"Needles hurt." He touched her cheek with his fingertips. "And I don't want to hurt you, Romy."

"So *don't* hurt me." Her smile failed. "Please don't, Matt."

He choked on what might have been a sob if he knew how to cry, and stepped back out of harm's way. And that's when he noticed she was wearing a silk dress and high heels. Her hair had been styled, her makeup carefully applied and there was a hint of Chanel in the air.

"You're going out," he said.

He saw her physically pull herself together. "My monthly dinner with my parents, which I completely forgot about until Mum called me this afternoon!" Pause, as she reapplied her smile. "If you want to come, I can wait a few minutes…?"

He swallowed. Shook his head. Took another step back, then stepped forward again because that was just too pathetic. What was he scared of—that she'd *love* him to death?

She took a gusty breath. "Okay then. I've left some menus on the kitchen counter—several restaurants nearby do home delivery. Or…or maybe you already have plans?" Pause, during which she very clearly braced while he said nothing. "Well, whatever. If you stay in and want to…to talk, about…about anything, I don't expect to be out too late."

She started to move past him but he stopped her. "Is Teague going to be there?"

"No."

"Has he met your parents, Romy?"

"Yes, he's been to a few of these dinners."

"So why did *I* never meet them on one of my trips?"

She looked at him for a long moment. He got the feeling she was choosing and discarding words. Then she shrugged and said simply: "Because it didn't work out that way."

"Why didn't it?" he pushed, because he wanted to know. Maybe it would help him to make sense of their relationship.

"Because we've never had the kind of…of friendship that would make such a meeting easy."

"How can he have been enough of a friend to meet them but not me?"

"Probably the same reason you took Teague home to meet your parents but not me."

"That's…different."

"Yes, and you and I are different from me and Teague or you and Teague. Or you and Veronica and Rafael and Artie and— Oh, Matt, can't you see that we're not friends in the same way? That we never were? We *couldn't* be, because I—" She broke off. Shook her head. "Look, you don't want to hear it and I'm late—I really have to go."

She tried to move past him again—again he stopped her.

"Do they know about me, Romy?"

"My parents? Yes. They know we were friends in college. They know we've been friends ever since. They know you're staying here. They want to meet you because they know about the sperm—in fact they half expect you to come with me tonight."

"Have you told them how we did it? The sperm? That it wasn't—"

"No. There didn't seem to be much point since… Well, let's just say I discuss almost everything with my parents, but not one-night stands."

"Three nights."

"Different number, same principle."

His head felt like it might explode. "I think…" Trailing off. Clearing his throat. "Doesn't matter. Have a nice time at— Where did you say you were going?"

"Petit Diable. I took you there last year, when I was dating the sous chef, Jules."

"Oh, Jules—yeah, I remember."

"That was the time you met Poppy." She took her overcoat off the coat stand by the door and slipped it on. "And you insisted Jules and I meet up with the two of you for brunch."

"Why are you mentioning that, Romy?"

She faced him. "Because I've decided there are some things I won't do anymore. Like having brunch or lunch or dinner or drinks or anything else with you and your latest hookup. I don't want to talk to them on the phone or see them on video calls or read their emails. I just... don't."

"You have to do that, Romy! I need you there."

"Why?"

"Stops them giving me ultimatums. Them, or you. I have to...to show them—"

"That I'm not a threat? Well, that makes sense. They meet me, they can tell what I mean to you and all is well in your world and theirs."

"I choose you. I *always* choose you."

She shook her head at him sadly. "Oh, Matt, that's not a choice. That's called having your cake and eating it, too. And I'm tired of being the vanilla sponge you refresh your palate with between bites of chocolate gâteau. I want to be the gâteau."

"That's not fair, Romy. I've never—"

"Don't!" She held up a hand. "It doesn't matter, Matt. It really doesn't." She opened the door, but stopped on the threshold, turned back. "You said something last night about old times and new times. Well, I'll find a way to accept that the new times are over—San Francisco, last night, done. But in return, you need to know that what we've had for the past ten years has to be over, too, because I'm not going back to the old times. I *can't* go back, even if what we end up with is nothing."

* * *

I can't go back, even if what we end up with is nothing.

Matt knew what nothing felt like—it was how he'd describe those four weeks after Romy had left San Francisco. But even in the midst of the full-blown freak-out that separation had brought on, he'd known that if he could have gone back and changed what had happened that night, he wouldn't have done it.

The miracle was that he'd held himself back from her for so long. He should have known he'd wouldn't be able to keep his hands off her forever. It was what he was like, the real him, not the hero she thought he was. *Of course* he was going to engineer a way to have her eventually. And the fact that she'd been the one to suggest that infamous Plan B didn't change it. He'd leaped at Plan B! And look what had happened when her email had arrived—not pregnant, off the hook! He should have taken that as a sign that it wasn't meant to be—instead he'd thrown the first things to come to hand in his duffel, snatched up his passport and headed for the airport to get to her and try again, and if Teague hadn't been there, he would have beaten his chest and dragged her by her hair to the nearest flat surface like a Neanderthal.

Hell, that's what he *had* done! He'd taken her on the floor like an animal. What more proof did he need that he didn't deserve her?

Ever since that night in San Francisco, he'd been trapped in a game of up and down. Take her, save her, take her, save her. It was a miracle her head wasn't spinning off her damn neck with how hot and cold he'd blown.

But she'd told him she loved him anyway.

Why couldn't he just accept that she did, no matter

when she said it to him? What was the problem with her feeling close enough to him when they were having sex to say it then? He felt close enough to her when they were having sex to *merge* with her!

So…couldn't he *try* to accept it?

What if he asked Romy what he should do to be a better person? Already all she had to do was tsk-tsk him to get him rethinking shit like drinking beer in the morning. She could tsk-tsk him some more, couldn't she?

He could stop swearing as a first step. That'd have to go for the baby's sake anyway.

And he could take a few leaves out of Teague's book of saints—ones that didn't involve stealing the guy's interior-design flair. Teague had been to therapy after his sister died, and wasn't ashamed to admit it. So couldn't Matt give therapy a try—deal with his demons that way instead of locking himself in the tower? Wasn't Romy worth at least giving it a go?

What did he *want* out of the rest of his life, anyway? Not to fuck every girl he met the way he'd been doing forever—that was the way to turn into his father. Jesus! Scary.

The rest of his life… Forever… Ha. It was simple, really. His forever was tied up with Romy Allen—that's how all this had started. The baby was his gateway to forever with her. She'd said that night in San Francisco they had a window of opportunity that was like fate. Neither of them had someone in their lives at that precise moment when she needed him, they were together, she needed his sperm, he needed a release.

What if she was right about it being fate?

What if he ignored fate, and *didn't* get her into the

tower with him and she got tired of trying to scale the wall and ended up with Teague?

Teague, who'd met her parents when Matt had not.

Well, fuck that! (Okay, stopping swearing would be a work in progress.) *He* should be the one meeting Romy's parents, not Teague. They were *his* baby's grandparents! And this wasn't petty jealousy, it *wasn't*. It was nothing to do with Teague personally, because he *liked* Teague, he did. No, it was about the past ten years and the past five weeks and…and finding his place in Romy's life and not letting her hate him and…and…and God, he needed a shower and clean jeans and a half-decent shirt and a taxi to Petit Diable.

And Romy, he needed Romy.

CHAPTER NINETEEN

MATT ARRIVED AT Petit Diable forty minutes later and looked in through the glass frontage until he found the Allens.

He watched for a few minutes, assessing the dynamics of the small group and growing anxious without understanding why—unless it was that they seemed so *nice*. Laughing, talking, helping serve each other from the platters on the table, focused completely on each other instead of the potential talent at other tables. Vastly different from the rare get-togethers he endured with his parents, during which the only indication they were a family came from his obvious physical resemblance to them both.

Romy didn't look anything like either of her parents— her father was stick thin and dark, her tiny mother looked like a damn movie star—but you could tell they were a solid unit. Assessing them, he wondered if the way he'd visualized his daughter, as a Matt/Romy combination with hazel eyes and red hair, might be way off the mark.

Something flickered through him like quicksilver—a sense of…disquiet. He stared at Romy's parents, trying to anchor the thought, but before he could latch onto it his view was blocked by servers clearing their table and he realized he'd have a better chance of latching onto whatever was bothering him if he actually joined them.

The moment he entered the restaurant, Romy looked straight at him—as though she sensed him. Her parents swiveled in their chairs to see what she was looking at, Romy dipped her head and said something to them, and next second they were on their feet, beaming at him.

Matt beckoned to the maître d' and after a quick explanation, the guy conducted some weird wordless cross-restaurant communication with Romy, and then he was allowed to make his way to them.

"Sorry I'm late," he announced upon arrival at the table.

Romy's father grabbed his hand and pumped it enthusiastically. "No need for apologies, son," he said.

Matt blocked a start at the "son" a fraction too late, and then started again when Romy's mother opened her arms. Shit. She was going to hug him. He didn't want that. He hadn't earned that. Didn't...*deserve* it.

Matt considered side-stepping her, making an excuse about needing the restroom, but it was too late; he was folded against her. And then that wasn't enough for her: her hands reached up, his head was dragged down and he was kissed soundly on each cheek. Another hug, and he was released, only to have both his hands held, gripped.

"I'm so very glad to meet you, Matthew," she gushed. "I've been wanting to thank you, personally, for what you're doing for Romy." And sure enough, there were tears swimming in her eyes! He wasn't going to cope with this. He shouldn't have come. He didn't belong here. He had to leave. But then she rubbed a rueful thumb against his cheek and said, "Lipstick, my darling, sorry," and his resistance melted because she was adorable.

His place setting was arranged as if by magic, his chair positioned opposite Romy and between her parents, and Mrs. Allen fussed him into his seat.

She smiled at her husband, who was seated on Matt's left. "Pour Matthew some wine, my love." Back to Matt. "Or would you prefer beer? Romy says you like beer."

"Wine," Matt said. "Wine is great, Mrs. Allen."

"Now, Matthew," she chirped on, taking her seat on his right, "none of this *Mrs. Allen* business. My name is Lenore and the handsome gentleman on your other side is Graham. And we should warn you that we're already half in love with you, but if we get too embarrassing give us a stern word and we'll stop." She shot him a little twinkling smile. "Or at least we'll *try* to stop, but I can't promise absolutely."

"Mum!" Romy shook her head. "Matt's not demonstrative."

Lenore reached for Matt's hand. "Matthew can be whatever he wants to be and we'll still love him." She gave his hand a squeeze before releasing it. "We've had our appetizers, I'm afraid, and Romy's already ordered share plates for our main course. But I'm sure we can increase the portions. Romy—shall I call the waiter over and ask for Jules?" Back to Matt. "Jules is one of the chefs here, an old boyfriend of—"

"He knows Jules," Romy put in quickly. "I'll ask Francois to get a message to the kitchen."

Lenore leaned toward Matt conspiratorially. "It's over with Jules, of course. A lovely young man but not for Romy."

Romy got to her feet with a screech of chair. "Mum! Matt doesn't care about my boyfriends."

Lenore raised an eyebrow at her. "I thought you were going to find Francois?"

She waited until Romy had walked over to the maître d', then focused on Matt again. "So! Now! Matthew! Romy may not have told you this, but Graham and I met at university just as you two did…"

By the time Romy returned a few minutes later, Matt had learned that Lenore and Graham had been married for thirty years, that they lived in Barnes (only thirty minutes away from central London but a world away in its "village family feel," which was "perfect for grand-children"), were planning to renew their vows in two months' time (because "love should be celebrated") and that he was invited to attend the ceremony (because he was "practically family").

So far, so…what? Good? Bad? He had no fucking idea.

Romy took her seat and asked him apprehensively, "Are you okay?" which he assumed meant she had no fucking idea, either.

"Fine," he said, and took a giant sip of wine.

He did his best to keep up with the conversation, but as Romy reached for her water glass, that goddamn plati-num ring on her pinky finger flashed, distracting him. Why did that ring bother him so much?

He sifted through his memories of the past ten years of the three of them—him, Romy, Teague—trying to find one that exposed some deep-seated jealousy that would explain his unexpected ring paranoia. The night he and Romy had met three months into their freshman year and they'd almost kissed, but he'd rewound and pushed Teague's barrow instead. Romy asking his advice ahead of her first date with Teague: What should she talk about? The night she broke up with Teague. Her twenty-first birthday dinner—and yeah, Teague producing the ring had seemed an over-the-top gift, but hey, it suited her. The Fourth of July ball at Teague's family estate. Matt had been too busy with one of the other guests— Leah Carnegie-Phillips—to resent Teague monopolizing Romy; Matt had described himself as Leah's bit of rough when he'd told Romy about it, and called Teague Romy's bit of smooth, which had irritated her so much he'd ended up getting her in a headlock and telling her to get over herself—but they'd been friends again within half an hour.

So many memories. Harmless memories.

He heard a clatter and snapped his attention back to the present. Romy had dropped her fork to her plate and was directing a pinch-mouthed headshake at her mother.

What had he missed?

Lenore smiled at him, a faint stain of pink on her cheeks. Remorse. "I apologize. I thought it was all settled."

"It is," Romy said.

"What's settled?" Matt asked, because it was clearly something to do with him.

Lenore looked from Matt to Romy to Matt. "The adoption," she said.

Matt frowned at her, uncomprehending. "Adoption?"

She patted his hand. "There's no difficulty with it, so don't worry that it will be an inconvenience."

"Huh?"

"If you were going to be named on the birth certificate, we'd have to get your consent, and Romy's told us you don't like being bothered with paperwork."

"I don't— Wh—? I thought this baby was—" He looked at Romy. "You're keeping the baby." Not a question—a demand for confirmation.

"Yes, of course I am," she said, flustered. "Mum means when I marry, should my husband want to be-come…become…"

"The legal father instead of a stepfather," Lenore fin-ished for her. "Romy's birth father *was* on the birth cer-tificate, you see, so he had to give consent, and it took a while to track him down."

"Hang—" Head spinning. He looked to Romy. "You're *adopted*?"

"Yes. I thought…you knew."

"No."

"I guess… You see we don't…don't think of it, we just… I just know Mum and Dad are my parents, even though I do…I do write to my birth mother, so…" She looked ill. Stricken. "It's not a big deal."

Matt stared at her. "Not a big deal?"

"No, that didn't come out right. I mean things…things have changed, so… Oh God."

He was still staring at her, but he couldn't speak, al-most couldn't find the will to breathe.

"Matt, this is something we can talk about," she said, and reached across the table for his hand.

He jerked his hand away from her touch, pushed his chair back and stood. "Excuse me," he said. "I have to… have to…go."

Romy made a move, as though she'd go with him, and he shot her a do-not-even-think-about-it look and headed out of the restaurant.

CHAPTER TWENTY

MATT LET HIMSELF into the apartment, went to the bathroom, splashed water on his face and then just stood there, holding on to the sink. Holding on, on, on.

Was he in shock? It felt like he might be. He needed a cup of something warm to take the ice out of his veins. Or someone to hold him and tell him everything would be okay.

He laughed at that. A harsh, ugly, mirthless sound. Who was there to do that for him, when Romy was the architect of his pain?

Funny, he'd been so busy telling himself a baby would make him irreplaceable to Romy, too busy thinking she'd always *been* his and always *would* be his, to consider what he'd actually be to the baby once some other man came on the scene. He'd just assumed he'd never be *off* the scene. But now he knew he couldn't act the part of the benevolent godfather from a world away, smiling from the sidelines while some other guy lived with his kid, loved his kid, was loved *by* his kid.

Godfather. What did that even mean? He couldn't remember who his own godfather was—some guy who'd been a friend of his parents twenty-eight years ago but hadn't been in their lives for at least twenty years. Easily forgotten.

As *he* would be.

"Aaarrrggghhh!" The cry tore out of him, doubling him over. His child, oh God, oh *God*, his child wouldn't be his. He couldn't breathe; it hurt too much to breathe, hurt so much he wanted to die.

How could Romy think it would be okay for some guy to adopt his kid? How could she tell him she loved him and then give his baby to someone else? How could she sit there with her parents and listen to them tell him *they* wanted to love him, too, and then let them talk about someone else taking his child as though it was as easy as scrawling a signature across a page, cutting him out of the picture?

He raised his head, looked at himself in the mirror. His face was white, bloodless, and yet there was a wildness in his eyes he recognized. His father's wildness, his father's eyes. He wished he could tear the mirror off the wall, smash it and use a piece of the broken glass to cut them out and deny that truth.

But what difference would that make? The evil wasn't in his eyes any more than it was in his red hair. It was bred in him deeper than the bone.

And there it was—the truth of that quicksilver glimmer of disquiet he'd felt when he'd seen Romy with her parents in the restaurant and wondered what his child would look like. The truth was it didn't *matter* if his child was a hazel-eyed redhead or a green-eyed brunette or anything else—what mattered was the hidden stuff, the soullessness he might pass down. The soullessness that wasn't just part of him, but had been actively encouraged by his parents. What right did he have to want to spawn a child let alone raise one, hammered as he was on both sides of the nature/nurture debate?

He heard the door open…close…then nothing.

But he knew Romy. She'd be wanting to talk, ready to convince him that adoption would be a *good* thing, that it was all about *protecting* him, that this way there was nothing that could *impinge* on his *lifestyle*. She'd tell him she'd make sure the child was as happy as *she'd* been with her adoptive parents. She'd say he could still be as involved as he wanted, if he was sure that was what he wanted, as long as there was *certainty* because children *needed* certainty! Well, the best way to give her certainty was to take himself out of the picture altogether. Because Romy, for all her comments about his revolving bedroom door and his jumbo boxes of condoms and the moans, grunts and squeals she was tired of hearing and the women she was tired of him flaunting in front of her, didn't know the half of what he'd seen, what he'd done, what he was.

But it was time she did.

He straightened. Splashed more water on his face. Shook out his hands. Reset his brain.

She was out there, preparing to talk things through. And this time, he *would* talk. He'd tell her everything at last, and end the game of make-believe he'd been playing with her for ten years so that she finally saw him as he truly was: not a superhero, but a soulless, heartless, worthless bastard.

And all it would cost him was his child.

CHAPTER TWENTY-ONE

NERVOUS DIDN'T BEGIN to describe how Romy felt waiting for Matt to come out of the bathroom.

And when he did emerge, nervous ratcheted right up to terrified at the look on his face. She knew, in that moment, she was about to lose him.

So she decided she might as well go straight for the jugular and said, "I love you."

Miraculously, a crack appeared in his facade. It was blink-and-you'd-miss-it—just his hand jerking an inch upward—but it convinced her that Teague was right when he'd said the way to reach Matt was to make him hear those words.

"And before we begin this conversation," she continued, striking while the iron was hot, "I should tell you my parents think you love me, too. Me…and the baby."

"Don't, Romy."

"Why not?"

"Because it's too late."

"It's not even ten o'clock."

"I mean it's twenty-eight years too late."

"I don't…understand."

He sent her a brief, chilling smile, and took his old position on the extreme left end of the couch, waving a hand at her old position on the right. "Then take a seat, Romy, because I'm going to make you."

She did as he bid her, her heart lurching. "That sounds ominous."

"I'm just going to tell you the truth," he said. "It's time you heard it." He took a deep breath, waited a moment and then began. "Earlier tonight, I asked you why I'd never met your parents."

"Y-yes."

"And you said you and I didn't have the kind of friendship that would make such a meeting easy."

"Yes, but I meant—"

"It doesn't matter, Romy. What really matters is why I didn't introduce you to mine."

She said nothing, but she watched him like a hawk.

"You see," he continued, "the last time I took a girl home to meet my parents, I was seventeen."

"Seventeen…" she said, as dread worked its way down her spine. "Gail."

"I should explain that sex was allowed in my parents' house—they were…permissive—so it was assumed that Gail and I would sleep together. It wasn't the first time for either of us, but it was the first time in my bedroom at home and it felt…important. The first night, we professed undying love for each other, the next I gave her a promise ring, like the romantic idiot I was." He laughed suddenly, but it trailed away as he frowned as though trying to recapture a memory. "And then at the end of that week I found her in bed with my father."

Romy, taken aback by the conversational tone of such an obscene utterance, sucked in a shocked breath, then wanted to kick herself when it made him laugh again.

"Yeah, it took me by surprise, too," he said.

"What happened?"

"Oh, it wasn't all that exciting. My father is a charismatic man. He groomed her, seduced her. She was a year older than me, more sophisticated than I was, but she didn't stand a chance. Not her fault—mine, for not warning her what to expect, not protecting her."

"No I mean what happened *after*, Matt. You, Gail, your mother..."

"Well, Romy, my mother was...involved...elsewhere at the time, so she didn't see the point in taking the moral high ground. I, however, made an embarrassing scene. My father didn't see the problem because it was DC, where the age of consent is sixteen, and Gail was two years over it. He wasn't breaking any laws, and it wasn't like he wanted to date her. But he found the whole thing so tedious, he promised to stay away from my girlfriends after that. Gail was dutifully embarrassed—so much so, she cut ties with me and who could blame her? But I learned my lesson and never took another girl home."

She reached out a hand to him.

"I knew you'd do that," he said dismissively. "But I don't need petting. I'm only telling you so you get the full picture of who I am. So...what fun story should I share next?" He shot her a look that got her heart racing. This was going to be bad. "How about the one starring my mother and Teague Hamilton?"

She couldn't find enough air to suck in a breath this time. "No," she whispered. "No, please."

"Don't worry, Romy. Our saint comes out of it with his halo intact. It happened the year of the Fourth of July ball. Wanting to repay the favor, I invited Teague home for Thanksgiving. He was at a loose end because his family was sailing the Mediterranean. Veronica had dragged

Rafael home to her folks' in some desperate attempt to get them to accept him, Artie was getting up close and personal with his first-ever electric drill, and you were off at some Cordon Bleu cooking school. My parents were supposed to be in Florida shooting movies—more on that later—but at the last minute Mom changed her mind. I suspect because she'd seen a photo of Teague and was intrigued by his preppy good looks. Long story short, one minute we were eating turkey, next minute Mom was trying to eat *him*! And I mean *eat* him. Didn't succeed, of course—you know Teague, loyal to a fault. Still, it was… I mean, Teague… Oh God, Teague…" He faltered, shook his head as though trying to get something out of it, took a breath. "Teague pretended it wasn't disgusting, and he…he hugged me." His voice was hoarse, cracked, hitching. "And he t-told me all m-mothers find him irresistible." Another breath. "He h-hugged me! Can you believe that?"

She wanted to reach for him, fold him in, cry for him. But he was already pulling it all together, so she did nothing but sit there, aching for him…waiting for him, as ever.

When he continued, his voice was devoid of life. "So anyway, as you might have guessed, my parents are what you might call highly sexed. If you were a porn aficionado, you'd be aware of their channel, where you'd see all sorts of things that have nothing to do with vanilla sponge cake. Chet and Cherry Carter—real names Kevin and Marsha—why not look them up, expand your repertoire, get a cheap thrill, whatever. It was a popular site when I was a kid, but the appeal has dwindled lately. Dad blames Mom—the MILF thing isn't working so well for her."

"MILF?"

"Mothers I'd Like to Fuck." He made an impatient, chopping movement with his hand. "You understand what I'm saying, Romy?"

"Yes. Your parents like sex—sometimes with people quite a bit younger than they are, and they're porn stars."

"They've been married as long as your parents have, but they've had so many sex partners they'd never remember them all. You can't approve of that."

"I doubt they're seeking my approval."

"How about if I tell you they didn't care what I saw when I was a kid? That nudity was a normal thing in the house so I couldn't bring friends home, that I could watch porn from puberty, that they laughed and told me not to be a prude when I caught them fucking?"

"I know you're trying to get a reaction from me, Matt—why don't you just tell me what it is you want me to say?"

"That you want me out of your life. I want you to tell me you won't let me near your kid."

And all her bravado crumbled. Her eyes welled. "I'm not saying that. I can't say that, because I love you and I want you as the father of my child. No, *our* child. And I wish I could…could tell you what you mean to me. I wish you could understand what a hero you are, to have come through that and still be you."

"I can't *believe* you!" He jumped to his feet, glared down at her. "I'm not a fucking hero. Stop saying it, stop!"

"I'll keep saying it, Matt, because that's what you are. A hero. My hero. Better than Captain America because you're real and you're here and you're trying to save me from yourself. That's what your tower is about—the one with the moat. Not to protect you, but to protect me! To protect *all* of us. But we love you anyway. And I…I know what you mean when you say we're twenty-eight years too late, because I feel like I've been waiting for you for twenty-eight years and it's *too late* to tell me not to wait anymore. I don't want to be saved, you see. I want to be yours."

"You can't be mine! I'm a sex addict, Romy! That's it! That's all there is to me."

"If you were a sex addict, you'd wouldn't have gone without sex for two weeks after my phone call. You'd never have lasted four weeks after I left San Francisco. And you probably wouldn't have lasted Monday to Friday this week, either."

"For all you know I was with another woman last night."

"I know you weren't."

"You can't know that."

"I can, and I do."

He ran his hands into his hair. "Why won't you listen?"

"I will if you say something worth listening to."

"Then hear this, Romy. If you're pregnant, I don't want to see you again. I'll set up the trust fund, and we're done. Will that prove to you I'm not some fucking hero?"

"No, because setting up a trust fund doesn't gel with the whole anti-Christ vibe you're aiming for."

"I'm not joking."

"I never joke about the anti-Christ. So move along. And if I'm not pregnant…?"

"If you're not pregnant, you can consider you've had a lucky escape and find a new donor."

"I don't want a new donor."

"You said you did in that email."

"I lied."

"You…you must see why I have to back out."

"Well, I don't."

"I've just *told* you!"

"You said things about your parents—that's all. And I'm sorry they weren't better role models, but I can't see what that has to do with you impregnating me."

"Bad genes," he said.

"Hmm. I don't think sexual adventurousness is inherited."

"Addiction can be."

"You're not an addict—we already covered that. And in any case, addictions are treatable. Who's to say *I* don't have a wacky sex gene? I mean, there has to be some reason I want to bite some poor unsuspecting man, right?"

"Romy, I'm serious. No more sperm."

She stood, faced him. "Okay then, when we have sex tonight, we'll use a condom. Or I'll use my hands…or my mouth."

He did a double take that would have been funny if she hadn't been so desperate. "I'm not touching you, Romy," he said.

"Now you see, a *real* sex addict would let me take advantage of him."

"I don't want to take advantage of *you*."

"Then do it as a favor. It won't be easy finding a casual sex partner once I'm pregnant, so I'd be grateful if you'd fuck me while I'm still a viable option."

"No."

"Why not?"

"Because you're too vanilla sponge, okay? I've been with women who want it harder than you do, rougher, wilder. What makes you think you can keep me interested even for one night?"

"I don't know if I can keep you interested, Matt. But I'm happy to take the dare."

"I'm not daring you, Romy."

She shook her head at him, as though disgusted. "You talk about vanilla sponge. You rave about your sexual escapades. You throw out words like *addiction*. But it seems to me you're the tame one. If we've barely moved past the missionary position, it's not my fault, it's yours—you've been directing almost all the action. Maybe I *should* choose Teague! Maybe I'll call him tomorrow."

"You do that, Romy," he said, and the blaze in his eyes as he grabbed her hand and yanked her in was electrifying.

He lifted the hand he held, wrenched off her pinky ring and threw it. Romy heard it ping off a wall but she refused to let her eyes follow its trajectory.

"Okay—here's a choice for you," he said. "Go and find the ring…or have sex with me." He released her hand, spun her to face the room, gave her a push. "Where could it be, hmm? I know you want to find it—it's the right choice, so go do it."

She wrenched herself out from under his hands and faced him again. "I know what you're doing, Matt. Trying to make me choose Teague over you because of some stupid idea that Teague's better than you. That's what this is about, isn't it?"

"Yes! Yes! I'm jealous of Teague because he's better than me! Everything about him is better. Better looking, richer, kinder. He's got a family to be proud of. He's a better man, better father material."

"If you really feel that, Matt, then be better for me yourself. Be the man I know you are. The man I love more tonight, knowing what I know, than I loved ten years ago, knowing nothing except that you were made for me."

"I don't *know* how to be better. God, I hope you're not pregnant—I hope it with every breath in my body."

"I saw the cradle, Matt. I know you want the baby."

One of his hands came up, shielding his eyes—but not before she saw the flash of devastation. His breaths were heaving—one, two, three, four. His mouth tightened— long moment—and then the hand dropped from his eyes to reveal blankness again. "That was…boredom. I had to do something while you were at work."

"I *know*, Matt. I know you."

"Go find the ring," he said through gritted teeth. "Choose Teague. You were always meant for someone like him, not me. Never me. You *know* that."

"I'm choosing you."

"If you choose me, it really will be only one night, Romy—that's all, no more."

"So shut up and give it to me," she said, and reached her arms up around his neck, nestling against him.

For a moment, his arms closed around her, tightened… but then he pushed her away. "Not like that," he said. "If you really want to do this, not like that. Not now, I can't stand it."

"Then how?"

"Like this," he said, and grabbed her hard by the upper arms. He shove-shove-shoved her over to the wall until she was backed against it. For one fraught moment he stared down at her, and then he kissed her so hard the corner of her lip split. She thought he'd stop then, and he did. He stepped back, looked at her mouth and then very deliberately leaned down again to lick at the bead of blood. "Now stop me. Tell me you made a mistake choosing me. Tell me you've changed your mind."

"No."

"I'm going to be rough with you."

"Then I'll be rough back."

That seemed to make him furious—so furious, he reached for her dress and ripped it down the middle. He flicked a glance at her body as though what was on display wasn't important, despite the fact she was wearing her best underwear and sheer stay-up stockings. But then, of course he'd seen every kind of underwear on a woman, all degrees of nakedness, stockings in every color and every style.

"Tell me you love me," he demanded.

"Why?"

"So I can remind you that *I don't love you*. It took me ten years to be interested enough to *fuck* you. What does that tell you?"

"That you were scared to lose me."

He flinched, but quickly rallied. "Yeah, well, I did do it in the end because it's what I'm good for and it's all I need. Now get that through your head and leave me the hell alone before I hurt you."

"You won't hurt me."

"I split your lip."

For answer, she grabbed his shirt and tore it the way he'd done to her dress, buttons flying in every direction. "There, are we even? Now will you shut up and do this?"

He grabbed her hands then, wrenched them up, slammed them against the wall, imprisoned them in one large hand.

She surged against his hold—not to break it but to strain her face toward his. "Kiss me, Matt. Hard as you want."

Keeping her hands imprisoned, he put his mouth on hers and savaged it, sucking and licking and biting. She savaged him right back, tugging against his grip.

"I need my hands," she begged. "I need to touch you."

"I want you to do something very specific, Romy. Say yes, and I'll let go."

"Yes…yes…" she panted. "I'll do anything for you… everything…all the things."

He let her wrists go, and instantly her hands went to his fly.

He stopped her. "Not that, this," he said, and grabbed the back of Romy's head, bringing her face to his naked chest. "Bite me, Romy. Through the skin until you draw blood. Your deepest, darkest fantasy."

"Why do you want me to do it?"

He laughed—a taunt in it. "Because you won't, vanilla girl."

"I will!"

"All you have to do is tell me you've changed your mind and I'll let you go. And you go find the ring and we'll be done."

But she shook her head, fierce, and lowered her head to lick across his left nipple. She was not done. She would do this.

His chest muscles tensed. He drew in a sharp breath through his nostrils. "You can't do it, Romy. Admit it."

Her answer was to suck his nipple into her mouth. One of her hands came up, palm resting then rubbing over his right nipple. He started to tremble, and she took courage from that, trailing her tongue up to his pectoral muscle to choose a spot. She measured it with her teeth, and then started licking there. He stiffened—he knew she was preparing him. But a half moment later he relaxed—he'd *forced* that, she knew he'd forced it.

"Do it, Romy," he urged. "Do it. I need it. This pain to cancel out the other."

She stopped, looked up at him. "What other pain?"

"The pain of wanting..." He paused there, closed his eyes. "Wanting what I can't have, what I *won't* have. Do it. I need it."

She was blinking again, but the tears came anyway, unstoppable. She dipped her head to lick again and her tears dripped onto his chest, mixing with the dampness from her tongue. She switched to sucking him, increasing the pressure. Suck, suck, suck, drawing his blood to the surface. And as she did that, she unzipped his jeans, delved a hand into his underwear, gripped him. One, two, three pumps, and he was gasping, then groaning, thrusting himself into her hand. She kept going, urging him with her hand, alternately licking and kissing and sucking his chest to distract him, forcing his words into her mind—*Do it. I need it. This pain to cancel out the other. The pain of wanting what I can't have, what I won't have.*

Oh God, oh God, she had to do it *now*, because he'd be ready to come in just a few thrusts and she wanted to give him a more intense pleasure to replace the pain she was about to inflict. *Do it—get it over with*, and before she could talk herself out of it she closed her eyes and bit down as hard as she could bear to.

Matt stiffened, a strangled "Fuck" erupting from him as she felt the give, the infinitesimal crunch of skin, a metallic tang. Blood—a tiny drop, no more. Enough, it was enough. She dropped to her knees, pulled his jeans and underwear down, took him in her hand again but only to hold him steady for her mouth.

"Don't," he said.

She licked all the way up the shaft, then looked up. "You said you wanted me to suck your cock. And here I am…on my knees for you…ready. I'm not stopping, Matt."

And with that, she slid her mouth over the tip of his cock, rejoicing when his legs went rigid and a cry gargled up from his throat. She started with tiny sucks, just over the tip, as her free hand delved between his legs to cup and press his balls, gently squeezing and releasing. She soon lost herself to the rhythm, to the male smell of him, the velvety feel, playing with speed and pressure until one deeper, harder suck caused him to cry out again, his head flinging back.

He was going to come. She could feel it building. Powerful, glorious. *Do it—let go*, she begged in her mind and next second his hands tightened painfully in her hair and he shouted her name: "Romy! Jesus God, Romy, Romy, arrrgggghh!"

A long, long moment later, when Matt's violent thrusts had stopped and his head was slumped forward against the wall above her, Romy sat back on her heels and looked up at him, licking her lips, tasting him still. Musk, salt, a little hit of lime.

He reached down for her, pulled her to her feet. "Your turn," he said.

CHAPTER TWENTY-TWO

MATT STRIPPED ROMY'S ruined dress from her and dragged her panties down her legs. "Step," he said, when they were around her ankles, "I want your legs wide open tonight." As she stepped, he yanked up his jeans and underwear, fastening them. He didn't intend to stumble over them when he had a point to prove.

He cast a lascivious look at her, lingering on her breasts, which looked ready to burst out of her bra as usual. He nodded at the front clasp. "Undo it," he ordered, and the moment the cups separated he was on her, rubbing and sucking brutally at her nipples. "I want them out…red…raw…aching for me," he said between sucks, and let out a triumphant roar as they came out of hiding one after the other.

He pulled back, looked at them, half-crazed at the sight of them, at the sight of *her*, in her stockings and high heels and nothing else. "Mouths and hands, right, Romy?" he said, and crowded her against the wall before dropping to his knees in front of her the way she'd done for him.

He wrenched at her thighs, opening them wide, and licked hard and long along the length of her. Delicious, fucking delicious. He licked harder, and harder, and when her hands gripped his hair and pulled it the way he'd done to hers, he licked harder still. He wished he could suck the essence right out of her, drink everything inside her, gulp it down.

He tore his mouth away, looked up into her shocked face. "Listen to me," he said, and the urgency in his voice must have communicated his desperation because she nodded once, twice, eager and resolute. "Brace your shoulders against the wall—I'm going to make you come fast."

"Oh God," she said, as her legs trembled in his hands.

He hoisted one of her thighs over his shoulder, giving himself better access. "I want my mouth buried in you so I'm drowning in the taste of your cum," he said. "Understand?"

"Yes."

His response was to lap at her. "Ahhh," he breathed against her sex. "Yes" kiss "good" lick "perfect." He slid his tongue inside her, using it like a small cock. In, out, in out, as her hips twitched in time.

"Keep going," she said, but as though to torment her he pulled out, and when she kicked her heel onto his back in protest he laughed softly and sucked her clit into his mouth while simultaneously tongue-tipping it so hard her protest ended in a gasping scream.

He started to lick seriously then, up and down, side to side, occasionally plunging his tongue into her. He kept her guessing, using tongue and lips, a graze of teeth, but always returning to her clit, growling low in his throat as he suckled it, lusting so badly for its tiny hardness he couldn't be quiet, then using his lips to squeeze around it, then going back to licking over it sure and strong, until she was a moaning mess, jerking against his mouth.

"I'm coming," she gasped. "I'm coming, Matt!" She tensed all over, her gasps becoming breathless huffing sounds, which built and built, her head thrashing from side to side against the wall as she shoved herself onto his mouth. "I'm coooooooomiiing-oooohhh. Oh God, Matt, God, GOOOOOOOOD."

He kept tonguing her, then suckling her, then licking, licking, licking, until her legs went limp, and the thigh on his shoulder loosened. Matt felt her weight give, as though she were about to collapse, and before she could slump to the floor he was up, spinning her to the wall.

"Hands on the wall," he commanded.

With a whimper, she obeyed.

"Now tell me what you want," he said, but he was already insinuating himself between her thighs from behind.

"You, I want you."

"Be specific. Where do you want me?"

"Inside me."

"Be specific, Romy."

"I want your cock in me."

"How?"

"Hard. Rough. Now. Fuck me."

But he didn't plunge straight in. Instead his arms came around her and he rubbed himself against her back. "Let's get you back up there first," he said, plunging his cock between her legs and rubbing it back and forth against her clit.

"Do you like that, Romy?"

"Yes, yes, you know I do."

"Then show me—squeeze me tight."

And so she arched her back, tightening her thighs

around him, thrusting her pelvis back and forth so that he slid along the length of her.

"What else do you want?"

"I want your hands on my breasts."

His hands came around her, cupped her breasts. "Like this?"

"Squeeze them."

"Like this?"

"Harder. I want you to do it hard."

As he squeezed, he kicked her legs wider, bent his knees slightly to give himself extra thrusting power, then slowly straightened as he guided himself into her. "Tight and hot and very wet," he said in her ear, and bit her neck. "Just the way I like it. Now hang the fuck on."

And with that, he pulled all the way out of her, then slammed straight back in so that she banged forward, flattened against the wall. Merciless, he yanked her back. "Take it, take me," he said harshly, and then he took her hips in his hands hard enough to bruise, anchoring her. "Ready?"

"Yes, yes, ready, do it."

And he let fly—shoving into her hard, pulling all the way out, then slamming into her again. "Fuck me back, Romy, fuck me back."

She leaned forward and backward, hands pushing at the wall to give her extra leverage while she shoved her bottom at him, grunting as he smacked into her. But the pace was too frantic, too forceful, and she ended up flat against the wall again with Matt against her back, shoving into her for all he was worth. Soon that wasn't enough for him, he wanted his fingers on her, too, so he spun them again and his back was now to the wall. He jerked her back against him, buried his cock in her again, thrusting rhythmically as his hands left her hips to go between her legs. One hand held her labia open, the other fingered her wildly, fast, furious, out of control. "I want to make you come so hard you'll never forget it, Romy."

"You, too," she said, and squeezed her internal muscles, as though she'd milk him of everything he had. "I want you to come like that for me. Unforgettable."

And then there was nothing but groans and gasps and grunts and hoarsely whispered words of encouragement, sex words, fuck words, as they sped up, racing, reaching, needing. A keening cry from Romy, a guttural curse from Matt, as the peak rushed and roared at them.

Oh God, God, no sperm, he reminded himself, as Romy's internal muscles convulsed and she started to come. He stayed, stayed, staaaayed until the very last second, and then pulled out of her, jerking once before spilling against her back.

Her head lolled against his shoulder. She was exhausted; he knew it. And so was he. Tired...and unutterably depressed. That damn stinging was behind his nose again. What a way to leave things. Rough sex, his semen on her back, used up.

No. No. He needed something else. He couldn't find the will to deny himself one last thing, something he wanted more than sex, something he needed. Closeness and comfort.

"Romy, darling?" he said, and kissed her temple.

"Hmmm?" Languid, drowsy.

"Come and let me wash you and then...then I want to sleep with you. Just...sleep. With you."

CHAPTER TWENTY-THREE

WHEN ROMY WOKE the next morning, she knew instantly and instinctively that Matt was not only absent from her bed, but that he'd left the flat altogether—and the grief of it almost suffocated her, so that it took a long, long time for her to force her legs over the side of the bed.

When she finally did, the first thing her eyes alighted on was the platinum signet ring on the bedside table. No note, but why would he need to leave a note? The message was obvious: Teague was the man she deserved, and Matt was handing her over to him, as he'd handed her over all those years ago.

She slid the ring back onto her pinky finger, seeing very clearly why Matt was right to say it wasn't jealousy, what he felt about her and Teague. It was more heroic than jealousy. There was something almost ceremonial in his giving her up because he didn't want to defile her.

How hard it must have been for Matt to come to terms with the fact that although he didn't want anyone else to have her, he *did* want someone else to have her. That he not only wanted her, he loved her.

Not that he'd ever tell her that.

That night in San Francisco, he'd said there were better words than *love* for what they had, words that couldn't be *desecrated*. And yes, maybe he'd heard *I love you* so many times it really was meaningless, but she would have given anything to hear those words from him, because they had to be very special for him to be so careful with them.

Well, she couldn't reproach herself with not having thrown herself into the moat and swum like crazy to reach the tower—that was something. But she also knew ten years was long enough to wait for a man who wouldn't let himself have you. A man who pushed and pulled you and tied you up in knots, who made you yearn for impossibilities and then gave them to you only to snatch them away.

But how much easier it would be to let him go if he'd left things at sex against the wall last night. If he hadn't taken her into the shower and washed himself off her like he was a stain. If he hadn't towel-dried her like she was made of delicate glass. If he hadn't gathered her into his arms in bed, and held her close and stroked her hair and kissed her in a way that had nothing to do with sex and everything to do with deep and lonely love.

She took a painful breath…held it…blew it slowly out.

Okay, enough wallowing. Just…enough.

It was Sunday and she had a typical English roast dinner to prepare for Teague if he could be persuaded to join her, because she not only owed him for the steak and ale pie but she needed a friend now more than she'd ever needed one in her life. A friend who could never, ever be more, not because of who he was but because of who he wasn't.

But first, she would clear Matt out of the nursery—a symbolic fresh start.

She strode purposefully to the spare room, but as she

grabbed the pillow off the bed to remove the pillowcase for washing, Matt's scent—the scent under the soap—flooded her, and she stumbled. She couldn't take off the pillowcase. The sheets, either. Because that would mean he was really gone. That what was between them was really over. Not just five weeks of insane passion, but ten years of irreplaceable love.

She looked at the crib, with its misshapen stars and paint drips, and before she knew what she was doing, she'd crawled into Matt's discarded bed, drawn up the covers, buried her face in his pillow, and she was crying like a troll.

CHAPTER TWENTY-FOUR

MATT WAS ON the deck, hungover, drinking beer and not enjoying the view of San Francisco Bay.

It had been two weeks since he'd left London and his need to know if Romy was pregnant was eating him alive.

His heart felt like it had been scrubbed up and down a stone wall until its entire outer layer had been scraped off and it hurt like hell. His head hurt, too, from thinking about her so relentlessly. The only part of him that didn't hurt was his dick, which seemed to have dropped dead. He guessed that was something to be thankful for; his current broken state shouldn't be inflicted upon any woman. But he wished it would give an intermittent pulse so he knew resuscitation wasn't completely out of the question at some future date. Light at the end of the tunnel. Evidence he wasn't going to feel this awful forever.

Okay, he needed more beer.

He wandered into the house he'd decided he hated on the basis that it was too *Teague*-like, and made for the kitchen—which he hated on principle because Romy had never seen it.

He'd just grabbed a bottle from the fridge when the

doorbell rang, and he experienced the first surge of energy he'd had for two weeks. For a moment, he didn't recognize it—and then he was racing for the door, yanking it open, his heart surging...then tumbling.

Not Romy.

The disappointment was bitter.

"What the fuck do *you* want?" he asked his father.

"Is that the best greeting you can manage?"

"For you, yes."

His father laughed. "Aren't you going to let me in?"

Matt didn't move so much as an inch.

"You'll be interested in what I have to tell you," his father wheedled.

Matt turned sharply on his heel—not inviting him in but not barring the entrance—and headed back to the deck.

"I'll take a beer if you're offering," Chet/Kevin said to his back, which was when Matt realized he'd been so eager to answer the door he'd taken his beer with him.

"I'm not offering," he said, without turning around.

Matt took his regular seat, stretching out his legs, leaning back in his chair. Being near his father always made Matt want to occupy more space than usual. "What do you want, Kevin?" he asked.

His father grimaced—he hated being called Kevin but knew better than to ask Matt to call him anything else. "To impart some news."

"So impart it."

"Your mother and I are getting divorced."

Matt waited for surprise to hit, for sorrow, regret, *something*. But he felt nothing.

"She's met someone," his father continued. And then, when Matt still said nothing, "Well?"

"Well, what?"

"Don't you have anything to say?"

"How do you feel about it? About her loving someone else?" Matt finally asked.

His father shrugged. "I doubt it's love that's motivating her. More likely to be because he's ten years younger and hung like a horse. I know—I hired him for a film."

"That's *it*?"

"It's time for greener pastures for both of us."

Matt sat up straighter. "You two have been frolicking in greener pastures your whole fucking lives."

"Thirty years is a long time to stay with the one partner."

Matt thought of Romy's parents, about to renew their vows. "No, it's not," he said. "That's why you *get* married. To stay with someone."

"Yeah, well, I daresay it won't last. I mean, a ten-year age gap? He can do better."

"You're a prick."

"I don't know why you always have to be so hostile."

"Sure you do."

"If you're still bitter about Gail—"

"Don't say her name!"

"—that happened a long time ago. It's not as though you were ever going to marry her."

"A *pathetic* prick."

"Sex is just sex. That shouldn't have come between us."

"Seems like Mom found out sex isn't just sex."

"Matthew, I'll have a replacement for your mother within a week. In my bed, and for the channel. And a fuck really is just a fuck at the end of the day."

A fuck's a fuck.

Matt recalled all the things he'd said to Romy about fucking and he seriously thought he might throw up. He

stared at his father as though he'd never seen him before, the truth coming at him like some sign from the
fucking universe.

Was it really as simple as it suddenly seemed? A matter of asking himself what he wanted his life to be? Because if so, he'd known the answer all along: he wanted
his life to belong to Romy.

He wanted today what he'd wanted from the night
he'd met her: everything, forever. Her thoughts, her
laugh, her touch. He wanted the way she looked and
the way she spoke, the way she smelled. He wanted her
baby to be his. He wanted sex with her, and friendship,
and everything between those things. He wanted every
word either of them could think of for two people who
belonged together, and if they discovered new words,
then he wanted them, too.

And of course he knew the only word for all those
things he wanted. The best word. The only word. The
word was *love*.

"I'm nothing like you," he said wonderingly to his
father. "I'm really, truly nothing like you, and I have no
idea why I always thought I was."

His father let out a bark of laughter. "Funny you
should say that, because we weren't so sure ourselves.
But we had you tested and you're mine all right."

"No, I'm not," Matt said. "I'm not yours and I'm not
hers, either. I would *never* test my child's DNA because
all I want it to be is *ours*. You see, Kevin, I've come to
the conclusion that a family isn't about blood, it's about
love. I don't want to be the bystander in a sexual menag-
erie, I want to be part of a real family. Because I'm *not*
a sex addict even though you tried to make me one, and

I know that sex isn't just sex, that it's a big deal, and it's an even bigger deal when you're in love."

Love—the word burst inside him and he fucking loved it. Loved *her*, with her steadiness and her paperwork and that tiny streak of wild that meant she could try to bite him through the skin but do a piss-poor job of it just because she didn't want to hurt him. He loved her so much he could have died on the spot with the realization of it and died happy.

But his father was laughing dismissively. "Love is a bourgeois emotion."

Matt got to his feet. "Then call me bourgeois, because I feel it and I want it and I'm going to go and get it. So see yourself out, Kevin—I have to pack."

Talk about déjà vu! Throwing clothes in his duffel, grabbing his passport, heading out the door and—

"Shit!" as he whacked straight into someone. He stepped back. "What the *fuck*, Teague."

"Those were going to be my words to you. What the fuck have you done to her?"

"I don't have time to talk. I have to fly to London," he said, and made to barge past.

Teague grabbed his shoulder, stopping him. "Don't you think you've done enough damage?"

"Whatever damage I've done, I'm going to undo it. Now let go."

"You won't undo it in London, because she's not there."

Matt fixed him with a gimlet eye. "Where is she? And don't say at your apartment in Manhattan if you value your life."

"I'm not in Manhattan, dodo."

"You know what I mean. At your apartment, when she should be here."

"As it turns out, she *is* here in San Francisco—albeit not with you."

Matt dropped his duffel bag and stood rooted to the spot, staring at Teague but comprehending nothing.

"Now," Teague said calmly. "Can we go inside and discuss what happens next?"

"*You* go inside and do whatever you like—but first, tell me *exactly* where she is."

"She's here for Lennie. I'm sorry but she doesn't want to see you. That's why she sent me."

"I don't underst—"

"I have a waiver for you to sign."

"Waiver…? Is she… Is she…" He closed his eyes, opened them. "Oh God, she is, isn't she?"

"If you mean pregnant, then yes. And before you try to kill me, no, it's not mine."

"I know that. It's mine."

"Biologically, yes."

"Not just biologically."

"Not just— Okaaay, I see. I think. But my understanding is that you were never going to be registered on the birth certificate so the only way you can gain parental rights is to—"

"Apply to the court for a PR order if she won't work out an agreement with me."

"Been doing some research, I see."

Matt shrugged a shoulder.

"She doesn't want to work out an agreement. And she seems to think you'll be fine with that." Pause. "She wants to move on, Matt."

"Where is she?"

"It won't do you any good to see her."

Matt's hand shot out and grabbed Teague by the throat. "Where. Is. She?"

Teague tried to nod his head.

"Does that mean you're going to tell me?" Matt asked.

Another attempted nod…and Matt released him.

"Jesus, Matt," Teague said, rubbing his neck.

"Sorry."

"No, you're not."

"No, I'm not. So where is she?"

"Ah, geez! This sucks, you know? I'm not supposed to tell you."

"I'll kill you if you don't."

Teague sighed…laughed…sighed again. "If I tell you, it's only because I think you love her."

Matt's jaw tightened. "I do. Now. Where *is* she, goddamn you?"

"She's having lunch with three business associates at a restaurant called Persini's. One of them is probably going to be a client, so don't barge in there being a dick and embarrassing her."

"Shut up, Teague." He turned to unlock the door. "Go in and make yourself a drink." He laughed. "You'll like the place—*that* much I can promise you. But I don't like it and neither does Romy, so if you're looking for a house in San Francisco, make me an offer. Pick a bedroom if you want to stay." Another laugh. "The walls are thick so it won't worry us."

"What does that—? No, don't tell me. But seriously, can't you at least shave before you go and see her?"

Matt thought about it. And then said, "No. It'll take too long."

CHAPTER TWENTY-FIVE

ROMY KNEW THE moment Matt entered the restaurant when her three dining companions' gazes fixed on a point behind her and their jaws dropped.

She estimated Teague had reached Matt's house fifteen minutes ago, so he was here faster than she'd expected. But he was wasting his time.

She refused to turn around, even though the tingling of her skin told her he was barreling toward her, and she stayed stubbornly in place when the smell of his pine-scented soap announced he'd arrived at the table.

"Good afternoon," he said to her companions, his voice sending a quiver through every nerve ending in her body. "Please excuse Romy for a few minutes."

And she found herself lifted out of her chair and—unbelievably—swung up into his arms.

She wanted to tell him to put her down, but one look into his green eyes obliterated every thought in her head so that even the gasps, titters and laughs from throughout the restaurant as he kissed her barely registered.

And then, "God, that felt good," he said, and headed out of the restaurant with her held against his chest and she still said nothing.

"There's an alley at the back of the restaurant out of

the wind," he said once they were outside. "Hang on and we'll go there so I can kiss you properly."

At last she found her voice. "You already kissed me properly."

"So I'll kiss you properly twice. Maybe even ten times. Or a hundred."

"Put me down!" Belated, but hey, she'd said it.

"It's warmer in my arms," he said, and kept walking.

"Matt!"

"Okay, okay, sorry, we're here," he said, and slowly released her so that she slid all the way along his body until she was standing plastered against him—at which point he kissed her again, long and passionately, before pulling back to stare at her face, his mouth quirking up in the same rueful smile he'd worn when he turned up unexpectedly at her flat in London. "I've missed you, Romy!" And yes, that was the same breathless voice he'd used then, too. He was uncertain of her.

Oh God, it was hard to put her hand on his chest and stop him from taking her back into his arms. "You can't do this to me again," she said, and was distressed to hear the wobble in her voice.

"What do you mean? I've never done this before."

"Yes, you have."

"What? I've walked into a restaurant and carried a woman out like a scene in a movie, have I? I'd have sworn I'd remember that. It's better than *The Proposal*, you know, what I just did. Demonstrative. Tell your mother."

"I mean sex."

"I haven't had sex in a restaurant, either—but I'm up for it if you are."

"I mean if you're here to have sex with me again *anywhere*, I can't do it."

"Is it because of the baby? Is it dangerous? What does the doctor say?"

"Because of the—? No! Stop researching pregnancy! It's because of how you make me feel after sex. Like... like I've *taken* something from you. I don't have it in me to go through it again. And anyway, you told me that when a woman says it's over, it's over—no questions asked. So why are you here?"

"Well, that's easy—I'm here because I love you."

Her heart gave one huge thump and then started beating in operatic, percussive surges, making her wonder if she was about to have a coronary. She couldn't speak, could barely think, because Matt—*Matt!*—had just told her he loved her.

"But on the subject of no questions," he went on without seeming to realize the effect his words had had on her, "I find there is, in fact, a question to be asked before I accept it's over. But this is a one-off, won't work with any other woman. It's this: What can I do to make you not want to leave me?"

"Oh, Matt! This isn't fair. I didn't want to leave you— you left me!"

"I know. I'll spend forever making that up to you. I'll even eat Lennie's snails and tell him I like them."

"It's not funny."

"Damn straight it's not. I hate Lennie *and* his fucking snails. Oh, but by the way, we need to work on my swearing. We've got nine months to cure me of the need."

"You're making me laugh, *it's not funny.* I offered you everything I am, in every way I know, and you still left me. I have nothing left to give you."

"Then don't give it to me. Make me earn it. Tell me what I need to do and I'll do it. I'll keep doing it until you tell me to stop. Until you beg me to stop. Until you say, *Jesus, Matt, enough already.* And— Hey! Hey, no crying! No crying or you'll make *me* cry, and I look worse than a troll!"

"You never cry."

"Oh, Romy, I've been crying for two weeks straight."

"You have not."

"In my heart, I have. Tears of blood."

"I thought you didn't have a heart."

"Yeah, well, I was wrong." He took her hands in his. "My heart, as it turns out, was waiting for you." He put her hands, both of them, over his heart. "There it is— you can feel it. It's doing its damnedest to beat itself out of my chest and find a way into yours. Might take some work to get its muscles strong enough to do that, because it's been knocked around over the years. It's not as good as yours, but it wants to be. It's kind of battered but it's trying to heal so that it can beat to the same rhythm as yours every day of our lives." He released her hands, his arms going around her, holding on. "Please, Romy, please!"

"I don't know if I can, Matt," she said, but she was clinging close all the same, her heart yearning to believe. "I need certainty, for me and the baby. I need you to *be* there."

"I've been there for ten years."

"That's different."

"It's not, you know. I've been protecting you for ten years, because I've loved you all that time—but what I was protecting you from was me, and lately I've started to think I'm redeemable. You see, you asked me that night in London to be a better man, but the better man was in there—it was the part of me protecting you. I reckon there might even be a soul in there somewhere if we get a torch and have a good look. Not all black, either." He leaned down for a quick, hard kiss. "What do you say? Will you help me look for it?"

"Okay, let me tally this up. I get the heart. I get the soul. But what about the other thing you said you had to offer?"

"Other thing?"

"The very big thing. I'd want that, too, you know."

He hooted out a laugh. "Oh, hell yeah, you can have the very big cock, that goes without saying—no biting that, though."

She threw her arms around his neck. "Oh, Matt, Matt! I want to kill you and kiss you at the same time."

"Better get the kiss in first, because I know I keep telling you I've done most things, but necrophilia is not on."

"You are *so* not as deviant as you pretend," she said, laughing helplessly.

And then she kissed him, pouring her own heart and soul in there, and maybe she was crazy, but she was sure she could feel them connecting with his.

When she pulled back, he cupped her face in his hands. "You know, Romy, if I could go back in time, I'd kiss you that first night, the night we met, and I'd never stop. I'd tell you I love you and never stop. Never, ever stop." Another kiss. "Just one thing I want to clarify: Isn't it customary for the girl to say *I love you* back to the guy who says it to her? Because that would be you saying it to me, in case you're in any doubt."

"I thought you didn't want to hear it."

"Ah, hell! Of course I want to hear it."

"What happened to sex being just sex?"

"I'm too bourgeois for that!" he said, and kissed her

yet again. "I want to be able to do that, to press my mouth to yours and know it might end up with me buried inside you…or it might just as easily not. It's better than sex…and worse than sex, because you can hurt me in so many ways, none of which have anything to do with sinking your teeth into my skin in a moment of kink. But on the subject of kink, and specifically necrophilia, I should just give you a little warning that I might actually keel over and die in a minute if you don't tell me you love me, and you said something once about the need for sex as a pregnant woman and you won't want to do it with a dead guy, will you?"

"Fine—I love you!" she said, laughing, laughing, laughing.

"Okay, now I'm going to have to kiss you again," he said, and drew her into his arms. "But you know that thing I said about being able to kiss you and not have it go any further? I meant that, I really did, but I have one confession to make on behalf of my very big cock. It's gone rogue on me. It's refusing to let anyone touch it except you—it won't even let me take it in hand myself. So you're going to have to take it in hand for me—well, hand, or mouth, or body, I'm equal opportunity when it comes to my cock. And when I kiss you, it's going to start clamoring for attention. So just be aware, okay?"

"You're depraved."

"And aren't you the lucky one?"

"Yes," she said, and snuggled closer, "I guess I am."

"Okay, one rogue penis coming up," he said, and he lowered his mouth to hers.

* * * * *

MILLS & BOON

THE HEART OF ROMANCE

A ROMANCE FOR EVERY READER

MODERN

Prepare to be swept off your feet by sophisticated, sexy and seductive heroes, in some of the world's most glamourous and romantic locations, where power and passion collide.

HISTORICAL

Escape with historical heroes from time gone by. Whether your passion is for wicked Regency Rakes, muscled Vikings or rugged Highlanders, awaken the romance of the past.

MEDICAL

Set your pulse racing with dedicated, delectable doctors in the high-pressure world of medicine, where emotions run high and passion, comfort and love are the best medicine.

True Love

Celebrate true love with tender stories of heartfelt romance, from the rush of falling in love to the joy a new baby can bring, and a focus on the emotional heart of a relationship.

Desire

Indulge in secrets and scandal, intense drama and sizzling hot action with heroes who have it all: wealth, status, good looks…everything but the right woman.

HEROES

The excitement of a gripping thriller, with intense romance at its heart. Resourceful, true-to-life women and strong, fearless men face danger and desire - a killer combination!

To see which titles are coming soon, please visit

millsandboon.co.uk/nextmonth

JOIN US ON SOCIAL MEDIA!

Stay up to date with our latest releases, author news and gossip, special offers and discounts, and all the behind-the-scenes action from Mills & Boon...

 @millsandboon

 @millsandboonuk

 facebook.com/millsandboon

 @millsandboonuk

It might just be true love...

GET YOUR ROMANCE FIX!

Get the latest romance news, exclusive author interviews, story extracts and much more!

blog.millsandboon.co.uk